Michael Foley was born in Derry in 1947 and was educated at St Columb's College, Derry, and Queen's University Belfast. He was joint editor of the *Honest Ulsterman* from 1970 to 1971 and contributed a regular satirical column 'The Wrassler' to *Fortnight* magazine throughout the early 1970s. His first novel was serialised in *Fortnight* and published in book form in 1984. He has also published a collection of translations of French poetry, and three poetry collections with Blackstaff Press. He currently lives in London where he lectures in Information Technology at the University of Westminster. He is married with one daughter.

ALSO BY MICHAEL FOLEY

FICTION

The Passion of Jamesie Coyle

POETRY

True Life Love Stories

The GO Situation

Insomnia in the Afternoon

TRANSLATION

The Irish Frog

(versions of French poems)

The Road to Notown

MICHAEL FOLEY

To Anne
who provided a
never-to-be-forgotten
window of opportunity

Michael

THE
BLACKSTAFF
PRESS
BELFAST

• A BLACKSTAFF PRESS PAPERBACK ORIGINAL •

Blackstaff Paperback Originals present new writing, previously unpublished in Britain and Ireland, at an affordable price.

First published in 1996 by
The Blackstaff Press Limited
3 Galway Park, Dundonald, Belfast BT16 0AN, Northern Ireland
with the assistance of
The Arts Council of Northern Ireland

Typeset by Paragon Typesetters, Newton-le-Willows, Merseyside

Printed in England by
Cox and Wyman Limited

A CIP catalogue record for this book
is available from the British Library

ISBN 0-85640-576-0

to

James Simmons,

mentor and friend

North

1

We went along a dark odorous hall and down a short flight of steps. Ahead was a dim kitchen but John turned left into a living room that looked out on a yard and a sagging brick wall. Only a little light got through, enough to reveal a few unmatched armchairs with broken springs and tattered upholstery. By the window was a big old table covered with oilcloth, and in the centre of a huge ornate fireplace a largely dead fire glowed feebly in places. I experienced a profound sense of wellbeing, almost enchantment.

What it recalled was the paradise from which I had been expelled at the end of my studies six months before – the darkness and elephants' graveyard peace of the Students' Union Male Common Room, that murmurous haunt of deadbeats and games players (poker for the hard men and chess for the creeps) in whose perpetual twilight the soul could take refuge from the tyrannies of ambition and promise. John Herron was a fellow chess creep. I knew him only slightly but when we ran into each other and he suggested a game at his home I took him up on it at once. It was the old business of adversity bringing people together. We were both in the real world now and discovering the hideous twin truths of adulthood: first, that malign reality gorges on nutritious young essence and second, that nobody else gives a shit.

John went for the set and my rapture was complete. The frayed board, battered wooden box and chipped discoloured pieces – not merely similar, it was an actual stamped Students' Union set. I assumed he had stolen it for sentimental reasons but soon enough I would realise that the motivation was brutally practical. Paying for leisure activity was entirely alien to the Herron ethos. Now John dragged a chair to the fire, threw himself down and shocked me to the core by putting his feet on the mantelpiece. In my own home such a thing could never have happened. With its clock centrepiece and symmetrical arrangement of vases and candlesticks, our mantelpiece was a shrine that could scarcely be touched by the duster of an acolyte never mind the dirty boots of a corner boy.

It was hard to concentrate on the game. For a start, our style of play was deeply unexciting, a process of cautious attrition motivated less by hunger for victory than fear of losing pieces. I was beginning to see it as further evidence of depressing character defects. Also, John was explaining his background. They were peasant stock from Galway, a family of five, three girls and two boys, brought up over a shop run by the mother and the sole means of support after the father's early death. So successful was the mother that they were able to move to this three-storeyed house in Harvey Terrace, formerly home to the exhausted and reclusive end of a Protestant dynasty, two elderly sisters and their disabled brother. Nothing had been done to the house in a lifetime, nor were the Herrons disposed to make changes. I was impressed by such Olympian indifference, so unlike the usual peasant urge to bury the past under beauty board and Formica. Even the disablement fittings were all still in place, something no other family would have permitted.

As John talked people came and went but there were no introductions beyond a casual 'How're ye doin'?'. The tall grim authoritative woman I took to be the mother. Another middle-aged woman must have been a neighbour. One of the daughters came for an extended stay, setting up an iron on the table and switching on a radio without consulting us.

'Any danger of a cup of tea?' John asked after a time, without looking up from the game.

'Hah!' she cried, carefully folding a blouse. 'What'd your last servant die of?'

'Ahve this boy nearly beat,' John explained. 'And something to eat. Ahm starvin'. Fadin'away altogether.'

'Fadin'away tay a mountain,' the girl said.

Nevertheless, a while later she brought in a battered tin bar tray bearing two mugs of milky tea and a few ginger snaps. Not even a plate for the biscuits! At home there would have been a china tea set (milk jug, sugar bowl, saucers, cups and plates), at least two different sweet items tastefully arranged on a cake stand covered with doilies and of course a fervent apology for the inadequacy of the offering.

'*Would yese lift this tea before it spills.*'

By now my position was irretrievable, though John lacked the character to claim a swift victory.

Towards teatime another sister burst in and rushed towards the fire. 'God Ahm foundered,' she cried. 'Get up and give us a bit a heat.'

Like Napoleon at the gates of Moscow, John was poised for the triumphant climax of a long and arduous campaign.

'Naw,' he snapped crossly, without taking his eyes from the board.

She seized him and attempted to drag him out of his chair. He resisted. Letting go at last, she made do with warming herself standing up. After a time she turned to get her back done and only now, when it was convenient, took a long critical look at me.

'*Where's the scissors?*' came a sudden terrible screech from somewhere in the depths of the house.

'Up me back for a hump,' the girl screamed, dropping back to a conversational tone with disconcerting abruptness. 'Are you one of the Trainors of Magazine Street?'

'No.'

'Are ye *sure?* Ye're the image of Mickey Trainor.'

Now I was in total disarray. John at last applied a definitive checkmate.

Magnanimous in victory, he walked me to the end of the road. It was a fine November day and Harvey Terrace was at its most distinguished, an imposing Victorian cul-de-sac on the side of a hill, its single uniform row of houses looking down on a wooded embankment. But its days of grandeur were numbered. It too would have to suffer its tragic destiny. At the bottom of the hill was a burgeoning Catholic ghetto and on its summit was a new Catholic estate already a legend for barbarity. Protestants had abandoned Harvey Terrace long ago, the professional Catholics more recently, leaving to the impoverished genteel the thankless task of imposing standards on Catholic nouveaus and worse. At the city end of the street several houses had been converted into flats, let to what John described as 'problem families', and in the end house, the one with the large fenced garden, was a Chinese family, or rather community, since, as John explained, it was owned by the proprietors of the China Garden and housed a constantly changing population of kitchen staff and waiters.

The social mix was precisely that of the terrace I grew up in. Here again it was genteels versus nouveaus and both of these versus the problem people, with a foreign household too far off the end of the social scale to be measured, my analogue for the Chinese the Indian proprietors of a drapery business prominently advertised as 'the House of Quality' but universally known as 'the Black Man's'. It pleased me that so many familiar dramas were being acted out afresh. Harvey Terrace, too, was reliving an old story.

I went back for more chess, intrigued by the street, the house, the family. A matriarchy (show me the Catholic family that isn't): Mrs Herron set the standards and wielded the power, her theory refreshingly easy to grasp if not to accept – that the Herrons were true aristocrats, those of the spirit rather than birth, an innately and effortlessly superior breed who would bestow upon a grateful world the gift of their sublime contempt. Apparently immune to social and religious inferiority, they seemed to me a mythical race, half brute and half divine, sprung from some legendary mating of god and beast.

Betty, the eldest sister, was in America. The other four were *all* superior and contemptuous, though with individual variations. Hugo had been brutalised by working on a building site whereas John had been mellowed by the education process. Rebecca, known as Reba ('What did your last servant die of?'), was devoted to slagging in a benevolent way, softened by two illusions – that it was all merely fun and that you were free to reply in kind if you had the talent and the nerve. With Frances ('Up me back for a hump') the contempt was unmitigated and undisguised. It was as though Mrs Herron, sensing that it was her last child, had injected into the egg all her reserves of ferocity and venom. With Frances there was no pretence of humour or equal rights. Frances manacled you to the wall and viciously flayed your hide off.

What attracted me to such a household? Certainly not John Herron or the indifferent chess. Perhaps the fascination of strong women, the intoxication of contempt? Or the need to atone for my own disgraceful upbringing? Imagine, if you can, that to the shame of being an only child in a culture of fecundity was added the ignominy of growing up in a house of women ruled by an aunt lacking the reassuring appearance of a male but with a prodigious and implacable virility possessed by no biological father I knew. I fed the Herron girls the shameful details and they punished me with zest.

'So Lily wore the trousers in your house,' Reba said.

'Yes . . . except she didn't allow women to wear trousers.' And I told the story of a niece's farcically involved manoeuvrings to avoid being seen in golfing slacks. 'She didn't let *me* wear long trousers until I was fourteen.'

'I bet you were a real creep,' Frances said viciously. 'A real nancy boy.'

'Oh yes. Only the best of clothes from Brownlow's.'

This was the outfitter to the Protestant gentry. There was a chorus of horror and revulsion.

'*We* got everything in the Black Man's,' Frances said with pride.

'Or Paddy Canning's,' Reba corrected. 'Until he drank heeself out of it.'

'Viyella shirts,' I said, to groans. 'Brown brogues.' More groans. 'Crombie coats.' Yet wilder groans. And still the catalogue of shame was not complete. In an ecstasy of self-flagellation I handed them the most humiliating detail of all. 'Remember those ties with permanent knots and elastic neck bands?' They most certainly did, a memory vivid and poignant enough to draw from even these hearts of stone a profound sigh of pity and compassion.

Such was my willingness to testify that I was granted the astounding privilege of an invitation to eat with the family. Not even an academician freshly elected could have felt so honoured. Happy to lose yet another game to John, I lay back on the sofa to watch *Top of the Pops* and await the diners – first Frances, then Reba, then, last and extremely late, Hugo with his empty lunch box.

'The dinner's burnt to nothin',' Frances accused. 'Where were ye?'

Hugo, with more of the brute than the divine, did not take kindly to being questioned.

'Up a dog's arse pickin' gooseberries.'

'Ye missed Pan's People,' John informed him, shivering at the memory of a vibrant carnality.

Hugo was typically terse and dismissive. 'Six big rides,' he replied at once.

The meal was stew (or 'stews', as they called it), served in huge soup bowls. I wondered if they were testing my resolve, already established beyond all doubt. Had I not been using their toilet, a fearsome rite of passage for a boy from a house of women? Instead of the fragrance of talc a foul stench of man dung, instead of the pink suite an ancient bowl violently streaked with discolorations, instead of soft toilet tissue roughly torn squares of newspaper hung on a nail, instead of the matching pink light switch a greasy black cord with a knot at the end. My courage had already been tested almost to destruction. I laid into the stews with a vengeance.

'I suppose you were always a pukey eater,' Reba suggested.

'The worst. Never touched my greens. Lily used to try and force me. *You'll eat it before it eats you.*'

'And did you?'

'My mother always gave in and threw it out.'

I finished along with the others, although I could not make my bowl shine like theirs. Luckily seconds were offered only to Hugo the working man.

'All slops go into the big pot,' Frances said sourly.

But not even a starving labourer could finish such an enormous second helping.

'Ees lost ees appetite,' Reba marvelled.

Frances snorted. 'Lost ees appetite and found a donkey's.'

'Leave the young fella alone,' Mrs Herron said. 'Ye need somethin' in your stomach goin' out to a buildin' site.'

If only I could have kept my mouth shut and enjoyed the banter. Instead I made the classic error of the charity case, that of claiming parity with the benefactor. It began with the story of how Lily and my mother moved out of my beloved Wellington Street without informing me.

'I arrived home at the end of the first term – or what I thought was home. Everybody gone. Not a sinner. The whole place boarded up and empty. Can you imagine it? Christmas time. The house I grew up in.'

'They were too scarred tay tell ye?' Reba intuited.

'Even Lily. They knew I loved that street.' I paused grimly. 'And that wasn't the worst.'

'What happened?'

'They moved to a bungalow.'

As they laughed I recalled Lily screeching, 'Ahm not able for all those stairs, Ahm not able for all those stairs' – that Catholic mixture of shame and apology and defiance that I hate so much and have inherited. Then, carried away by success, I set out an analogy between the Wellington Street of my youth and the Harvey Terrace of the present. From that I progressed to a general theory of Irish Catholic evolution – the birth of consciousness in the primeval slime, the move from country to town, the accumulation of capital, the exchange of slum for swanky terrace, the education of the children and the final progression to the paradise of the suburbs. We were one species, I tried to explain, though at different stages of evolution. The Herrons were insulted and outraged. The idea of becoming paltry creatures like me! With one voice they rose up to proclaim themselves and their descendants for ever the salt of the earth. Only Hugo was not passionately involved.

'Will yese fuck up,' he roared. 'Ahm tryin' tay watch *Z Cars.*'

'We're workin' class and you're a middle-class creep,' Frances shrieked.

'And when you marry and move to the suburbs what will your children be?'

'*Workin'-class. Workin'-class like me.*'

'WILL YESE FIR FUCK'S SAKE FUCK UP,' Hugo bellowed.

And of course my degraded status was as immutable as their noble one. When I claimed to have rejected the bourgeois world by refusing to join a profession or even work full time, they laughed in bitter scorn. However tragic your destiny, it was not to be escaped. Evasive action only made you look an even bigger fool. It was play-acting, play-acting, play-acting. Acting the tin man. Acting the maggot.

'Sittin' in a bedsitter all day,' Frances sneered. 'What's that supposed to prove. *Who're ye kiddin'?*'

Frances prowling like a galley boss with a cat-o'-nine-tails. Since she worked in a shirt factory it was possible to avoid her by visiting the Herrons at their daytime court, the sweet shop in Great George Street run by Reba and her mother. This sweet shop was an aristocrat of the confectionery trade (naturally), and any comparison with the backstreet 'wee shop' was taken an extremely dim view of. Here, instead of gobstoppers and penny chews, there was a range of quality confectionery starting where the wee shops left off, with Buttered Brazils at one and six a quarter and going right up to the insane luxury of Cardinal Creams at three and three. And instead of runny-nosed children with the arse out of their trousers, the typical client was an affluent sybarite in search of an appropriately classy treat for himself and the wife in the Rialto balcony during *My Fair Lady.* In a way the Herrons were like drug dealers pandering to the depraved rich. I never saw one of them eat a Cardinal Cream.

For loungers there was an unwritten but rigorous code – no more than two in the shop at a time, no reductions or free samples, no bantering with serious customers and no sitting down, least of all on the seats behind the counter by the paraffin heater which were strictly reserved for the Herrons. Not only was it unthinkable to ask for titbits, it was usually a good idea to purchase something by way of rent. (Despite my own straitened circumstances I nearly always bought a Granny Smith or a bar of Whole Nut.) Never once did I see the code breached, not even by drunks. Even the most deranged of winos obeyed the Herron etiquette.

Like all stable regimes, it was maintained not by sanctions but by the supreme confidence of those in authority. I always enjoyed Reba's relaxed skill with drunks, for instance the little bald man, radiant with admiration, who made his unsteady way to the counter to stare in ineffable wonder.

'How're ye doin', Sammy?' she said in humorous resignation.

What Sammy Mullen wanted was more luxurious and unattainable than Cardinal Creams. Moving with great care and circumspection, he gently touched the outer strands of her hair with the tips of his fingers. 'Gossamer,' he sighed in rapture, looking to me for confirmation. I nodded at once and he sang, looking from one of us to the other, out of tune but with infinite tenderness, 'A trip to the moooooo . . . oon on gossamer wings'.

'More like a whin bush,' Reba said drily. And indeed there was nothing delicate about her wild head of thick wavy hair. Or about the rest of her either. She could have toyed with Sammy like the ladies of Brobdingnag with Gulliver.

'Beautiful girl,' he sighed, turning completely to me. 'But the best lookin's Betty.'

'Betty's in America,' Reba said.

'Sure Ah know that. Ah know that. But she's the best lookin' one.'

'Betty got all the looks goin',' Reba conceded, with such good grace that Sammy fell in love with her afresh and repeated his gossamer wings performance.

'But what about Frances?' I asked him.

'Ah Jesus,' Sammy said, suddenly serious. Lifting an arm as

though to forestall an attack, he retreated in mock horror. Safe in the doorway, he dropped his guard and gave us a last gossamer wings before disappearing with a laugh.

I regretted driving him off because in Herron company it was advisable to have someone else as buffoon-of-the-day. Especially as John and Hugo soon arrived. I could have taken a beating any minute when in off the street walked a young French sailor, tiny but cute as lace pants. Even more delightful, he was lonely and lost and spoke practically no English. After the token purchase he introduced himself as Michel and explained in sign language and broken English that he wanted to find the docks and his ship.

Reba regarded him in wonder. 'God he's a wee dote. Ye could put him on the mantelpiece if he didn't shite.'

There was probably an edge to our laughter, but Michel joined in just the same, with a truly engaging innocence that demonstrated what can be achieved if we become as little children.

Even Hugo the brute was captivated. 'Guess who's turned fruit?' he asked the uncomprehending youth. 'Give us a kiss and Ahll tell ye.'

Reba was carrying out the unabashed examination Herrons considered their right. And indeed Michel seemed to be enjoying it.

'He's the image of Murty Quinn,' she decided at last. Speaking with exaggerated slowness, she addressed herself to Michel. 'Do ye know Murty Quinn? Singer? Not very tall? With the Miami Showband?'

Hugo helpfully illustrated with a song, altering it for the amusement of the English-speaking company:

Do the Hucklebuck, do the Hucklebuck,
If you dunno how to do it I don't give a fuck.

'That's not the Miami,' Reba snapped. 'That's the Royal Showband. That slabber Brendan Bowyer. Bacon Lips.'

John translated, explaining to the youth that Reba was struck by his resemblance to an Irish singer. Michel glanced at her in truly adorable embarrassment.

'God he's gorgeous,' Reba breathed. 'Ast if there's any more like him on board. Dotes like him – but maybe a wee bit taller.'

John translated dotes as 'handsome matelots' and omitted the height requirement.

'Oui, oui,' Michel eagerly nodded to Reba.

'Moneybags as well? Beaucoup d'argent?'

'Oui, oui.'

'Ahm gonnay do the boats the night.'

John offered to conduct him to the docks but Michel turned beseechingly to Reba.

'Mind the shop!' she cried to Hugo. 'Ahm runnin' away wi' a sailor.'

'For fuck's sake.'

'Sure Jacinta'll probably be in. She's a wild notion of you.'

'That wagon,' Hugo grunted. 'She was rid-out when she was fifteen.'

Three of us set out with Michel, who made no secret of his preference.

'God Ahm mortified,' Reba laughed. 'Ahll never lift me head in this town again.'

It was a bright spring day and we were in no hurry. Michel explained through John that he was seventeen years old and a native of Marseilles. John suggested to Reba that she was baby-snatching.

'Wise up! Sure Ahm only nineteen meself.'

The Herrons always acted older than their years but today Reba seemed determined to enjoy the frivolity of youth. When we reached the boat she did not resist Michel's French-style farewell. As their lips met and remained in contact John and I gave an awkward cheer and laugh. They were certainly an odd couple, the tall big-boned girl with the wild hair bending as though to devour the little sailor boy. Her heavy hair even fell across him, hiding his face. Maybe after all it was wiser to be a sweetheart than a smartass. Eventually Reba disengaged and Michel made an emotional departure, pausing at the top of the gangway for a final wave. We lingered, reluctant to leave the docks. Spring, love, youth, the warmth of Provence and the adventure of the high seas – not even the Herrons were immune to such a combination. But of course Reba could never acknowledge tenderness and yearning.

'Me neck's broke bendin'down.'

'We should have brought a box for him to stand on,' John said. 'That's what they did for Alan Ladd when he made that film with Sophia Loren.'

I too acted blasé despite being troubled. 'I thought they made Sophia stand in a hole.'

The afternoon was a revelation because Reba had never seemed in the least romantic with her boyfriend, or 'bars', as she described him, a colloquial term of baffling etymology which seemed to imply a relationship more lightweight than that of fiancé, despite its lasting several years. A regular in Harvey Terrace, Danny Deery had endeared himself, even to the misanthropic mother, by his constant crack, imperviousness to insult, and fantastic willingness to oblige (Frances: 'He's that civil he'd let ye shite in his hands'). In Herron parlance he was a 'Big McGlundy', the kind of good-natured halfwit it is impossible to dislike. Certainly not a rival to be feared. Success in the upper air of social relations makes it unlikely in the furtive underworld of the flesh. A Big McGlundy is rarely a stick man.

Regarding John's beloved, there was no evidence since he never brought her to the house and never discussed her, from which the Herrons deduced swankiness and a brother shaping up to become a class traitor.

Hugo's girl was only too keen to get into Harvey Terrace.

'That wee girl has me fuckin' head deeved. *Ahm goin' wi' you six months, Hugo Herron, and Ah never seen one o' your family. Ahm gonnay haftay go into the shop and introduce meself.*'

'What do you say to that, Hugo?'

'I just tell her: *You're goin' into no fuckin' shop.*'

The dispensation accorded to Frances was extreme and unprecedented but justified by an iron logic none dared challenge. Since Sean worked for a building firm seventy miles away he could be with his love only at weekends and after a drive so exhausting as to preclude further travel. Since they were entitled to be alone together the only solution was a private sitting room in Harvey Terrace. No one else had been given such an amenity but any suggestion of casual hedonism was ruled out by Sean's maturity and high seriousness.

I saw one of his token appearances in the living room. Tall, strongly built and self-contained, with regular features and unfashionably short curly hair, he was handsome in a heavy, vapid way, like a garda or customs official in the South, a trusty custodian of inherited and unquestioned values. I could see how this might attract Frances, who would provide him with a full set of laws to implement – but what did he see in her? Why did he tolerate her vitriol? How did he get excited by her bony frame and her face of sharp overlapping planes, like an exercise in analytical cubism?

Making no attempt at ingratiation, he nodded briefly at everyone and answered a few questions while Frances watched for smart-aleckry. No one was foolhardy enough to try it in her presence. There was silence until they were gone, and caution even then.

'A grand big sensible fella,' Reba said, the irony indicated by her unnaturally straight face and long direct stare at me.

'Any girl would be proud of a bars like that,' I solemnly agreed, meeting her gaze with a po face. We were into the electric world of the sexual subtext. 'But sure Danny's a grand big sensible fella too.'

She held my gaze for a long crucial moment. Gradually I let my face assume its true configuration – the sacred sign of the monster. She laughed, experiencing first the joy of betrayal and then the guilt, clapping a hand on her vile mouth. 'God forgive me and pardon me.'

But after the first betrayal everything is easy. A few days later Reba answered my knock on the door of Harvey Terrace. John was helping the mother clear up after a break-in at the shop. He would be back as soon as possible for the chess.

'Ah,' I said, the banter that flowed so freely in public suddenly drying up in private.

Reba leaned against the doorframe and watched me gaze uneasily up and down the street. I felt like a Big McGlundy. Behind her the hall was profoundly silent.

'Frances in there?' I managed at last, an attempt at a joke that came out inane.

But I had stumbled by accident on the code. She seized my sleeve, jerking her head towards the stairs with an air of inscrutable mystery.

'Come on.'

We climbed past the foul toilet to an unknown region, a second-floor landing stacked with boxes of confectionery. I jokingly made to open one. Reba dared me to try. In this family, pilfering shop stock was the ultimate offence, invariably detected and punished with unyielding severity. She described the flogging and humiliation of Hugo when he was caught with two packets of Treets and a Mytee Bar. Of course that was when the father was alive . . . but all the same.

Our destination was the second-floor return. Sure of my surprise and wonder, Reba flung open the door and stepped aside. My reaction was all she could have wished. As the child of a bourgeois house will establish anarchy in a private room, so in this family indifferent to cosiness someone had created a miniature suburban dream home. There was a two-seater sofa arranged before a tiny television on top of a glass-fronted unit whose bottom half contained neatly stacked LPs and whose top half was a cocktail cabinet with Dubonnet, white lemonade and two glasses. Against the wall stood a sideboard bearing the tiniest fridge I had ever seen.

The love nest of Frances and Sean – of course!

'Christ!' I said. 'Where did this stuff *come from?*'

'Sean gets most of it through his work some way.'

'Too much.' I went to the cocktail cabinet. 'I need a drink.'

'Are you kidding?' Blasphemy might be acceptable; pillage was not.

Instead I bent to the LPs. Rock music was the universal culture of youth but here the first two records were *Dream with Dean*, Dean Martin slurring his way through romantic slush, and *Love is a Many-splendoured Thing* by Nat King Cole.

'That's their song,' Reba said.

'What?'

'Love is a Many-splendoured Thing.'

'But how do they play these?'

'Frances takes the record player from downstairs. There's terrible rows with Hugo.'

I moved across to the fridge.

'Don't touch that – we'll be killed.'

It was a freezer packed with beefburgers, frozen vegetables, crinkle-cut potatoes.

'Sean's mad about curly chips.'

What shocked me was the idea of creating such a horror *in advance of* marriage. Not to drift or slump into suburban living but to embrace the concept with conviction and fervour.

And why was Reba showing me this? Was it her dream too? She had certainly defended the freezer with spirit. I caught her eye, and saw the unmistakable glitter of the heresiarch. She had come not to worship but to defile the holy place. She wanted stinking barbarians and horse dung in the temple. She wanted profane love in the sacred shrine.

I kissed her, pushing her back against the wall. Her hand came up to rest lightly on my arm, acquiescent if not passionate. After a while I broke off to see how she was taking it. On her face tenderness mingled with irony in a light sweet-'n'-sour. Looking into her eyes, I took her gently by the waist and moved my hands lightly up and down her body. A cold and calculating advance, with neither the excuse of passion or alcohol nor the cover of compassionate darkness.

'You're a bad animal,' she murmured contentedly.

I moved in, not withholding the loathsome knob. Even this further vileness was accepted. What would she not have accepted? Her ironic passivity was deeply seductive, but my own nerve failed me, as so often at this crucial point. I am better at making the sign of the monster than behaving like one.

But if it was difficult to go forward it was equally hard to return to safe ground. There ensued a period of furtive, hectic encounters in the house and longer, more leisurely conversations in the shop. There she revealed, in typically ironic fashion, that not only were she and Danny not doing the nasty, they were not doing anything at all.

'Ah thought at the start he was bein' a gentleman . . . ye know? Workin' up to it gradually, like.' She laughed in the now familiar half-guilty way. 'But two years is a bit long to wait for a court.'

She also fleshed out the bare Herron data supplied by John. Unlikely as it seemed now, the mother had been swept off her feet by a charmer who took her from Galway to the North with dazzling talk of moneymaking schemes. Soon enough it was apparent that he was not a free-market visionary but a standard Irish alcoholic. His problem was aristomania, a hunger for singularity, for distinguishing himself at all times from the vulgar herd. Hence the crazy schemes and scorn for anything commonplace. For Reba, the guard-dog saga was a perfect illustration. When the mother, in despair, proposed to open a small shop, the husband refused to cooperate in a typically squalid peasant enterprise. Later he relented and promised to supply a guard dog. After weeks of enquiries in bars he bought from a sailor (no – 'a seaman with a first mate's ticket') an animal of fabulous ferocity, 'half husky and half wolf'. Alas its savagery was aroused as much by its owners as by potential intruders. It had to be chained to the back of the coal house and fed by means of a long pole. A constant threat to the children, it was eventually put down.

'But how did she get the shop started?'

Brothers in Galway and America put up money on condition that the husband could not get at it. Naturally the aristocrat despised their dependable mediocrity. In return the brothers memorably summed up his fecklessness: 'That man would shite the bed if there was a hundred houlin' him.'

Then the early death of the husband, adding one more to the widows of Erin, a burgeoning group more embittered than merry. What Reba remembered most vividly was her mother's threat to abandon them. In fact she never went further than sulking for hours in the coal house but Reba would carry to her grave the precise phrasing and intonation of certain sentences: 'Ah lived before Ah saw one of yese', 'Ahm puttin' me coat on me now' and, most terrifying of all, 'Ahm puttin' me foot on the Scotch boat.'

How had the father treated Reba?

'All right.' She shrugged. 'Betty was always his favourite.' A pause. 'Frances hated him. I didn't.'

'But it wouldn't dispose you to marriage,' I suggested, with a smirk of the pure evil I knew she found stimulating.

'Doesn't seem to put Frances off.'

Apparently Sean could not be married soon enough. An engineering student with a steady, he had been moving smoothly towards a profession and a wife when his girl threw him over for the traditional charming wastrel. Sean failed his finals and attempted suicide, twin disasters which were never to be mentioned or even approached, for instance by questions about the precise nature of his job in the building trade. Hard to imagine big Sean crazed with passion, but the suicide attempt confirmed a frightful symmetry. In accordance with the parental model, the Herron men fell for strong women and the Herron women for weak men.

But Reba became embarrassed by my hanging about the shop. People were making jokes about her 'new bars'. I took to visiting Harvey Terrace later in the evening and discovered that the Herrons had preserved the peasant custom of ceilidhing, that is, providing your own in-house entertainment. Several nights a week family and guests gathered in the living room to exchange conspiracy theories and to celebrate the Catholic heritage of aristocratic opposition. Scepticism and derision are common with Fenians (adoption of the perjorative term 'Fenian' an example of self-mockery), but only the Herrons took the attitude to its logical conclusion. For them every known form of human achievement was charlatanism.

Disdaining vulgar and demeaning worldly show, the true Fenian prince wears an infinitely more dazzling raiment – the invisible but haughty robes of total rejection. A difficult tradition to uphold in the age of conspicuous consumption. Much denunciation was required on these social evenings, orchestrated by the family largely without the assistance of alcohol. Jester guests on the other hand were encouraged to get drunk and make fools of themselves. Of course you had to bring your own, plus a few bottles of stout for Sammy Mullen, the resident clown.

'Give us a wee blirt, Sammy,' Mrs Herron would say, in good spirits after more denouncing of quislings and traitors. With a look of profound solemnity and concentration, Sammy would launch into the personal favourite that was perhaps his secret dream, 'From the Candy Store on the Corner to the Chapel on the Hill'.

Then he would try to get me to perform. 'What about some of these young ones for a change. Come on now. Somethin' with it. Somethin' be that fella . . . what ye call him . . . *Mick Jaguar.* Come on now' – grabbing my sleeve – 'Mick Jaguar for a song.'

In the end his sentimentality required dashes of vinegar from the hostess.

'Lovely children ye have,' he said to her, with a fond glance at Reba. 'Lovely . . . lovely . . .'

'It's well seen ye didn't have the rearing of them.'

'Ah but children . . . children . . .' Though he himself had abandoned a wife and family, the contemplation of little ones always filled him with awe. 'Sure a million poun' wouldn't buy them,' he managed at last.

Mrs Herron had her own view of child rearing. 'Sorrow and shite,' she declared at once.

Her other views were as unconventional. The language might be that of the medieval peasant but the thought was late-twentieth-century pessimism of the blackest hue. A guiding principle: 'Think the worst of everybody and ye won't go far wrong.' On shrewd businessmen: 'As cute as the fly that shites on the fly.' On social climbers: 'Hit shite wi' a stick and it flies high.' On the pretensions of the mighty: 'The Queen shites too.' On the predominance of image over content: 'Get the name of an early riser and ye can roll in yer bed till the cows come home.' On the futility of existence and the desolation of fulfilment: 'What does the terrier do when it catches the cart?'

Another regular was Danny Deery, the Big McGlundy Reba betrayed in the kitchen while he entertained her family in the living room. Did he know? It seems likely. Probably the Herrons also knew – obtuseness was not one of their virtues. But no one said anything and I was free to enjoy the rewards of courtship without the tedium or expense.

Still Reba set no limits to our baseness. The evenings were charged with imminence. And now there was an additional excitement, for after fifty years of stagnation the North suddenly burst into a dramatic life caused in part by the activities of a Protestant minister regarded with fondness by many Fenians despite or actually because of his outspoken bigotry.

'Have yese heard the latest?' Sammy asked. 'Ees wife went to the dentist and says the dentist, *How's the mouth?* and says she, *Aw he's grand, he's givin' a rally in Ballymena.*'

'Say nothin' about that man,' Danny Deery countered, looking shrewdly round to see if we could grasp the sophistication of the point. 'Sure isn't he the best friend we ever had?'

No one disagreed. The real enemies were the fearful moderates trying to calm things down. With the wisdom of hindsight we might have been less enthusiastic, but then the only thought was to keep it going at all costs. Turn the heat up! Keep it on the boil! On top of the natural imminence of youth there was the intoxication of an apparently permanent hegemony about to crumble to dust. A thrilling first lesson in mutability. It seems that nothing will ever change, then all at once the brazen axioms collapse. Apocalypse was only a news bulletin away and many, including the Herrons, became lifelong news addicts.

As yet there was no death and little suffering. Property still bore the brunt and compensation for riot damage was handsome and prompt. It was even possible to do well out of the turmoil. Danny Deery told a typical story with typical relish.

'See, Mickey Hutton's shop was broke into. Wrecked the place. Shite everywhere. So Mickey goes to his solicitor. *How Ahm Ah fixed?* says Mickey. And the solicitor says to him, *It's this way now, if there were less than five of them it's malicious damage and not so good, but if there were five or more it's riotous assembly and you're in business for compensation.* So he leans across the desk to Mickey, dead serious – as po-faced, ye know – and says he, *Michael, I'd like you to think carefully and answer one question. Now think hard, Michael,* he says, *was there enough shite for five?*'

Shite as a weapon in the class war. Foojie McGuire breaking into school to do big business in the head's desk, a bitter student friend leaving a disconcerting mark of Zorro in the locker of a rich boy. Many instances come to mind. Research would provide the basis for a monograph: 'Uses of Excrement by the Underclass'. A weapon of devastating effect, no more potent symbol of the hated and feared sordid reality the privileged wish to forget. For those too squeamish to use the substance the word is an effective substitute. Note its predominance in the Herron vocabulary.

Hence Danny's story brought the house down. I never thought to see Mrs Herron in ecstasy.

'*Was there enough shite for five?*' Danny repeated in a solemn drawl, milking the anecdote for all its considerable worth, enjoying his greatest social success with the mother just as his relations with her daughter touched bottom. I discovered a pleasing symmetry in this.

But in the intoxication of falling monuments much that is valuable can also be destroyed.

'I finished with Danny,' Reba sighed as I came to her side to dry the dishes. Abruptly she stopped work to stare out regretfully at the yard.

'But he was in there all night yarning away?'

'Even so, I finished with him.' As so often, just to articulate the deed gave it an intoxicating reality and sanction. Her natural insouciance flooded back and she turned to me with a wry grin. 'Blew him out like a wet snotter.'

Now it was my turn to gape in surmise. The problem with demolishing institutions is that you have to put something in their place, and when there is only one model you can end up re-creating what you destroyed. Now I would be the official fiancé – doing the Hucklebuck to Bacon Lips in the Cameo, eating Buttered Brazils in the Rialto balcony, buying vodka and white as Seamus and the Big Two mangled Jim Reeves in the Hayloft.

Already she could read my negative thoughts. 'Don't panic. I'm not asking *you* for anything.'

On the contrary, she seemed prepared to give. History was being made on all sides. As we waited for the living room to clear I stimulated her with the look of one who carries evil coiled like a serpent in his bosom.

'Can we put some more coal on the fire?'

How shockingly early the tragic flaw, the fatal contradiction, my desire to run free while enjoying the comforts of home. What appalled Reba was the idea of burning Herron fuel to warm a bourgeois boy.

'Everybody's in bed. Are ye mad?'

'The blow heater at least.'

Her voice was soft with affection, but unequivocal mockery danced in her eyes.

'Sean and Frances have it in the love nest.'

2

If you are setting off to start a new life, never use the family car. Especially if it is the vehicle in which your mother, after many years of widowhood, served a long and profoundly fearful apprenticeship. Even after passing her test she could never be confident with Lily at her side providing a stream of peevish criticisms and warnings. On this occasion as always I put on a good show – window down, elbow out – but Fear sits in the back with one hand on the passenger seat and the other braced against a wheel arch.

Of course it is a foolhardy and possibly dangerous mission. For a start, the man I am going to see is a Protestant. Has not our own bishop clearly defined the risks? 'If you allow your children to be contaminated by those who are not of the fold then you can expect nothing but disaster.' And Kyle Magee is not a God-fearing Protestant but a novelist opposed to established religions, and preaching the joys of the flesh. Practising it too, if his books are anything to go by. At last Irish letters has something to rival the French, for it seems likely that history will place Kyle on a par with Simenon who has penetrated ten thousand women (although there is disagreement as to whether whores count – many commentators allow him as few as two thousand).

The explanation is that Kyle is half-Continental himself. His father was the pure article, a Presbyterian businessman from Ballymena, but the mother is French, albeit a Protestant from northern France who seems from the books to disapprove of her son's philandering. This is not surprising, since Kyle favours the wrong side of the tracks, being one of those who prefers his pleasure spiced with danger. In *Over the State Line*, his first novel based on his American wanderings, he describes the farcical difficulties in getting a black whore out of a Deep South student hall. *Bolt the Stable Door*, which covers his early years, has initiation by a stable girl and a love affair with a Fenian. Only *Market Forces* describes a relationship within his own class – the affair with an American WASP that ended in the stormy and short-lived first marriage.

Even in less repressive times it is consoling to hear of the Irish enjoying a bit – and what more heart-warming than a home-grown Henry Miller, succeeding not just at home but in Hank's own back yard? Also exciting were the immediacy and directness, the absence of craft-of-fiction machinery and the sense of a man grappling furiously with his own life. The style was often naïve and gauche, but better the clumsiest confrontation than the most elegant sidestep.

In a student magazine I published an article that turned out to be the first on Kyle's work as a whole. It would never have occurred to me to get in touch with an author but as soon as the article appeared a long, friendly letter arrived. I seemed to have lively ideas on fiction – was I at it myself? I sent him a few stories and the response was instant and electrifying. Excited by 'the number of talented young writers springing up in the North', nothing would give Kyle more pleasure than to help with encouragement and advice.

Unfortunately, his home is deep in the Protestant heartland. I am heartily glad to draw into the driveway of Altnagarvin. Yet the arrival is disturbing in a different way. In a lifetime of reading, both voluntary and prescribed, I have never found anything directly related to my own experience. Even the history and geography I studied concerned different countries. Now the word is made flesh, the scene before me corresponding exactly to the description in a lurid-covered paperback in my bag. A big two-storey grey stone building with many extensions and outhouses, Altnagarvin looks out over a gentle slope which falls to a little lake with a dilapidated boathouse and rises on the other side to a densely wooded hill.

Surely this is not meant to be – mistake mistake mistake mistake. But then Kyle himself is jumping down the steps, laughing and waving. Despite the baggy cords and torn sweater, he is as handsome as his jacket photographs: dark-complexioned, with classic French features and Alain-Delon-style straight black hair through which he continually drives his hand and which always falls back into the kind of elegant disarray I try in vain to create in front of the bathroom mirror. You have to be born with such naturalness. Go home now, back to the Fenian world of rotten teeth and puffy blotched skin. But Kyle is pumping my hand and hugging me in the warmth and solidarity of fellow soldiers in the war against repression, fellow preachers in the ministry of truth. At the top of the steps he suddenly jumps into the air and kicks his heels together.

'We gonna have such a time,' he cries. 'Such a time. Such a time.'

And why not? Kyle is the Zorba of the North and will surely change my life for ever. Zorba, teach me to dance!

Straight away there is a challenge. Approaching across the hall is a woman with black hair and dark skin, obviously related to Kyle, but with nothing shabby in her appearance. Blouse of fine, light, expensive, semi-transparent material, buttons open to the shadow. Expensive knee-length leather boots, Levi's packed as a Sonny Rollins coda. Above the waist all woman and below it all man. No – her head combines the sexes. Feminine the bobbed hair, make-up and silver earrings; manly the twin grooves from nostrils to mouth like ancient Heidelberg duelling scars. Never have I experienced such disturbing virility and glamour in a woman. A sense of profound unworthiness possesses me.

But instead of horsewhipping the presumptuous Fenian she turns calmly to Kyle. 'Can I have the car keys now? I have to go into town for something.'

'My sister Renee,' Kyle says. 'A fine actress.'

She hoots in scorn. 'That was years ago.'

A Kyle trait: he defines everyone in terms of creativity, however short-lived and long past.

We set out on a tour of orientation that has the opposite effect. Extended at many different times, the house has a bewildering infrastructure of stairways and corridors. It is impossible to get the hang of its layout, perhaps because so many rooms teem with distracting life – animals, children of Renee and Kyle by various marriages, friends and lovers of these children, and a host of talented, youthful artists on the verge of astounding the Western world. Kyle introduces the creators with particular affection and pride. Fine actor and playwright. Gifted musician. Promising poet. Altogether there are three living rooms. It's like talking to a man with three heads.

Such a relief to settle finally in Kyle's study, where he reveals that he is a Lawrence man. The purpose of literature is to provide the courage to reject lies and stop being a Willy Wetlegs. Liberated and inspired by books, individuals will refuse the compromises on offer and insist on a better society. Although not a practising Protestant, Kyle has retained the evangelical fervour of his people. They believe that a man can be born again by immersion in water; Kyle promises the same result by immersion in literature.

Not for me such a Salvation Army aesthetic. I want something bizarre and wild. Transgression and outrage are my dark siren songs. Aberration and deviance call to my soul. My head might acknowledge humanism – but my heart belongs to Dada. I mention Burroughs and Genet.

'Don't they merely set out to shock and disgust? Where are their positives?'

More used to concealing than defending my enthusiasms, I make a noise like a halfwitted churl with his tongue cut out.

'But don't you feel literature has to offer something positive, a moral dimension? Not conventional morality, of course. Just the seriousness of caring about improving people's lives. Lawrence and Henry Miller, for instance.'

'*Morals?*' I almost shout, stung into life. 'Good writers have been everything under the sun – fascists, thieves, pimps . . . murderers . . .'

'Who's a murderer?'

I regard him in amazement. 'William Burroughs shot his wife.'

Kyle nods gravely. Either he does not know the shooting was an accident or he is letting me off the hook.

'I can't think of a writer I like who subscribes to liberal orthodoxy.'

Kyle chuckles with delight and drives a hand back through his hair. 'What about me then? I'm a perfectly orthodox liberal humanist.' He has me, but declines to press home the advantage. 'What do you dislike so much about liberalism?'

Just to hear the word makes me sick to my stomach. 'Wishy-washy ... safe ... middle-class ... middle of the road. Liberal writers are always dull. Only the reactionaries have style.'

Kyle is musing to himself, nodding gently. 'I can see how a fastidious young man would hate it. Liberalism's the official creed of the West so the language and principles are hopelessly degraded. No one puts the ideas into practice but everyone pays them hypocritical lip service.'

'Like our preacher friend. Roaring about democracy when all he wants is Protestant domination.'

Cool it, Action! Whoa, there! Northern Ireland politics is forbidden territory: inadvisable with a lifelong Catholic friend, never mind a Protestant you've just met.

'Exactly,' Kyle murmurs. 'Presumably you've marched with the civil rights people.' He cocks his head quizzically. 'Perhaps even thrown stones at the police?'

Like all timid creatures, I have terrific sensory apparatus. Now the entire early-warning system is on red alert, all the delicate antennae are fully extended and listening like crazy for evidence of an ugly unregenerate core beneath the friendly exterior. No signals at all, nothing negative or sinister. Kyle seems detached and curious, possibly even sympathetic, like the foreign journalists in the North at the moment – relaxed, mature, glamorous, 'not from around here'.

'I've thrown a few stones,' I admit at last.

'I appreciate – and support – the civil rights case. But I'm saddened by the hatred and crudity of the slogans. The visual and verbal ugliness of it. The imaginative poverty of chanting *S ... S ... R ... U ... C.*'

'I've never done that,' I snap, though in fact I have bayed primitive slogans as joyously as the rest of the pack. 'I'm basically nonpolitical. I'd rather read and go to the cinema.'

Which movies?

Zorba the Greek. The Hustler. Fast Eddie Felson, with his love of pool and dazzling talent, accurately assessed by the perceptive gambler – *You're a loser, kid.* Kyle nods, but with obvious perplexity. If you have talent and opportunity, how can you lose?

Suddenly he jumps to his feet. 'Perhaps you'd like a game of snooker?'

I presume there is a table in the house. In fact it is four miles away. Since Renee has Kyle's car, I have to drive, concerned both about the journey and the prospect of intruding on strangers. Kyle has no such inhibitions. Between the idea and the reality there falls no shadow. Indeed, there is rarely even a time lag.

Another big house, but of a more conventional nature. A temple to the god of Money rather than Truth.

The courtesy of the greeting could scarcely be faulted, but there is just enough perplexity to show that the visit is bad form. Kyle appears not to notice and proceeds with enthusiasm to a basement games room with a full-sized snooker table. Two sons come to watch in relaxed, sardonic disdain. Most likely they pick up the smell of Fenian. If not, my pathetic snooker talent is sufficient grounds for contempt. No squeaks or jumps, the ball roughly on target – but instead of going in, it invariably bounces around the rim of the pocket.

'My speciality shot,' I declare grimly. 'The respectable miss.'

Kyle chuckles and once again drives a hand through his hair. '*Respectable Misses* – great title for an anthology of Ulster verse.'

Luckily Kyle is almost as bad. He is better at pool, he explains, going on to reminisce about a game with a famous black jazz pianist, in the course of which they consumed a crate of beer and a bottle of Wild Turkey.

How had he met the pianist?

Stupid question. Between the idea and the reality falls no

shadow. 'Hitchhiked to his house and knocked on the door.'

By now I should be getting the hang of it but when Kyle proposes jazz on the way back I assume he means recorded music. Instead he sets me on the study sofa and produces a real-life tenor saxophone, something I have never seen at close range. It is certainly a magnificent totem, burnished and numinous and characterful, worn patches on the metal eloquent testimony to the hard life on which the music is based.

'It's a Selmer Mark 6. They've made a lot of models since, but never one as good. This is the horn all the greats played – Rollins, Coltrane, Webster, Hawkins.'

He launches into a ballad, eyes closed in soulful intensity, lifting the instrument high in the air at passionate crescendos – an apparently total commitment entirely wasted on his audience. Knowing nothing about jazz, and in any case now suffering from severe sensory overload, I would be unable to distinguish a provincial amateur from the greatest innovator since Bird.

'Of course it needs a rhythm section,' Kyle explains. 'I'm trying to get a quartet together again. Know of anyone who might be interested?'

Of course. My mother plays great walking bass and Lily's a real heavy cooker on drums.

'Playing always makes me thirsty. Do you take a drink?' One suggestion that is not at odds with the Fenian experience.

But as a so-called man of the arts I must be a bitter disappointment. In need of more stimulating company, Kyle goes around the house inviting people to the pub. Not for him the compartmentalisation so essential to neurotics. Why try to separate family and literary friends? Why not bring your children, your sister – your aged mother, even?

The children decline the invitation, as does Kyle's wife Olivia, who wants to stay behind to prepare a meal. As Kyle is making arrangements with her there is an unexpected arrival. I turn to see Tom McKenna quietly observing us. He must have let himself in at the front and waited in the kitchen doorway for the attention due a leading Irish poet: though his physical presence alone is commanding (he is over six feet tall and 'built according', more like a rugby player gone to seed than a poet). It is hard to believe that this robust frame houses one of the most delicate lyric talents of the age. Harder still to grasp the fact that he is actually *here.* A second major literary figure. Buy one, get one free.

'The artist . . . *en famille*,' McKenna says at last, looking ironically about the kitchen. 'Now I know what happens when you settle down.'

'And we know what happens when you stay in the States,' Kyle says, going up to him and slapping his enormous belly. 'It's bigger than ever, Tom.'

Among McKenna's prodigious gifts is a priceless talent for turning a liability into an asset. Instead of registering embarrassment and shame, he begins to move the great belly back and forth in the most obscenely suggestive manner, grunting with pleasure at the end of each thrust.

'Ever see an elephant coming?'

Olivia approaches, laughing, and they seal a tender embrace with a protracted kiss on the mouth. Keeping his arm round her, Tom looks into her eyes and says, in a deep, resonant tone, squeezing her after each sentence. 'You're wasted on that character. Get out of this Presbyterian backwater. Come away with a Gaelic poet.'

Kyle introduces me as one of the new young Catholic writers.

'The Fenians are risin' everywhere.' McKenna appraises me swiftly and sharply. Apparently there is nothing to fear. 'Promising, eh?' he says to Kyle with a laugh that makes it sound like an insult. Already we are seeing his gift in action. Who else could load a banal phrase with such significance, even to the extent of reversing its meaning?

Kyle, Tom, Renee and I set off for the local on foot. The old mother, a bit weak on her pins, is to follow by car.

Kyle makes a fuss when she arrives. 'The first woman in the county to have a licence,' he says proudly. 'And still as fond as ever of big cars.'

Again the comparison: my mother and Lily hunched in terror in the front of the Mini.

'I didn't want to be isolated in the country,' the old lady explains, 'but in those days people were shocked . . . oh yes.' She leans forward to Tom and me. 'I had to tell them all the women in France drove cars. Of course that wasn't true at all.' Chuckle of mischievous delight. 'I got off with a lot being French.'

The local is Niall's (a Fenian bar, McKenna informs me with a meaningful laugh), whose tiny back room already seems crowded when the five of us have settled. Niall waits on us in person and Kyle engages him in conversation, expressing keen interest in his business, family and personal wellbeing. To me Niall has the look of a typically two-faced Catholic gombeen man, contemptuous of liberal do-gooding and interested in nothing other than money. To Niall and his customers Kyle is surely the ultimate Big McGlundy. I can imagine the behind-backs talk, the scornful anecdotes, the sniggering. However, Kyle finishes by asking if he can cash a cheque – perhaps he is not so naïve after all. Niall agrees at once.

Signing with a flourish, Kyle looks at Tom. 'Cries like dead letters sent to Dearest Him that lives . . . alas . . . away.'

McKenna throws back his head in a loud, appreciative laugh. 'That's very good . . . very good.'

It takes me a few moments to grasp the import of this. Altnagarvin and its inhabitants are *living on credit*. But of course it is hardly surprising. You would expect a contemporary Zorba to be running an overdraft. And I with no commitments or dependants have several hundred pounds saved. *No one here must ever know.*

McKenna explains that he is back in the North for the funeral of an aunt. 'The undertaker says to me, says he, *Tom, that's an awful big woman to wash down.*' He leans forward to peer shrewdly at the company, convincing us once again of multilayered richness and significance. '*An awful big woman to wash down,*' he repeats.

I enquire reverently about his career and he mentions a *Selected Poems* due in the States, where his work is more respected than in England, which is neither surprising nor regrettable. The English scene has been dead for fifty years or more. Insular, smug, safe ... dead. For some reason Kyle is still attached to England and blind to the real achievements elsewhere.

'What would you say,' McKenna asks me, 'about a half-Irish writer who's scarcely looked at Joyce and a half-French writer who's never looked at Proust?'

Since I myself have never read *Finnegans Wake* or word one of Marcel, I have nothing at all to say on the matter.

Luckily Renee comes in on McKenna with startling intensity. 'But don't you find Proust so sentimental about his old grandmother?'

She is not only magnificently brutal but also an astute critic of Proust. Ferocious dark eyes burn into McKenna. This is no Irish colleen. Anyone looking for Mary of Dungloe is absolutely in the wrong shop.

'Exactly,' McKenna murmurs, unintimidated, relaxed, knowing, assured, actually laying a Fenian paw on her bare brown arm. 'The weakest thing in the book. But at least he killed her off early. And he had the sense not to put his mother in much. He knew how soft he was on her.'

Looking around for corroboration, he finds himself staring at another novelist's beloved French mother. We have all forgotten the old lady.

'What's wrong with being soft on your mother?'

She is not offended, merely perplexed, and it comes to me that Kyle is right after all. Why be a secretive Fenian? Why be furtive and separatist? Why not bring everyone together as equals, frankly stating and defending their positions?

I signal to Niall in wild jubilation. 'Pint of stout, two Jimmys, Tio Pepe and a G and T!'

All too soon it is over. Tom has to get back to his native village (though he promises to return the next day) and wants to get through the police patrols before dark. On his way to Altnagarvin he has been stopped several times, a routine experience for most, but for the poet a source of potent symbol and myth.

'I passed five rings of steel,' Tom solemnly declares.

On the walk back to the house Renee tells me about her acting career. Small parts in British comedies as saucy French maids – even a movie or two – then marriage and children. She is trying to get back in but it is phenomenally difficult. The young producers are so insolent now. Often you do not even get opening your mouth. Her last audition, for instance.

She pauses, overcome by emotion. I take a quick peek. Shadows lurk in the deep cheek grooves. Cruelty and carnage flame in her eyes.

'Sorry, darling, he said to me, but I just can't see you as a victim.'

At the house the mother is waiting in her car. As Kyle and Renee go forward to help her, McKenna falls back and, nodding towards Renee, speaks to me out of the side of his mouth. Beneath the worldliness and sophistication exists a standard Fenian corner boy.

'Is she . . . uh . . . ye know . . . *with you?*'

First, shock – then elation. *He actually thinks this is possible.* Of course I take care to let nothing show, shrugging with a weary laugh of surfeit and boredom. *He actually thinks this is possible. He really does.*

I have made a hit with the mother too, it seems. In the hall she seizes my arm and drags me away from the others towards a painting that fills the wall opposite the door. It is a gigantic female nude, minus the head and legs but painted in a stylised manner that refutes any charge of pornography.

'What do you think of that?' she whispers in hideous intimacy. Can she see right through to my bourgeois soul? I look to the others but they offer no help.

'I like it,' I have to say at last.

'But why?'

I am conscious of profound mental fatigue. It is not easy to come from a culture where nothing has been questioned for centuries into one where almost every statement has to be justified by logical argument.

She considers the painting carefully. Whatever her objections, they are not based on fear. 'If they'd left her head on at least. *Why did they cut her head off?*'

Once again I fail to reply. Not important, for we are getting to the real issue. Squeezing my arm, she puts her face close to mine. Familiar hideous emotional pressure. 'And what do you think of these awful books of Kyle's?'

She *can* see my bourgeois soul. Sensing the absence of true bohemianism, she is calling in much-needed support. Certainly Kyle cannot be the easiest of sons. As Genet has pointed out, being the mother of divinity is more arduous and problematic than the state of divinity itself.

'I think his books are excellent,' I say, without much conviction. At least I have managed not to recant.

It is a relief to proceed to the meal and the anonymous crowd. No one asks me to testify – until near the end.

'So!' Kyle cries to me with impresario's pride. 'You enjoyed Tom McKenna?'

'I certainly agreed with his views on England.'

Kyle chuckles. 'I'd be more impressed if I didn't know the facts. I have contacts there, as you know. Tom's famous for bad-mouthing England but every time a book comes out he's all over London knocking on doors to get it reviewed.'

'And what do you think of his poetry?'

'A forty-watt bulb.'

After the meal Renee and the mother disappear. Kyle and Olivia take me to a grand room looking west over the lake. Possibly intimidating once, it is now comfortably battered and run-down, with even a touch of senescent peace. Kyle goes to a huge sideboard and produces a bottle of Jameson and glasses. After an unfortunate earlier experience I have never been able to drink whiskey.

'This all right for you?'

'Sure.'

'Perhaps you'd like something in it?'

'No no no no no.'

One wall is shelved from end to end and packed to bursting with books. On the floor below the bottom shelf, a row of LPs stretches from the back wall to the window. Kyle flips around and comes up with a boxed set.

'Christ!' Olivia shouts. 'Not *Uncle Vanya!*'

'We can always learn from Chekhov.'

Up to now Olivia has seemed the self-effacing type. She takes a ferocious belt of hooch, a wild unfocused gaze roaming round the room. 'Fuck!' she shouts with startling violence, the soldier's word disconcerting in this environment dedicated to rational discourse.

Undeterred, Kyle puts on the record and we are into Olivier as Astrov, bored by life in the provinces – dull, stupid, sordid – surrounded by cranks and becoming a drunken ageing crank himself. What can a sensitive man do in the provinces but drink? As though in confirmation, all the last westerly light seems to converge on my Jameson, glowing with mysterious golden power in its chunky, bottom-heavy glass.

We are microbes ... microbes. Olivier's mature adult chuckle, marvellously combining amusement and despair. How those two hundred years from now will despise us for living such stupid, insipid lives!

Outside, a gentle slope leads down to the calm and shining lake. Opposite, a wooded hill cut by diagonal paths. By the boathouse, facing the lake, is the seat where everyone will meet in Act One. Altnagarvin is the perfect setting for Chekhov. Except that no one here is in despair. No abdications in favour of those two hundred years hence. Here there are only today people fulfilling themselves like crazy. In Altnagarvin, now is the time.

Certainly no one is inhibited or repressed. Halfway through Act One Olivia jumps up and rushes out with another frightful oath. Kyle does not respond. In fact he seems to be asleep, except that he keeps getting up to replenish our glasses and change the record. I match him glass for glass. It is important to get used to the Jameson, whose effects will resemble those of my new life, that is, harsh and unsettling at first but eventually flooding the soul with a sense of repletion and repose.

At last Sonia delivers her closing speech. 'We shall rest! We shall hear the angels. We shall see all heaven bright with many stars, shining like diamonds.'

A suitable note on which to retire – but Kyle wants to see the real stars.

'A little boat ride perhaps?'

Calm balmy night, the lake domesticated and placid. But for a journey of a few hundred yards it is surely excessive to be taking the car. Come to that, why are we going out through the main gate?

Kyle guns his car down the road with a manic Zorba cackle.

The 'boat' is not a pond skiff but a sailing dinghy moored on the coast. A bumpy dirt road leads to a small deserted jetty. The sea is as still as a mirror but not in the least reassuring. Genuinely serious threats are always silent and calm. To me it glitters with premeditated malice like a bourgeois delinquent.

Kneeling on the jetty, facing the water, Kyle closes his eyes, and, raising both arms above his head, palms outward, bends his upper body forward in solemn obeisance. After a few moments he rises gravely, dusting his cords.

'The secret of all successful relationships is mutual respect.'

For me Astrov is nearer the mark. 'It's the normal condition of a man to be a crank.'

Our voyage is cancelled due to mutiny even before embarkation. And it will not be the last time Kyle suffers from my cowardice. He has to settle for flinging the car about country lanes on the way back. As I grimly brace myself in the passenger seat, art is once again my solace and strength. 'We shall go on living, Uncle Vanya. We shall rejoice and look back with a smile on our tribulations. And we shall rest. I believe it, fervently, passionately. We shall rest! We shall rest! We shall rest!'

In the morning I awake to find Kyle calmly going through my pockets.

'Car keys?' he asks. 'Mine won't start.'

Kyle with the family Mini – one careful owner, a used-car

buyer's dream. Intoxicated by the dance, we forget the other side of Zorba – blowing the irrigation project money on a week in a brothel.

Anxiety reduces my pleasure in a splendid Ulster fry, but eventually Kyle breezes into the kitchen full of the beautiful morning. Perfect for a walk in the woods. We might see the deer. As with so many of his casual remarks, this gives rise to a host of questions. Are these animals wild or in any sense owned? If owned, then by whom? In either case where do they hang out, on what do they feed? How are they protected? How restrained? I am thinking not of hunters with rifles but the danger they would face in a Fenian area, gangs of eight-year-olds attempting to brick them to death.

And is it possible for someone like me to see such beautiful creatures? Can a corner boy commune with the shy, wild spirit of the woods? With Kyle along I might have been confident, but in the hall he suddenly veers towards the stairs.

'Now, children, I must leave you. There is work to be done.'

Making a gesture of benediction, he turns and mounts the stairs with stately tread. Even now it takes me a while to understand. He is going up to do the sacred thing. I watch his progress in reverent silence. Then something impels me to call out.

'Tell it like it is, Kyle!'

He comes to the banister, chuckling with delight, arms open wide in classic master-to-disciple posture.

'What beautiful friends I have.'

So it is Olivia and I for the walk. She talks freely and with conviction, most of what she is saying sensible enough. Yet there is a problem putting it together. I have always assumed that people make an impression. It may be unpleasant or misleading but there is always a definite impression. Now, for the first time, there is nothing. It refuses to add up.

After a while it becomes clear that everything she says is either an opinion of Kyle's or something she thinks is artistic currency. This invasion of the alien body-snatchers is common enough in the world of the arts, but the first encounter with it is disconcerting and eerie. Your hand reaches out to a person and goes through ectoplasm. Your legs lift to meet the stairs, but there are no stairs.

Not that there is anything ghostly about her appearance. A tall, gaunt, wild-faced woman, she wears an outfit as distinctive as Renee's, though it could scarcely be more different – wellies, men's baggy cords and a huge shapeless sweater hanging a foot below a construction worker's donkey jacket. Only someone very rich or English would cultivate such a gyppo look in Ireland. Olivia is in the second category and rounds off the effect with a strong Yorkshire accent. Perhaps it was the earthy dialect that attracted Kyle. Lord Chatterley's mistress, a female Mellors.

And on the subject of game she does seem genuine, explaining with animation that the deer are owned by the Forestry Commission and fed by local farmers.

'Very generous of them.'

'There's nothing generous about it. They're well paid by the commission. The farmers don't give a damn about the deer.' Suddenly she seems quite angry. 'You know the electrified fences they use for cattle? They're all right for cows, but people don't realise they can actually kill deer.'

I have to admit that I too have been ignorant in this respect.

'The herd's down thirty per cent in the last few years. The farmers couldn't care less and no one will make them take down their fences.'

Renee, Kyle and the mother join us for a late lunch. Also one of the younger group, Robbie Semple, a 'promising' actor–playwright, prematurely bald and with the sinister, ravaged appearance of Baudelaire in his final years. I have tremendous respect for anyone who can make alopecia swing and Semple has succeeded completely, so stylish he makes hair seem a vulgar absurdity, baldness the necessary precondition of existential sainthood. Beside him Kyle resembles a square fifties B-movie star.

'Well!' Kyle cries with typical ebullience. 'Did you see the deer?'

'Not a smell,' I have to admit. 'How did it go for you?'

'It was just a review,' Kyle says, naming an Irish contemporary.

'I hope you gutted him.'

Kyle smiles in gentle tolerance but Semple utters a sudden wild, whinnying laugh.

'So conventional.'

His virulent scorn rouses Renee. 'What's so great about being unconventional? There's Billy Connell down the road. Odd as two left feet. Hardly ever leaves the house. He's unconventional. What's so great about that?'

There is obviously a subtext here. She stares angrily at Semple, who lapses into silence, that modern medium for which he has such a natural affinity. In years to come he will work on the play-without-words, a genre whose possibilities he now illustrates by turning to the window with a sneer. With body language as expressive as this you could certainly lock up the word hoard and throw away the key.

Furious, unassuaged, Renee continues to turn on Semple eyes as dark and sinister as the Canal Orfano and in whose depths as many men have perished.

'You're confusing unconventional and eccentric.' Hopelessly committed to words, I take it upon myself to reply. 'The eccentric behaves differently because of neurosis. He has no choice. He's under compulsion. But the unconventional person makes a conscious decision to reject the values of the herd. The unconventional person is healthy. The eccentric is sick.'

It is my turn to receive the eyes, shining now, shivers of moonlight on the dark canal. She is flashing on me only to punish Semple. But it wasn't a bad speech either. At last I'm starting to get into the game.

'Why does no one I know talk like that?' Her voice, made for disdain and contumely, is actually now a yearning sigh. 'So . . . so . . . so . . .'

'Cogent?' I suggest.

Semple whinnies. Going for the Jameson, Kyle cackles, enjoying nothing better than friends and loved ones in mutual admiration and rapport.

In the wisdom of the years, old Mrs Magee can see only the human tragedy in Renee's example. 'Poor Billy,' she sighs. 'He was fine till his mother died.'

Now Olivia makes an eloquent wordless contribution – a harsh abrupt laugh, dark with bitter significance.

Semple declines a drink, wordlessly of course, leaving Kyle to explain. 'Robbie prefers drugs to alcohol.'

The others also decline and depart, much to my disappointment: just when my confidence is growing, when I'm getting in some big first serves, moving well round the court, returning serve early and low.

But here company is never a problem. In that uniquely harmonious moment at the end of the first glass, Tom McKenna makes another dramatic appearance in the doorway. The poet's psychic powers need no further proof – but he provides another just the same. Outside the main gate, several deer gathered in the road as though to stop his car. While from others they flee in distaste, Tom McKenna they seek and confront.

'There was a big fellow leading them,' Tom says, with a searching look at each of us in turn, 'and we had a good long look at each other . . . oh yes.'

Of course they did. Nobility of spirit will always recognise its like.

'He knew you were a poet, Tom,' I say. 'Born to mate with your own free kind on the crags.'

Relaxed by the whiskey, I now even have the confidence to make cheeky drop shots.

McKenna subjects me to one of his leisurely cool appraisals, the kind of look I remember from teacher-priests. *Just don't get too smart altogether, sonny.* And another message also. *I'm the one you have to reckon with here. What goes down with these dumb Prods won't wash with me.* Certainly not a man to underestimate – as cute as the fly that shites on the fly. He turns to Kyle, adopting a genial, ironic tone. 'You'll have to stop encouraging these young wans.'

Kyle, pouring shots, announces that the Jameson is finished. We will have to go to Niall's after this round.

Unhurried, solemn, foxy, McKenna sips Jameson and then considers his glass in profound appreciation. 'The salmon is healthy only when its mouth is wet.' Raising his eyes, he gives each of us a look of multilayered amusement. 'As soon as the mouth goes dry it dies.'

Obviously more drink will be consumed, but just as things are getting interesting it is time to go. I am already late for a date with Reba. Not only that, I have filled up with petrol and *forgotten to get a receipt.* All friends of the Herrons are solemnly pledged to collect receipts for Sean to add to his petrol claim and boost the savings for marriage to Frances. Reality returns in a bitter flood. Reba will knock my melt in.

As Kyle goes off to round up a party that will include his mother, McKenna leans across to me, resuming his posture of humorous conspiracy, and says, out of the corner of his mouth, 'The beloved son. The golden boy. He who can do no wrong.'

Fenian meanness assails me from all sides.

'Ye see, the mother never fitted in with the local Orangemen.' He leans even closer. 'Who would, eh?' Long humorous slug of whiskey. 'And the father was busy being a captain of industry. So everything was lavished on the beloved son.'

'What about his novels?'

Noticing my touch of irritation, McKenna laughs indulgently and sits back in his seat. After a few moments he comes forward again. 'He's a *writer,*' he says, with a laugh suggestive of dark complexities and profundities a youth like me could never begin to understand.

Kyle returns with Olivia, Renee, his mother – and shining hardback copies of his last two novels. Not to be outdone, Olivia presents me with a poetry anthology apparently plucked on the spur of the moment from a kitchen shelf (later I find an Alcoholics Anonymous leaflet tucked inside). The old mother pumps my hand (don't leave it too long, I know the way now). Renee steps in, seizing me firmly by the arms to plant on my gaping peasant mouth a kiss that instantly overwhelms the cerebral cortex.

Overcome, almost annihilated, I stand speechless, awkwardly hefting the books. Behind the Magees, McKenna remains seated, drinking Kyle's whiskey and smirking with the mean-spirited Fenian cuteness I have never despised so much.

'But you've an overdraft,' I protest feebly, raising the books.

As though such a negative thought could affect the Zorba of the North!

'There's always America in the summer,' Kyle cries. 'God bless America!'

3

I thought I had the Herrons classified, but life resists the schema as strenuously as the Gael opposes the Brit. When Betty came back from America for the wedding of Frances and Sean it was hard to believe she was a Herron. For a start she was not just attractive but pretty, an adjective I never thought could apply to this family. Ditto for petite. And she made the most of her looks. Where her sisters had coarse wavy hair pulled back into ponytails or jammed into place by huge clasps, Betty had the same fashionably straight bob as Kyle's sister Renee. Where the others largely scorned make-up, Betty had dramatic purple eye shadow with matching lipstick and nail polish. Where they favoured heavy dull sweaters and skirts, she knocked the eye out of your head with light, stylish, well-tailored outfits in bright colours. And her manner had none of the expected qualities – the aggressive superiority, sarcasm and contempt. Totally lacking Herron vinegar, everything about her was fragrant and exquisite. Any observer would have sworn she peed Moët et Chandon and shat Belgian chocolate.

What she did have was Herron hubris. Far from apologising for her presumption, she publicly proclaimed a rebirth. From now on she was to be known as Liz.

In the uproar it was ever-gallant Sammy Mullen who was first to grant official recognition. 'Here's to Liz,' he shouted, jumping up and bringing his Guinness against her Bacardi and Coke (this was another affectation – here everyone, including the girls, drank beer or stout).

Others were even more out of place. Hugo's girl, Rosemary, introduced at this homecoming, had brought Mrs Herron a bizarre art work – a framed canvas with a centrepiece of a Celtic fort composed of matchsticks.

'The internees made it,' Rosemary announced with pride and misplaced confidence.

Like many another, she assumed the Herron dislike of England implied a commitment to the republican cause. In fact they were just as contemptuous of romantic nationalism. No ideology could enslave them. They were Nietzschean anarchists. And Rosemary compounded the error by chatting with the insane common sense of a middle-aged maiden aunt.

Caroline, John's girl, was also talkative, though in a radiant, bourgeois way that confirmed the Herrons' worst fears. I watched her offer a plate of white bread with a smile of unchippable polyurethane.

The appalling thing about these girls was not so much their style as their failure to register its effect. To me, an adult without a feedback mechanism is as shocking as a child without limbs.

Liz saved the evening with amazing stories about America, where it was common for young girls to be violated and butchered in bizarre, gruesome ways. Years later I discovered these were urban folk myths, but at the time I swallowed them as avidly as the others. So much for scepticism.

Everyone's favourite was *The Babysitter and the Man Upstairs.* No sooner has the young girl settled in front of the TV than the bumps, knocks, taps et cetera begin. When the phone rings she rushes to it in relief – only to recoil in horror. *I am in the apartment above you.* She locks herself in the bedroom with the children and phones her boyfriend, who arrives to find her on a landing, completely dismembered but not discouraged, pluckily making her way downstairs by means of her chin.

'With her *chin?*' Caroline repeated in wonder.

'With her chin.' Liz nodded solemnly, suggesting that in similar circumstances she would have shown the same determination.

'And you travelled round America on your own?' Reba said.

'I was all up and down the east coast. Canada's the only place I didn't reach.'

'Sure Canada's an Orange hole,' Mrs Herron said at once.

'But how did you afford that?' I wanted to know. 'Was it expensive?'

While Hugo launched into a story about a hunchback immigrant being quoted astronomical prices in the States ('Everything's high up in America'), Liz leaned intimately towards me and explained that she had worked as a waitress in her uncle's roadhouse.

'I had to wear this uniform – checked blouse, hair bow and really skimpy, skimpy skirt. Up to here, honest to God.' She marked a line across the top of her thighs and chuckled, indicating that while the outfit was of course absurd it had looked sweet on her. Already there was a bond between us. Only we two were cosmopolitan, only we wished to brave the American nightmare. Leaning closer, she said: 'Go and stay with the uncles. They love anyone from Ireland. They're just two big Paddies, but they're really generous.'

To make use of the Herron connection, this was an idea I could never have conceived. Yet here it was, offering me a ticket to the States. Imminence was everywhere these days.

Hugo was finishing his story with the hunchback's riposte to an insult. 'That's not a hump, that's me arse. Everything's high up in America.'

Rosemary punched him in ritual outrage. It was becoming a classic Herron night after all.

Helping Reba with drinks in the kitchen, I enquired about Liz. Had she always been like this, or did America turn everyone into sweetie-pie starlets?

'She's just the same,' Reba said. 'Except for that American accent. God, that's hard to stick.'

'But how did she come out of *this* family?'

Being pretty and petite, Liz had always been her father's favourite – dandled on his knee, indulged, dressed up, taken on visits – whereas her sisters were described as 'big lumps' and expected to stay home and do the housework. Of the two big lumps Reba came off slightly better. She got to go to the ball occasionally, but Frances was always Cinderella. Thus we had a schema after all. According to Reba's testimony, the father's treatment of the daughters mapped directly onto their temperaments: Liz the candy-ass sweet-pants and Frances the mad dog; Reba herself somewhere in between. There was a famous family incident. During a game in which Frances was pushing Betty in a wheelbarrow, Betty ended up at the bottom of a flight of concrete steps. Did the angel fall – or was she thrown? In any case Betty sustained damaged teeth and a scar on her nose and Frances was 'battered soft' by the outraged father.

Choking with laughter, Betty/Liz came into the kitchen and put a hand on my arm to steady herself. 'God what's she not like, that wee girl. That Rosemary one.' Already she was slipping back into the vernacular. Again unlike her family, Liz adapted herself to her surroundings instead of the other way round. 'Know what me mother just said to me? I said, Rosemary does go on a bit and me mother said, *She talks like a goose dungin'*. I had to come out or I'd wet meself.'

As she laughed again I noticed the crooked teeth and the scar on the bridge of her nose, imperfections that made her prettiness achingly human. America would probably have remedied these – she had escaped just in time from the land of regularity and blandness.

Still she leaned on my arm. After hearing of Reba's deprived childhood I should not have been offering her sister yet more admiration. But Liz inclined unto me with a sweet spontaneity that was impossible to resist. Goddam it, I too was deprived.

'And such a loud voice,' I said. 'She'd drown a fuckin' Orange band.'

With a terrible squawk Liz thrust her spilling Bacardi at Reba. Gripping my arm even more tightly, she crossed her legs at the thighs and bent almost double. 'Oh don't . . . *don't!*'

Reba took a cautious sip of Bacardi and Coke and, as with a hen-house child at its first experience of human kindness, touching awkward innocent wonder flooded her sceptical features. Up to now she had drunk only beer or stout, an inexpensive taste I would have been happy to preserve.

'God, that's gorgeous,' she sighed, converted, taking another hefty snort.

But who could be cross with sweet-pants Liz? She brought wonder and delight to us all.

With a rapturous cry Sammy Mullen came in pursuit of his love. 'Beautiful,' he murmured to me, taking Liz by the hands and attempting to dance her. 'Beautiful wee girl.'

'Go and dance with Rosemary,' Liz laughed. 'Rosemary's beautiful too.'

Even considering such a thing brought a touch of cold sobriety. Releasing Liz, Sammy stepped back and spoke in a remarkably level tone.

'Jesus,' he said, 'if that wee girl's good-lookin' my arsehole's too long covered.'

It was the time of imminence. The Protestant State was in ruins. Excited by the potential for change, Kyle prevailed upon the local radio to grant him a half-hour show which he called, only partly in mischief, *Born-again Ulster.* Convinced he could save the province, he began each fortnightly show with a talk encouraging listeners to cast off the influence of dead institutions and beliefs and use their imaginations to invent new ways of living. Only now did I realise the extent of his ambition. A kind of Presbyterian Lorenzo the Magnificent, he would make grey sullen Ulster as effulgent as Quattrocento Florence. Needless to say, I was sceptical. Like most Irish Catholics I am a Manichean by temperament. Belief in the imperfectibility of man is part of my gene code.

'What's the only thing that unites all the Irish?' I asked Kyle. 'North and South, urban and rural, Fenian and Prod?'

'Love of rugby,' he said. 'And weren't the Irish great against the French last week?'

'Not love of rugby. Hatred of liberalism. Hatred of do-gooding. Hatred of reform.'

But who can resist the temptations of stardom? I was recruited as a Catholic basher, making fun of RC education and mores. Even Robbie Semple contributed a few satirical sketches. Renee was in London trying to resuscitate her acting career but Semple remained in Altnagarvin, apparently living off Kyle, about whom he was contemptuous behind backs. Gratitude and loyalty were no part of Semple's ethos.

There was no shortage of jeerers and mockers, but something more positive was needed, something *con* and not *de*structive. Kyle put out a call for humanists and had an instant response: a retired professor who, instead of slippers and country cottage, had taken on the difficult and perhaps dangerous task of establishing an Ulster branch of the British Humanist Association. Ulster could not have found a more appropriate figurehead. Wise, dignified, grave, with a fine head of grey hair and a trim grey goatee, he resembled the bust that Rodin would surely have left the world had he ever been commissioned to sculpt the Humanist.

As soon as he arrived in Altnagarvin he disparaged his Protestant background.

'This mindless worship of King Billy. What would they say if they knew he was a homosexual dwarf?'

Quick as a flash, Kyle was down on the humanist heresy.

'But of course homosexual dwarfs can be wonderful human beings too.'

'Some of your best friends?' I suggested to Kyle, drawing an angry look from the guest at this cheap flippancy.

'Exactly,' Kyle said, naming a well-known English critic.

The humanist described his career – Chair of Physics at the University of Singapore, undying hatred for the regime, undying love for the East itself.

'The sari, for instance, is such a beautiful garment. Becoming on women of every age. You don't have the generations separated by style of dress. That's a profoundly divisive thing in Western culture.'

At once this was seized on by Kyle the promoter. 'Perhaps you'd like to develop that idea for the next programme?'

For me a different question. Could this be the father figure I sought? Brought up by provincial, philistine women, I badly needed a male role model heavy on experience and principle. Kyle scarcely fitted the bill. Already I was starting to feel like *his* da. What I had in mind was someone like Conrad's Marlow, the wise old narrator who advises foolhardy, impetuous youth.

Humanism, goatee, the East, this candidate was perfect except for one thing – an immediate and intense dislike for me. As far as I could judge from his manner, he saw me as an insolent and opportunistic guttersnipe. My God, if only that were true.

'I believe in decorum,' he said to me at one point in a meaningful way, leaning up out of the sofa to stare me down. I should have proved to him that this was inconsistent with humanism but at the time I could think of nothing to say.

By and by, another possible motive for hostility crossed my mind: that I was a Fenian with ideas above my station. Paranoia or perceptiveness? You can never be sure. Of course he rejected Protestant bigotry and professed his love for Asians, but this was no proof of universal brotherhood. It is easier to love foreign natives than the ones at your own back door. No doubt he would have found me adorable if I had been brown-skinned, but now he behaved as though I had usurped his rightful place at Altnagarvin.

Unable to win in debate, I still had one crucial advantage: I was invited to stay the night and he was not. After the script conference the talk grew desultory and I could feel him trying to freeze me out. In the end it was he who had to go.

We moved in a leisurely way to the front steps where I stood at Kyle's shoulder in casual, negligent ease.

'And how's the Ulster branch?' Kyle asked.

'Booming. Membership trebled. Meetings packed out.' Marlow laughed at one of the little ironies so beloved of the cultured. 'London can't understand it at all, of course. The most religious region in the British Isles, and yet with one of the largest humanist groups.'

I let him chortle a while and then said in a light, offhand, almost absent-minded way: 'I'll just get my stuff from the car.'

Marlow darted me a grieved look, stricken.

Suck on that, you mother.

In the room we had just left, Semple was lacing his coffee with Kyle's Jameson.

'Thought you didn't drink alcohol.'

He replied with an evil whinny.

'That was Ulster's top humanist.' Although he was contemptuous about *Born-again Ulster*, I knew Semple followed its progress with interest. He let loose another wild, derisive shriek.

No doubt he jeered at me too, but I always found him strangely sympathetic. I suspect that the great despisers will always claim a place in my heart. Semple's sublime contempt was tonic whereas Kyle was beginning to seem like a plodder. Why are the Nietzscheans always so stylish and the liberals always so dull?

Laying down his coffee, Semple spoke in sudden uncharacteristic excitement.

'Did you hear they were busted in Chicago?'

'Who?'

'Burroughs and Genet. They were on a march.'

'I didn't know that.'

'Fuck they'll be here next.'

And why not? No longer a stagnant backwater, Northern Ireland was main news all over the world. Now aberration and frenzy were available on the doorstep.

It was the time of imminence. Anything could happen.

Liz applied her sweet shoulder to the wheel by doing voluntary work for Garvin Dodd, a Protestant solicitor standing for parliament as an independent liberal opposed to the unionist hegemony. Naturally his support was largely Catholic, but the older generation had a familiar problem. As so often before, liberal was synonymous with libertine and Mrs Herron was always reminding Liz of this: 'That fella has an eye for the girls. Watch yourself with that fella.' And behind her daughter's back she issued dire prophecies: 'That wee girl'll end up in the body o' the jail.'

Yet she herself was consulting Dodd. When it came to business, Catholic morals yielded to respect for Protestant efficiency. Her problem was the devastation of Great George Street. Largely destroyed by riot, arson and looting, the area was to be redeveloped and she was threatened with a compulsory purchase order on the shop. Given these serious circumstances, she was outraged when Dodd spent the first fifteen minutes of the interview singing the praises of her daughter. It was as bad as attending a Fenian GP. Nor was she consoled by his legal advice. Compensation was based on income, which was determined by tax returns. Had she been declaring her income and paying her tax? *A Catholic widda woman with five children paying tax to the Protestant State! A Nietzschean anarchist paying tax to anyone!*

In Harvey Terrace residents and visitors tiptoed around the suffering woman of the house. Just as well that Liz's electioneering had halted her studies (she was taking A levels at the tech and worked in the living room) and her attempts to learn the flute at a newly acquired music stand in the living room ('That wee girl has me head deeved,' Mrs Herron shrieked, even in pre-trauma days). In a way I admired the old girl's consistency. Like most Irish bourgeois, my mother and Lily lived in a state of perpetual peevishness, but they could switch to gaiety and insouciance the instant a visitor arrived. Mrs Herron's outrage was visceral and absolute. When she was in one of her black moods she was equally vile to everyone. No one else's problems or plans could be discussed at such a time. Though, of course, Rosemary could not refrain from mentioning her marriage to Hugo.

'I seen a lovely wee house out in Silvertown that'd do us. I went back to it yesterday and threw a miraculous medal into the garden.'

Magical coercion – the religion of primitive man. Liz caught my eye.

'Mrs Herron,' Rosemary went on, 'I'll get ye a miraculous medal for the shop.'

Another grotesque misjudgement. Though she observed the

conventions of Catholicism, Mrs Herron was scarcely in the mainstream, much less on the saints-'n'-sorcery fringe.

'For the love of God, wee girl,' she screamed, 'have ye no wit at all?'

This was a good start to the evening. Already Liz and I felt sophisticated and superior and now we were on our way to the tech cinema club. It was a Swedish movie Liz badly wanted to see, and since Reba was working (and anyway hated subtitles) Liz asked me along. I was familiar with the venue, a lecture theatre where the wooden seats tortured your arse, cold seeped into your bones and harsh white light leaked in around the blackout curtains. Many gladly endured this on a regular basis. In the provinces you expected to suffer for art.

At least the audience was attractive, youthful and animated, chattering noisily. Liz also chattered, pointing out classmates and college characters. The difference was that she continued after the lights went down. All that changed was her subject matter, now drawn from the appearance of the characters on screen. 'Oh, she's really nice-looking'... 'Would you look at the state of him.' It reminded me of my mother and Lily purporting to watch television, continually going in and out of the room, passing cups of tea and snacks back and forth, adjusting mats, ornaments, lamps, heaters, chairs and all the time babbling, babbling, what was happening on screen something vague and distant on which to let the eye rest in the odd moments of silence and stasis.

Now a girl was brushing her hair. 'Counting the strokes,' Liz said in a loud, cheerful tone.

'Shut the fuck up,' someone snarled viciously from behind.

Liz made a rum face, but my sympathies were all with the plaintive. How would Reba have behaved? She would have hated the movie, probably even walked out. But while she was there she would have given it her full attention. She would have shut up.

Afterwards Liz took my arm with an air of high expectation, as though the main business of the evening were yet to come. All I had planned was to walk her home. We hovered outside the tech and then set off in the direction of Harvey Terrace, but in a languid, aimless way, as though without a specific destination. The film was not mentioned. Instead she enquired about *Born-again Ulster* in a tone of respect and concern. We were fellow right-thinking progressives, responsible and far-sighted, joining forces with like-minded people from the Protestant community in order to defeat the powerful forces of reaction.

'It's chuntering along,' I said. 'Kyle's wife's getting fed up with all the admin.'

'You know everyone in our house takes the piss out of it,' Liz confided sorrowfully. 'They go around mimicking Kyle and laughing themselves sick. And they do your polite radio voice.'

I was neither surprised nor shocked. Who would expect approbation from the Herrons? I, too, often found Kyle ridiculous, my own careful public voice always grotesque.

Reba was not mentioned, but the message was clear. A traitor herself, she deserved no loyalty from me.

'It's the same when I practise the flute,' Liz was saying. 'The slagging never stops.' Another bond between us; we were fellow sensitive artists surrounded by philistines. 'Hugo tells everyone I'm trying to get into an Orange band. This is what I get for helping Garvin.'

'And how's that going?'

'We think he might scrape in. If not, it won't be for want of trying.'

Thanks to his young team, Dodd was certainly winning the poster campaign. Everywhere his smiling liberal face was pasted over the heavy jowls of his opponents. DODD FOR HARMONY AND GROWTH. Often a more pragmatic slogan was scrawled underneath: *Vote for Dodd the Fenian Prod.*

'I've been collecting sick votes,' Liz said, all her old insouciance back in play.

'Is there another kind in Ireland?'

She punched me playfully. 'People who can't get out of the house get their voting forms weeks before the election. So when you're knocking on doors the first thing you do is ask if there's any sick votes. Mostly there aren't, so you canvas in the usual way. But if there are, you try to collect them as if you're official. Most people hand them out.'

'And what do you do with the ones not for Dodd?'

Let no one think of Liz as a dull goody-goody. Within her, effrontery yearned for freedom like the bubbles in champagne. Laying a hand on my arm, she collapsed against me, giddy with deviance. 'We have a bonfire in headquarters every night.'

For an advocate of transgression and outrage, I was suprisingly shocked by this. Goddam it, surely the liberals shouldn't cheat. But then everything was overwhelmed by her fragrance, a heady blend of discreet cosmetics and freshly washed youthful hair and skin. I had a sense of nature at its most magnanimous, of sap swelling and juice flowing, hypersecretions impregnating pants with nectar pure as honey made by monks in remote mountain monasteries.

'You're a terrible case, Liz.'

'I know.'

She snuggled in like a mischievous child. Then a sigh, as though another hot honey-gush had taken the last crispness out of her pants. Now was the time for a transfer of allegiance. Liz would be the writer's dream woman – fan, agent, manager and roadie rolled into one. And these were just her day jobs. What had Reba to offer but indifference and scorn?

Why was I even thinking about it? Imagine trying to explain to Zorba.

'She want you, boss?'

'The girl was hypersecreting, Zorba.'

'Then what's your problem, boss?'

'She talked all through the movie.'

'Must be some movie, boss?'

'Actually it was a terrible movie, Zorba.'

But after all, the potential was not infinite. Imminence was starting to fade a little.

Already Harvey Terrace had paid the price for delirium. During the last riot, shrubs and trees had been cut down for barricades. Now the once-gracious street was as painful to behold as a scalped woman. The Chinese end house was worst hit. In the big side garden the fence had been torn down, every tree and shrub uprooted, the grass flattened and churned to mud. It was urban wasteland, littered with papers, packets, Coke cans, even an empty oil drum. All it needed was a scavenging three-legged dog.

Liz explained the oil drum. 'Ye know Dirty Butter? Mickey McCallion? He was stopping cars for petrol to make bombs. I think most people told him to piss off, but he had this impressive big drum. The little Chinese woman came running out shouting, *No safe, No safe.* Mickey slaps the drum: *This make house safe, lady.*'

I got to Altnagarvin late after a long and badly signposted police diversion through the back roads of the Ulster heartland. Kyle was in the front lounge with Semple and a placid white-haired man he introduced as 'Elvin McCready, the transcendental humanist'. As I sat down, Semple leaned forward with a po face and handed me a pamphlet.

MULTI-DIMENSIONAL CONSCIOUSNESS

Dwell above the Level of Destruction in the Body of Light

There was a bottle of Jameson on the table. I went for a glass and filled it.

> Ninety per cent of mankind will heed the call to develop a multi-dimensional Body of Light. Our physical world will fade away like soft Irish morning mist and we will abandon three-dimensional time and space to voyage freely, discovering planets earthly instruments cannot detect, meeting and conversing with other interplanetary travellers and performing painless surgery without anaesthetics.

I had yet to speak, but I can radiate scepticism like no man's business. Obviously Elvin decided at once that I belonged to the ten per cent who would not heed the call. Hoisting his large three-dimensional body out of the sofa, he announced that he would have to be on his way as he had calls in the morning. I assumed he meant calls to or from one of the extra dimensions.

'Elvin's a Betterware salesman,' Kyle explained.

Now imminence was not merely fading. It was deteriorating into farce.

'You're not putting this fruitcake on the air,' I said to Kyle when he got back. Semple laughed shrilly.

'Of course his work isn't literature. The ideas are badly expressed, but they're often genuine enough. He's opposed to selfishness and materialism and committed to renewal. His moral values aren't so different from ours.'

'Speak for yourself.'

Semple shrieked wildly. 'I think he's *terrific*.'

'And there's something very sweet and sincere about the man himself. I offered him a glass of Jameson and he said he didn't drink but would take it to make me feel at ease.'

'He should have drunk it without saying anything,' I said. 'Goodness has to be invisible, as Hannah Arendt says.'

Kyle suddenly adopted a strong rural Ulster accent. 'Hannah Arendt now,' he cackled like a toothless backwoods creature, 'who would she be at all?'

The Jameson was well down, I noticed.

Semple shrieked again. 'The female commandant of Treblinka.'

'Yese are too clever for me, sor,' Kyle said, refilling the glasses.

'Has that lunatic gone?' It was Olivia, gaunt and wild-eyed in the doorway. 'Your children waited all day for you to take them to the beach.'

'Why do they want a crowded, filthy beach?' Kyle cried. 'Haven't they the most beautiful spot in the province to enjoy? Woods, deer, a lake. This was a paradise for me as a child. And why fuss over them when they're perfectly healthy. Let them grow up beautiful and free – like wild flowers.'

Olivia regarded him angrily. 'This beautiful estate,' she said slowly, 'is falling down round your ears.'

Kyle fortified himself with a strong snort of Jameson.

'*You're an arrested adolescent,*' she screamed, slamming the door.

Kyle went after her and there was an altercation in the hall.

'This normal?' I asked Semple.

'Absolutely,' he said with scorn, detaching himself from such squalor. 'Well ... maybe a bit worse. Kyle had a fling with an American poet and she was staying here last week.'

'With Olivia and the family? *Here?*'

'Things were a little tense. And when that happens Kyle always takes to the boat. There were four of us – Renee and myself and Kyle and his girl. It was too rough really – but you can't talk to Kyle. As soon as we hit the open sea the mast snapped and we had a hell of a job getting back in. Didn't think we'd make it myself. Anyway, Kyle brought the mast home and put it in his bedroom. To remind him of mortality and good fortune, he said.' Semple paused for a pensive sip of Jameson. 'And oddly enough, it saved his life the very next day.'

He took another leisurely sip. For a man despairing of words, he certainly knew how to tell an anecdote.

'How was that?' I had to beg.

'Well he was in bed with the poetess and used the mast to prop the door shut. Olivia tried to break it down with an axe, but she didn't get in.'

There was a sharp cry in the corridor. Kyle returned, relaxed and calm, and put on a record.

'Kenneth McKellar,' he said briskly. 'The great Scottish tenor. And one of his finest performances – "Annie Laurie".'

For a smart boy I'm terribly slow on the uptake sometimes. Probably I was still fascinated by the story of The Mast and the Axe. Or perhaps my unconscious tried to withhold the terrible knowledge from an overtaxed brain. If so it was a misguided effort, for when the truth finally burst through it swept away every trace of deference.

'Kenneth McKellar!' I shouted. '*For fuck's sake.*'

For me McKellar was the vilest kind of cosy bad taste. It was not just the man himself – phoney tradition and heartiness in a kilt – but the fact that my mother and Lily adored him. I had come to the King of Bohemia and been served the middlebrow vomit I was desperate to escape.

'For fuck's sake!' I shouted again, with a violence most would have heeded. But Kyle interpreted criticism simply as failure to understand. I could not be listening properly. He turned up the volume.

'Listen to the timbre. The confidence. No Irish singer has that.'

'Thank Christ. We've enough to be ashamed of.'

Arguing with Kyle only made him retrench. I took a sharp belt of Jameson instead.

Now he was disputing with Semple. 'If we want to reach people we have to use popular forms and existing institutions. Your approach of shocking and insulting won't work. Anger and rudeness bring only anger and rudeness in return.'

'Fine by me.' Semple looked in my direction but I lacked the heart to offer support.

'If you want to stop people believing in lies you have to get through to them in the first place. Reform involves hard work. You have to get into institutions and change them from the inside. Take the existing apparatus and use it for something superior. What I'm doing with local radio at the moment.'

Semple threw back his head and roared with laughter. It was dark outside and we had yet to start the script conference, but at the thought of scheduling myself with an interplanetary traveller a great weariness came upon my spirit.

Kyle was only getting into his stride. 'We have to take popular forms and invest them with more passion and subtlety and truth. Like Shakespeare and Billie Holiday . . . and Kenneth McKellar.'

Now it was my turn to utter a laugh – abrupt, harsh and infinitely disabused.

Kyle finished his Jameson in an eager gulp. 'Two thousand years ago when Christ wanted to change things he didn't become a high priest and try to bully and intimidate people. Instead he talked to them in the street. He told them stories using everyday language and experience. And the passers-by were impressed. They stopped to listen. The man was a great entertainer.'

'Do you write?' Kyle enquired of Reba straight away.

'No.'

'Paint a little, perhaps?'

'No.'

'Play an instrument?'

'No.'

'She's not the arty type, Kyle,' Olivia said, directing at Reba a woman's smile implying earth-mother gifts older and more valuable than the arts.

Needing so much time to explain Kyle, I had forgotten to mention Olivia. For Reba, who always bought quality brand names, only gyppos and winos wore cast-offs like Olivia's.

'But everyone can *appreciate* the arts,' Kyle was saying. 'What do you think of *Born-again Ulster?*'

Reba made a kind of death rattle. She could scarcely admit that she laughed her fanny off mimicking Kyle and me. In fact, faced with Kyle, she seemed to have lost every trace of the spirited, inventive mockery that had been her chief asset. Perhaps mockery requires a degree of collusion and she could only make fun of hangdog Fenians profoundly aware of their own deficiencies. Every Fenian knows in his heart he's an eejit – but Kyle, although as idiotic as any, was protected by impregnable self-belief. Whatever the reason, Reba had gone to pieces and slumped on the sofa, a heavy, inert, hapless thing.

Olivia addressed her with the exclusive intimacy of an old friend. 'It's all very well for Kyle. He doesn't deal with these maniacs who ring up and give dog's abuse. They think *Born-again Ulster* is some sort of fundamentalist gospel show, and instead they find it's full of blasphemy and sex. So they're understandably annoyed. Then they ring me up.' She gave Kyle an accusing look. 'I never wanted to use that name.'

'These are frightened people,' Kyle said, with just a touch of irritation. 'You have to persuade them they have nothing to fear. Encourage them to go on listening to the programme – they might learn something.'

'I just shout back at them,' Olivia said with a smile at Reba.

'But that's no good. We have to break down the barriers and reach these people who think we're their enemies.'

Now Olivia was talking exclusively to Reba. 'He thinks I have time to reason with lunatics as well as working as his secretary. His unpaid secretary.'

'Why do you do it?' Reba suddenly asked, startling Olivia into silence.

'It's part of the work,' she said at last.

Meantime Kyle had been thinking and had come up with a solution.

'Tennis!' he cried, springing up. If Reba was not artistic she must be a sports girl.

I raised my eyebrows. Reba shrugged wearily – anything was better than this torture. Since Olivia did not play, Kyle hunted up one of his teenage daughters and we went out to a court at the back of the house. Looking as though she had never held a racquet in her life, Reba lunged wildly, missing balls or blasting them right out of court. To make matters worse, Olivia and the daughter's boyfriend stayed to watch. If someone had at least made a joke – but the non-game jerked along in killing silence and gravity. Score-taking was soon abandoned and then any attempt at competition. Kyle and his daughter patted the ball straight to Reba. She missed or blasted it out of court.

After a while Reba called it a day. In silence we trooped back to the house.

'Niall's?' Kyle suggested. I said we would have to get back. 'Perhaps one for the road here?'

'Stay the night!' Olivia cried to Reba, who rolled her eyes in sudden terror.

'We have to get back.'

'But you'll have a drink first.'

Reba accepted a tumbler of Jameson and gulped at it. Olivia went off with the daughter to cook, leaving us with Kyle and the boyfriend, a bank clerk who looked the part but turned out to be a serious student of jazz. While Reba and I sat like two lumpish sacks of dried turf from the bog, Kyle and the clerk argued passionately over jazz saxophone. The clerk claimed he could identify any of the giants from a few bars. Kyle took him on at tuppence a go. Kneeling by the record player, he played a brief snatch of music and looked up.

'Johnny Hodges,' the clerk said, grinning at Reba and me.

'Tuppence!' Kyle cried, making a great performance of springing across the room and presenting the youth with his prize.

'Coleman Hawkins.'

'Tuppence!'

'Ben Webster.'

'Tuppence!'

Now Kyle brought me back into it. 'Have you change of a ten pence piece?'

I handed it over, an insane grin concealing the murderous fury beneath. For the smartass, hell is a seminar on a topic you know nothing about. To be humiliated in front of a mentor by a creep of a bank clerk! Nothing like this must ever happen again. I would have to learn jazz at once. (Reba suffered the opposite reaction – an incurable lifelong aversion to jazz.)

Kyle was running out of change again. He could cover only one last shot.

'Another great original,' the clerk cried. 'Kyle Magee!'

Not just a creep, a ball-licker as well. Driving a hand happily through his hair, Kyle rushed across to present the last twopence piece, glancing at Reba and me for audience feedback. We responded like sacks of compressed peat briquettes.

'Didn't know you'd scored a plate,' the clerk said.

'Just a demo tape,' Kyle sighed

On the way home nothing was said. It seemed to me that I would never again be touched by a human emotion. I was occluded and annealed, a blackened, cauterised stump.

After a while Reba began to make the occasional remark, more like musing aloud than attempts to start a conversation.

'She buys all her clothes in Oxfam.'

'Who?'

'Olivia.'

We passed through a heartland town. Two posters: *Gospel Meeting with Eternity Dennis Lyle in the Iron Trades Hall* and *Streetwise Promotions present The Bitch Vipers from eight till late in the Union Hall.* Protestant Ulster, land of contrasts.

Reba again: 'There wasn't any tennis at St Teresa's. You know it? A secondary modern. But I was good at netball. Goal Shoot, I was. The whole team played to me. And we won everything.'

We were back in rich farmland, broken by the odd roadhouse and filling station.

'Only Liz played tennis. At the convent. She was the only one went to grammar school. She never lets you forget it either.'

I started out to say something, then thought the better of it. Reba understood and laughed.

'Did I fail the eleven-plus, you mean? Me and Frances never did the eleven-plus. No one gave us the chance.'

'Why not?' My own indignation surprised me. The stump was coming back to life.

'You didn't ask questions like that.' Reba too was surprised at my vehemence. I was demanding a form of behaviour – rational, just, consistent, sensitive – scarcely known in Irish family life. She laughed again. 'Ask me no questions and I'll tell ye no lies.'

Another silence, but calmer, more meditative. 'It's Liz you should have brought today,' Reba said suddenly.

'What?' I pretended surprise although the thought had occurred to me. What a day it might have been with Champagne Lizzie instead of Reba the Peat Briquette.

'It's Liz you should be going with instead of me.'

Not a trace of resentment or self-pity. This was not a ploy but a statement of fact. Protest and bluster would have been an insult. I said nothing.

'I'm not right for you. I'm only getting in your way.' She paused. 'We should break it off now.'

So – Reba was letting me out and Liz was asking me in. The passive man's dream. All I had to do was roll with it. But is there anything more terrifying than being offered what you want?

'If it's just today...'

'Today has nothing to do with it. I've meant to say this before now.'

I wished to God we were stationary. It's not easy to drive and decide your life at the same time, especially if you're seriously deficient in both skills.

'Has Liz...?'

'Liz has said nothing. We don't discuss you, much as you'd like to think we do.' The old mocking spirit was back. 'So Ahll love ye and leave ye – all right?'

Still I said nothing. No one could accuse me of impulsiveness. She was offering what I wanted, but how convoluted we are. The fact of her making it so easy was what made it hard. She faced the truth and asked for nothing. Either is rare, and the combination has a price above rubies. I did not take up the offer, but neither did I make a declaration of love. In any case the language of romance embarrassed and irritated Reba.

The issue was decided in Harvey Terrace with one of those banal exchanges that set the course of a life.

Reba: 'You don't have to come in.'

Yrs. Tly.: 'I always come in.'

As so often, the decision was immediately challenged. In the living room Rosemary was modelling various going-away suits 'out on appro' (the wedding was only a few weeks away). These expensive, hideous outfits were bad enough, but what froze my heart was the appearance of the girl herself. For Rosemary had undergone the Irish equivalent of female circumcision: the long straight natural girl hair had been shorn off and replaced by the crown of matronhood, the wrought-iron perm. She even seemed to have acquired a matron's hunch, osteoporosis forty years early.

Mrs Herron also looked dejected. Certainly none of the outfits impressed her, despite the quality and expense. When the girl went out to the kitchen to change she turned to us with a weary sigh. 'Sure ye could put the whole of Austin's on her and she'd look like nothin'.'

Two rows of houses faced each other across a dirt road. Raw wind shivered muddy puddles and the scant leaves of saplings strapped to stakes in protective cages of wire mesh. Older children roamed the wilderness in packs, like wild dogs. Younger children performed a savage dance on a sand heap left by builders. On a bald hummock at the end of the road a cement mixer stood against the skyline like a prehistoric monument. Silent here, it would be churning somewhere else, for this was the empire of the outer suburbs where the cement never sets.

Cold wind numbed my face; the thought of living here numbed my mind. It must have been miles to the nearest bus route, never mind a shop. A freshly excavated mass grave would have possessed more imminence. With a hideous cackle, Mother Ireland reached from her shawl and squeezed my heart with a bony claw.

Who had chosen the place of desolation? Frances and Sean. Sean's employers built the houses so Sean could choose a prime site (an end house with a bigger garden) and arrange for extras, like a stone fireplace, oak kitchen units and an avocado bathroom suite with the stupendous innovation of a bidet. While Sean attended to structure and fittings, Frances organised the contents. Even culture had been taken care of. As well as the pots and pans to which we were formally pledged for a wedding gift, Frances put a request through Reba for books to fill the two empty shelves in the lounge alcove.

'What sort of books?' I asked. 'I've never seen either of

them reading.'

Reba, embarrassed: 'They don't want to actually read them.'

It was a good chance to unload Irish crap, but as I was growing tired of Burroughs and Genet I included among the wholesome traditional fare *Our Lady of the Flowers* and *The Naked Lunch*, experiencing once again the fierce joy of gratuitous mischief. It was like slipping two tape worms into a pot of Irish stew.

Sean was at work so Frances showed us round, allaying my horror by allocating us the master bedroom, a fabulous confection in salmon pink with a marshmallow bed as the centrepiece. In the boxroom was a new pram.

'No!'

'Yes!'

The girls went to the kitchen to talk and Reba returned with an anguished expression I had come to know.

'Ye see, Sean's planning to go out on his own. He does other work at weekends – he's out on an extra job now. But it's not easy on his own . . . He was sort of hoping you'd give him a bit of a hand tomorrow.'

Of course, forced labour usually goes with exile. All the same I was shocked.

'What? On a building site? On a Saturday?'

'He's trying to go out on his own.'

'But where exactly? To do what?'

'He'll explain himself when he comes in.'

It was almost midnight when Sean returned, a strong smell of drink suggesting that his labours had not been without respite. But he offered no details of the Saturday job. The man of the house does not explain.

Even on the site there were only commands. Get out here, stand over there, hold this. Closer, back a bit, that's it. Under similar conditions (Siberian exile and forced labour) Ivan Denisovich was happy building a wall. A man can lose himself in any kind of activity. Happiness is absorption, says the sage. Providing that you know what you're trying to achieve. Fetching and placing bricks,

Ivan could see the wall rise.

On the way home Sean, without any consultation, pulled into a roadhouse and ordered two hot Paddys. For once my literary training stood me in good stead. Kyle may not have made me a life force but at least he had taught me to drink whiskey.

We were going out with the girls in the evening. Already it was getting late, but Sean ordered another round. Sipping in leisurely relish, he turned to me with a new kind of look – prolonged, assessing, half ironic. The sort *I* should have been giving *him*.

'Listen . . . ah,' he began, carefully. 'There's a couple of weeman down the road there . . . know what Ah mean?'

I had no idea. Brothel? Amateurs? Mistress and accommodating friend? And was this the other half of my wage packet? Hot Paddy followed by hot pussy – what more could a red-blooded Irishman ask? On the other hand he might have been winding me up. The way to find out was to string along.

'But the girls . . . we're late already.' An instinctive blurt. He lifted his glass and took a slow drink. I heard the familiar clang of metal shutters coming down. 'What women? Who are they anyway?' First we provoke the shutters, then we beat on them with desperate cries.

He leaned across to land a playful punch on my shoulder – playful by the standards of the building trade.

'Ah was only kidding. There's no weeman.'

And of course the reward for loyalty was anger and outrage from Reba at the notion of delay caused by sitting in a bar.

'None of this was my idea,' I hissed.

'Get changed. And don't be all night in the bathroom.'

I changed without washing. Sean, of course, took a leisurely shower. While Reba talked to Frances in the kitchen I lifted *Our Lady of the Flowers* and placed it carefully between Cardinal Heenan's autobiography and *A Pope Laughs: The Wit of Pope John.* Sean and Frances did not read but it was my hope that a baby-sitting aunt would mistake the Genet for a religious work and find that Our Lady was not the Blessed Virgin but a homosexual prostitute besotted by murderers with huge cocks. It is thoughts like this that sustain me in the bitter servitude of the days.

Is it in this work that Genet exhorts us to acknowledge all our children, however monstrous? I have to admit that I dried my arse on the sumptuous face towels that were a wedding present from Caroline and John.

All through his work Genet exhorts us to betray. In the roadhouse (the same one as earlier) I ratted on Sean at the first opportunity. Reba simply refused to believe it, claiming I had a grudge against Sean and an interest in poisoning the suburban idyll.

'It was no joke,' I insisted. 'There were two women somewhere.'

'Get us another drink and give me head peace.'

Indeed, the girls set a brisk pace, as though to show us they too could hang tough. Sean put away doubles without apparent effort or effect, making no concessions to the need to drive.

Not even my whiskey courage was enough for Sean's spanking pace on the way home. When he overtook two cars at once a cry of protest was torn from my lips. Turning in the passenger seat, Frances presented features radiant with Bacardi and the priceless trust of young love.

'Sean drives better when he's had a few drinks.'

We got to the turn-off safely, but Sean went by without a glance. No one cried out or protested. We went around in a wide circle and approached a second time. Never had a dirt road looked so inviting, but no one turned to stare as it went by. All eyes were fixed on the road. The silence was tense but disciplined – like that of a U-boat crew with a British destroyer overhead. Another silent circling. Once again we passed the turn-off.

Perhaps I should explain that there had been banter during the evening. The avocado bathroom suite was mentioned. I believe I sang a short medley from *Dream with Dean.*

As we roared away from the house it occurred to me that the visit was a nightmare mirror image of Reba's experience in Altnagarvin. Reba's agony in the world of the arts; mine in the suburbs. On the fourth approach Sean decided to spare us and turn in. When he pulled up outside the house no one moved or spoke in case it set him off again. Also, of course, the luxury of stasis was something to relish.

After a while Sean turned and looked at me. 'That was the scenic route,' he said. 'Thought ye'd like to see a bit of the country.'

At last the Little Theatre was moving into purpose-built premises. Here the community could come to terms with itself, marvel and groan at past iniquities and learn a new spirit for the future. The opening was a great day for the Friends of the Little Theatre, from those who had bought a brick at one pound through the purchasers of silver and gold bricks (twenty-five pounds and fifty pounds) to the Life Associates like Kyle who had donated one hundred pounds or more and had their names engraved in stone in the foyer. But above all it was a personal triumph for Deirdre Mannion, the handsome and forceful founder of the company, sustained in twenty years of dedication by the dream of her own theatre.

Deirdre was the celebrity of the moment, but in absolute terms Tom McKenna was the brightest star. Poetry lovers thrill to an atmosphere of menace and, as a result of obscure but reverberant warnings in his early work, McKenna was considered a prophet of the current unrest and had a growing international reputation ('his are the most sensitive antennae' – *New York Review of Books*). Poets are often thought to be solitary creatures, but McKenna's natural habitat was the crowd. It was a privilege to watch him move around the Little Theatre foyer, winning hearts and minds everywhere but never letting himself be detained. First he remembered not only who you were but the date and location of his previous encounter with you and the names of your children and spouse. Then, leaning too close, he would seize some part of your person, look round as though in fear of eavesdroppers, and finally, inclining a head to yours, address you out of the corner of the mouth in a conspiratorial whisper. The sensation of privilege was overwhelming. Only *your* company was a pleasure, that of the others a duty. For them polite conversation, for you confidences and intimacy.

Beneath such a benign sun who would not blossom? Then a joke for the getaway. As you leaned back to roar with laughter he nodded and winked and was gone.

What I admired most of all was his talent for refuse disposal. Getting rid of seducees is harder than attracting them in the first place. I kept getting stuck with people desperate to get on the radio. For instance McFeely, a bearded giant who described himself as a poet resigned to writing plays for a living. Of course they would never be staged in this province.

'You'd have to screw Deirdre,' I suggested, expecting a cheap laugh. But opportunists never joke about career moves.

'Does she take a length?' McFeely asked with sudden dark interest, turning round to stare at Deirdre in conversation with Kyle.

As he went to the bar for a refill, his place was taken by an aspiring young actress doing menial work for Deirdre in the hope of a part. For her, acting was an experience of almost unbearable intensity, on a par with regarding the face of God.

'The most incredible thing in the world,' she said, 'is to enter another human being.'

Wide liquid eyes looked into mine. There was not a trace of irony.

'Introduce us,' McFeely said to me, looking only at the girl.

'Maeve,' she said in quiet sincerity.

McFeely, about to hand me a glass, paused and beheld her with shining eyes. 'Queen Maeve,' he said at last, in a deep and richly resonant tone – my chance to escape. As though also in flight, Renee was pushing through the crowd, bearing safely aloft her glass of wine.

'Dame Deirdre!' she cried when we had made a space. 'Mother Superior. I know how she treats the company. Of which I will never be a member, needless to say.' She paused for a swift refreshing swig. 'Great ladies of the theatre ... don't talk to me. You know Vivien Leigh – who always played delicate and cultivated ladies? I was in a dressing room with her once. She was dressed for the part – you know, the great ball gown and so forth. She just lifted it up, put her leg against the wall and pissed in the wash-hand basin like a *dog*.' Renee stressed the last word with a loud relish that made several people look round. 'There were at least five others in the room at the time. And of course her language. Every other word was *fuck*.' Again the expletive was pronounced with gusto. There was obviously drink taken.

I was looking forward to more scurrilous backstage gossip, but Kyle approached with a grave expression.

'I hope you took Mother Superior down a peg or two,' Renee cried.

'She was complaining about inadequate grants. But I told her I didn't think the arts should be kept on a life-support machine. She's a curious mixture of elitism and piety. She keeps putting on classics and expecting homage and gratitude. When no one turns up she blames philistine Ulster. But the relevance . . . the *value* of her productions is never questioned. These actors with wonderful voices that sound like verse-speaking competitors . . . Maybe people really do know what's good for them' – he made a sweeping gesture with a wine glass – 'I mean, is Chekhov any better than *Coronation Street*?'

'She'll never do your play now,' Renee laughed.

'Why not? I was offering positive advice. Pointing out what a tremendous force for good a new theatre could be.'

'If it does your play, you mean.'

'If it uses all the wonderful talent available.' Kyle opened his arms to include me, Renee and the just-arrived Robbie Semple, who ignored him to speak to Renee.

'Let's get out of here,' he said harshly.

Renee stepped back to give him a look whose message was searingly unequivocal: *kiss my pantyhose, sperm bank*.

Undeterred, Semple gripped her elbow. 'Before the speeches.'

Renee shook him off and leaned into me. 'Are you going down to the Arts Club after?'

Deirdre was calling for attention. Despite Kyle's protestations, he must have demoralised the great lady, for instead of celebrating her hour of triumph she cast herself as tragic victim – Deirdre of the Sorrows. To the naïve she might appear a successful person. In reality her life had been a lonely struggle.

'Why do they hate me so much?' she cried. 'Twenty years of hostile notices.' She swept us with a fierce accusing gaze. 'Hugh – the cuttings.' Her husband rushed off, reminding me of a sacristan scurrying behind the robed celebrants. But it was not herself Deirdre was thinking of. *She* was only a foolish old woman. Cries of protest were silenced with a wave. It was the players she felt for most, the players who had given everything and borne the brunt of the vilification. Hugh returned with a large cardboard box in which, without taking her eyes from us, Deirdre plunged both arms to the elbow, withdrawing an armful of cuttings which she raised shoulder high and released in a silent expressive shower. How well she understood that actions speak louder than words. Here was theatre at its most magnificent and moving, and once again the Ulster audience displayed the responsiveness for which it is renowned. Groaning, wincing, sighing, we looked down at the carpet in guilt and shame.

It was not easy for McKenna to lift the mood, but he succeeded with a masterly enumeration of Deirdre's achievements.

'What a po-faced bastard,' Renee laughed in admiration, leaning against me and putting her arm across my back. Semple stood to one side with a scowl of Baudelairean disgust. It was wonderful fun.

But as McKenna finished his eulogy, the hand on my back thrust me forward and Renee said in a loud voice. 'Let's hear from the younger generation for a change. We've had enough from the old guard.'

'The younger generation,' McKenna agreed, turning with the crowd in our direction.

A sea of encouraging smiles. The famous Ulster audience.

'For fuck's sake,' I said through clenched teeth to Renee.

'Go on,' she hissed – the crazy bitch. I was a back-seat sniggerer not an Oscar Wilde. My body went into a violent spasm of denial, like a dog shaking off water after being pushed into the sea.

'The younger generation has much to say,' McKenna smirked, 'but appears to be not quite ready at the moment.'

Everyone laughed. Even Semple now had a smile.

Renee leaned forward with some slobbering apology or consolation but I pushed her away and went to the bar. Only to be accosted by a small earnest man who accused *Born-again Ulster* of fiddling while the province burned. We were elitist and complacent, he complained, as smug and blind as the bourgeoisie. 'You know when that place up the Malone Road was bombed? It's getting a bit near home, they said. *Where do you think it's been all along?* I said.'

McKenna came by and could not resist twisting the knife. 'I see Magee's wiped your eye,' he said, nodding at Kyle and Queen Maeve in intimate conversation.

'The girl is an imbecile,' I snapped. 'Nothing there at all.'

McKenna turned in mock astonishment, as though Maeve's full figure had been some kind of optical illusion.

'Jaysus,' he breathed, 'I wouldn't say there was nothing there.'

Shortly after, Kyle himself approached me. 'Perhaps if you're going on to the Arts Club you could lend Maeve and me the keys to your flat?'

Why does Kyle's calm assurance always render me helpless? I wanted to go home instead of the Arts Club but I surrendered my keys without a word.

More theatre was to follow, including a sordid public scene between Renee and Semple. Shouting. Swearing. Throwing the contents of glasses. In the end Semple hit her and had to be dragged off.

Such a juicy scene should not be skimped, but narrators are only human. The appetite for life cannot be consistently voracious. As Montherlant says somewhere in one of his novels: 'The whole thing is so vile that I haven't the stomach to go on.'

Someone had to host *Born-again Ulster* when Kyle made his annual trip to the States. The two long-serving regulars were Marlow the humanist and myself, with Marlow the obvious choice for front man. He had the right sonorous authority, the measured and richly harmonious tone that is the fruit of Western civilisation at its most ripe. Instead Kyle chose a Fenian with his tribe's nasal bark and Gatling-gun speed of delivery. I assumed that Marlow would tender a grave and dignified resignation. In fact he accepted the situation without a murmur. No indignity is too high a price for fame. He was friendly, charming, deferential. Or as Burroughs has put it: *Shit on me, boss man, I'll wash your used condoms.*

It was a perfect post: the interesting job of selecting material without the tedious detail of getting it on the air. A producer took care of all that, selecting actors, sound effects, filler music. The only interference was on the issue of time, and authors were invited to trim their own pieces when necessary. For the first few shows there was nothing to do but present the material Kyle had left. I used the time to write a piece on the Little Theatre opening. The younger generation might not have the balls to speak in public, but it could sit down in private with a Biro in its hand.

The producer, Martin Patterson, asked me to meet him in the Arts Club. Despite my period of celebrity, I had never been there and I was shocked by its atmosphere of relaxed and comfortable venality, of mutual favours and accommodations and deals. Whatever went on here it was nothing to do with the arts.

Patterson arrived late, all apology and solicitude. The hours he had to work were a scandal. He could never get away. This elaborate courtesy was disturbing. It was not just that we were the same age, I was sure he was also a Fenian. Of course it would have been unspeakably vulgar to mention this. The Ulster professional classes like to pretend you can play golf with someone for years without being aware of religion. In practice the knowledge is instinctive and its application immediate. Martin Patterson is a neutral name but one look and the radar said 'bourgeois Fenian'. Pale, soft-spoken, clever, fastidious, plump – in a less materialistic age the youth would have made a lovely priest.

He invited me to join him in a meal. I declined, feeling obscurely but strongly that I could let him buy me drink but not food. How do we evolve these bizarre codes of honour? Patterson called a waiter, an elderly man with a perfect death mask of servitude.

'A sirloin, medium-rare, and a salad. No dressing.' He glanced at me.

'Gin and tonic.'

'Gordon's and Slimline Schweppes for me,' Patterson said.

For 'priest' substitute 'bishop'. No, not exactly, too flagrant. He was more the power behind the throne. A monsignor, that was it! *Monsignor Patterson will see you now.*

Ignoring the sparkling Gordon's and Schweppes placed at his elbow, he leaned earnestly across the table and addressed me in a tone – soft, humble, almost supplicatory – I had often heard from those of the Ulster professional classes too intelligent and fastidious to display brutal arrogance. You had to be careful with this apparent humility. What it eschewed was vulgarity, not power.

'That piece,' he began, shaking his head in wonder, 'that piece about the Little Theatre – it just has to be the best thing you've ever done. One of the funniest things I've ever read, in fact. I mean, I almost fell out of my chair laughing.' He leaned across to lay his hand on my arm, as though for support in case of another laughing fit. Suddenly noticing his G and T, he seized it and drank half. 'I've been showing it round to everybody ever since. They think you must have exaggerated, but I tell them it's *cinéma-vérité*, it's documentary realism. I mean, I was there. I know.' Seeing my glass almost empty, he waved for another round. 'You know what you should do?'

'No.'

'You should write a satirical novel tearing the shite out of the whole crowd.' Somehow his precise enunciation robbed the coarse phrase of power. 'Have you ever thought of that?'

'It has crossed my mind.'

'You should do it. Seriously. I mean, this place is ripe for it. Crying out for it. Deirdre Mannion, for instance. My boss is on the Little Theatre board so I get the whole inside story. If all he says is true, then that woman is impossible. Practically insane.'

Fresh drinks arrived, along with the steak, which absorbed his attention for a while. 'You're sure you won't have one of these?'

'No no no no.'

'Or even some of mine? It's really not bad. The food here is awful stodge – the vegetables always cooked to mush, Irish-style – but they do a reasonable steak if you warn them not to char it.'

'No no no no.'

The steak reminded me of another occasion. I had a summer job in a factory and was enjoying steak and chips in the canteen when two men sat down next to me. One looked on in silence while the friendly one spoke.

'Now . . . don't get me wrong. I mean, personally I don't give a damn. But some of the lads have noticed that *every Friday ye eat meat.* Not that they mind either. But this is a mixed work force . . . and what we're thinkin' about is the way it looks to the other crowd. Gives them somethin' to talk about.' Then the hand gently laid on my arm. 'Know what Ah mean, son?'

Patterson was in the course of rejecting the Deirdre piece and we were now in the personally-I-don't-give-a-damn stage. Next would come the interesting part – the justification. I thought he would simply say it was too long, but this was to underestimate the ingenuity of the monsignor.

The thing was this, he explained, leaving his meal unfinished in his enthusiasm for truth. It was not that he or his colleagues disapproved of Deirdre-baiting. On the contrary, they would have to drop the piece not because of any objection to the content, but because they agreed with it *all too well*, so they were now scared the public might think they had embarked on some kind of totally insane vendetta.

Fantastic casuistry! Not hands off Deirdre because we protect public figures but hands off because we've already almost beaten her to death. Wonderful complexity of power in our time! No longer can you shout, Chop his head off and have his woman brought to my bed. Now you have to convince yourself and your underlings that decapitation and rape are just what the lucky couple need. Occasionally a bright underling will convince himself first. This is the one you must immediately promote.

I was fairly sure there had been no attacks on Deirdre, perhaps an occasional mild reservation. But Patterson wanted me to accept his argument. 'You see our position?' he said. 'You understand what I'm saying?'

'Yes. Yes. I understand perfectly.'

'And of course this is not a rejection, just a postponement. It's a terrific piece. We'd be delighted to use it ... after we've had a breathing space. Of course I could understand if you insisted on taking it back ...'

'No ... no ...'

'I'd like to hang on to it ...'

'Hang on to it.'

I told Kyle his show had been censored and showed him the piece. He agreed it was amusing and ought to be used. This in spite of certain trouble with the producer and a play of his own under consideration at the Little Theatre. You certainly couldn't accuse the guy of cowardice or self-interest.

'But why didn't you object yourself?' he said, with only the mildest hint of irritation. 'You seem to have been *totally pusillanimous*.'

Prepared for this, I protested that I had no authority. It was his show, I was only filling in – the implication being that, in his shoes, I would have fought to the death. When it comes to self-justification we are all as eloquent and subtle as top defence lawyers. And indeed, Kyle seemed to believe that his deputy was not a hyena but a lion.

Patterson repeated his argument to Kyle but at the crucial stage Kyle said: 'What attacks? As far as I can see, no one's ever said boo to the woman. She's frightened everyone for years, making out to be queen of the arts.'

This was tantamount to calling Patterson a liar and he responded with the outrage of an offended monsignor. The Little Theatre piece would not be used and that was the end of it. And so it should have been, except that Kyle perpetrated the enormity of going over his producer's head to the boss above. In bureaucracies what counts is not the attainment of objectives but the appearance of calm. Nothing matters as long as the shit is contained. The golden rule of middle management is that shit must never rise a level. So although it seemed perfectly reasonable to Kyle, going higher was both futile (the irritated boss of course supported his boy) and, from Patterson's point of view, an act of almost unthinkable vindictiveness and spite.

In the Arts Club there was a stand-up row that was the talk of the cultural community for weeks. Apparently a white-faced and trembling Patterson went straight up to hiss in Kyle's face: 'What do you think you're doing going over my head?'

Professional etiquette was never a strong point of Kyle's. 'Answer me a question first,' he said. 'Why do you make such lazy tenth-rate programmes?'

Probably Kyle was genuinely curious, but this was not a common interpretation. In the Arts Club, nothing so outrageous had ever been heard. From now on Kyle was an irresponsible nutcase, a dangerous crank whom the habitués of the place of accommodations neutralised by treating him as a figure of fun. Much of what I have to say will also make him look absurd – I can tell it no other way – but it should never obscure an important truth. Among the lackeys and parasites of the Arts Club, Kyle was a noble shining prince.

Inevitable consequence: Patterson refused to work with Kyle and the show was dropped. Not only had Kyle failed to foresee this, he was incapable of understanding it after it happened. We are familiar with the depravity of the privileged, but there is also the innocence of the privileged. Kyle was as bewildered and hurt as a struck child. How could a man be punished for trying to save his beloved province? Of course I felt guilty at being the cause of all this, but Kyle seemed to bear me no grudge. It was a character test as severe as the British dismantling of the Stormont parliament. Even the most liberal of Protestants must have smarted a little and even the most moderate of Catholics could scarcely suppress a gleam of triumph. For the destruction of the Protestant State was a stunningly elemental victory, totally different from the usual dilatory half-measures of politics. When I met Kyle the day after it happened, my speech may have been circumspect but my face was almost certainly ablaze with barbaric triumphalism. Without a trace of resentment he sighed and said, 'Perhaps it was necessary. Perhaps good will come of it.'

As for the show, I was not really sorry. I had never believed in it anyway. Also, I was becoming aware of the distance between Kyle and myself. You can break through the barriers of class and religion but there remains the deep difference of temperament these bring about. It seemed to me that we could never truly come together. I was never young; Kyle would never be old.

It was a good time to move on. The mood in Northern Ireland was increasingly ugly. Garvin Dodd's narrow defeat had turned out to be the last gasp of liberalism in Ulster. Now the IRA had re-emerged to shoot British soldiers and car-bomb town centres. Protestant gangs were assassinating Catholics at random. Squalid killings on the street were taking all the sexiness out of murder.

And even before this it was clear that transgression and outrage would not be my destiny. Once I came home from recording a show to find the bedsit transformed into an art gallery. Bookshelves, bed, window ledge, chairs – every available space was covered with insipid watercolours. Standing in the centre of the room were a desperate-looking Reba and a mild-mannered man in his late sixties. She introduced him like a friend of long standing – which was probably how it felt: a retired civil servant now devoting himself to the arts.

Surely for once I had an irrefutable argument: we could not use art work on a radio show. Nevertheless he flushed in displeasure –

the rejected are never content – and with an expression of resolve produced from a briefcase the biggest wadge of poems I have ever seen. I cleared a chair and sat down. They were like the watercolours, but without the skill. I knew that if I looked at Reba all was lost. In the end I had to come up for air. Immediately Reba assumed a pleading grimace – *take something for chrissake.* Although my mind was resisting the knowledge, I had already known in my heart that my fate was sealed.

Advertise for murderers and you get a retired civil servant. Call for aberration and lunacy and you get holiday-cottage poems. Set out for the Nietzschean crags and some lame dog grabs your trouser leg.

South

4

We are in the computer room, attempting to run the machine without the aid of manuals. Or rather the bright student is attempting to run it. Since a class of thirty has been chosen from nine hundred applicants, the bright students are extremely bright. And since they are used to Irish education, that is, teaching themselves, they are also resourceful and independent. Here in careless profusion, without planning or husbandry, indeed in circumstances of indifference and neglect, is the species cultivated ardently throughout the West: the results-oriented self-starter.

With a hunter's sharp cry of involvement, he whips the back off the central processor and stares eagerly at the switches and lights. I suppress a shudder of revulsion. Despite my comprehensive retraining, I still have the arts man's primitive fear of technology. In particular, staring at wire-dense innards causes a cloud of unknowing to descend on my brain. There is probably a medical name for this condition, irrational fear of the insides of machines. Of course I put up a good front, standing a couple of paces back and apparently overseeing the proceedings with a terrific frown of concentration. Already I am familiar with one of the basic principles of teaching and, indeed, all authority, that expressed in the Russian proverb: When you see a dog running towards you, whistle for it.

Suddenly I am aware of someone else in the room. A tall and powerful man of sixty, with silver hair and a well-cut suit, he is perfect for the resonant wisdom of a distinguished American senator in a made-for-TV movie. But at the moment he is possessed by the inarticulate rage of the hooligan. My first thought is that we have violated some code of practice by taking the back off the machine. But no, his outstretched arm is pointing up and away. Following, I see another great device throbbing patiently at the junction of ceiling and back wall. What is this machine and what have we done to offend it? The cloud of unknowing is denser than ever.

'I paid ten f. . . g thousand pounds for that,' he screams, finding words at last, turning upon me his inflamed countenance and taking a step forward.

His way of communicating the f-word requires explanation. Although the rest of the sentence is enunciated clearly, the expletive is indicated only by the fricative followed by appropriate lip movements and violent head jerks, so that the word is unequivocally communicated without actually being pronounced. This is an Irish solution to an Irish problem: how to enjoy the virility of swearing without endangering your immortal soul. (An alternative is to use words that sound like the king of expletives and hence can partake of its lurid splendour: 'fack', 'feck', 'fake' and 'buck' are all widely employed.)

I stare blankly at the apparatus in question.

'It's a f. . . g air-conditioning unit,' he screams. 'I was forced to buy that to keep this f. . . g room at the right f. . . g temperature. Ten f. . . g thousand pounds I paid for that f. . . g thing. And what f. . . g use is it when stupid f. . . ers like you go and leave the door open?'

Once again I follow his arm. No doubt about it, the door is ajar.

'No one told me,' I rashly protest. Now he is aware of me as an individual, focusing his gaze in incredulous contempt. He takes another menacing step forward.

'Who the f. . . are *you* anyway?'

'The new lecturer in Computing.'

By now his face is in mine. 'Ye'd think ye'd f. . . g know better,' he roars. The bright student backs away, slack-mouthed and ashen. No more support from that quarter. This is me and the maniac.

Then, as suddenly as he has arrived, the man appears to lose interest, turning away in disgust and impatience.

I am brushed by the wind of the wing of madness myself. 'And who are *you?*' I hear my voice say.

'Who am *I?*' He swings back, fury rekindled, perhaps even

intensified. Hunching for the struggle, I realise that, phobia notwithstanding, I have almost climbed into the back of the machine. His right arm swings up – but backwards, away from me, in the grand encompassing sweep of the absolute monarch. '*I am the f . . . g principal of this f . . . g college.*'

Dear Fearful Fenian

Your cagey funny letters are always a good read . . . better than your fiction, dare I say it.

I'm pleased that you got the job you wanted in Dublin. I know how plausible you can be when you apply yourself though I agree it was highly fortuitous that the priest on the interview panel was asleep. Your cunning and evasiveness seem to be in good working order, though I wonder if you are not missing valuable experience by all this 'trick cycling' as you call it (always an outlandish phrase to distract the attention). You are pleased with your ingenuity in avoiding an Irish (presumably Gaelic?) exam – but we need someone intelligent and objective to learn the language and scrutinise the culture and myths. Why let the nationalists hog it?

Everywhere you go you are fending off people and experiences. You give nothing a chance.

And where are your positives? I thought you weren't terribly keen on computers when you were doing the course in England. Does it suddenly get interesting if you have to teach it for a living? 'Good holidays and not too demanding' sounds appalling to me. Craven and defeatist, without even the excuse of trying to change things from the inside. I expected more from the wild young bedsit rebel living on national assistance, his brain on fire and his values strong, simultaneously devouring Penguin Classics and tuna fish salads.

And settling in Dublin because of your in-laws' blind hatred for England! Worried about your children having English accents!

If you are sinking back into Catholic middle-class life perhaps at least it will teach you some understanding. Perhaps you will be nicer to your mother and Aunt Lily.

My own mother still speaks of you with affection.

And if your work is not too demanding you will be able to put your free time to good use. As also the college photo-copying machine. I suffer grievously from lack of access to duplicating facilities. Copy the enclosed career résumé and circulate it among your literary friends in Dublin. My work is not as well known as it could be in the South. Are there still those ridiculous censorship laws?

It will need to be updated soon. Fantastic new imaginative work is in the pipeline.

Give my regards to your nice wife whose name always eludes me.

Love
Kyle

Liz had also gone to England for an education, but with less of a career orientation than I, graduating with a degree in Social Science and an illegitimate child. Not as anti-British as the rest of the Herrons, she would have stayed on in England but for the difficulties of being a single parent far from support. Nor was going back to Mother an option, given Mrs Herron's sorrow-and-shite view of child rearing. From Harvey Terrace there came only one pledge of support: Hugo's offer to travel across and give the father an unmerciful hammering.

Instead Liz turned to Reba, despite the fact that we too were struggling with many new factors, including our own first child, Emma. The idea of acquiring more dependants was extremely unattractive, but Liz had the key attribute of the manager. She could make people do what she wished by convincing them that the benefits were all theirs. Instead of adding to our burden, she would help us by contributing to the mortgage, helping about the house and, of course, providing a free baby-sitting service. I pointed out the financial disadvantages of life in the Republic – the miserable child benefit, the health and education costs that would not apply in the UK. Liz argued that everything would be fine as soon as she was established in her chosen field of journalism. The important thing was the mutual support. Instead of the conventional nuclear family we would have a hippie-style commune. As she poured me another glass of wine, her eyes promised rewards beyond the family man's wildest dreams. What were state benefits compared to this bounty?

Horrified by the Dublin suburbs, we had bought a house in a somnolent terrace off the South Circular Road. Gentrification was unknown in central Dublin so the terraces were dilapidated and cheap, preserving a smokey, dreamy, timeless decrepitude that embodied our vision of urban pastoral (formed for me by student bedsit land and for Reba by Harvey Terrace). Liz and her infant son David moved into the third bedroom on the return, the study where I meant to write a novel at the fine old leather-topped desk that had been a wedding present from Lily.

What a splendid strew covered its top – pages, folders, binders, Biros, notebooks. From this formless chaos would emerge a unified creation. Every God adores disorder.

But at the moment it was all I could do to write an occasional letter to Kyle. Caught in the pincer jaws of marriage and work, I held on to Kyle as my link with the world of the spirit. Even this tenuous link had barely survived my failure to invite him to our wedding. The thought of him soloing on tenor sax and being honest with the relatives was simply too bizarre to countenance – and of course Reba was violently opposed. The wedding was a Mafia thing, I explained to Kyle, a meaningless experience to be got over as quickly and cheaply as possible. But the idea of the empty ritual, so central to the Catholic experience, was completely alien to Kyle. Why did it have to be awful? Why could I not enlist his help to redeem it? Where was the problem? What was I afraid of? It was the *Born-again Ulster* rejection all over again. He was shocked, he was hurt, he could not understand.

Only belief in my promise made him persevere. If Kyle convinced himself of your talent, he was a friend for life. Lack of fulfilment was not a problem. Nor lack of response. He kept the letters coming even when I failed to reply.

Now Liz had a carrycot on top of the desk, cosmetics on the bookshelves, baby equipment everywhere. A new and uninspiring chaos. Every god adores disorder, but the presence of disorder does not imply the divine.

Terrifying revelation: once again I was trapped in a house of women. Fondly imagining audacity and freedom, we set about re-creating the familiar conditions of servitude. Perhaps my poor broken father was once excited at the thought of Lily coming to stay.

And once we had dreamed of escape to the United States, where the uncles would provide a launch pad and safety net. In the midst of emigration plans Reba discovered she was pregnant. Since she would not consider England we had to compromise on Dublin.

A few weeks after Liz moved in I made an atrocious but unsurprising discovery. Beneath the carrycot the leather desk top was cruelly and irremediably scored.

'An antique desk ruined,' I said to Reba. 'Utterly ruined.'

'It's not antique. It's only reproduction.'

'Valuable . . . all right?'

What more cruelly symbolic: the place of creation obliterated, burdened, secretly and viciously gouged; instead of imaginative life, real life, a monstrous human cuckoo crapping, pissing, vomiting, howling, ruthlessly seeking attention by every means at its disposal.

Here was my destiny – sorrow and shite.

According to Roche, the senior lecturer with responsibility for Computing, the manuals for the college machine are in the office of the vice-principal, who denies all knowledge of their whereabouts. Charged with managing the machine but knowing nothing about it, Leonard retains control by locking up the crucial component, like an Irish mother keeping her son's testicles in her handbag.

At least this is Roche's story. But is Roche to be trusted? I have never laid eyes on the vice-principal (staff induction is unknown to the Gael). Before bearding him I undertake some research.

Not easy when most colleagues have second and even third jobs (referred to as 'nixers'). They work for ad agencies, they install back boilers, they sell insurance. The instant a class is over they leave, abandoning the staff room to the Terrible Grey-haired Boy-Men of Ireland, a group of fortyish single men who live with their mothers and spend their days in armchairs playing cards and talking sport.

'Bridge player?'

'No.'

'Follow the horses?'

'No.'

Sure ye'll be among your own kind, Lily said of the move south.

'Play golf at all?'

'No.'

So far our exchanges have not been promising. I sit down next to a bridge match and wait for a break to solicit views on Leonard.

'All vice and no principle,' says a diffident type, his gold-rimmed glasses, tweed tie and sports coat standing out among the shapeless cardigans and open-necked shirts. For Boy-Men offer all the variety one would expect in adolescents, everything from quivering sensitivity to sprawling loutishness. One of the louts now intervenes with three almost simultaneous actions – noisily drawing phlegm from his nasal cavity, delivering a definitive opinion, and flinging down a greasy card: 'Leonard's a cunt.'

The leader of the Boy-Men is actually a family man and not grey but white. Leaning his puce features towards me, Paddy McGrath offers an explanation that itself must be explained. For in Ireland character is accounted for solely by regional difference. Although the English caste system has been slavishly copied, dislike of the

English and the illusion of independence make it impossible to acknowledge class distinctions in Ireland. Also, contempt for psychology and reverence for the family prevent the acceptance of upbringing as a determinant. All that remains is place of origin and there is a system, perhaps consistent and complete, for distributing human characteristics around the towns and counties of Ireland.

So now, after establishing eye contact, Paddy offers the crucial insight. 'Leonard's a Listowel man, ye know.'

'Ah,' I sigh, nodding wisely.

As well as the Boy-Men the college has a sprinkling of international dissidents, eccentrics rejecting Western civilisation for the simple timeless ways of the Gael. Successful or not in their quest, they have had to stay. Civilisation is easy to get out of, but a bitch to re-enter at exit level. In a corner is Hector Spadavecchia, a US navy scientist who quit in disgust at the Vietnam War. A math genius with languages as a hobby, Hector is fluent in several European tongues, has long ago mastered Gaelic (in which he occasionally converses with Paddy McGrath and the Boy-Men) and is currently working on Mandarin Chinese, a project that involves accosting Chinese waiters (who must think he's CIA or queer or both). The only language Hector is reluctant to practise is English.

Next door is the room that serves staff as office accommodation. Peeling paintwork, scarred and twisted lockers, a few broken-down tables and chairs. Single opaque, filthy window nothing ever penetrates. Instead a ghastly nightmarish twilight from one row of buzzing fluorescent tubes (the other row cannot be switched on as one of the tubes flickers insanely). No one but me ever works in this room. Here I hole up like a mutant in the ruins of a nuked-out city.

A dissident comes in to his locker: Digby Howard, upper-class English and one-time nuclear physicist with the Atomic Energy Commission in Geneva. Roche tells a good story about him being shown round the college. 'Where's my office?' Digby has to enquire at last. They bring him here and the physicist sees in a flash that he has achieved the wildest quantum leap in Europe – from fantastic Swiss efficiency and comfort to Irish slovenliness and squalor.

'Got the machine going?' Digby asks now.

'No.'

'Even if you did, it's totally unsuitable for a college.'

'Why was it bought?'

'Chicanery. Someone got a backhander?'

'Is this college run by maniacs?'

Often Digby claims to be happily forgetting his physics and submitting to the hegemony of essence. However, habits of analysis and definition die hard.

'Don't use such a vague term,' he snaps. 'The principal is schizo – but Leonard is paranoid.'

Nothing for it but to beard the monster in his lair. Less imposing than the principal, Leonard is still very much the dignified and experienced administrator, solemn of voice and grave of mien, with tidy grey hair and suit and heavy horn-rimmed spectacles. Perhaps the overpowering smell of aftershave should alert me to mania and obsession. Not many senior administrators are as violently fragrant as this. But he seems so much like an old-fashioned GP or bank manager, one of those whose abrupt and forbidding manner is balanced by fantastic dedication and probity.

Except that behind him are the unmistakable red plastic binders of documentation for the machine. The full set by the look of it, innocuously lined along a back shelf but as charged with mystery and turbulence as the tablets of the Law. My salvation, and practically within arm's reach.

Leonard holds his office door three-quarters open. Not obviously keeping me out, but certainly not letting me in either. One masterful shoulder shove, two swift strides . . .

'I'm looking for the computer manuals.'

Leonard frowns with the puzzlement of a man anxious to help but faced with a question that relates to nothing in his frame of reference. 'Computer manuals?'

'We need them to run the machine.'

'Ah.' He takes a step closer, though without letting go of the door. Where English sincerity would involve a withdrawal in mild outrage, the Irish version requires a coming forward, a softening and lowering of tone, a laying on of hands in solidarity and benediction. *How could one of your own deceive you?* Eye contact, proximity, touch. The hideous intimacy of the race. *Sure isn't it only ourselves.*

Leonard lays the fingertips of his free hand on my sleeve, his face gently troubled like a soft Liffey dawn, his voice supremely patient and consolatory, like a priest explaining to a convert the necessity of accepting the Trinity on faith.

'I know nothing of any manuals.'

One coping strategy is to turn sordid reality into a purely intellectual problem. With Liz, the challenge was to get her to cook even one meal. Later, to make even one cup of tea. Not that we ever imagined she could become a *Hausfrau.* All we wanted was to penetrate her defensive shield once, the intellectual satisfaction of knowing such a result was possible if sufficient resources were deployed.

Tactics were various. If Liz joined us for breakfast, Reba and I would discuss the evening menu with enthusiasm and dedication. Often I would insist on being chef, hushing Reba's protest with a tender sensitivity to the strains of motherhood and housekeeping. Then Reba would express to Liz her gratitude for an Irish husband willing to cook for his loved ones after a hard day at the office. Sometimes we would announce the menu, leave the ingredients in the kitchen and take ourselves and Emma and David out of the house so that Liz would come in hungry and be forced to cook. This involved us in inconvenience and discomfort, but the use of martyrdom as a weapon comes naturally to the Fenian – my mother used it with devastating effectiveness throughout her marriage. In the interests of a symbolic victory, Reba and I were prepared to wander a wet and cold South Circular Road with a pushchair apiece.

This extreme tactic was as ineffective as the others. The success of martyrdom as a weapon depends on a guilt reaction in the opponent. Astoundingly for a Fenian, Liz appeared to be incapable of experiencing even the slightest twinge of guilt. For her the only duty in life was to sparkle and enchant. We were the backcloth and she was the jewel. We were the parents and she was the child.

Then there was the money problem. Reba could not get work and Liz earned only tiny sums at irregular intervals. This left one salary for five mouths, a mortgage and the hefty repayments on a leather suite. Also the roof leaked, the hot-water heater was knackered, ancient lead pipes and wiring badly needed to be replaced.

Liz did not contribute. Once she replaced a sick journalist for ten days and got a tidy sum, but she immediately bought an expensive camera and signed on for a photography course. Essential for her career, she explained, though after a few months of ostentatious snapping she dropped out of the class and put the camera with her flute and squash racket in the Museum of Cultural and Leisure Artefacts.

Instead of contributions there was extra expense. She got occasional work compiling the news for a commercial radio station and this involved ringing round police stations to wheedle for titbits. Our phone was in the hall and since the calls were not short she would sit on the stairs across from the phone so that movement through the house involved ducking under the cord or squeezing past her on the staircase. Naturally we did more of both than was strictly necessary. Totally ignoring us, profoundly untroubled, Liz would release into the mouthpiece one of her silvery laughs laden with intimacy and promise. Almost broke, we were footing the bill for a pornographic talk line. Every garda in Dublin was getting a hard-on at our expense.

Only one dirty trick was effective: encouraging David to throw himself on his mother. Not even Liz could shake David off. For he was a classic product of the neglect/indulgence cycle. Liz left him most of the day with Reba and often went out again in the evening, usually slipping away without letting him know. When she was with him she lacked the heart to impose discipline. As a result he was a problem eater and sleeper, perpetually suspicious and insanely possessive of his mother.

Of course Liz was prepared to baby-sit at any time, but as Reba and I had no money this was a limited advantage. Occasionally we went to the Irish Film Theatre, Dublin's nearest equivalent to a London-style art house (uncut foreign films but no filter coffee or banana cake). On the way home we stopped off in Cassidy's for a pint, discussing not the Continental movie but the problem of Liz.

Once we came in off a wet and freezing South Circular to find Liz and David on the living-room floor surrounded by every pot and pan in the house partially filled with water. David happily poured from one to the other, creating a new wet patch on the shag pile each time. Liz looked up with a fond chuckle, fully expecting us to share her fascination and amusement. Reba stared at the sopping carpet. Explaining curtly that I was cooking chick pea curry next day and needed to steep the peas, I seized a large pot by the handle. David gripped the rim on the other side. Of course the steeping could have waited. It was another attempt to make Liz suffer. Some chance.

'Now you'll have to let go, David,' she said mildly. 'We have to cook tomorrow's dinner with this pot.'

We have to cook! *We!*

I gave her one of my looks, the flash of concentrated malevolent fury that shrivels the flesh. Every living creature withers under this look. Everything but Liz. Nor was she affected by my terrible transcendent silences, the lengthy periods of withdrawal when I scowl on the leather sofa, remote and unknowable as Calvin's God. I have a unique talent for making people ill at ease, but once, after an hour of this, she actually turned to me and said: 'You know what I like about you? You don't feel the need to talk all the time. You can just sit there saying nothing. I don't mind that at all. I feel really at ease with you. Really comfortable.'

Of course she knew I had the hots. This was the root of the problem, the factor that undermined all the strategies. Even as I pulled at the pot and glared she could see I was aware of her position on the carpet, tight skirt riding up the spread thighs. She knew her sexual power made a mockery of righteousness. A man with a hard-on has no moral weight.

Dear(ish) Fatalistic Fenian

This phrase of yours 'the failure of imminence' is absolutely typical. Resonant, clever, arresting – but the worst sort of lie, defeatism masquerading as maturity. And isn't it an example of the very thing you claim to detest? Cowardice taking refuge behind rhetoric. The wonder of life is that imminence never fails.

At least it's good to know you are savouring the delights of jazz although your black = good, white = bad is far too simplistic. Try Judy Garland singing 'The Trolley Song'. You probably know it already – 'Boom boom boom went my heartbeat, ding ding ding went the bell'. Judy is often thought of as a lugubrious performer but this song has an exuberance and spirit that always lifts my heart. A great classic of popular art.

If you can't get the record I will make you a tape. Plus, at no extra charge, Kenneth McKellar's superb 'Annie Laurie'.

Your renunciation of writing also has an unpleasant ring. A case of turning your face to the wall and murmuring, Lord I am not worthy. And even in this, as with so much you write and say, a kind of superiority. Secretly you believe you're better than the rest of us who do what we can.

Though rereading your stories, I see it's nearly all the one-character sketch about a terrified Fenian unable to live and love because of these hang-ups caused by insensitive parents and teachers. But a failure of personal courage cannot be compensated for by endless angry attacks on attitudes long since discredited. People who don't share your background must wonder what you're on about.

You are good at describing grotesque behaviour but not so good at breaking through to the felt personal experience. What is needed is energy, commitment, courage. Perhaps the enclosed will inspire you – a chapter of a novel in progress and a marvellous marriage of important truths and individual quirkiness. I seem to be getting better and better. If I could tell you the secret I would.

The trouble with this yellow paper is that the error correcting shows up flagrantly. You would think an electric typewriter would make fewer mistakes.

If your own work is flagging you might be glad of the chance to support someone else. Robbie Semple's latest project is a version of *The Balcony* by Genet. More of an adaptation than a translation. He's moved it to Ulster, with the setting still a brothel but the Chief of Police now the head of the RUC, the General an English army officer, the Judge an official in the Orange Order, the Bishop a southern Catholic with a brogue and the rebels, needless to say, the IRA. I have reservations about the piece but it's certainly marvellous theatre with lots of good local references. For instance, when the young Fenian whore, Carmen, dresses up as the Immaculate Conception of Lourdes for an Ulster bank official.

CARMEN (*timidly*): I'm with your bank.
OFFICIAL (*pleased*): Really? Why us?
CARMEN: Because you're *The Bank That Likes To Say Yes.*

The Little Theatre wouldn't touch it so we're setting up our own company. What we desperately need is money for costumes, props and so on. Aren't you a great Genet fan? I'm sure it would do you good to invest in a project after your own heart. Five hundred pounds would cover most of our expenses

and, of course, entitle you to a handsome percentage of profits.
Try to enjoy your days and nights. I do.

Love
Kyle

Wearing a grey business suit and carrying a slimline executive case, the man from the computer company has the frowning impatience of the few who get things done while the benefiting majority sits on its arse and complains. Despite the Irish name, Terry Finnegan, it is obvious at once that his allegiance is to the world of the multinational corporation. Only the beard offers hope of residual Celtic indulgence and warmth, and even this is shaped and trimmed with unGaelic severity.

He sets his slimline on the disc unit and glances about with distaste. 'Are you the computer manager?'

'There is no computer manager.'

He lets this hang in the air. 'Technicians?'

'There are no technicians.'

He nods grimly. 'I personally gave Leonard a complete set of manuals. He was also offered free training for whoever would be running the machine.'

'He denies all knowledge of manuals.'

Another pause. He looks me up and down, coldly assessing. 'If you want another set you'll have to buy them.'

'How much?'

'A few hundred – at least.'

I fail to suppress a bark of helplessness and disbelief.

'Go to the principal,' he snaps with ruthless achiever's logic.

Allowing myself to fall against the disc unit, with appropriate gestures and accents I describe my encounter with the principal in this very room. Halfway through I realise I am attempting the conspiratorial intimacy of auld crack – the very technique I despise in colleagues. From his unsympathetic response I can see how I must look to them – cold, ruthless, implacable, slashing the Celtic mist to tatters with a cutthroat razor. It is true that we must suffer to attain compassion. Humiliated, I feel a surge of empathy for my broken compatriots.

Now he snaps open the slimline. 'I shouldn't be doing this. Shouldn't be here at all if there's no machine failure.' He thrusts a folder at me. 'Basic start-up commands. Photocopy it and bring it back straight away.'

There is one ancient photocopier in a room to which only departmental secretaries have the key. Their reluctance to part with this is a legend. Here all the zeal is proprietorial and negative. We are powered by the twin motors of suspicion and fear.

Also by the need for frequent lengthy rest periods. The secretary's office is locked – coffee time.

I return with a heavy heart – to find Terry in shirt sleeves happily wrestling the machine. He has got it going, and components throb and glow with reassuring futuristic power. God is in the CPU and all's right with the world.

'The photocopier room is locked.'

'Anyway, I've powered it up for you now,' Terry happily cries over throbs and hums. 'It's going fine. No problems at all.' He puts the folder back in his case and hands me a brochure. 'Think about your migration path.'

Nothing about the current machine. Instead a glossy card announcing a new system in an inspirational shade of orange known as hot tango.

Terry puts his jacket on, snaps shut the slimline and hefts it with happy finality.

Inertia. Paralysis. Overpowering desire to freeze in panic like a timid furry thing.

'But I still don't know how to get it going myself.'

Terry regards me across the huge gulf that separates the professionals from the messers. Setting down his case, he removes his jacket once again and strides about the room, furiously throwing switches and banging keys. Devices go dark with peevish whirrs of disappointment.

'Now,' he says, with fantastic tolerance. 'Watch what I do. *Note this down.*'

Within a few weeks of her arrival Liz had more friends than we had made in a year. For instance Madge Dillon, a freelance journalist established to the extent of television appearances and a successful book, *Stretch Marks*. This was a compilation of interviews with women (a single mother, a battered wife, a rape victim, a former prostitute, among others) who had suffered at the hands of men but won through to independence and dignity in the end. Madge herself had fought bravely in the feminist cause, a veteran of landmark engagements like the invasion of the Forty Foot male bathing area and the occupation of the men's toilet in the Dáil.

Liz told a story about Madge on a junket to France for the Beaujolais Nouveau. Although the private plane was full of so-called men, Madge was the only one with balls. When the Frogs offered only the year's *nouveau* for tasting, Madge demanded the older wines, the *real* wine. Beaujolais Nouveau was, of course, a marketing trick for shifting inferior new stuff. While spineless men stood about helplessly, Madge forced the Frogs to cough up vintage wine.

Liz admired such fearlessness and was sure I would respect Madge's opposition to the Catholic Church. We watched her on a chat show with a bishop known to be suffering from leukaemia. Madge offered to donate her own bone marrow – in return for a family planning clinic in his diocese. The bishop roared with laughter. The craven host roared with laughter. The audience roared with laughter. Liz looked to us in triumph. We roared with laughter. But secretly I was horrified. Madge was exactly what I had feared to become as a result of *Born-again Ulster* – a character, a colourful rowdy, a licensed clown. Not merely harmless, she was a positive asset to so-called opponents. As long as she was letting off smoke bombs, they could claim to be tolerating dangerous subversion.

Liz also had older male friends, with whom she was grave, mature, dignified, concerned. Typical of this group was Campbell Stanway, a senior reporter on an Irish daily but a model of English cultivation: silver-haired, sensitive, courteous, reserved. At least reserved with everyone but Liz. They met for coffee and carrot cake in Kilkenny Design, an oasis of refinement and taste which encouraged Campbell to bare his heart. Like many another he had come to Ireland *in escape from* rather than *in search of*. In his case in flight from a broken marriage. But just as he was settling into Irish journalism, British paratroopers shot dead thirteen Catholics in Derry, and in Dublin an angry mob burned down the British embassy. Slumbering nationalism and anti-British sentiment burst out afresh, but by now the English newspaper industry was in serious decline and it was impossible to get back in. Exiled among nationalist colleagues, even getting to see his children was a problem. The short air route to England was the most expensive in Europe.

Liz listened with profound sympathy and repeated it all to us, alternately shrieking with laughter and beating her breast in contrition ('God this is a sin'). And after seeing her boyfriends she was equally frank. It got so that Reba and I, without admitting it, would wait for Liz to come home with her titillating news of the world.

Subdued indirect light in the through lounge. The two of us slump in silence on the leather sofa. On the coffee table an empty sherry bottle. Not that we particularly like sherry but in Dublin at the time it is the cheapest way to get an effect. Beside us the record player, aglow but emitting no sound. We have been quarrelling again about what to play. As my interest in jazz has developed, so Reba's aversion has intensified.

Dramatic entry of Liz! Great news! Madge will sponsor her NUJ application. How can she fail with such pedigree backing? And with an NUJ card comes the chance of a full-time job instead of bits and pieces. But what a night! With Madge to cover a beauty contest in a luxury hotel. Madge demanding the cocktail menu. Free cocktails all night for everyone, including Liz and Wafi. Nevertheless, Madge will take the piss something terrible when she writes her piece. Cocktails all night but the toilet jammed with nervous contestants. Outside, who but Campbell Stanway on foot, because his car has been stolen yet again. Sky-high journalists' premiums about to go even higher.

'By this time I'm *bursting,*' Liz cries. 'So Wafi has to keep a lookout while I go up an entry. Then doesn't this big garda come up to Wafi. *Have ye no fuckin' home to go to?* And Wafi absolutely shitin' himself. He's terrified about getting involved with the police in case they send him home.'

'Where he'll be executed at once?'

'Exactly.'

Not only non-Irish and non-Catholic, most of Liz's boyfriends have something dramatic in their backgrounds or circumstances.

'And he's not exactly welcome here either. You know what the Irish are like. He's just been thrown out of his flat.' Now that our liberal and human sympathies are engaged, she offers us a way of compensating for racist compatriots. 'He needs somewhere to leave his sunbed for a couple of weeks.'

'A sunbed!' I shout. 'What's an Arab want with a sunbed?'

Reba has an explanation. 'He lets women use it and then jumps in on them.'

Liz shrieks in the euphoria of a night of free cocktails. 'Wafi likes to jump on.' Another peal of delight. 'He likes to watch me use the vibrator and then finish it himself.'

We have crossed the portals of the infinite. We have rent the veil. We have passed beyond. Half a bottle of sherry scarcely prepares for such a vertiginous journey. 'You prefer . . . brutal men,' I suggest at last.

'No no no no. Wafi's very affectionate, really. Very tender. He has a wife back home.' Liz leans forward and lays a hand on my arm. 'I always prefer married men.' Her voice is low and profoundly sincere, eyes on mine. 'They're so *considerate.*'

Dear Snuffling Sniveller

If your financial problems are as bad as you claim, you will have to start writing on both sides of the paper. And surely, unlike the rest of us, you have adapted to the contemporary world. You should set yourself up as a computer consultant. Private enterprises make a lot more money and there must be a great sense of adventure in offering yourself for sale and finding everyone wants to buy.

Money problems are a feature of most people's lives. Altnagarvin has been an economic nightmare for as long as I can remember. Usually the American revenue stabilises things but this year even that has not done the trick. Olivia and Renee beset me daily with dire warnings and harebrained recovery schemes. As soon as I finish the novel, I will have to apply myself.

One of your odd Americanisms comes to mind. 'There's some things a man just can't ride around.' I have to say, though, that I find Randolph Scott a most unlikely source of wisdom. Especially for someone of your generation. Even in my day he seemed disgustingly old. Was he ever young and attractive in a Western? In any film? Though I remember a stable boy who was a great fan. Used to jump on the horses and shout: 'Ahm Randiloff Scott so Ah am.' When I pointed out the mis-pronunciation he pushed me into a heap of horse dung. An early lesson in ingratitude.

Perhaps Randolph Scott has fine inspirational qualities which are only apparent to Fenians?

As you are always pointing out, I have much to learn about my Catholic neighbours. However, it is not true that I resist unwelcome truths. No truth should ever be unwelcome. I listen to all your pronouncements with attention and humility.

For instance, your scolding at my neglect of my French heritage. I have just joined the *Sunday Times* Wine Club, a marvellous institution that sends cases of very tasty cheap French wine.

You must visit with your nice wife and child. My daughters are very good with young children.

The Balcony has gone into rehearsal. I am playing the General and have interesting business with a young whore (look up the details). Robbie himself is Arthur the pimp and Robbie's new girlfriend is the Fenian whore Carmen. Renee plays Irma, the brothel madam. It's wonderful to see her working again. The scene where Irma almost expresses desire for Carmen is electrifying. You would think Renee was about to eat the girl. She's also marvellously bitter in the final address to the audience: 'You must go home now where you can be sure everything will be falser than here.'

We hope to get it on as part of the Dublin Theatre Festival in the autumn. If you can't be a financial backer you can at least help by putting up as many as possible of the cast.

Love
Kyle

Like the rest of her family, Reba regarded Liz as an eejit who would eventually be brought to her senses. Sooner or later she would have to find a sensible job or go home. A view I tended to share, knowing from my radio days how fragile is the ecology of flattery and cash. An insult to someone like Campbell Stanway would cut her income in half.

Yet she was making her way. She got her NUJ card. She had work every week. Mostly routine court attendance, but it was work. Campbell Stanway passed her stories from his paper's news desk, the sort of flagrant security leak I thought would bring terrible retribution. Liz laughed at my naïveté – everyone gave stories to everyone else. She got her first by-line. Standing in for a sick education correspondent, she succeeded in placing her name at the top of a brief report on a teachers' conference. There it was – *Liz Herron.* Both Reba and I were startled by the resonance – the authenticity –

of the name in print. Instead of the eejit we knew, it suggested an established figure, one of the new breed of confident, achieving women. Above all, it had a today feel. Strong but light, authoritative but casual, distinctive but short. No marketing man could have given her a more potent sign.

The article itself simply quoted speakers. 'Here is the great challenge – can Irish poets sing as well in a world of concrete and steel as in a world of cottages and turf?' 'If we allow pupils to choose their own curricula we will have modules on *Star Wars* and Michael Jackson. Would the medical profession be happy to let patients write their own prescriptions?' Liz was disconcerted when I burst out laughing, but when she realised it was not at her expense she was happy to join in. All that mattered was the aura of the name at the top, the integrity of the sign.

To celebrate, Liz took us out for a meal and got Madge to babysit. Reba had always imagined journalists to be a self-important and snobbish elite, but Madge turned up in tatty duffel coat, jeans and lumberjack shirt and talked in a broad Belfast accent that made us sound like genteel West Brits. *How're ye doin', Reba? How dye like it down here? Dye go back home much? Ahm never out of Belfast meself. Down here they think the North's all barbed wire and Berlin walls. They think it's terrible – but it's great, like, ye know.* It seemed to me that she was laying it on with a trowel, a classic case of inverse snobbery, but I may have been prejudiced by the fact that she ignored me. Reba certainly bought the whole package. If the Herron scepticism has an Achilles heel it is for this kind of salt-of-the-earth, one-of-the-people act.

Madge suggested that Reba go out with Liz and her. Up to now Reba had avoided the journalist circle but this time she accepted the invitation. Hence a dramatic realignment. Instead of Reba and I isolating Liz, Reba and Liz were now isolating me. It was a lesson in the dynamic nature of power. Perpetually restless, it is forever shifting and turning and assuming new constellations. Only when these are complete can we see the gradual process of change. What I had failed to observe was Reba's altering perception of Liz.

Yet the evidence could hardly have been more striking. For some time Reba had been shopping with Liz and replacing her nondescript good-quality wardrobe. Now she had white bootees, tight pink jeans, several tight-fitting low-necked T-shirts, and a fashionably faded denim bomber jacket. Not that she had entirely shed her puritan guilt, buying only in markets, bargain basements, stock clearances. The denim jacket cost a pound in a bedroom sale. Also, her newly exposed breast tended to flush in public. She covered it with a pink scarf (from War on Want) tied in the Western bandanna style that was all the rage.

Then there was the new hairstyle. Like many another, Reba had spent a despairing youth trying to flatten her wild Irish waves into the long straight hair that was the ideal of the age. Once I came upon a sight that would have been traumatic for a child and was disturbing even for an adult: Reba frightfully contorted over an ironing board actually ironing her own hair. But now the wild look was in. Instead of fighting her waves she could ride them in jubilation. Now it was Liz who had to struggle, needing a perm to conform with fashion.

Finishing touches: pink or purple eye shadow and big, cheap, more-or-less disposable earrings.

All her life Reba had been denied: first by the embittered mother, then by the shutdown of nightlife in the North, then by marriage and lack of money and the demands of a young child. But now she was ready in herself, and at her doorstep lay a city as hedonistic as Vienna in its prime. Now the wire was off the bottle and the champagne about to blow its cork.

The technical college is a place of acrid labs and howling machine rooms. Pungent chemical odours sting the nostrils and the shriek of power tools assails the ears. In addition, most of the classrooms have been vandalised and the heating has never worked properly, so that the environment is squalid and cold. Needing warmth, comfort and silence, man has created a freezing, desolate pandemonium. Yet all is not horror and alienation. The building harbours a surprise in its depths, a warm and fragrant secret pith – a bakery.

Here students learn their trade and offer the results to initiates at irregular intervals. It is a good place to catch certain long-serving members of staff – Roche, for instance, emerging now with a bag of buns. According to the Boy-Men, Roche is from Cork (or Cork City, as it is usually known, whereas Dublin is generally plain Dublin – you don't have to pretend to be what you are), a place of origin that confers a complex set of characteristics endlessly amusing to the Dubliner. The extent of my own knowledge is that Roche is not a Boy-Man but a relaxed and contented paterfamilias, a man with many children, interests and incomes, his involvement with the college the most stable and least demanding.

'It's the eager beaver,' he cries in affectionate greeting, shifting the buns to his left hand so he can deliver a manly back slap with the right. 'Did that computer man show up?'

'He did.'

'Any joy?'

'Not exactly.' Roche shrieks in perverse delight. You would never guess that the machine is in fact his responsibility. 'Do you want a full report?'

At this very moment Roche has students awaiting a lecture for which he is already fifteen minutes late. He also knows that I know, but the hunger for anecdote is too strong.

'The boss has to be briefed.' And, indeed, he attends to my account with lively interest and amusement. 'So you watched what he did and tried it later yourself?'

'Yes.'

'And did it work?'

'No.'

Against my many Dublin failures must be set an outstanding success as a straight man. Roche is possessed by such unbridled merriment that he can scarcely hold on to his bag of buns. This is another good anecdote for his collection. I do his job and then get mocked as 'the eager beaver'. Not that one expects anything else.

Gratitude in Ireland is scarcer than balls on a heifer.

'There's one last chance,' I explain. 'I phoned the guy again and he's prepared to break all the rules and photocopy crucial pages from a few of the manuals. But he insists on a nominal charge. Fifteen quid for the time and costs.'

Roche whinnies again at my pitiful naïveté. 'I have no budget. No access to cash of any kind. It'll have to come out of Maths Department funds. You'll have to speak to Uncle John.' Realising the danger of involvement, he suddenly remembers his waiting class. 'Listen . . . I have to teach' – backing off down the corridor clutching his buns – 'and I'm really up to the eyes at the moment. Under a lot of pressure.' For a moment his expression is serious – but almost immediately it dissolves into another knowing laugh.

For where English hypocrisy requires the appearance of sincerity, the Irish version does not. In Ireland the hand does one thing, the voice says something else, and the eye winks at you in humorous complicity.

Nor can he deny another cultural imperative – the need to exit on a strong punch line. Coming back towards me, he shifts his buns and seizes my sleeve. 'And you're just in the right spot. John had only one requirement in the planning of the college. He insisted on an office next door to the bakery.'

So the journalists encountered Reba in the first wild innocence of her freedom. Expecting to be overawed by the company, she found it was quite the reverse. Mostly Boy-Men like the college staff, the journalists affected a tough and worldly manner but were in fact easily surprised and shocked. Everything about Reba astounded them – height, mad hair, bright clothes, ability to drink stout, sense of humour, mockery, disrespect, foul mouth, wicked tongue and northern accent harsh as a chain saw cutting tin. Utterly different from the docile women they knew, Reba effortlessly beat the men at their own hard-boiled game, expressing Olympian indifference with a sip of stout and a careless shrug: 'That's no hair off my balls.'

Now, as soon as she appeared in Mulligan's, Boy-Men queued up to buy her pints and be crucified for hypocrisy and gormlessness. Fearful mammy's boys and masochists, they adored being abused by a giantess who drank like a navvy and used language you wouldn't lift on a shovel. Without even trying, Reba became a sensation and experienced the intoxication of homage.

At home on the leather sofa I was able to catch up on Joyce and Proust, appropriate heroes for the death of imminence. In fact, I got through so many novels I had to write to Kyle for more. Books were hideously expensive in the South, the Dublin libraries hopeless after generations of censorship. Often I had to give in and go to bed, but stamina could be handsomely rewarded in the early hours. You never knew how the girls would be, hyperactive or comatose or each in turn.

An example of a hyperactive night. The girls burst in and regard with surprise and compassion this morose otherworldly creature in a leather armchair.

'Did you miss us?' Liz cries.

It is hard to be merry after a solitary small-hours vigil. 'I've been communing with the void.'

'What did you tell it?'

'That I oppose to its icy malevolence the terrible lucidity of self-knowledge.'

'And what did the void say to that?'

'Keep believin' it, Shit-for-Brains.'

Liz laughs dutifully but, tired of this badinage, goes to the radio in the corner.

Swaying in the doorway, Reba produces a Free State tenner from the pocket of the denim jacket. 'Didn't spend a penny. No one would let me buy a drink.'

The radio plays 'Kung Fu Fighting' (*those cats are fast as lightning*).

'Get up!' Liz shouts at me, adopting a stern martial arts pose and making chopping motions in the air with her hands.

'You're wanted on Planet Earth,' Reba says to me.

'The sad hospital. Our monotonous and unworthy fatherland.'

'Are ye gonnay talk like this all night?'

'I have resigned myself to eloquence.'

'Hah!' Liz shouts, taking a martial spring forward.

Reba proposes a more Irish approach. 'Get ees trousers off!'

I fight like a tiger, not out of modesty but because the back of my shorts may well reveal a disgraceful stain. How do regular stickmen cope with the perennial male problem of russet gusset? Even Kyle, frankest of reporters on love, has nothing to say on this vexing issue. Once again the commentators fail us.

And one example of a comatose night. Late late late late. I hold out on the sofa, exhausted and ashen. What keeps me awake is the manuscript of Kyle's latest novel, *Home Fires*. All of his life with Olivia is there: affairs, rows, degradations, humiliations, departures, returns. Apparently Olivia, too, has had her flings. Every page is engrossing. O blessed rage for ordure, the dirt that reveals the truth behind the public mask! This is the foul fertiliser from which wisdom grows. But not easy to come by, especially in the cosy blandness of Irish fiction. I read avidly, appalled by the frequent misspellings (Catholic education warps you for life but by Christ you can spell) and electrified by the frankness. *Don't tell them that, Kyle! I can take it – but can they?*

What are misspellings and gaucheness compared to honesty like this? We must acknowledge excellence where we find it, even among our friends.

The world is silent – apart from the return of the teenage daughter next door. Her father is waiting in the hall. Violent door slam. Blows and shrieks. 'Get in outa that, ye shaggin' bastard ye!'

Eventually Reba and Liz roll in, comatose. I haul Reba upstairs first. Dropping her onto the bed, I take off the denim jacket, white bootees and pink jeans. When I try to remove the T-shirt she starts throwing punches.

Liz has passed out on the sofa. As I support her upstairs, she falls against me, murmuring endearments: 'You're . . . so good. So . . . tolerant.' Pause to kiss – sickly-sweet smell of booze. In her room the sofa bed is still a sofa. Liz collapses onto it. After a time she unzips her skirt – and falls back.

'You want the skirt off?'

Liz grunts. Interpreting this as assent, I take hold of the hem and draw the skirt down. She grunts again and lifts her legs to let it pass. Beneath her black tights are faded blue cotton pants with the elastic of one leg detached from the fabric. Life in its heart-rending beauty has no need of artifice. A little whimper of compassion escapes my stern self-control.

The problem is this: all the Herron girls are prone to thrush and permitting Liz to sleep in her tights is tantamount to giving her a dose. And, of course, removing them would raise another spectre – necrophiliac incest. Long terrible pause. It is the hour of the wolf, when the moral imperatives of the hunter are in abeyance and the resistance of the prey is at its lowest ebb. Now the goon squads burst in on terrified suspects. Pitiless moonlight. Terror and madness. Burials in unmarked graves.

Reba is in a coma. The Catholic State is profoundly silent.

Whiff of fragrance from the skirt in my hand. The terrible rigid member, pent. I start to shake – fever of the tomb-robber given an opportunity of violation, lusting for gold but scared of a frightful curse on his life and the lives of the generations to come.

Dear Frigid Fenian

Surely living with two spirited young women is no cause for complaint. Who said that marriage is a chain forged of such heavy links it requires two to carry it and sometimes three? I offer the following as evidence of what can be achieved with a little imagination and courage within the framework of provincial society.

A few weeks ago a dozen or so married couples met in a local hotel and the men threw their car keys into a kind of ornamental fountain in the lobby. I'm not happy with this sentimental wish-fulfilment aspect, *Three Coins in the Fountain* and so forth, but perhaps it is necessary. Many rituals which seem an irritating waste of time turn out to have great psychological validity. My keys were lifted by a considerably older woman who became extremely embarrassed and wanted to withdraw. I assured her that the randomness and lack of romantic preliminaries were the point of the thing. We were trying to escape the conventions. Isn't it well known that Asian arranged marriages often work better than those based on romantic choice? Also, older women have their own attractions, everyone has something to offer. So we drove to the coast and swam naked for half an hour or so, an exhilarating experience in its own right. Afterwards we lay on the sand and tasted the salt on each other's bodies. Still she was reluctant, not in a coy way but with a genuine feeling of unworthiness. It was a great privilege to be able to convince her of her value and I was rewarded by an experience that would not have been possible with a woman who had a high opinion of her charms.

When I left her home we talked for a long time over mugs of hot chocolate. She was neither stupid nor insensitive though she lives in a bungalow full of gimcrack ornaments and appallingly sentimental reproductions of animals and glorious sunsets. A terrible failure of the imagination.

Talking of intimate conversation reminds me of how long it is since we met. Why don't you visit? It now looks as though my own Dublin debut will be as a saxophonist rather than an actor. What are the venues for a saxophone-led quartet playing modern classics and standards? I know very little of the Dublin jazz scene.

The Balcony finally blew up last night after a row between Renee, Robbie and Robbie's new girl. Drink was taken and intimate home truths uttered on all sides. It's terribly depressing after all the work and commitment.

But this morning was fine and clear and sharp. I climbed through the wood to the top of the hill, from where on a good day you can see all the way to the coast, seven miles or so. I should have been a painter. The appearance of things is an unfailing source of renewal and joy.

And I have almost mastered the chords of 'I'll Be Seeing You'.

Every day wonderful things are happening. Every day is a miracle.

Love
Kyle

Neither corrupt nor insane, John Kinsella represents the most enlightened form of Irish authority – benign despotism. From behind the desk in his tiny office permeated by aromas from the bakery, his soft and ample form radiates harmony and wellbeing, a kind of Irish Buddha. Nor is he merely Oriental in appearance. His stewardship of the Mathematics Department is firmly based on Taoist precepts: 'Hold fast to the way of antiquity in order to keep in control the realm of today' (*Tao-te-Ching*, XIV.34), 'Do that which consists in taking no action and order will prevail' (III.10), 'That which goes against the Way will come to an early end' (XXX.70).

Despite the commitment to inaction, his presence is enormously reassuring and positive. By means of faith alone he has raised the famous Joycean paralysis to a mystical, transcendent level. In the matter of the computer that will not function he seems the most likely prospect in a chain of command that runs: chancer (Roche), benign despot (Kinsella), paranoid (Leonard), schizo (principal). Seated across the desk from him, I explain the situation in clear and confident terms, approaching by means of inexorable logic the one feasible solution – fifteen quid from petty cash for a photocopied mini-manual. As well as being calm and reasonable I take care to avoid anything that could be interpreted as criticism of others in the chain of command.

It is a performance that would have an English administrator eating out of my hand, but against the ancient wisdom of the East it is powerless. Not that Kinsella says anything ('One who knows does not speak' – LVI.128), nor do his impassive features betray any hint of displeasure or impatience. Nevertheless my confidence, initially absolute, drains away in the course of the exposition ('One who speaks does not know' – LVI.128). Bit by bit my resonant and resolute voice comes to sound scratchy, feeble, peevish, even slightly repellent, like the mandibles of an insect attempting to shift a large smooth stone basking in the sun.

A warm fragrant blast from the bakery serves to emphasise my alien logic and outsider status. Every visit there finds empty shelves and trays and indifferent shrugs from the men in white hats. If I stay to retirement age I will never be privy to the schedule of the bakery.

Obviously I am not to be granted the fifteen quid, but did I actually ask for the money or merely fade away at the crucial point? It is possible that no direct request has been made. Under perfect authoritarianism, demands need never be refused because they wither away themselves prior to expression. Without speaking, Kinsella has filled the cubicle with a massive and unassailable truth: young smart alecks who play with new machines should not come crying to their elders for help. Least of all if it requires the elder to put his hand in his pocket (when it comes to money there is no detachment; here all official expenditure is experienced in a bitterly personal way). Smart alecks must accept the inevitable consequences of their pride. For is it not written: 'Woe to him who wilfully innovates' (XVI.38)?

It is silent in the tiny cubicle, sparsely furnished with two chairs, a bare desk and a metal filing cabinet. The institution-green walls are also unadorned so the eye is drawn inexorably to the two bulging paper bags on top of the cabinet. One is filled with fresh loaves, the other with buns.

'Was there something else?' Kinsella murmurs, after a time.

Yes, the disappearance of one of the few female students, not only very bright but a useful counterbalance to the male ethos of the class.

'I know about that,' Kinsella says. 'A very nice girl.'

From the satisfaction in his voice it is obvious that this student has found the Way and that it does not involve wilful innovation. At one time it could only have meant the convent, but of course the Catholic State is more secular now.

'Where has she gone?'

Startled at first by the brutal directness of the question, Kinsella is soon content once more. He leans forward, radiant, joyful, benign.

'She got the bank.'

Within the new Reba–Liz alliance the balance of power quickly shifted to Reba. Expecting to introduce a country cousin to society, Liz in fact had trouble keeping up with her protégée. Creative abuse was the new style, but Liz had neither Reba's natural acerbity nor the primal authenticity of her delayed adolescence. Only once can we enter our kingdom in triumph.

Inevitably Reba acquired a serious admirer, an attractive young Marxist reporter who shocked her by returning the abuse and despising her little South Circular nest as a 'bourgeois family unit'. Not in any way a Boy-Man or a Mulligan's bar fly, he cultivated many interests, not only unusual in themselves but intriguingly inconsistent in combination. For instance, despite his Marxism he was devoted to opera and bemoaned Ireland's lack of a professional company as bitterly as its failure to become a socialist republic. Would Reba care to see a visiting production of *Carmen* at the Olympia?

This was another revelation for Reba. Carmen was the perfect role model – haughty, tempestuous, independent, wild-haired. The whole story was a perfect paradigm. Reba was Carmen, her reporter Escamillo the sexy toreador, yrs. tly. Don José the mammy's boy and asshole. And not just the story, the flamenco dancing, stamping of feet and tossing of heads: bad temper as art form. The whole show was a hymn to hubris, the distinguishing quality of the Herrons. It was the gypsy in their souls – like the Galway black hair and dark skin, inherited from Spanish Armada sailors who had come ashore from wrecked ships to sow their fiery seed among the colleens. Such was the Herron belief. In fact, I discovered a less romantic explanation, that the dark look came from an earlier wave of pre-Celts pushed out to the western seaboard by later arrivals. I never had the heart to offer Reba this theory.

The experience also gave Reba a respectable alternative to my accursed jazz and Liz's AOR (adult-oriented rock). She bought a record of *Carmen* highlights and played it incessantly, stamping her bootees as best she could on the shag pile.

But when Reba took to going out for a drink with the reporter, away from the gang in Mulligan's, Liz decided I needed a talking to. As soon as the children were in bed she came down to the living room and sat facing me with an expression of stern disapproval.

'Drink, Liz?' We had now adopted the desperate measure of making our own wine from a kit – or rather a red liquid that resembled wine.

Liz grunted impatiently. This was not a social call. I assumed she was annoyed at the impertinence of Reba and her friend meeting outside the journalist circle. But as I filled the glasses another possibility occurred to me – Liz herself had been rejected by the reporter. No one gets righteous quicker than a spurned libertine.

'I told Reba this wasn't fair on you,' Liz said, with a grimness that told me Reba had not been co-operative. Being Carmen's big sister is no easy task. 'I mean, what do you feel about this whole thing, anyway?' Noticing the glass in her hand, she took a swift swig and came forward on the seat with revealing eagerness. Not so much interested in my feelings, she was fishing for information. *Reba was not confiding in her.* Good old Reba!

On the other hand I did not want to reveal to Liz that I knew as little as she. Not normally a role player, I do have a weakness for acting the weary sophisticate. Also, the idea of making her suffer was not entirely displeasing. I gave a light, ironic shrug calculated to annoy. It was plain that she wanted me raving and desolate like Lear on the heath.

Liz, annoyed: 'I told her she was taking a hell of a chance.'

'What sort of chance?'

'I told her you'd just do the same on her and that your marriage would soon be in trouble.' Liz the home-wrecker, indefatigable husband-stealer ('Married men are so considerate'). 'I said, have you no concern for the marriage?'

I laughed out loud. 'When did you develop this respect for marriage?'

'I just meant you could go off with someone as quick as she did.' Now that righteousness had failed, she was trying more familiar ploys. 'After all, you're an attractive guy.' The old silvery laugh of transgression. 'A good catch, as they say.'

The curse of it was this: her wiles always worked. So much for the weary sophisticate. Tender feelings stirred in my bowels like a brood of fledgelings in a nest.

And over another glass of wine she begged forgiveness for her sins. 'Of course it's all my fault really. I should never have taken her into a crowd like that. Something like this was bound to happen.'

Now we were the two mature ones, Reba the irresponsible eejit. Yet another power shift. Yet another new alliance. Now we had experienced every combination of two out of three. Dangerous waters, though. A lot of stuff swirling around in the murk. As the injured party I was entitled to seek compensation from Liz. But things were not that simple. For a start I was getting a lot of spin-off from Reba's break-out. We were making use of Liz's vibrator, for instance. I was far from being a rejected and desperate guy. Then there was Liz's dubious motivation. It could be more a question of punishing Reba than of succumbing to me. I always felt Liz despised me a little for allowing stardom to slip away.

We went on drinking wine until Reba got back, sensing at once the power shift.

'Any wine left?' she asked, in a slightly sardonic tone.

'It's taken a bit of a beating,' I had to admit.

Liz laughed suddenly, a provocative, confident sound.

Reba poured herself wine and put *Carmen* on. For 'L'Amour est un oiseau rebel', she laid aside the empty glass and got up to dance, taking off the denim jacket and raising her bare arms above her head. Liz immediately followed suit, her loose long skirt more appropriate than Reba's jeans, but her lifted arms ruling her out at once.

'Flamenco dancers never shave their pits, Liz,' I had to say. 'You're too much of a sweetie. Not hairy enough.'

With a cry of triumph Reba flaunted the uncurtailed earthy unkemptness for which I can claim some credit. A sanitised and circumscribed modern man in most ways, I have successfully entreated Reba not to shave her armpits.

Without losing the rhythm of the dance, Liz bent her left hand to the hem of her skirt and swept it up in a single fluid motion. She was not wearing tights this evening. Chuckling a little, but still in step, she hooked the thumb of her right hand into her pants and drew them down.

In absolute terms she was probably no more richly endowed than Reba, but her slight build and prettiness intensified a hundredfold the effect of fantastic untamed abundance. She let loose a wild laugh, not of challenge but victory. *How do you like it now, Mr Smart-ass Cold-Balls?*

Dear Fenian Faintheart

It is never 'unbelievably tiresome' to ask for books. What are friends for? What are books for? It gives me nothing but pleasure to pass on a work of art.

There is no 'inconvenience', as you seem to think. I go to the post office every day, a delightful walk past a stream and the ruins of the old linen mill. It is run by two marvellous old God-fearing sisters who have a quotation from scripture stuck on the front of the till – perfect symbol of Protestant Ulster.

When an old humanist friend came to visit last month he turned up extremely late, unusual for humanists and this man in particular. He apologised but said he felt obliged to stop and remove all the religious material nailed to fences and trees.

Knowing your taste for such things, I have kept two of the finest examples – HELL HAS NO FIRE ESCAPE and DRINK IS THE DEVIL'S VOMIT.

And the countryside at this time. Hints of spring seem to get more ecstatic each year. The curious blend of blinding white and modest deportment in the snowdrop clumps. I will have to get down to some painting. Van Gogh did all his work in ten years.

What a beautiful province this is in spite of everything. Do you never miss the splendours of your native place? Perhaps now is the time to come home. Since the collapse of the power-sharing executive (I supported the executive wholeheartedly), there has been a dangerous pessimism and inertia. Ulster needs all its talented sons. You may be some kind of crippled neurotic but you are right often enough to get people's minds moving.

It strikes me that you have a lot in common with Robbie Semple. In particular a tendency to see all in authority as corrupt and/or buffoonish figures who must be swept aside but will inevitably be replaced by something even more stupid and vicious. And your most violent scorn is reserved for the compromised but good man struggling in a world of corruption and indifference. Any hope of improvement is fatuous, you seem to be saying, a dangerously nihilistic view that you cover up with jokes.

Does this universal contempt come from Nietzsche? Or is it Catholic Manichaeism in your case? Semple is certainly a great Nietzsche fan and I have been looking at the work to try to understand the attraction. Certainly it is stylish, but the style only conceals the lack of content. Perhaps this is often the function of style? There are wonderful fireworks, but nothing you can take away to apply in life. Roman candles, sky rockets, catherine wheels – but when the firework display is over you are back in the dark.

Robbie is certainly displaying an alarming lack of character. Since the failure of *The Balcony* he has sunk into despair and apathy. Instead of putting his talent to use he is drinking heavily, fantasising about America and beating up his girlfriend.

Yet how much you could both achieve with a little more courage and concern.

Cancel everything next Thursday evening. There is a repeat of a Judy Garland special in which I am almost sure she does 'The Trolley Song'.

Love
Kyle

I put it to Roche that our students of computing must at some point actually use a computer and that even these most docile and tolerant of young people are beginning to show signs of dissatisfaction and restlessness. Ditto for this most patient of colleagues. Roche could not agree or sympathise more. Eye contact, proximity, touching – every tool in the Irish sincerity kit. This is no longer a laughing matter. What we need is a conference of all interested parties – myself, him, Kinsella, Leonard, and Darcy the principal. And not merely to get the machine going but to sort out finally who is responsible for running it and who provides the budget. No more evasions and messing. A crisis meeting in the boardroom.

This is the only room of any distinction in the college, a building purpose-built in the early sixties but as shockingly faded as the other products of that sanguine decade. I am the first to arrive, at eleven o'clock, and can enjoy for a moment in private an opulence different from the tacky decrepitude of the rest of the college. This floor is higher than the neighbouring buildings, which cut out the light lower down, and from a picture window overlooking south Dublin, sunlight floods in on the long wooden table, the padded leather-covered chairs, the enormous glass ashtrays of marvellous solidity and heft. The room's atmosphere is of benign paternalism and old-fashioned comfort. It reminds me of being taken for a drive in my uncle's big Humber.

At twenty past eleven Roche rushes in, the very picture of

executive commitment and decisiveness. 'No one here yet? Be back in a second.'

I was interviewed in this room, but it holds no painful memories. A somnolent panel knowing nothing of computers, drinking tea from china cups and a silver service. The friendly tone almost apologetic. The one priest asleep.

Below, smoke accumulates over the little terraces. By now all the fires are lit and the fresh baps fetched. Morning tea in the parlour. RTÉ Radio murmurs. Budgies scuffle in cages. Cats doze on chairs. On the scrubbed floors of bars the sun lays tiles of gold. Men open virgin newspapers and taste the first drink of the day – the sweetest, the most exquisite, the nonpareil.

Our own house is out of sight behind a church. Reba should be back from the shops and Liz should be up, drinking black coffee in the kitchen in her dressing gown – she seldom eats a breakfast – and shrieking with laughter as she recounts the events of the evening before to Reba. Perhaps reticent Reba is also opening her heart ... David rushes in and flings himself against his mother. Liz lifts him onto her knee. He seizes her lapel for support and pulls the dressing gown off her shoulder...

Exquisite, drowsy tumescence, disturbed by an arrival at 11.35. As I watch in fascination, a mouse emerges from a corner of the room and ambles along three sides before disappearing at the far end.

Rustle. Scratch. A mouse
tours the resonant
boardroom: *profound harmony.*

For of course the only solution is to become an Irish Buddha oneself – squat, impassive and imperturbable in the sun – and let the mandibles of the insects scratch at your smooth surface in vain.

At 11.40 Roche returns to do business. It is a measure of his seriousness that although he has almost certainly been to the bakery, he has taken the trouble to stash his buns before coming back.

'Where is everybody?'

I respond with a shrug. He who speaks does not know the Way.

Roche darts exasperated glances about the room, as though expecting to discover imperfectly concealed executives. 'This is very disappointing.'

Liz was moving out, Reba was thirty – party time. Reba's plan was that she would invite the rumbustious journalists and I would have zeros from the college, my little clan of female language teachers dedicated to replacing Irish male brutishness with liberal values, love of the arts and vegetarian/health food (Ireland untwee will never be at peace). I shook her by rejecting this group and insisting on Kyle (as Montesquiou said of Proust: 'Beneath a timid exterior he is not entirely devoid of resourcefulness').

Frances and Sean arrived in the late afternoon and when Frances saw Reba's new look she immediately abandoned her own party outfit for Reba's tight pink jeans and one of her low-necked T-shirts. After almost a decade of infants and suburbs she too was ready to bust loose. Already, after a telephone conversation with Reba, she had given her wild locks their freedom. In the area of hair-straightening she and Reba advanced, roped together like Picasso and Braque in the heady dawn of Cubism. Always on the appliance side in the Appliance versus Lotion debate, they had endlessly researched and tested devices, their technology never more than a few months behind state of the art. Now all that was over and they could toss heads as magnificent as those of the wild stags above Glendalough. But for the moment Frances bided her time on the sofa, quietly drinking home brew.

Kyle arrived with a classic example of what my mother and Mrs Herron would have described as 'a cheeky article'. You could tell from the way she strode into the room and stood apart, one foot forward, left hand supporting right elbow, head thrown back to release a contemptuous blast of cigarette smoke towards the ceiling. In extreme cases such as this the adjective would be dropped. 'Oooooooh' – shudder of deep and bitter certainty – 'an *article*'.

Seeing Kyle for the first time in years, I experienced an overpowering urge to apologise, to confess and seek absolution for my many lapses and sins: the betrayal of the arts and alignment with the information age; the bourgeois leather suite, shag pile and Chinese saucers on the mantelpiece (I tried to remove these on the pretext of avoiding breakages but Reba immediately detected the true motive); the coarse-grained music we were playing (AOR instead of jazz); the backward Catholic State we inhabited (barely recovered from the hysteria of the pope's visit); the boring company I was subjecting him to (not only Fenians but suburban-zero in-laws); and the plague of hack journalists who would descend on him at closing time. A full confession would have taken all night. I made do with an apology for exposing a real writer to hacks.

Kyle absolved not only me but the journalists themselves. 'It's childish to think papers have to be as bad as they are. They could be redeemed. The struggle to be a good journalist in a bad society is a very real one.'

Kyle was apparently as tolerant as ever, leaning against the wall and happily sipping a glass of home brew. A murky maleficent liquid. Dublin Bay Effluent. Freshly squeezed juice of Liffey King Turd.

'Have you vodka?' the article asked.

Then they conferred in private and Kyle came back to me.

'Can we use your bedroom?'

Reba and Sean were out for more drink. Kyle had written in praise of hurried love, torn through the iron gates of life. Maybe he would be finished before Reba got back.

Frances came to me from the sofa. 'They've gone up' – she jerked her head towards the ceiling – 'up to . . . ah . . .'

I nodded casually, as though lovers used my bed every night of the week. Is there anything more fun than playing the decadent to an innocent sweetheart?

'Where are they?' was Reba's first question.

'Upstairs.'

'What are they doing up there?'

Remember that the child had only just come of age.

'Saying yes to life.'

Even now it took a second.

'You mean he's screwing her?' The poor child was never meant to be Mistress of Revels. 'In *my* bed? That . . . *fucking huer?*'

It could have been nasty had not the journalists arrived.

Madge Dillon seized the fingers of my right hand and worked them like the teats of a cow, keeping her eyes fixed on mine and eventually intoning gravely, 'Bord Bainne.'

'Huh?'

'I interviewed the head of Bord Bainne today. The Milk Board . . . yeah? This is how he shakes hands with everyone.'

Liz removed her coat to reveal a backless black cocktail dress that recalled a Sammy Mullen comment on one of her earlier outfits: 'No more cloth on her nor would tighten the head of a spade.' The shock made me regress to the patois. 'God you're a great wee girl.'

She laughed in acknowledgement of the first adjective, a low chuckle magically freighted with transgression. Then admonished me on the second: 'Less of the *wee*.'

In the doorway was a scornful youth with fashionably slicked-back hair and an expensive trench coat open on a well-cut dark suit, red-and-white striped shirt and solid bright-red tie, an appearance of international elegance spoiled by the bottle of Paddy he drew from the pocket of the coat. But even with the Irish whiskey, he was more like a tourist than a son of the Gael. Reba went to him in silence. It is true that the strongest emotions are dumb. He put the bottle to his mouth and took a bracing shot. Reba emptied her glass and held it out. He poured her a stiff one. She drank half, her left hand straying towards the lapel of the trench coat, *actually almost touching the hem of his garment.* Still no words, but the body language was deafening.

Sober, grave, Liz put her mouth to my ear and employed the journalist's gift for presenting the obvious as revelation.

'That's the one that's after Reba.'

'I'm not blind, Liz.'

'But people will notice. He doesn't give a shit. That's the

kind of him.'

In fact I rather approved of the disdain. What I could not have endured was Reba taking up with a buffoon.

'So what do you suggest I do?' This came out with more acerbity than I intended. Liz presented her bare back and walked off – to be immediately replaced by Frances, increasingly equivocal and disturbing in Reba's clothes. Her face had lost its severe angular look but she was still slim and the low neck revealed deep clefts between collarbone and shoulder. A man could lose himself for twenty years in sleepy hollows like that.

'Aren't you going to do anything?' Unlike Liz she did not seem to be angry. 'Sean would have done his nut.' Her tone was wondering, tentative. Instead of anger, I heard respect and the urge to console. She wanted to admire me like a father and mother me like a hurt child. Daddy *me*, I'll mammy *you*. A devastating combination. Who would have thought there was so much mileage in being a cuckold?

Under cover of the hubbub, Kyle slipped back in, alone and almost unnoticed.

'Good sport fucking, Kyle?'

He winced. 'These outlandish phrases.'

I had hit on another anti-mantra – a word or phrase which produces, instead of wellbeing, acute discomfort or even pain. Discovering these appears to be a natural talent. Of course I would rather have been a concert pianist, but we have to use the gifts God gave.

But a celebrity could not go unremarked among journalists. Madge Dillon came across and soon had Kyle agog at stories of her derring-do in the bad old censorship days when she brought banned Lawrence and Henry Miller books into the Catholic State concealed on her person and challenged embarrassed customs officials to search her and remove them. Kyle listened enthralled. He had merely read his heroes. Madge had risked prison for them – and this in spite of disapproving of their male chauvinism.

Reba's boyfriend came across to Kyle but got off to a bad start by attempting to sell John Le Carré, a writer of *spy thrillers*, as a major novelist. His tone was distinctly adversarial, and waving a bottle of Paddy did nothing to mitigate the effect. Then he mentioned that he had just been in Kyle's part of the world to cover an IRA funeral that had been attacked by the RUC. Reporters and mourners both beaten. Women bleeding, children screaming.

'Yes,' Kyle said, after listening patiently, 'but it seems only Catholics suffer. What did the dead man do, may we ask?'

With a guffaw of contempt the Paddy was hoisted aloft and brandished. 'To the freedom fighters of the North!'

If he was hoping for support he must have been disappointed. The silence was instant and total.

'Donal,' Reba whispered.

Madge put her mouth to my ear. 'It's his family. Falls Road. A brother killed. Heavy diggers ... ye know?' Reba had never mentioned this. A true son of the Gael after all.

'But what sort of freedom are they fighting for?' Kyle cried. 'Will there be freedom for Protestants?'

'We have no quarrel with Protestants.'

'But you've been murdering them for years. How do you expect them to be reasonable?'

'As soon as the Brits agree to go the hand of friendship will be extended.'

Donal said this with a great air of magnanimity, as though major concessions were being offered. The Irish notion of compromise – promising to be nice to the other guy after he does what you want.

'But what are your plans for the arts? For education? For social welfare?'

'Social welfare!' Donal threw back his head to release towards the ceiling a magnificently contemptuous laugh. 'Hitler's social welfare was the best in Europe.'

I had never thought to see Kyle incoherent. 'You see that's ... that's ... ' He swung his glass in inarticulate rage. 'That's the sort of ... cheap ... evasive ... '

Donal put his face to Kyle's and demonstrated what Pearse

praised as 'the Irish power of clear, vivid, unadorned speech': '*Fuckin' liberal shite!*' he roared.

This was the crux of the argument. What infuriated people about Kyle was his outspoken liberal values. An extremist they could understand but not a fatuous middle-class do-gooder. In Ireland liberalism is the love that dare not speak its name.

Several journalists closed around Donal. Seizing an elbow each, Reba and Liz pointed him to the door. For me it was a fantasy scenario – remaining calm and rational and ironic while your rival noisily self-destructs in public.

Instead of being depressed, the Herron girls were galvanised by the incident. Bursting with surplus *esprit sauvage*, Frances pulled me out onto the floor to dance. I was wearing a cowboy shirt with metal studs instead of buttons. Uttering a terrible cry, she seized each side of the collar and, with the ferocious concentration of will and self-belief required to smash a breeze block with your bare hand or whip a tablecloth from under a dinner service, ripped the shirt open to the waist in a moment of searing incandescence. Of course the element of surprise contributed to the effect. But when she did it a second time, I experienced the same overwhelming ecstasy of thralldom.

It is memories like this that will linger when the caravanserai has passed and the tumult has died away in silence. A blue-and-green-checked shirt from the Emperor of Wyoming. Many claim such boutique clothes are shoddily made. I can only say that this garment was violently ripped open three times without shedding a stud.

A belly-pusher with Liz. I laid a hand on her naked back and she swung against me, sweet 'n' low, apparently welcoming the arrant knob.

It occurred to me that the way was clear at last. Before, Liz had always been embedded in families. Now she had her own place. And on the unfashionable north side, well out of the way. Never one of those for whom danger spices the act, my ideal is the untroubled ruminating pleasure of the sultan.

Strange equivocal sensation – the rebirth of imminence.

'Isn't Frances terrific?' she murmured. For 'Frances' substitute 'Liz'.

I accepted both primary meaning and subtext. 'Terrific!'

Reba, too, sought me out, touching, appealing, establishing and holding deep eye contact. 'Aw . . . honey.' It was the wild extravagant generosity that possesses women at times but can neither be predicted nor induced. All we can do is accept it gratefully when it comes. She started to laugh. 'What a night, eh? You know when we were out for the drink Sean asked me to hold his cock.'

Of course the initial reaction was surprise. After this came more tranquil emotions: empathy, wonder, compassion, tenderness. If a woman would handle Sean's brutal fillet there was hope for us all.

Full technical details would, of course, be required. For the moment one question. 'What did he say?'

She sighed, reliving Sean's fervent sincerity. '*Aw Jesus, Reba, hold me lad a wee minute.*'

In the end no one could keep up with the Herron girls. The revellers fell back and left them the floor. For once Kyle, too, was content to watch, chuckling happily, knowing he was not up to dithyrambic frenzy on this occasion. Even being a life force is subject to the tedium of habit.

Liz swept across the floor, executing sinuous arabesques with cool Mozartean elegance, presenting to us her bare back, shoulder blades rippling beneath the skin like the wings of some great exotic moth. Reba too was compelling, though not as mobile, preferring to stamp the floor flamenco-style. The Carmen of South Circular. Mistress of Contumely. Madonna of Scorn. Yet the performance of these two, for all its fervour, was marred by the poisonous taint of professionalism. The frenzy was practised – a competence. Frances was more of an athlete than a dancer, but her frank, bumptious leaping had the authentic wild innocence. Like Billie with Lester or Bird at the birth of bebop, you could tell at once that the lyric joy was fresh.

We stood back and watched them, applauding and cheering.

These three sisters did not long for Moscow. Wherever they were, that was Moscow. I turned to Kyle with a triumphant look. How do you like it now, Mr Hot-shot Novelist? How does your cheeky huer compare to this? Profoundly foolish boastfulness. Never flaunt your treasure before a desperate world. Hide everything of value. Cover it over instantly like a cat with its shit.

5

Back room of Mulligan's in Poolbeg Street. Ancient hard wooden chairs, long scarred wooden table, discoloured wallpaper, empty grate. Draughty, shabby, bleak, it exudes an atmosphere of futile meetings in the service of lost causes, the long familiar road of impotence, factionalism and acrimony. Into this place of futility comes Kyle the Evangelist, handsome and youthful in a new black leather bomber jacket, radiant with optimism and hope for a society in which the shrivelled and desiccated will attain their full potential, bearing with him the materials with which to effect this transformation, namely a briefcaseful of his own writings, and having just arranged a means of nationwide dissemination, namely an agreement to review for a prominent Southern Irish newspaper books on the Irish Literary Revival.

'Jesus, Kyle.'

If he intends to become an expert on Irish life he might as well get used to the prevalent Fenian disease – universal contempt.

'A lot of it was worthless. But I suppose Yeats thought the ferment and publicity might create an audience, a popular culture.'

No skulking in back rooms for such a man. Out to the bar for wine of the country. Not that our presence is appreciated.

'Hey, Christie,' someone behind us calls to the barman, 'what's all these wooden planks?'

Christie glances disparagingly at us, then speaks out of the corner of his mouth to those behind, like a footballer bending a free kick round a defensive wall.

'Germans,' he says.

I suggest to Kyle that, like the hero of the Joyce story set in this bar, he should offer to arm-wrestle the author of the 'wooden planks' jibe.

'I never understood how *Dubliners* was supposed to be a chapter in the moral history of Ireland. It always seemed to me frigid and full of disgust.'

'Not hard to see why it was rejected by Mills & Boon.'

We go out into bright autumn sunshine, up Tara Street and Pearse Street and right into Westland Row. Lucky chance for Kyle to see the Grosvenor Hotel before it disappears for ever. Already it is roofless and partly demolished, the front plastered with show-band posters – *Sean Ryan and the Buckshot, Philomena Begley and Her Rambling Men* – stout country lads and lasses in cowboy hats. Genuine Irish popular culture. I explain that this is where Leopold Bloom paused to enjoy a flash of leg as a rich woman came out of the hotel and got into her carriage. Kyle attends without enthusiasm. Of course voyeurism would not be his bag at all. Nor indeed any of the furtive parasexual activity of the Fenian.

'Tell me this, Kyle, on the basis of your vast experience. Which is the true ecstasy – vertiginous coition, resonant penetration . . . or unsolicited appropriation of the burning tool?'

What I am after is acknowledgement of the primacy of imminence over fulfilment – but I am prepared to accept that over-valuing expectation may be a feature of the underclass. However, Kyle produces no glib response, staying true to his principles of calm reflection and impartiality.

'I think there's a great deal to be said for all three.'

As we proceed up the street Kyle expresses belated gratitude. 'All this Joycean lore is very interesting. We had none of this at the Bloomsday do itself.'

'You were too busy getting your hole.'

As always Kyle resists the profane and familiar approach, responding with grave dignity. 'That was only in the afternoon. In the morning we unveiled that plaque at the birthplace of Bloom. How does it go? *Citizen, Husband, Father, Wanderer.*'

'Far too pompous. Should be *Coward, West Brit, Cuckold, Wanker.*'

'The ceremony was anything but pompous. This little woman who owned the house turned up in the middle of it carrying two Quinnsworth bags. She'd forgotten all about it and was utterly bewildered. So I was present for a truly Joycean moment, after all. And of course I was at the banquet that night.'

The glittering banquet in Dublin Castle, famous writers and Joyceans from all over the world, among them Kyle, relaxed and grinning and confident despite his almost total ignorance of the master's oeuvre. You would think that, as a novelist, he could render a lively eyewitness account. Not a bit of it. He was reluctant, indifferent, incurious, vague, apparently with no sense of the uniqueness of the occasion or the incredible street value of original gossip. Every detail had to be dragged out of him. My heart was very nearly broken.

'But what about Borges?' I almost sob once again. Goddam it, a Milton/Homer blind genius sitting down at the same table – surely *something* would register? 'What about Borges?'

Kyle appears helpless and hunted. 'Didn't speak to him myself . . . but I seem to remember Tom McKenna and he . . .'

'Yes . . . *yes?*'

'In the hotel corridor in the early hours. Quoting Tennyson at each other.'

'What Tennyson?'

We are at the top of Westland Row, waiting to cross. Kyle gets off the hook by a show of mock alarm at a street name.

'Fenian Street!' he cries, shielding his face as though from a blow. Then he pretends to be brought round by the sight of the Protestant Merrion Hall, extending his arms in gratitude to its squat hideous bulk, blackened as though by long immersion in the hell of the Catholic State. 'SO THEN EVERY ONE OF US SHALL GIVE ACCOUNT OF HIMSELF TO GOD – Romans 14.12'. I hope the Creator has less trouble extracting Kyle's story.

'Who else was there?'

Kyle sighs. 'Borges's secretary or companion or minder or whatever. Stunning Latin American woman. But of course Borges is blind so McKenna says, rather solemnly and grandly, you know his style, *Have you ever seen her?* Borges shakes his head and McKenna turns to her and gives her this long, long look. Then he drops his voice even further. *She's very beautiful.*'

At last something worth digging for. A little moment of quintessential McKenna.

'Was he trying to score?' I question tersely. '*Did* he score?'

But Kyle's patience has been stretched to the limit. 'Oh I don't know,' he snaps wearily. 'I really don't know. It was very late by this time. And a long eventful day. It's not every day a man falls in love after all.'

Over a glass of duty-free Calvados I told an anecdote about going to the Grand Hotel in Cabourg to see Proust's bedroom, now a little museum. In the foyer were signs for Salle Marcel Proust but in the dining room the signs seemed to run out.

'Salle Marcel Proust?' I asked a young waiter, glancing about for stairs.

'Oui,' he said with curious finality.

Behind him whitecaps tossed on an unquiet sea. Closer, rich geriatrics lapped soup with big heavy hotel spoons. As if a posh hotel would waste space on a museum. Salle Marcel Proust was the dining room.

Not a great story, but well told. Like a housewife on a budget, I have learned to work wonders with limited ingredients. Reba laughed in spite of having heard it before. Liz also laughed, but in a perfunctory, secretive way, drinking off half her Calvados with startling abruptness.

What could she produce from a week in Connemara? Her holiday snaps, which she laid down one at a time like a gambler displaying a royal flush.

Ten of hearts – Kyle in a rowing boat with unidentified adults.

Jack of hearts – Kyle in the doorway of a country pub, triumphantly holding aloft a pint of Guinness.

Queen of hearts – Kyle playing ball with David on a beach.

King of hearts – Kyle hugging Liz at the door of a country cottage.

Ace of hearts, scooping the pot – Kyle and Liz, naked, face down and side by side on the beach, heads turned back to the photographer in humorous mock consternation.

Many claim such moments of revelation are rich in reaction and surmise. Connections, memories, speculations, regrets, et cetera. But these so-called reactions are retrospective. All you feel at the time is a kind of vertiginous nullity.

Savouring the moment to the full, Liz regarded us staring dumbly at the snaps. Then she drained her *digestif* with a flourish and released a wild peal of triumph and delight.

'My God,' Reba said at last, lifting to her eyes for intensive scrutiny Kyle's phosphorescent bare ass.

Garçon! Encore trois Calvados!

'We didn't want to tell anyone till we were sure,' Liz explained.

'Sure!'

'Sure of what?'

With a laugh and a gesture, Liz expressed the eternal response of the intuitive genius – anyone who had to ask would never get to know.

'And how long has this been going on?'

'Of course we met at that party here – but he had another girl with him. Then we bumped into each other on Grafton Street during that Bloomsday thing.' For the first time, her voice betrayed signs of alarm. She might have no doubts about the future but her retrospective terror was acute. 'You know, Kyle was only invited to that at the last minute? After somebody else dropped out.'

'I know that.'

'And he only spent the summer in Ireland because his mother had a stroke.'

Once again I nodded solemnly.

'I mean, you hate to wish sickness on anyone . . . but if it wasn't for that stroke . . .'

A new phenomenon in Irish history: instead of a breakthrough that should have happened but did not, one that should not have happened but did.

'And thank God she's coming round again. She's really great.

Her speech was affected and down one side, but she's starting to come round a bit.'

Naturally, the mother of Zorba would herself be an indomitable spirit.

'The terrible thing is, they've taken her driving licence away. She really relied on the car for getting about.' Liz brooded darkly in sorrow and indignation. 'You know she was the first woman driver in the North?'

'Wait a minute,' Reba said. 'You mean you've actually met her? You've met the mother *already?*'

'Kyle took me up after the holiday.' Liz laughed at the ease and inevitability of it all, these apparently impossible developments achieved by her own incredible charm and the incredible readiness of the Magees. 'She was really brilliant. Told me she never got on with Olivia.'

'This was in Altnagarvin?'

'Renee's place. Kyle wanted me to stay with him in Altnagarvin, but I didn't fancy that. We spent an afternoon with Kyle's friend Robbie and his girl and then went on to Renee's for the night.'

'Semple and his girl?'

In Reba's eyes Kyle was impossible, but Semple was the Antichrist. Once, when he and Kyle were touring with a revue they had written, Kyle had asked if the company could drop by my bedsit for a snack. I recruited Reba to help with the catering. Of the six guests, five instantly flung themselves on the bed and chairs, leaving Kyle, twenty years their senior, to sit on the floor with his back to the wall. Far from being annoyed, he was radiantly happy, repeatedly chuckling and driving a hand through his hair. Reba had produced the ultimate Herron extravagance: tinned red salmon, garnished Herron-style with whole tomatoes, whole boiled eggs and whole spring onions. Semple shrieked with laughter. His girl-to-be jumped up – an arresting figure, tall, thin, highly strung, dressed in a black leather suit that enhanced the translucent pallor of her skin. Pale enough to play mime without make-up, but entirely lacking in the pathos of the clown.

'Christ!' she shouted, violently stubbing out a cigarette before advancing on Kyle with her hand out. 'Keys.'

'What?'

'Van keys.'

'Where are you going?'

'I'm not going anywhere.' She tossed her head at the obtuseness of old buffoons. Semple whinnied. 'I just want to wait in the van.'

'So how did you find Semple and his girlfriend?' Reba asked Liz now.

'Couldn't have been nicer. Good fun.'

There was a silence in which each pursued no doubt vastly different trains of thought. Visage clouded by memory and longing, Liz cradled her Calvados and fell back in the chair. Overwhelmed, bewildered, granulated, Reba reviewed the evidence from the beginning, that is, the snap of Kyle's bare ass.

'And you even got sun in Connemara,' she marvelled. 'It drizzled the whole time in France.'

I swirled and sipped Calvados, glad of anything that might put a sophisticated front on the howling maelstrom within.

'So what happened on Bloomsday?'

Liz covered her mouth with her hand, unsuccessfully attempting to suppress criminal laughter. 'Well, we bumped into each other and Kyle suggested a drink in honour of Joyce. So we went up to Rice's and had a Jameson.' Further laughter. 'You remember there was a big sort of poster thing . . . a map with all the times and details of the Bloomsday business . . . a really big thing you had to open right out?' I nodded, recalling the difficulties of consulting it in a breeze. 'Well, you see . . . we had that spread out on our laps . . .' Almost incapacitated by laughter, she took a bracing drink. 'We had that right over us, you know . . . and . . . and . . . my God, didn't Kyle drop the hand.' She shrieked and jackknifed violently, as though only now releasing reactions suppressed at the time. 'You know me wee pink canvas mini . . .' Shudder and groan of ecstasy. 'I was wearing that and no tights . . .'

*

So now Kyle is looking for any excuse to come south. In spite of the Catholic hysteria generated by the pope's visit. In spite of the nationalist hysteria generated by hunger strikes in the North. Undeterred, Kyle drives south to his love on roads lined with black flags and gigantic photographs of the dead.

On our quest for the soul of the South we turn into Nassau Street, where Joyce met Nora coming from Finn's Hotel in 1904. The name of the hotel is supposed to persist on a façade, but I have never seen it. Here it is now, faded but legible, high on a gable end facing into Trinity.

'Kyle, you jammy bastard! You make everything happen.'

In fact, the legend is visible because a tree in front of the gable is bare – I must always have looked when it was in leaf – but Kyle laughs as happily as if his cosmic life force has really brought this to pass.

'Where Nora worked as a chambermaid. A domestic servant. The sort of girl you exploited, Kyle.'

'Don't be so quick to condemn. Certainly there were girls who had to call me Master Kyle – even when I was a child. It's easy and fashionable to sneer at that now. But why deny the satisfactions of the faithful servant? Many had their best moments in that context. You know ... the servant genuinely wanting to please a good master ...'

Ooooh-scooby-do-bop! Lay it on me, liberal humanist!

'The slaves adore their servitude! Eternal justification of the masters.'

'No no no,' Kyle insists. 'A few years back I ran into one of our old maids in London. That seedy area round King's Cross. God knows what she was doing for a living. In bad shape, anyway – but really glad to see me. We bought a half-bottle and went back to her place – one room in someone else's flat, fairly sordid – and over the whiskey she said the time she had to call me Master Kyle was the best of her life. That seemed to me a sincere statement – not just the drink.' He falls silent, brooding on the memory.

'Did you dick her?' I slyly enquire.

He draws back, as at some obscene advance. 'These grotesque expressions. You know, I've developed a theory. You're profoundly afraid of sex and try to neutralise it with this American argot.'

'Very likely. But did you burp her?'

The marvellous thing about Kyle is his inability to refuse a direct question.

'She was a bit too far gone for that.'

Arriving at Merrion Square, it suddenly occurs to me that engrossing conversation has banished all thought of lunch. I meant to have smoked trout and tabouleh in Kilkenny Design.

'So Nora should have appreciated her servitude? Stayed in Finn's Hotel instead of running off with Jim.'

'Joyce was as hard a taskmaster as any. Have you read those letters?'

'Coprophilia and so forth? That's all standard for Fenians. Shite has always been a Fenian obsession, Kyle. Though more as a weapon, of course. Think of the dirty protest.'

We consider the elegant enclosed green of Merrion Square. Kyle frowns in concentration, furiously probing to the heart of the southern experience.

'I know what's different about Dublin,' he suddenly exclaims. 'It's the old iron railings. In Britain and Ulster those were all pulled down for the war effort. We Protestants took the war very seriously, you know.'

I point across at Sir William Wilde's house. 'That's where they were supposed to meet on their first date. Nora stood him up – and Jim was in a bad way.'

'He really did fall for her.'

'Love at first shite?'

Lying on the beach at Killiney, we watched the three children running in and out of the sea. It was a sunny Saturday at the end of September. Teaching resumed on the Monday and I was happy to drain the last dregs of idleness.

But the voluptuous delights of torpor were not for Kyle. He got up to organise the children and soon they were all at work on a mixed-media face in the sand – seaweed face, stick nose, shell eyes and teeth. You had to hand it to the guy. Prepared not just to visit the Catholic State but to spend time with his loved one's relations and even participate in the nurturing function.

For her part, Liz was working through Kyle's novels with the wonder, ecstasy and admiration essential in the companion of an artist. Importance, like charity, begins at home.

Kyle's novels, my books. With typically reckless abandon, Kyle had given away all his copies of the out-of-print novels. Liz had to borrow mine and was currently reading *Home Fires*, a mint-condition hardback never opened (I read it in manuscript) much less carted around in a beach bag with Eversun Factor 6 and sugar-free drinks for the kids. I had a horror of book fetish but something in me died a little when she hauled it out of the bag.

'Enjoying it?'

'Brilliant.' She sighed in voluptuous veneration, drawing her legs up like a child getting cosy in bed. 'He's just bursting with talent.'

Another thing – she marked her place by turning down the page. Wanton vandalism. In a hardback the flap of the dust jacket can always be used as a bookmark. Cracking the spine a little to hold the book open, Liz propped herself on one elbow and held it up at arm's length between her face and the sun. Clashing bracelets slid down her forearm. Her half-sleeve was a cool tunnel ending in a moist mossy grove.

'You know, all that in the book really happened,' I said, perhaps a trifle snappishly.

Liz released the laugh of privilege – condescending, rich, provocative, assured. 'Kyle told me all those stories already. I love the one about the mast against the door and Olivia trying to smash it down with an axe.'

Boundless arrogance of the youthful usurpers! For them history is not an inescapable nightmare but a source of amusing anecdotes. Nothing easier than to establish the new utopian regime. They will lift the old winding river out of its bed and set it down in a straight new course.

'A mast of a boat,' Reba murmured drowsily, renewing an old wonder.

I thought of how Des Esseintes paid a ventriloquist to stimulate his feeble desire by throwing her voice and creating the effect of an angry spouse pounding on the door. What the Frenchman had to finance and script came to Kyle as the leaves to the trees.

Kyle returned up the beach but, far from flopping down in exhaustion, proposed, in the most casual, offhand way, as though it were merely popping in on a neighbour, a visit to an internationally known English star of stage and screen. Wearily I commenced the familiar dogged, detailed enquiry. Friend of Renee's from way back. Currently filming in Ireland. Sent address to Renee with an invitation to call.

'It'd be great to see him,' Liz cried. 'Why didn't you tell me, Kyle? Could I do a piece?'

'He's a big dote,' Reba purred. 'Ah could eat 'im wi' a spoon.'

'But seven people, Kyle. None of them on the invitation. Three dirty wet weans. We're talking about a movie star, for crissake.'

'He's just an ordinary fellow,' Kyle snapped. 'Diffident. Humble. Unsure of his talent. Worried about his career.'

'He still won't want to see us.'

'You're intelligent, cultivated, attractive people. Why wouldn't he want to see you?'

This was almost in a shout. Far from sinking into Fenian inertia, Kyle was determined to lift us all up to the high, bracing air of liberty, equality and fraternity. He strode off towards the car. Liz pursued him.

'So that's what we are,' Reba mused.

'We're *fucking gyppos*,' I told her. 'Never forget it.'

The house in the Wicklow hills was not easy to find. Each time we got out of the cars to confer, I suggested giving up and going home – but the more you try to ditch a plan, the more determined Kyle becomes. Eventually we found a gateway and a long curving drive that disappeared among trees.

Outside, the aloof hush of privilege; inside, the whingeing of tired, fretful children. Liz and Kyle were also still in their car. Had he lost his nerve? If so, it was only for a moment. He got out and awaited his bedraggled platoon.

'Wish Ahd worn me good bra,' Reba complained, frowning into a hand mirror.

'This is ridiculous.' I appealed to Liz, relying on her cultural weakness for the cheap sneer. Very few Fenians can resist the lure of derision.

She burst out sniggering, immediately having to cross her legs. 'I'll have to get to a toilet.'

'Not before me,' Reba said. 'I need to change a Tampax. It's coming through me jeans.'

Thankfully there was no one at home. After hammering long and hard, Kyle went round the house to the back door. As he re-emerged at the front, Sarah shut her eyes and grunted with pleasure and satisfaction. Inspection revealed a neat bundle stretching her pants like fruit in a string bag. Her nappy had been removed at the beach and not replaced when Kyle rushed us away. Reba and Liz were off among the mature shrubs. I set about the task with a kind of fierce relish, hefting the packed pants like a chunk of paving stone. Shite is the ammo of the dispossessed.

'Children, Kyle. A million pounds wouldn't buy them.'

He was scribbling on a diary page. 'What's your phone number?'

'Ah?'

'Your phone number?'

I snatched the note.

> Called with intelligent, interesting friends. Have to go north myself tonight but the others live in Dublin. Get in touch at the number below.
>
> Renee sends her regards. Incapacitated by pregnancy but looking forward to the child. A million pounds wouldn't buy them.
>
> Love
>
> Kyle Magee

For jammy Kyle the gods relent. Ancient signs appear on buildings and, rarer than Halley's Comet, a Vermeer is on show in the National Gallery, left for safekeeping while its owner is on holiday. Already the painting has been stolen and returned. Little do we know that it will soon be stolen a second time. We are even more privileged than we realise. Two very fortunate fellows.

And a late Vermeer, one of the very best of the tiny oeuvre. At a table sits a woman writing a letter – calm, untroubled, bland face. Behind her a maid, standing, with folded arms, looking out of the window with an expression so inscrutable and mysterious it makes the *Mona Lisa* seem as subtle as Wonder Woman. And whereas the more famous lady of the Louvre has a permanent crowd of admirers dodging and ducking like a group of men trying to shave in the same mirror, here there are no tourists blocking the view. In fact there is no one in the room but an attendant and ourselves.

'A masterpiece,' Kyle says at last, with calm finality.

'And no one even knows it's here. Not that it would make any difference if they did. In Proust a character dies for a glimpse of a Vermeer exhibited in Paris. Here they wouldn't cross the street. The indifference. The torpor.'

We study it in silence, eyes always drawn back to the face of the maid.

'The Fenian servant,' Kyle says. 'Docile but smirking. Full of secret pride and superiority. Just like yourself.'

Certainly the maid is the more interesting character: erect, detached, aware, simultaneously looking out at the world and enjoying a rich inner life, understanding her environment and hence in control of it. Knowledge is the power of the slave.

'Sure haven't yese had the best of it always,' Kyle says, adopting a humorous Ulster accent. 'I don't know what all the complaining's about.'

'The mistress certainly knows nothing. Look at that empty bap face.'

'Mrs Vermeer, perhaps?'

'If it's her, she used the painting to pay the baker.'

Kyle broadens his accent even further. 'A good, sensible, thrifty Presbyterian. Just like the Ulster women I grew up with. A bit limited in some ways, but has anyone the bate of them for crab-apple jelly?'

During this loud performance the attendant has been edging suspiciously towards us round the walls of the gallery. In Ireland animation is always suspect.

Unperturbed, Kyle addresses him directly. 'You're very fortunate to have such a great masterpiece.'

'Ah?' the man says, playing for time, glancing swiftly from one to the other of us for evidence of mockery. Obviously not the superior, knowing type of slave. 'Ah sure, I wouldn't understand that at all now.'

Kyle can never resist an opportunity to proselytise. 'But there's nothing to understand. All you have to do is look at it.' He indicates the Vermeer with an inviting wave.

The attendant darts it a quick look and draws back with an uneasy laugh. 'Ah sure, it's too late for me, like. An auld wan like me. It's all right for young fellas like yourselves.'

'What age are you?' Kyle asks, with a brutal directness that has the man rolling his head in desperation, but the cavernous empty gallery offers him no protection or support.

'Ah, there's a few miles on the auld clock, ye know? Like, I'd be within shoutin' distance o' fifty, like.'

'I'm forty-nine myself,' Kyle says, 'and only beginning to learn about painting.'

On the attendant's mottled, veined features, uneasiness is replaced by perplexity and wonder. He approaches to study the perfectly preserved masterpiece that is Kyle Magee's face. Close together for a moment, the peers present a startling contrast. Whatever else is true of the master–servant relationship, one thing at least is indisputable – only the masters retain their looks.

The attendant's hand rises, tentative, involuntary, as though to touch Kyle's clear, glowing skin. 'Forty-nine,' he whispers. 'But like . . . like your face hasn't broke out yet.'

*

Liz invited us to her flat for a meal with herself and Kyle. Fearing that we might be dull company for two such free, adventurous, pro-life spirits, we found them engaged in the most stultifying activity ever devised by Western man (who has devoted much of his ingenuity to the encouragement of stultification). I refer, of course, to watching snooker on television.

While Liz went to check the food, Kyle prepared aperitifs with one eye on the screen.

'For Jesus' sake, Kyle,' I had to say at last. At least I knew him well enough to be able to voice a protest.

'Aren't you enjoying it? Weren't you a great fan of *The Hustler?*'

'For Jesus' sake.'

I waited for Liz to put us out of our misery. After fifteen minutes she came back in a Guinness apron, wielding a large wooden spoon (a new role – Liz the master chef) and went straight to the screen with a look of profound concern.

'What's the score?' she asked Kyle with quiet intensity.

'Davis just got a break of sixty. Silvano needs snookers.'

'Aaaaww,' Liz groaned. 'Silvano was lovely.'

Reba and I looked up at this display of emotion. Liz turned to us, already brightening, an incorrigible optimist. 'But at least Alex Higgins is through.'

Reba gaped at her. 'Hah?'

'You mean you don't know Alex Higgins? Hurricane Higgins? From Belfast?'

It could scarcely have got worse. Not only required to watch sport, we were being asked to subscribe to regional chauvinism.

Perhaps, as part of his quest for understanding, Kyle was attempting to penetrate to the very heart of the Fenian experience, the killer-foam sofa of inertia and impotence. Perhaps he was an adept of submission and passivity. Of course any such attempt was doomed to failure. He could no more enter the Fenian experience than a Westerner could know the true Tao.

The television stayed on during the meal but at least the topic of conversation was Kyle's family rather than snooker.

'Renee's brilliant!' Liz cried. 'I mean, she's just *full* of go. She heard Grotowski was giving a workshop in Florence, so she just said, *Fuck it, I'm away to Florence*.'

'Who's Grotowski?'

Liz stared at me in outrage. First Hurricane Higgins, now this. 'You mean you've never heard of Grotowski? He's probably the most famous theatre guru in the world.'

'How do you spell it?'

'For God's sake. *Everyone* knows Grotowski. As soon as Renee heard, she headed straight for Florence.'

'And was it worth the trip?'

'Actually, it wasn't a workshop, it was only a press conference.' At this Liz relaxed enough to laugh a little. 'But that's the kind of her – game for anything. And she was not long married and five months pregnant at the time. Actually, I haven't seen the baby yet – but I'm going up next weekend. Dying to see it.'

Reba turned to me with one of her totally blank looks that are yet so expressive. When Liz went off with Kyle she left us David, who quarrelled with our children, got carsick on even the shortest journeys, slept badly, ate practically nothing. And always, now, there was the threat of an asthma attack. Once, she even went off with his ventilator in her bag.

The snooker went on till after midnight, but at least we had a break. During this Kyle watched *Match of the Day* and confessed to a foolhardy passion for Arsenal.

'A lot of Fenians play for the Gunners and it's considered a Fenian team in the North. As much as your life's worth to praise them in certain company.'

As always with Kyle, excellence transcended tribal loyalty. Liz was also soon intoxicated by the quality of their football. After half an hour of recorded highlights she too was an ardent Gunners fan.

Reba was so outraged that she made no attempt to help Kyle and Liz clear up. Initially dreading a highbrow soirée, she was even more enraged by the proletarian vulgarity. 'I'd go to Hugo and

Rosemary if I wanted to fucking watch football and snooker all night.' Then sheer wonder overcame her rage. 'And Liz sitting there all through it, raving about everything.'

There was a question that had to be asked.

'To the best of your knowledge, has Liz at any time revealed an interest in football, snooker ... *any* sport?'

The answer was what I expected and deserved – a stream of the most foul and violent oaths ever to issue from the mouth of a woman.

Blessed cloister calm of Merrion Square West, perfect for ruminating *flâneurs*, elegant, spacious, cool, far from the fevers and vulgarities of O'Connell Street – the GPO republicans, the slot-machine palaces and the maniac driving up and down with a life-sized Virgin Mary strapped to the roof of his car.

We proceed across Baggot Street and then into Ely Place, where the great town houses of the Anglo-Irish gentry have been taken over by the new forward-looking, professional, business-suited Ireland. Leaving Kyle to wait, I climb to the offices of Emerald Computer Training, where David Hayes is accepting a credit card payment, making a joke of his clumsiness with the machine. 'I'm more used to this from the other side ... you know?' But even when we're alone he maintains his jovial manner. 'And how are things up above?'

Himself a model of probity and dynamism, David loves to hear of the chicanery and torpor that prevail in the college. I feed him a new horror story about cheap trashy terminals which won't jive with the mainframe.

'God Almighty!' David shakes his head in disbelief. 'And this is what we're paying these *incredible* taxes for.'

I wait to establish eye contact before continuing. 'You know, it's such a pleasure to come here in the evening. It really is. I mean, just to know everything's going to be organised.'

Earnest, business-suited, diligent, David looks down in quiet pleasure. 'We do our best ... you know.'

I allow a little interval of solidarity and respect. 'Listen, David ... what I want to ask ... ' Now it is my turn to look down. 'I was wondering if ... ah ... if you could, you know ... let me have a cheque today?'

'No problem,' he comes in at once.

'I know I still have a few weeks to teach on this course. But you know ... Christmas coming ...'

Silencing the babble with an upraised palm, he produces a chequebook and an expensive fountain pen. 'No problem. It's a moveable feast.' He writes boldly, blithely, without a hint of irritation or reluctance. 'Same arrangement? Make it out in your wife's maiden name? Rebecca Herron? Two *rs*?' Do you see David using a teleprompter or notes? His notes are on the screen of his mind. He adds the name and briskly snaps off the cheque. 'A tidy sum. Why give away half in tax ... hn?'

Emerging into sunlight, agitated and flushed, I suppress an overpowering desire to apologise to Kyle. The bad old attitudes. Instead I flourish the cheque. 'The new Ireland, Kyle. Building a power base in sunrise industries. The Silicon Valley of Europe. We have fifty Nigerians coming in for training next week.'

We go up the east side of Stephen's Green and make a brief incursion into Earlsfort Terrace to check the programme at the Irish Film Theatre. *Last Tango in Paris* – immensely encouraging. Not that I want to see it again, but it's such a comfort to know that European nihilism is available.

Kyle is also moved. 'You know Liz was deeply affected by that film.'

'Oh yes. Got a curly perm like Maria Schneider.'

'Not just that. She bought half a pound of butter and went out and used it the way they did in the film.'

A bizarre image comes to mind. Not of Liz but of a giant hoarding that dominates the dual carriageway:

FOR A DEEPER AND RICHER EXPERIENCE
SPREAD IRISH BUTTER – THE NATURAL WAY

'Don't you think that was courageous?' Kyle asks.

It takes a little time to formulate an answer to this. Kyle provides it himself in the end. 'She's a great girl . . . a great girl.'

Certainly she has been an inspiration to us all. Like the baton in a relay race, her vibrator was passed from Liz to Reba and from Reba on to Frances after her dramatic coming of age at the party. By this time it was rather the worse for the wear, sellotaped where I had trodden on it in a moment of sensual stupefaction. Frances's rage to live overrode her reservations about the state of the device, but the gods had apparently decreed that she was not to be a swinger. After a fortnight she developed an infection and Sean a hideous outbreak of spongy dick. Despite the certainty of incurring her wrath, I could not resist a remark to Reba: 'If you held his lad now, it would come away in your hand.'

We pass the former Catholic university, its mighty portals topped by a lugubrious stone lion, a disheartened defender of the faith sadly dreaming of the time when a colleen would never crave artificial stimulation or consider putting butter on anything but poundies and soda bread.

'And Madge is a great girl too,' Kyle adds. 'A marvellous girl. It's journalists like her that change attitudes. Without the likes of Madge you wouldn't have dirty foreign movies.'

Has he read her new book – *Only the Wind Blows Free: Northern Women Tell Their Stories?* A collection of taped interviews with female (but exclusively Catholic) victims of the trouble in the North – wives of men killed or serving prison sentences, mothers of children blinded by rubber bullets. The Fenian as eternal victim, exactly the partial view that enraged Kyle before.

But I ought to concentrate on the new, outward-looking, international Ireland. 'Eddie Lockjaw Davis played the Gresham last week.'

Yet jazz is also a tricky topic. Even Kyle cannot fail to see that my 'blacks only' attitude implies a low opinion of his playing. And if I am contemptuous of British jazz, what must I feel about the Northern Irish variety?

'I never cared for the later Basie sidemen,' he says.

'Lockjaw was *bloody good.* And the Gresham was packed out. It was a terrific evening.'

'If there's such an enthusiastic audience, how come you haven't got me any bookings yet?'

'Kyle, I'm not an impresario. If Bird did actually live I couldn't get him a gig.'

On the corner of the Green, waiting to cross, Kyle has one of his bright ideas. 'Isn't your college round here? Perhaps you'd like to make amends by doing me some photocopies.'

The thought of Kyle in the college, possibly being accosted by the insane principal – 'Who the f... are you?' I explain that, far from being state-of-the-art, the college adheres to the old principle of sure-it'll-do-rightly, the photocopier an ancient machine that labours mightily to produce shiny, blotchy grey sheets equally repulsive to sight, touch and smell.

'The copies are almost certainly carcinogenic, Kyle.'

But for the evangelist, dissemination is essential.

'Sure it'll do rightly.'

Not only do I hate going in on my day off, the college itself has become less congenial. I used to be tempted by the life of the Boy-Men. To become a voluptuary of torpor and sprawl in the dreaming staff room far from the sway of tyrant Destiny. But there is no escape. Destiny invaded the staff room. When hunger strikers began to die in the North it did not remain a haven of indifference and inertia. Instead it became a hotbed of protest, with Paddy McGrath organising Boy-Men for marches on the British embassy. Now international dissidents are rarely seen and English staff like Digby Howard have vanished from the face of the earth.

And of course there is no access to the photocopier room. Carmel, zealous guardian of the key, must be on a coffee break.

In the staff room she is filling a mug at the urn, Paddy McGrath and the Boy-Men lined up behind and openly admiring her tight jeans (possible only because Madge Dillon pilloried the insane principal for trying to stop the female admin staff wearing trousers).

'Finished?' a Boy-Man brightly asks Carmel as she steps aside.

Paddy coolly appraises her. 'She's far from finished.'

They laugh.

'Hasn't started yet?' one suggests.

As though considering this, Paddy carries out another long, impertinent scrutiny. 'Oh I'd say she's started all right.'

This corpulent, purple-faced, white-haired ruin is actually strutting like a peacock before the slim girl. Even his cronies find the contrast grotesque.

'Young as ye feel, Paddy?' one asks ironically.

Paddy grabs Carmel by the waist. 'Young as the woman ye feel.'

She shrieks and pushes him off.

'Go on, Paddy!'

'That's the stuff, Carmel!'

Everyone follows the tussle with interest, but I have to look away. Beyond the soiled windows the sun is blotted out by gravid clouds racing inland to discharge their burdens.

Paddy retains a firm grip – but however delightful the encounter, he has to pause to alert his cronies to my peculiar expression. 'Jaysus would ye look at the face on him,' he cries. 'It's the fuckin' Antichrist.'

Part of a major refitting campaign, Kyle's leather bomber was bought at enormous expense in Dr Jacket and Mr Hide. Kyle protested that it would be cheaper in the North but Liz refused to tolerate for a moment longer his shapeless tattered cardigans and sweaters. The checked Joe Hill shirts he could keep but the baggy corduroys were replaced by jeans and the ponderous landed-gentry brogues by Italian moccasins as supple as gloves.

She also set to work on his habits. If men like he should live a thousand years (and who would deny it) then surely he had an obligation to co-operate with destiny. But even on the issue of smoking he would not concede in theory let alone practice. And as for healthy eating, the man was entirely impossible. Not only did he refuse to scan labels for carcinogenic additives, he actually went out of his way to insist on the proven killers – cream, butter, sugar, white bread and red meat. No mere inertia or conservatism, this was part of an active policy to identify fearfulness as the real enemy. Having successfully challenged the gods all his life, he was not about to be scared by the possible effects of Ulster fries.

So when we were cooking for them Liz came in advance to request white sugar, real milk and butter et cetera. Since it was she who had done so much to banish these during her stay, this was another exquisite *bouleversement*.

'You know the way of it,' she said with that sweet reasonableness that surmounted all inconsistency. 'Kyle's very traditional.'

'Jesus,' Reba said. 'Stand by your man.'

These meals were always unpredictable, Kyle and Liz bursting in late after some dramatic incident or adventure. For instance, being driven from the Charismatic Conference by a one-armed journalist. Concealing his left arm behind his back, Kyle imitated the eccentric steering style.

'It was all wild dramatic sweeps,' he cried, swinging his right arm back and forth. 'Probably deliberate aggression. When we were getting into the car I made the mistake of asking if he was all right. He really snapped at me. *Of course. Of course.*'

Stricken afresh, Liz leaned on her sister for support. 'I couldn't look at him, Reba.' Then she addressed us all. 'And after that Charismatic business. These two got up . . . hand in hand . . . this is in front of five thousand people . . . they got up and started on about how the movement changed their marriage. Every day they go upstairs and lie side by side on top of the bed . . . experiencing this communion . . . this *ecstasy.* And then they squeezed each other's hands and looked into each other's eyes . . . enough to make you puke.'

'I thought there was something in it,' Kyle said. Whenever possible he accompanied Liz on assignments, not just out of solidarity but to observe the strange ways of the Gael. 'Isn't it a kind of renewal? Better than the old-style Catholicism you're always complaining about?' He paused to emphasise his thought-provoking conclusion. 'Maybe you don't want things to change. Maybe you're in love with what you hate.' Opening his arms to encourage response, he looked at each of us with bright, committed eyes. First adventure and experience, then intelligent disputation.

'That carry-on gives me the *fucking pip*,' Reba snarled with a vehemence and bitterness that silenced even Kyle.

'Curry's ready!' I cried, genial host.

Liz came forward to touch my arm in sincere apology. 'Actually, we haven't time to eat now. You go ahead with yours and maybe we'll have some later. We want to go to this Beckett production downtown.'

'Everyone's raving about it,' Kyle said to me. 'Have you been?'

No ordinary company, the San Quentin Players were a group of convicted murderers who had taken up acting in prison and discovered a special affinity for the works of Beckett.

'But let's all go!' Liz cried. 'You can drop your kids with my baby-sitter.'

'It's been booked out for weeks.'

They already knew this and were undeterred. Reba and I declined to go to so much trouble for what would surely be disappointment. In any case I was less enamoured of murderers these days. Events in the North had robbed the calling of its singularity and luminescence. Now it was so commonplace that even I knew murderers personally. Two small-time crooks who once tried to hang about Herrons' shop (and were suspected of break-ins) had graduated to shooting a local boy who joined the British army and was foolhardy enough to come home on leave. To Genet they may have been sensual princes, but no one else was impressed. I kept the curry warm, confident that Kyle and Liz would be straight back. Wrong, wrong, wrong. Completely wrong.

Several hours later Kyle happily explained. 'We got the management out and I just said, I'm Kyle Magee, the Ulster novelist, and this is Liz Herron, a local journalist, we've heard this is a stunning production and we'd very much like to see it . . .'

'And they gave us seats,' Liz cried. 'Really good ones too.'

By now the smell of curry had thoroughly permeated the house, giving Kyle another opportunity for charming frankness.

'Can we eat?' he cried, sniffing in ecstasy. 'Nothing like futility to give you an appetite.'

'My God!' Kyle cries, rooted in the doorway. 'Is this it?'

'Grogan's – the literary pub.'

I throw it off blithely enough, but I am taken aback myself.

A small square space, undivided, with no rooms leading off – neither variety nor vista to pleasure the wandering eye. Nor is the detail any more seductive. None of the famous old Dublin pub fixtures – wooden snugs, mirrors, gas lamps et cetera – and nothing sufficiently sordid to merit a poetry of squalor. Instead, furniture and fittings in the style of that wave of cheap mass production in the fifties, described by its enthusiastic supporters as 'contempirry'. On the floor a mustard carpet, around the sides a bench seat in mustard plush dimpled with cloth-covered buttons. On the soiled walls one ghastly landscape and a sheet with the signatures of participants in some sporting fixture or draw.

'It's the inverse snobbery,' I explain. 'The literati could never drink in a pub of distinction.'

But my armour of sophisticated irony is immediately pierced. On the bar, beneath a discoloured and scored plastic hood, a white-bread cheese sandwich curls forlorn and useless wings. I experience a vicious stab of regret for the smoked trout and tabouleh in Kilkenny Design.

We sit on the bench seat, in front of us the plywood top and spindly splayed legs of a table designed for 'contempirry' drinks like Bacardi and Babycham. A dozen honest-to-God pints of stout and the thing would go down like a spavined horse.

Two Jamesons, served by a barman appropriately lacking the wit and charm of the Dublin curate. Solid, healthy, intolerant and vacuous, he would make a fine young garda.

'So these are all writers,' muses Kyle, glancing about.

'Absolutely. This is where I distributed your CV flyers.'

'I have a few spares in my briefcase.'

'But of course they don't look like writers. You'll never catch them reading anything but the racing pages. The country's leading novelist is actually a racing correspondent.'

Certainly the patrons resemble punters waiting for the betting shops to open. Mostly male, they sit apart, shabby, morose, disabused. A few miles on the auld clock. Faces broke out.

'Concealment and dissimulation, Kyle. Central to the Fenian experience.'

Gratefully sipping his Jameson, Kyle, the apostle of confession and frankness, ponders the tortuous ways of the Gael.

At the next table but one an atypical group, two couples in bright leisurewear, consume with relish Special Brew and vodka and white. Uncrushed by the years, avid and voluble, they are currently displaying a lively interest in Kyle.

'Have you de formula?' one of the men suddenly asks, leaning towards Kyle in a shrewd, intimate way.

'I'm sorry?'

The question is repeated. Kyle looks to his native interpreter, but I am just as much at a loss.

'Aren't you from de Nort?'

'Yes indeed.' Kyle laughs with relief.

'Well, have you de formula for solvin' de problem up der?'

Kyle drives a hand through his hair and releases one of his disarming chuckles. 'If only I had.'

'You'd be a popular fella . . . uh?'

'A national hero.'

Pondering Ulster's long travail, we solemnly apply ourselves to our drinks.

'Isn't it desperate?' mutters one of the women, with a strong rural accent.

Perplexed, heavy of heart, Kyle nods and sighs.

Frowning in concentration, the woman adds, 'But like . . . tell us this, like . . . is there a lot of harishment?'

Kyle suffers another moment of blankness. I lean forward and murmur discreetly. 'Ah,' he says. 'I've never actually been harassed myself.' Obviously they have taken him for a northern Fenian. Will he disillusion them? 'But I dare say a lot of it goes on.'

Her brow assumes an even deeper furrow. 'Like, I have a friend who goes up there to shop . . . she says the same . . . she's never seen any harishment.'

'Most of us live totally normal lives,' Kyle cries cheerfully.

They all laugh in relief and gratitude. Along with their concept of the North as alien, desolate and hostile is a concept of the northerner as a kind of neo-Cromwell – ardent, rational and cold, burning to decimate the sleepy South with insanely ruthless logic and competence.

Now the other woman is confident enough to contribute. 'But you'd hate to bring up kids der.'

'I've reared five. All happy and healthy. Touch wood.' Kyle slaps the plywood, human vulnerable guy. 'Children yourself?'

She sighs with pleasure. 'Ten. Fourteen pregnancies, eleven kids, ten alive. Little Connor, that was. Knocked down by a bin lorry. Only two and a half.'

We observe a sympathetic silence.

'You've had your troubles,' Kyle suggests.

'But I'd have another eleven if I could. I love kids.' She sighs deeply, voluptuously. 'Little Connor. A darlin'. He'd be sixteen now.'

A terminal silence descends. We sip our drinks, ruminant, grave.

'Well, Kyle,' I murmur finally. 'Here's the goal of our quest. The soul of the South. Mother Ireland at last.'

'How do we know they aren't writers?'

'The leisurewear. Inverse snobbery couldn't go that far. No Dublin writer could don leisurewear.'

We drain our Jamesons in an atmosphere of fulfilment and harmony. The quest completed in time to meet Reba and Liz for the afternoon. Then the barman sets two more wee Jimmys before us. Kyle looks up, startled. Mother Ireland waves and smiles.

'Salt of the earth, Kyle. Give you the shirt off their backs.'

'Must be playwrights. Only playwrights make money.'

'Salt of the earth for writers to mingle with. Inverse snobbery means that writers can only mix with manual workers. All the Dublin crowd used to drink with Pierrepoint the hangman. Ireland hadn't the work for a full-time post so they brought Pierrepoint over from England. One of the civillest fellas you could ever hope to meet.'

'A gentleman?'

'Exactly. They were desolate when he retired and bought his own pub in England.'

Kyle examines a beer mat. 'The Quick Drop?'

I study him in astonishment. 'Are you going native, Kyle? Setting up as a Dublin wit?'

Always fatal to encourage Kyle. At once he assumes a frightful stage-Irish brogue.

'Begob an shurr it must be the wather.' He looks across at the stolid barman. 'Youse do be after puttin' somethin' in the wather round here.'

When it was time for Kyle's American summer trip he insisted that he could not afford to put it off two years running and that he should go alone to give himself and Liz time to think. If their ardour cooled during this interlude, they would call the whole thing off with no hard feelings. On the other hand, if they felt as before, serious plans for the future would have to be made. And in the meantime, since it was a kind of retreat, a period of withdrawal and meditation, they would both have to keep it in their pants throughout the summer.

'Do you believe he'll do that?' Reba asked Liz.

'*What?*' Liz cried, shocked that anyone could even consider an alternative. '*Of course he will.*'

'And what if he doesn't?'

Considering that this was another novel hypothesis, Liz reacted with remarkable assurance and speed. 'What do you think I'd do?' she said, without a trace of amusement or irony. 'I'd put a fucking knife in him.'

Kyle had certainly brought out a new side of her character – a fanatically possessive, volatile, blade-wielding gypsy. Even Madge was not above suspicion and had to be warned off in no uncertain terms. For Madge was now a card-carrying fan and had published an admiring profile describing Kyle as 'a Protestant maverick' and 'a thorn in the flesh of the unionist establishment'. By word of mouth she circulated a less formal but even more flattering verdict – 'Kyle's fuckin' great'. For his part, Kyle seemed prepared to overlook Madge's republican sympathies. Whatever her political views, only someone pro-life would promote the major writers – D.H. Lawrence, Henry Miller, Kyle Magee.

Liz had a parallel success in the North when she went up for weekends to stay in Kyle's daughters' flat in Belfast. We put it to her tentatively that this was a rather bizarre arrangement. After all, daughters putting up *their own father* and what they probably regarded as his *Fenian huer.* Liz was outraged. If anyone had a negative attitude it was us and not the Magees. Everyone – mother, sister and daughters – had gone out of their way to make her welcome. Ruth and Susannah, the daughters, were down-to-earth, sensible girls with their father's honesty and bluntness. If they had any reservations, they would not be slow to make them public.

Ruth, the older girl, worked as a beautician and was usually out with her boyfriend. Susannah, a catering student, had fewer commitments and immediately took to Liz. Not only did she cook amazing meals in the flat, she invited Kyle and Liz to her college, where gourmet lunches prepared by students were available to the public at nominal prices. Friday tickets were scarcer than gold dust but if Liz made it in time for lunch Susannah always got them a booking. Undoubtedly a great future in catering awaited the girl – if she could just get through her compulsory Computing module.

And at this point in the narrative Liz withdrew from her bag a wadge of dog-eared printout which she dropped in my lap with an air of high expectation. 'I told her you knew all about computers.'

It was a lengthy program in one of the primitive early dialects of BASIC which encourage just the kind of indiscipline and lack of structure exhibited by the pages I was scanning – what in the trade we describe with distaste as a 'bowl of spaghetti' program.

'What am I supposed to do with this, Liz?'

'I told her you could help.'

'But what does she have to do? Use it? Understand it? Adapt it? Write one of her own?'

After a difficult weekend with David there was probably an edge to my tone. Liz gave me a hurt, reproachful look – the one displayed by my mother when I failed to make Aer Lingus seek out and return the lost suitcase of Father Joe Kielt.

'But all his presents were in it,' my mother said. 'Handmade things from the Philippines.'

Now Liz used the same irrefutable logic. 'She has to pass Computing to get through to the final year.'

So good was the relationship with Susannah that Liz even went up for a weekend when Kyle was in America. Susannah prepared an *incredible* meal, to which Renee and the mother were also invited. Much drink was consumed and a merry time had by all.

Liz returned in triumph. 'Susannah got her Computing.' Her face indicated a defiant subtext: *No thanks to you, asshole.*

'I knew Pearse was a teacher,' Kyle says, 'but I never realised he ran a school, much less a set-up as grand as this.'

Overwhelmed by involuntary memory, I am unable to reply. Instead of a confident adult in the Pearse Museum, I am once again a terrified child in my grandfather's house. A combination of silence, gloom, mustiness and heavy floor polish – the terrible, unmistakable cocktail of authority worshipped and obeyed. Unaffected, the rest of the party move noisily upstairs to the dormitory. When I recover the volition to join them, Liz takes my hand and draws me across to an ad for the original school – 'Domestic

Arrangements in Charge of an Experienced Lady'. She laughs, one of her low, deep chuckles, a startling sound in the hushed and musty dim which also throws into dramatic relief the red-gold glow of her exposed shoulders and back. Imagine the young boarders here waking to an apparition like this. The terrible Witch Queen who can assume any form to drive the warriors' wits astray. Sternest test for the Faith of Our Fathers impervious to dungeon, fire and sword.

'You've been using that sunbed again,' I accuse.

'I've done no such thing.' Outraged, Liz pulls aside T-shirt and bra strap to reveal a white strip. 'If I was lying under a sunbed I wouldn't have patches.' She allows me a generous silent interval to study the evidence. 'I've got a bit of colour sitting in the front garden. I had buck all else to do all summer waiting for Kyle.'

Approaching from behind, Reba leans against me and puts a warm mouth to my ear. 'How about *two* experienced ladies?' Pushing with her front, she drives me towards one of the beds, using the technique flamenco dancers are taught ('use your breasts like the horns of a bull – but soft').

Narrow metal cot, blanket of coarse grey – the spartan bed of a young Irish hero. For a moment I am seized by the delirium of desecration. Kyle's sexual games could never attain the ultimate intensity. Only one long repressed can become an adept of vertigo.

'But it's just like my public school,' Kyle cries. 'Just like an English public school.' He glances round. 'It's really taking me back.'

'Fruiting, Kyle?'

'Mutual masturbation was certainly common. As a boxing champion, I was much in demand.' He goes into a crouch that seems to compress and concentrate his body in a purposeful way. 'Famous for my right hook.' He gives a demonstration, stopping the punch just short of my chin.

Downstairs there are the glass cases of documents and manuscripts, the photographs of men in uniform and buildings in ruins after the Rising. Soon the children get restless and Reba and Liz are happy to take them out into the sun. What is Ireland's tragic history to the Herron girls? Gypsies acknowledge no nation state.

Kyle lingers over a section larger than the rest and described by a single word: *Sacrifice.*

> No failure judged as the world judges such things was ever more complete, more pathetic than Emmet's. And yet he has left us a prouder memory than the memory of Brian victorious at Clontarf or of Owen Roe victorious at Benburb. It is a memory of a sacrifice Christ-like in its perfection. Dowered with all things splendid and sweet, he left all things and elected to die.

'This use of martyrdom as a weapon is a funny business.'

'But highly successful in the hands of an expert,' I have to remind him. 'My mother used it for forty years with devastating effect.'

'I can't see Liz going in for Christ-like sacrifice.'

'But now you can appreciate the power of the dirty protest, gaunt men wrapped in blankets huddled in cells smeared with excrement. It fuses both Fenian weapons into one mighty instrument. To combine shite and martyrdom was a stroke of true genius.'

Kyle proceeds slowly, scrutinising every document in turn. 'He keeps mentioning his model for education. What is the Boy Corps of Emain Macha?'

'The legendary young Ulster warriors. Long hair, denims and Doc Marten boots. Tartan scarf tied round the wrist. Can of Special Brew in one hand, half a brick in the other.'

Kyle is not amused. This is a serious mission. He moves on to the next case – *An Claidheamh Soluis,* the Sword of Light – and frowns intently at a photograph of Pearse.

I follow with the negligent laugh of the undeceived. 'You know why Pearse was always photographed in profile?' No response. 'Because he had a googy eye.'

Kyle does not even look up.

Oppressive odour and hush of piety. Distant cries of children in the park. In the foyer an invisible attendant can be heard talking urgently. '. . . this character with a big brute of a dog an' it snappin' at fresh air, like. Says I, there's young children in this park. Says he, it's perfectly friendly. And another thing, says I, that dog's in heat. Ye'll have every dog for miles around here . . . ah?'

'They'd be comin' outa the fuckin' walls,' a second voice agrees.

Out into the sun and a rare treat for the voluptuary of random juxtaposition: on the grass against the plinth of a bust of Pearse (with clear, noble, *perfectly aligned* eyes) Reba and Liz with T-shirt necks pulled down and skirts hiked up. Liz is bringing Reba up to date. Olivia knows about the affair and has accepted the inevitability of divorce. Now that it is all out in the open, Kyle wants Liz to come to Altnagarvin, but even plucky Liz is wary of The Mad Axe Woman. Of course she can understand Kyle wanting to savour his last autumn on the ancestral estate. For Altnagarvin is to be sold, with what is left after payment of debts being divided between Olivia, Renee and Kyle, the main shares going to the women since Olivia is taking the younger children and Renee the disabled mother.

'Not that Renee needs it. Her husband's loaded.' Already Liz is revealing the instinct for bargaining that will make her such a formidable agent and roadie. Also, strange for a feminist, a new and passionate belief in primogeniture. 'Kyle's the eldest son and he's getting *buttons* out of it.'

Finally she turns to me. 'What's keeping him, anyway?'

A lazy contented wifely grumble, as though Kyle is pottering round any old musty museum when in fact he is sampling the Fenian cocktail at its most concentrated and potent – Christlike sacrifice, Faith of Our Fathers, Mother Ireland, Cuchulainn and Gaelic sports ('When it comes to a question of Ireland winning battles, her main reliance must be on her hurlers. To your *camáns*, O Boys of Banba'). Although Kyle is arriving at conclusions that will radically affect her, Liz dozes as complacently as if the sun will shine for ever in a land where the nightmare of history is past. Of course, I too have been unforgivably remiss. It was selfish and irresponsible to yield to an impulse of revulsion at mustiness and leave

Kyle without supervision or guidance.

What could be keeping him? What is he thinking in there?

The view of the dreeping yard was the same and the same handful of coals fitfully glowed in the grate – central heating remained an insane and impossible luxury – but the oilcloth was gone from the table and the cracked linoleum had been replaced by carpet squares. Instead of the torn and mismatched chairs there was a newish suite in stretch covers, and the mantelpiece, formerly bare but for unpaid bills and empty parish 'planned giving' envelopes, now had the usual clutter of glass animals, vases and photographs of smiling grandchildren in frothily ornamented silver frames. Yes, the Herron living room had lost its enchanted shabbiness and succumbed to cosiness and trinketry. I attributed the worst excesses to Rosemary, but it was bound to have happened in any case. Banality, like nature, abhors a vacuum.

But tonight my sense of wonder was entirely restored. Tonight the room presented an exquisite treat for the voluptuary of the grotesque, the epicurean of the absurd: in one of the stretch-cover chairs, cigarette in hand and legs casually crossed, was Kyle Magee in grey needlepoint cords and a muted M & S version of an *après-ski* sweater. For this momentous occasion Liz had wisely rejected both of Kyle's previous images – the eccentric bagginess of upper-class bohemia and the leather-'n'-moccasins porn king look. Instead she went for the Christmas Day outfit of a civil servant from the suburbs. Anonymity and blandness were the qualities sought – but no amount of image-making could dim the Zorba of the North. Or sway a bone-marrow sceptic like Mrs Herron.

'Liz thinks I don't know what age he is,' she said to Reba and me. 'Says I to her, *it's me he should be takin' out instead of you*. Though ye'd think at his age he'd want to sit down a minute. Says she to me, *he's very talented*, and says I to her, there's too many young ones runnin' around in rock-'n'-roll bands now. Says she, *it's jazz not rock-'n'-roll*. Says I, it's all the same, he's too old, that kind of sloosterin' around with guitars is only all right for young ones. So then she says to me, Madge is delighted, Madge is really pleased about it. And says I, *Madge . . . that eejit . . . that clift?* Sure what would a gulpin like Madge Dillon know about anything? And then she starts gettin' up on her high horse, she starts givin' me the third degree. How come I can't accept him when all *his* family have accepted *her*? And then, of course, she says I'm against him just because he's a Protestant. Says I, religion has nothin' to do with it, I know the kind of him and all belongin' to him. Oh you're just a Catholic bigot, says she.'

'He *is* very liberal, though,' Reba said. 'He's not a black Protestant.'

'I *know that*,' the mother screeched. 'It isn't that at all. Sure don't I know all about him. The father did just the same. He doesn't get it off the back stone.'

'Get what?'

'Aw my God!' Mrs Herron cried out. Not the least of life's burdens is having repeatedly to explain the obvious. 'The father was always a gadabout. Always leavin' his family to go off with some young one. I said that to Liz and she said, whatever about the father, Kyle stayed with his wife all those years to bring up the children. She says the marriage was a mistake, he was never in love with the wife and now he's in love with her and wants to settle down with her. Says I, that fella won't change for you. That fella's his bones made.'

'But they do seem very happy,' Reba suggested.

'God luck to her wit.' Mrs Herron looked out of the window at the indifferent heavens. 'She won't have all her sorrows to meet on the one day.'

There was a long silence. Reba's confidence in the liaison, never strong, was no match for her mother's scepticism.

I had yet to speak and was not about to commence. Mrs Herron almost certainly blamed the whole thing on me. Infatuated with the nonsense of artiness, I was cute enough not to let it affect my life, whereas Liz, without a titter of wit, was being lured to destruction.

'So she's tellin' everybody I'm against Protestants,' Mrs Herron resumed. 'Whatever I say about him she thinks it's because I'm anti-Protestant. *His* family are great and I'm the worst in the world.' She paused before concluding her long and eloquent speech. *'Ah can't open me mouth.'*

And now, as the momentous meeting got under way and everyone tried to appear relaxed, Mrs Herron hunched on the edge of a hard chair, unforgiving and loath, the ancient despot of a desert kingdom allotting a few moments to supplicants.

Only Kyle seemed to be genuinely at ease, springing out of his seat to distribute cigarettes, and even approaching the withered oligarch. 'Your daughter hopes to reform me,' he said to her. 'An energetic and determined girl. She may well succeed.'

Ostensibly a comment on smoking, this was really an offer of good will.

The mother laughed. 'I'd say you've your bones made by this time.'

Exactly the kind of unfortunate remark to be avoided on such an occasion. Yet she remained calm and controlled ('We have the strength and the peace of mind of those who never compromise' – Pearse).

'Mark Twain used to say giving up smoking was easy.' This literate commentator was none other than Sammy Mullen. 'He said it was no problem, he'd done it dozens of times himself.'

The laughter was feeble and short-lived. Sammy was trying to be refined and humour dies at the merest hint of pretension.

Kyle offered the packet to Hugo. 'And you work in a cigarette-machine factory. They must be finding life difficult these days.'

'Not as far as I can see. I'm on overtime every week.'

'Good money?'

'He spends it all on auld fish,' Rosemary burst in.

'Fishing?' Kyle suggested brightly to Hugo. 'I used to be very fond of fishing as a boy.'

'Naw,' Rosemary said. 'Tropical fish. They cost a fortune.'

Kyle was silenced. Even I was taken aback. So far as I knew the

Herrons' only pet had been a wolf. Coloured fish seemed impossibly insipid.

Sammy Mullen had the explanation. 'He has six piranhas.'

'I hate them things,' Rosemary muttered with bitter intensity.

'Took me in to see them,' Sammy said. '*Mere tay ye see this.* Drops a big lump a meat into the tank. Here's me jumpin' back. *Jesus, Hugo.* But they never touched it. Not a bite. Then he says, *now watch tay ye see.* Switches the light off and back on again. Not a sign a the meat. Nothin' left.'

'They only eat in the dark,' Hugo explained reluctantly.

'See during the day,' Sammy said, 'ye could put your hand right in and they wouldn't touch it.' Warming to the occasion at last, he leaned over to Kyle. 'Unless of course ye were a blackie.'

Kyle revealed no sign of annoyance at the racism, but he sat down rather heavily in the armchair. I was beginning to believe that he was genuinely in love. Why else would he dress like a suburban zero and soak up punishment like this?

Liz filled an awkward gap by taking orders for drinks, making a special effort to coax her mother. 'Would you not take a wee drop of port? Kyle got a bottle specially.'

'All I could get was Sandeman's,' Kyle apologised. 'I asked the woman if they had any port other than Sandeman's and she said to me, rather angrily, But Sandeman's *is* port.'

The Fenian off-licence – another harrowing first for Kyle. Although long-established, it resembled a makeshift black market in a disused air-raid shelter in postwar Berlin. Three bare concrete walls glistening with damp, the fourth covered with German sweet white wine. In the centre a massive leaning tower of some frightful cheap lager. Between the lager and the sweet wine an impatient, angry, ignorant woman with no time for airy-fairy nonsense about diversity and choice. Take what you get and be glad of it. Sandeman's *is* port.

Mrs Herron made a grimace of the utmost unhappiness and reluctance. 'Maybe a wee, wee glass.'

At last a concession. Like Bogart in *Casablanca*, Mrs Herron rarely drank with her guests. And in her case the break with tradition was even more difficult. Bogart never suffered from near-chronic cystitis.

Liz decided that the time was ripe to link these two people separated by sex, religion, class, temperament and belief system – Kyle the sunny humanist and Mrs Herron the nihilistic Nietzschean. What connected them was that Mrs Herron had begun her working life in the Golden Coffee Pot, an exclusive delicatessen owned by a relative of Kyle's. But of course the class and religious overtones made the subject a gamble.

Kyle immediately denounced the owner. 'A famous eccentric. A crazy woman.'

'Mad as a hatter,' Mrs Herron agreed.

'But with her moments of courage. You know the big coffee pot outside the shop was mentioned in a wartime broadcast by Lord Haw Haw? *The Golden Coffee Pot will be bombed tonight.*'

'I remember it well,' Mrs Herron said, neglecting to mention her fierce Fenian glee at the traitor's insults to the English. To this day she recalled many jibes with fondest nostalgia.

'The authorities told her to take the pot down and she refused. The bombing raid never came and the pot stayed up for another twenty years.'

'I wouldn't have been sorry to see it go. You know you had to actually pay her to serve your time as a shop girl? A shop girl! It's hard to believe now.'

We were getting into dangerous waters but Kyle produced some skilful navigation. 'Perhaps the experience was useful when you opened your own business?' Not only had he steered us out of danger but into the happy haven of Herron shop anecdotes.

Now everyone could reminisce about the characters from the old days, the outcasts of the universe who used the shop as a community centre. Eileen, the slavering simpleton who had a notion of John and was abused, Mrs Herron hinted bitterly, by 'manys a one passing out collection baskets at the back of the cathedral'. Vijay, the Pakistani rejected by his own community for going native with a Fenian girl, and then rejected in turn by the Fenian girl. Harry Big Eat, who consumed as a snack a half-pound box of Galtee cheese. Mickey McMenamin, who came in every day after work and bought a tin of Master McGrath and an onion; exhaustive enquiries produced no evidence of a dog.

Sammy Mullen: 'I used to say to Reba, *watch he doesn't lift his leg at the counter, Reba.*'

In this way the evening moved to the congenial climax of tea and ham sandwiches (neatly decrusted and quartered in yet another concession to delicacy and cosiness). As I carried a plate up from the kitchen I met Kyle on his way back from the toilet (now stench free and with a light switch instead of the greasy cord).

'Did you hear the old fellow quoting Mark Twain? I thought that was rather good.' Sammy, too, was part of the huge public thirsting for quality popular culture. It was only a matter of communication, which in turn was only a matter of effort. Kyle drove a happy hand through his hair. 'In fact it all seems to be going well.'

At once I thought of the old Fenian joke. Question: When does a liberal Protestant become a black orange bastard? Answer: As soon as he leaves the room.

Because the public relations work had been entirely in vain. Nothing said or done by Kyle had made any impression on the pungent and implacable scepticism of the Herrons. Even his celebrated dark-skinned good looks failed to charm. 'Yella as a duck's foot' was Hugo's comment – though Sammy Mullen at least appreciated the appearance of the guest: 'Jesus, if I looked like that I'd be runnin' to dances.' Not that Mrs Herron bore Kyle any ill will. It was Liz who had to shoulder the blame: 'That wee girl was born an eejit . . . and she'll die an eejit.' As for the prospects of the alliance: 'It's the road to Notown.'

6

As soon as Madge Dillon opened the door we greeted her with wild cries of gratitude and deliverance. It was not so much the drive to Belfast as the tension of following the vague directions Liz had given to Reba, whom I punished severely for the imprecision, causing a quarrel. Madge stood aside for Reba, then barred my path.

'Have ye a car?'

'How do you think we got here?'

'Go to North Street and get more tequila. An off-licence there stocks it.'

We knew this would not be an Irish wedding. Perhaps there was a Mexican theme instead – tequila slammers and a brass band with droopy moustaches. I could go with that. *Get me the guns and I will free Mehico.*

But Madge revealed it was strictly a personal taste. 'I'm really into tequila at the moment.'

'Settle for gin,' I told her, my moment of delirium replaced by the mature skills of evasiveness and equivocation. 'I'll go round the corner in a minute.'

'You're not wearing that waiter's coat?' Madge retaliated, casting a scornful look at the off-white Martini Terrace jacket I thought had the right raffish elegance for such a sophisticated occasion. Already the jacket had caused trouble, Reba insisting its whiteness would be seen to challenge the incandescent singularity of the bride. This was not an Irish wedding, I repeated, with faltering confidence. So far it had been as fraught and tense as the traditional version.

Reba had already disappeared. I followed Madge down a narrow hall and into a tiny living room with a sideboard, tiled fireplace and suite in imitation leather. There were two contrasting works of art:

above the mantelpiece a landscape made from pieces of coloured cloth and, taking up the sofa, a large, accomplished, semi-abstract painting of what may have been Celtic warriors in helmets and shields. Certainly the theme was as Celtic as the technique was contemporary.

'From Tom McKenna,' Madge explained. 'Apparently the artist is well known.' She regarded it with dislike. 'Dirty bugger he is too.'

'The artist?'

'McKenna. He was here last night.'

Before I could ask for details, Madge went on through and down three precipitous steps into an even tinier kitchen – pantry would be a better word – filthy gas cooker, ancient presses with wooden sliding doors, Formica-topped spindly table, gigantic discoloured jawbox with a mound of rotting tea bags underneath. I paused on the steps, entranced. Every detail was perfect. It could have served as an exhibit in the Ulster Folk and Transport Museum. Student house, early sixties. A lustrous, almost phosphorescent squalor.

In the centre of the room was Liz in an off-the-shoulder white cocktail dress that was presumably her wedding gown and entirely vindicated my jacket. Certainly it subverted the conventions and I would have been dazzled were it not for her hair, which had been elaborately woven and bedecked with what looked like sweet pea. I understood the intention. Sweet pea is charmingly unpretentious and natural – but entwined in your back fence, not your hair. She made a wild gesture of welcome that was inhibited by the glass in her hand and Reba crawling about at her feet adjusting the hem of the dress.

'Isn't it desperate!' Liz shrieked gaily, indicating the kitchen with a wave. 'Kyle's daughters offered me their flat, but I didn't want them around beforehand. Not that they aren't as civil. Ruth was in earlier doing my face.'

'Who lives here?' I asked Madge.

'Musicians I know. Three guys in a band. They're on tour at the moment.'

Reba spoke from the floor. 'Somebody get me a drink.'

'Liz has the last drop in the house,' Madge announced cheerfully. 'There was supposed to be champagne but it got drunk.'

Offering her a tenner, I pleaded nerves unstrung by diversions, cordons, security gates, army patrols.

'It's been *wild*,' Liz said when Madge left. 'Nonstop for three days. And Madge inviting everybody she meets to the wedding. She was on the phone to England the other night asking some character. I mean, there's only meals for a certain number.'

'Who's cooking?' Reba asked.

'These friends of Kyle are doing everything. Imagine.'

The hem finished, Reba went upstairs to change and I had my last intimate moment with Liz as a single woman.

'Here,' she murmured, pouring half her drink into a tumbler.

We raised our glasses and gazed into each other's eyes.

'Good luck, Liz.'

Was ever a banal phrase so rich in subtexts?

'I know you mean that,' she fervently murmured. 'Thanks.'

We drank – deeply, decisively, solemnly. Silence was the most effective form of communication, I felt – intense feeling held in check by fantastic restraint – the volcano blazing and heaving beneath a cool marble slab.

But one question had to be put before it was too late. 'Liz . . . my jacket . . . sort of white . . . does it . . . ?'

'*Honey* . . .'

Setting down her glass, she moved easily into my arms. We kissed lightly but with a tenderness and commitment unshadowed by impending change. If anything, she was more generous than before, as though to reassure of bonds that were long-established and durable. Ah mischievous Destiny that amused itself by teasing us so! What an elegant couple we must have looked. I could certainly have gone for French – and possibly even tried for knob.

'Kyle's here!' Madge called out cheerfully and we went out to the hall to meet him.

Descending the narrow staircase in a silk trouser suit from the closing-down sale at Pampered Belle, Reba had been brought to a halt by the sight of Kyle. A bridegroom about to see the bride *before the ceremony.* Only now did it fully come home to her that this was not an Irish wedding. Or perhaps she was merely surprised by his appearance – the shaven hair, shirt and tie and grey business suit.

'Jesus, Kyle,' Madge said, unwrapping her parcel, 'You look like some dickhead that sells double glazing.'

Normally Kyle would have laughed, but today he had a manner to go with his look. He was serious, dignified, mature . . . *statesman-like.* Even the offer of a drink was refused with a solemn shake of the head.

'Is this what you'll be like as a married man?' Liz wailed.

'We'll have to get up to my mother. I promised Renee.'

'How is your mother?' Reba asked.

'She's *terrific,*' Liz came in. 'Really fighting it.'

'What she hates most is incontinence,' Kyle said. 'Today'll be a long day and she's really worried about wetting her pants.'

Whenever strict regulation is eased there is always the problem of the headstrong mistaking relaxation for licence.

'But isn't the problem more serious, Kyle?' Madge said, handing out huge gins. 'Won't your mother *shite herself* when she sees you marrying a Fenian huer?'

Our chauffeurs were two fellow guests, a civil but decorous Protestant couple dedicated to the credo that sustains the Ulster bourgeoisie: ugliness ignored with sufficient conviction will eventually wither and disappear. Thus, as we drove through the rural Protestant heartland, no one remarked on the sectarian graffiti, the Bible quotes on gables and trees, the red white and blue kerb-stones of the villages or even, most startling of all, the message GO HOME YOU FENIAN BITCH painted in huge white letters across both lanes of the road. Even Madge, crushed between Reba and me in the back, was reduced to nudging and pointing out the choicer examples of fundamentalism.

At last, like mythical hunters stumbling on an enchanted valley, we emerged from the bellicose fiefdoms into a world of graciousness and elegance, a tiny humanist principality nestling in the heart of the tribal homelands. As soon as we turned into the drive I had a feeling of magical timelessness. News of the death of liberalism could not have reached this remote outpost. In fact, for most of the area, news of its birth had yet to arrive. As though aware of the spell that protected them, shrubbery burgeoned and blossomed more fully, birds carolled more sweetly and the sun shone with genial benevolence, striking fine fire from the windows of a solid old house that snuggled down in its ivy like Peter Rabbit under the bedclothes with his camomile tea.

Our hosts were greeting guests at the door. A fine old humanist couple, their eyes fairly sparkled with hospitality, tolerance, justice and love of the arts. Impossible to fault them, it was also unnerving to think of their life style as the apogee and terminus of Western civilisation.

The wife looked me over with amusement and interest. 'We only know you from the radio, of course. You're not at all as fierce as you sounded then.'

This was not just the humanist tendency to see everyone as essentially civilised and amenable. Even a cursory glance would reveal that the dazzling heresiarch was no more.

'That was a long time ago,' I said curtly, glancing about the discreet hall hung with paintings and feeling a twinge of my old incendiarism at this insufferable combination of right thinking, good taste and generous patronage of the arts.

We were ushered into a large front room, obviously used for recitals but now converted into a pseudo-church. At the far end, two individual pews looked out onto the lawn. Beside them an organ, microphone and lectern faced rows of chairs set out on either side of a central aisle. Just a few simple touches, but enough to create a sacerdotal atmosphere. We entered on tiptoe, the guests already present maintaining a respectful house-of-God silence or communicating in reluctant whispers.

Immediately there was a problem of affiliation. Kyle's people were on the right and the Herrons on the left. All the interesting guests were on the bridegroom's side: Tom McKenna and Madge (typically flouting convention) in the front row, behind them Renee in conversation with a tanned and handsome American hippy with a ponytail. Ever keen to reject the tribe, I was moving right when Reba seized my arm and guided me firmly in behind her mother.

A youth came up the central aisle and took his place at the organ. A humanist son, I presumed, with floppy untrained boy hair that covered his forehead to the top of a pair of spectacles whose thick plastic frames gradually changed from dark brown at the top to transparent at the bottom. What could be seen of his face had the pale translucency common in the better suburbs of provincial towns. With scrupulous, restrained movements he produced a sequence of soothing chords – sacred musak. Nowadays not even worship can be conducted in silence.

Or rather, pseudo-worship. It was obvious that we were about to see some sort of imitation religious ceremony, no doubt to propitiate the relatives. But if they were hoping to placate Mrs Herron, they were mistaken. I could see her left profile, a terrible, inscrutable mask of stone. Of course, for her religion was obeisance to meaningless ritual – but it had to be authentic meaningless ritual. Imitation was actually worse than forthright rejection – a cowardly and self-defeating concept, like that of the vegetarian sausage.

Nevertheless Kyle took his seat at the front and Liz, already his wife from the civil ceremony earlier, came in on John Herron's arm to the traditional music. Awaiting them was a first-rate impersonator, an ex-priest and liberal martyr hounded out by the hierarchy in a blaze of publicity. But again the attempted imitation badly misfired. Intended to stand in for the unbroken authority of the Catholic Church, the poor man actually embodied the chaos and anarchy of rebellion. Wearing a troubled frown, he spoke of the couple's courage in breaking down barriers and of their shining example to all in our divided community.

When it was time for the rings, Tom McKenna stood up and Madge leaned against him. From behind, it was not clear whether this was a tussle or a fumble, but as a result the rings were dropped. Here the true domestic nature of the room came into its own. On a hard surface rings would have bounced or rolled. Instead, the shag pile trapped them with silent ease. All the same, it revealed the essentially clownish and insecure nature of the proceedings, the total absence of the order and gravitas conferred by genuine ritual.

Then we had an innovation. Tom McKenna rose and went to the lectern. Not only internationally known for his poetry, he was much in demand for prizegivings, funerals, memorials and the like. To every occasion Tom afforded its correct light and shade, the precise combination of reverence and daring the audience craved but could not itself have defined. It was a sureness of touch that never failed to impress me. Only a rare natural talent can find the clit every time.

He began by reading a passage from a novel that was still controversial (highly daring) but also an established modern classic and as sacred as scripture to Kyle. It was the wedding scene from *The Rainbow*, where Tom Brangwen attempts to define marriage in spite of irreverent interruptions from intoxicated guests. McKenna read with perfect rhythm and timing, not exactly doing funny voices but varying the pace and inflection, glancing up to cue us and leaving space for us to laugh. After the platitudes of the pseudo-priest we were happy to oblige.

Having won us over completely, he put aside the novel and took up a slim volume with an expression of solemnity and reverence. It was time to put aside idle things for the revelation was at hand. 'Epithalamium,' he murmured. A hush came upon the room and many heads bowed, as at the consecration of the host. And, indeed, a similar transubstantiation was under way. Just as mere bread is transformed into the body and blood of Christ, so the words of ordinary speech became the truth of High Art.

Golden sun-shot sherry in rows of sparkling crystal glasses on a scintillant white tablecloth. A sight to knock the eye out of your head. Unconvincing in most respects, the fake ceremony had been every bit as fatiguing as the genuine article.

In an instant the room was full of relatives and literary people mingling in precisely the way I had thought impossible at my own miserable wedding. What a failure of nerve to try to compartmentalise your life. Let them all come together! Let them flourish in random proximity like beautiful wild free things in a ditch! Rosemary and Hugo were talking to Susannah and Ruth, Frances and Sean to Tom McKenna and Renee's businessman husband. Renee herself was chatting brightly to Caroline. Reba was with Ponytail – not so random, perhaps. She has a thing about ponytails. Again it's the gypsy in her soul. Kyle and Liz, of course, were everywhere, moving about like royalty, graciously acknowledging the congratulations and compliments coming from all sides. In a corner Mrs Herron was standing over Kyle's mother, who was very correct and grand in spite of being confined to a wheelchair. At intervals Mrs Herron would bend to speak and then straighten up to look ahead, every bit as imposing as her companion – remote and implacable as a pre-Christian God.

I gazed about me at the glorious plenitude, trying to decide which group to join. Before I could move, John Herron sidled up and twisted his face in familiar preparation for speaking out of the corner of his mouth. This was the last thing I wanted. Sniggering and tittering on the sidelines. The Fenian cheap sneer.

'And that's Kyle's *sister,*' he murmured, staring in wonder at Renee and then across the room at youthful Kyle. 'What are these people on, anyway – fuckin' royal jelly?'

'Liquor, sex and Ulster fries.'

John had returned his gaze to Renee, mesmerised by her house-of-correction looks. 'Jesus,' he muttered, out of the corner of his mouth. 'That woman'd give ye a terrible hidin'.' He regarded her, worshipful. 'She'd put marks on ye.'

I explained that Renee's face had been her undoing in the North. Most recently she had failed to get a job as a newsreader, although women readers were all the fashion and Renee had the necessary qualifications – mature glamour, perfect poise, grooming and diction. She was perfect for the post in every way but one: her face would scare the shit out of Northern Ireland's teatime viewers.

Seeing us watching her, Renee came across with Caroline in tow. 'Isn't it just beautiful here?' she flashed radiantly at me.

'Hasn't the character of Altnagarvin.'

'Hah! You know it's been sold. The council bought it as a home for mentally retarded children.' Moving closer, she adopted a confidential tone. 'Maybe that's what it always was.'

The old immediacy – but different, subdued. Marriage – or just the occasion? She had her hair done in pseudo-Grecian loops and wore an expensive but conventional dress with a ruff at the top of its choking high neck. Today she could almost pass for someone's aunt. Another mystery of wedding ritual: why do women who are normally devastating spend a fortune to look like shit?

'Who's the ponytail?' I casually enquired.

'Sam? He's Kyle's son from the American marriage. He happened to be doing Europe this year.'

'He's very good-looking,' Caroline said, with a smirk of bourgeois daring.

As we gazed in fascination at the throng, teenage humanist children moved around replenishing glasses. Not only was the drink free (already dangerous to Fenians) but the continual topping up confused the essential monitoring of consumption. Used to authoritarian control, the Fenian is not adept at replacing external constraints with self-discipline. I concluded that the humanists had a secret death wish.

And, even as I pondered, a smiling young girl approached with a bottle. Despite grave forebodings, I permitted her to top up my glass. A Fenian could do little else.

Renee, though, was on orange juice. 'I have to get Mammy home later. And there's the baby . . .'

'You must find it a bit of a shock,' suggested Caroline, no doubt expecting Renee to produce a catalogue of complaints.

Instead the older woman showed her spirit for the first time. In our enlightened age the sister of Zorba can be as much of a life force as a man. Laying a hand on Caroline's arm, Renee advanced as though to plunge a ravening mouth on the girl's bloodless lips.

'I *adore* babies,' she murmured, squeezing fiercely. 'They're so . . . *sensual*.'

Like a heat-seeking missile, Tom McKenna popped up at Renee's side but Renee went off to check on her mother, leaving the poet bereft but obliged to spend a few moments at least with the zeros.

Now the junior humanists were coming round with trays of cocktail sausages and vol-au-vents. I displayed no more restraint than with the drink.

'How do you keep your figure?' McKenna snapped with a sudden peevishness that fell upon me like a benison. Not content with monstro boss fame, he wanted to be pretty as well.

My satisfaction was short-lived.

'Suppose you've packed in the writing,' he said in a casual, indifferent tone, glancing about for a more interesting group to join.

It was only the simple truth, but his careless tone cut me to the quick. Not that he would have known it, even if he had wished to wound and had been paying careful attention. Never would I let a man like McKenna know he could hurt me. Turning away from him, I looked out of the window. Already the sharpness was gone from the afternoon, the light lush and overripe, poised for decay. On the lawn a single figure, stock still, stood with its back to the house. Black hair and grey suit – it could only be Kyle.

Even sweet golden sherry failed to wash away the bitter taste of failure and redundancy. All that was going to happen now was that time would run out. A sudden stabbing premonition. This was Gatsby's last party. It was the end of the summer.

At my elbow the youthful organist filled my empty glass with a smile. Simultaneously, from a hidden source but cutting laserlike through the hubbub, I heard a sentence of devastating clarity: 'I don't know what he's doing marrying a Fenian anyway.'

At the top of the table, by the window, the newlyweds had John Herron and the mothers on one side, McKenna and Madge on the other. And so thoroughly mixed were the guests that a tracking shot along the table revealed a series of conjunctions bizarre enough to excite the most sated voluptuary of the grotesque. Impossible to imagine the exquisite conversations I was missing. Impossible even to follow those within earshot. Not only too far gone to eavesdrop, I was scarcely able to see at all. Everything seemed to be happening on a distant and faulty TV screen. At intervals the picture would gently lift and tremble, eventually settling back in place with a disorienting shudder.

'Isn't Liz looking *absolutely beautiful?*' Renee leaned an intimate face into mine – an effect like a train coming out of the screen in 3D.

Certain reflexes survive even systematic derangement of all the senses. 'You're looking very well yourself,' I got out.

'Ugh! There's no hiding middle-aged spread.'

Here was a chance to express wonder and gratitude for mature female beauty. Youthful slenderness may be charming to look at but the rounded belly that has carried children is softer and warmer to lie upon.

'Ah no . . . don't . . . it's . . .'

Someone leaned over our shoulders with smoked salmon *hors-d'oeuvres.* I pecked out of duty, hunger long since left behind. Renee went at it with the gusto of the sober. Then there was a long delay that might have been tedious had not the Beaujolais replenished itself.

'There's a terrible panic in the kitchen,' Renee explained. 'I think a lot more turned up than they thought.' She surveyed the noisy revellers. 'It looks as though everyone either of them ever knew is here.'

'But not Robbie Semple. Where's old Robbie these days?'

'Gone to America, thank God. He's been impossible these last few years. All he did was drink and beat his girl.'

Rejected by the theatre establishment, Robbie had been living in a council flat with the Immaculate Conception actress and a baby. Even the Rimbaud of the North was trapped in sorrow and shite.

But of course the true artist can never be denied. Canvas

exhausted on Tahiti, Gauguin carved trees instead; manuscripts burned by his jailers, Genet began again, writing on stolen mail-bags. Denied access to conventional drama, Semple had evolved a new type of challenging street theatre: on his nightly way home from the pub he would stop every person he met and tell them to fuck off.

'Everyone?' I asked, my respect for his integrity flooding back. 'Absolutely everyone he met?'

'His greatest challenge was a party of nuns. There were seven of them and I think even Robbie hesitated for a moment. But he went through with it in the end apparently. He went round every one.'

Throwing back her head, Renee let loose a wild shriek that, even in this hubbub, caused heads to turn. I could see John Herron looking down from the top table, no doubt in anguish at the missed opportunity of seeing Renee read the teatime news.

At the moment the bulletins were profoundly disappointing to Fenians. Since the hunger strikes nothing had happened in Irish affairs. For the Catholic news junkie the sole consolation was the new breed of newsreader – women past the folly of youth but immune to the ravages of time: calm, authoritative and inviolable, offering a fixed point of dignity and compassionate strength. To submit to such a woman was a dream of redemption many shared. Over sherry John and I had exchanged fantasies. *He* wanted to handwash Angela Rippon's panties and *I* wanted to be urinated on by Jan Leeming.

Kyle, who was with us at the time, was profoundly irritated by this. 'You see I don't find that funny or interesting or anything.'

Humiliation was certainly never Kyle's bag. Remembering that uncharacteristic peevishness, I now gave him a careful scrutiny. In the midst of the merrymaking he was silent, solemn, grave, playing with a napkin ring as flustered humanist children served a superbly garnished Chateaubriand that in no way resembled the traditional Irish wedding fare of turkey and ham with soggy sprouts.

Renee leaned over. 'My present.'

'Huh?'

'My present to Kyle and Liz – these steaks.'

Still I could not bring myself to eat. The food was gorgeous but unreal, like a photograph in a cook book of *haute cuisine*.

'A boring sort of present.' Renee sighed. 'I'm sure *you* got them something wonderful.'

Indeed I had dreamed of a gift that would embody many things: my long and rewarding relationship with each of the couple, their wild, free, exemplary spirits, and of course my own more inhibited but nevertheless complex, rich and multilayered personality. But, as for Anthony Quinn in *Lawrence of Arabia*, frantically plundering trains in search of 'something honourable', the ideal gift proved frustratingly elusive. With a few days to go we plunged into a craft fair and after much bickering made a purchase which Reba warned me, on pain of the most severe penalties, not to denigrate or disown.

'Och it was just a sort of an auld mirror thing,' I said, with a wild dismissive gesture that almost overturned my glass.

McKenna rose to commence the speeches, but even with his stature and presence (and Liz hammering violently on her glass) it took some time to still the tumult.

'Flann O'Brien once said . . .' – he paused to allow an anticipatory ripple at the name of the comic genius – '. . . that there was no such thing as a large whiskey.' Roar of laughter from the throng. 'By the same token, there's no such thing as a short speech.' Further laughter, less loud.

By now he should have had undivided attention but already conversation was breaking out afresh, along with the public speaker's ultimate nightmare – unsolicited, autonomous mirth. I had no doubt that McKenna had a lengthy speech prepared – but one intended for a discerning audience, not a drunken mob. Swiftly proposing a toast, he handed over to Kyle.

Rising solemnly, the groom began by expressing detailed thanks to the humanists and, to Mrs Herron, a gratitude that was necessarily more vague (she had contributed nothing and offered no help). We turned to the old girl for a reaction shot. A stone God on the hillside of a remote and uninhabited island. Then the groom broached the subject of matrimony and we smiled in anticipation. After all, Kyle was a proponent of popular culture whose books revealed the farcical aspects of marriage: angry cuckolds attempting to run down lovers, demented wives breaking down locked bedroom doors. What we wanted was music-hall comedy, coarse traditional fare of the marriage-is-not-a-word-but-a-long-sentence variety. But, as demonstrated by McKenna, it is generally writers solemn on the page who are witty in the flesh. Kyle expressed his beliefs with a painful sincerity.

'Although I'm not religious myself I do think of marriage as a sacrament . . . a symbiotic union . . .'

The Word was the last thing we needed. We were rabble. We were low-life. We wanted Barabbas.

'For God's sake, Kyle!' Renee shouted, to uproarious laughter and applause.

McKenna had another stab at it, rising bravely with the telegrams, but as he waited to impose himself on the multitude Madge Dillon suddenly jumped to her feet and snatched the bunch from his hand.

Now this was more like it – music hall at last.

Laughing, she held the sheets up and away from a possible counterattack. Of course McKenna could not get involved in such slapstick. This was Ireland's Ambassador of Verse, a man several times quoted by the taoiseach. Madge began to read in a loud, exaggerated Belfast accent, mispronouncing words, misplacing emphases, pausing to frown at the print like a backward child. Whether this was affectation or drunkenness, the result was not amusing, destroying the impact of the messages and sometimes even their sense. And what we were being denied was the wit of celebrities from several continents. Protests were raised. Madge responded by laying it on even thicker. Like many another she mistook impertinence for wit. Finally shouted down, she escaped by a *coup de théâtre* as bold as the storming of the men's toilet in the Dáil.

'*Fuck I need a pee.*' And, still clutching the telegrams, she turned and climbed out of the open window behind the top table.

Liz was almost completely deflowered. Only a few blossoms remained and these were bedraggled and wilted. Sweet pea is not a robust bloom. She pushed me into a corner and released a cry of pent-up rage.

'I am just about ready to kill Madge. First that business with the rings – you know she tried to grab the rings from Tom. I warned her after that – and now this stunt with the telegrams.' Liz had to pause to choke back her fury. Nothing like a wedding to bring people together. 'Tom is livid and who could blame him? He was great to do best man and that reading was brilliant. He's been really great all day and all he's got is insults and hassle. I introduced him to my mother and she would hardly even speak. Know what she said to me afterwards? *That fella's a hook.* I said he's an internationally famous poet and she said *he's a hook.*'

I tried to nod gravely but my inhibitions were largely gone. Instead I laughed out loud.

'It's not funny.'

'I know. I'm sorry. What exactly is a hook?'

'And now she's going from bad to worse, whatever's got into her.'

'Madge?'

'My mother. She was all right up to the meal but now she's *impossible.* She insulted Rosemary and Rosemary had a fight with Hugo and took an asthma attack.'

'John can handle her though, can't he? Get John.'

'She's already had a row with John. Accused him of never darkening her door. John said he had to look after his own wife – Caroline's had back trouble and had to take it easy. So then my mother said to him *sure that's all only notions.* Notions! John had enough at this stage and tried to get Reba and Frances – but they wouldn't go near her in a mood like that.'

Through a drunken fog I was beginning to perceive the outline of something huge and terrible bearing straight down on me. Far from merely getting things off her chest, Liz was asking me to *intervene.* She was actually proposing that now, among the most dazzlingly sophisticated company I would ever know, these people charming in themselves and with so much in their gift, in my natural constituency at last for a few brief hours, I should yet turn aside and devote my Martini Terrace jacket to a vicious, embittered peasant woman.

'For Christ's sake, Liz. She'd murder me too. I mean, I'm the one brought you and Kyle together in the first place. I'm to blame for the whole business.'

'All I want is for you to occupy her for a while. Keep her from making a scene. As soon as Rosemary comes round a bit Hugo can drive them all home.'

She waited, not exerting her usual charm. She was calling it in, the years of sweetness and honey, the incredible offers. The fact that I had never taken her up was irrelevant. She was calling it in.

'I suppose I'll have to talk to her then.'

No smiles, no kisses, no hugs of gratitude.

I had been thinking of looking for coffee to clear my head – but now I went back to the kitchen for a gin and tonic. As I poured, a man in a group next to me said, and I swear this is accurate: 'The artist is shut out of heaven and denied an entry visa to hell.' This is the sort of thing I was swopping for the paranoia of an aged kulak.

She was in the room where the ceremony had been, standing well apart, clutching a handbag: righteous, outraged, impatient, a terrible fury held in check by an even more terrible rectitude. How much our visual artists have missed in their obsession with landscape and legend! Here was a classic pose, rich as Vermeer – *Irish Woman at a Wedding.*

There was no need to probe for the problem.

'I nearly *dropped* when I was introduced to that character with the ponytail. Says the mother, *Kyle's son by the first marriage.* I nearly went through the floor, look see. No one ever said to me he'd been married *twice* already. If it is only twice, that is.'

'Only twice.'

She snorted grimly, unappeased. 'They certainly kept the first one quiet. No one ever let on about that.' As so often, the damage was caused less by the offence than the cover-up. Particularly wounding to someone whose life blood was knowledge.

'It didn't last very long,' I suggested.

'That's what the old mother said. And I suppose that'd be nothin' to them, right enough. Oh they're a crowd ... they're a crowd right enough. That sister ... the actress one ... how many times is *she* married?'

'Twice.'

'And making a great job of the second, Ahm sure.' She laughed bitterly. 'I notice you're very great with her.'

As with all rogue animals the only solution was to put her down. But had I an elephant gun of sufficient calibre? In any case the deal with Liz was merely to hold her at bay and keep her from savaging the other guests.

'And she married money this time – like the mother. The mother looks very grand now – but she was only a country shop girl like myself. Nothin' to her name but good looks and the nerve o' Nelson. She latched on to this Ulster officer after the first war but when they got here she found he wasn't as well off as she thought ... even then all the officers weren't landed gentry ... so she looked around and got her hooks into someone with money ... Kyle's father ... who always had an eye for the girls himself ... Kyle didn't get that off the back stone. Of course the father was married already but they soon sorted that out ...'

I could see why news of the first marriage had been such a devastating blow. She knew everything else. And the extent of her knowledge made me feel like a naïve idiot, a clift, a gap, a Big McGlundy, a gawm. After all my years with the Magees I knew nothing about them. In particular, I had never suspected the humble nature of the French connection, imagining in a vague way fantastically symmetrical poplars leading to an austere and silent chateau.

'So this is what you discussed with Kyle's mother,' I said, with a touch of sarcasm, hoping she would reveal her informant.

'Indeed an' I did no such thing.'

She would never reveal her sources. She was not a gossip. Power rather than prurience was behind her hunger for knowledge. (Later Reba suggested a possibility: could it be Garvin Dodd, the Prod family solicitor?)

'So what *did* you talk to her about?' Now that I knew they were from the same background, the Clash of the Titans was even more fascinating.

'Och . . .' Mrs Herron grunted impatiently, discounting the conversation as polite tittle-tattle. 'She said she was very pleased about the marriage and very fond of Liz. She said Olivia never looked after Kyle and she had to do all his ironing herself. That's why she hates the stroke, she can't do his ironing any more. So . . .' Mrs Herron nodded grimly. 'There you are. Liz is going to have to look after him.' Turning to the window she instituted a pause so full of menace one might have thought her an adept of contemporary drama. 'She couldn't wait to get him. Now she can have her fill of him.' Another pause, followed by one of her gnomic summaries. 'A woman'll have her woman's day.'

She stared out of the window where the last of the light magically sustained the illusion of plenitude. An image entirely without substance. Whatever warmth there had been was long gone.

I finished the gin, immediately reactivating my drunkenness. I felt stupefied, muffled, ineffectual, dim. Behind Mrs Herron Liz appeared in the doorway of the room, signalling wildly to keep up the good work. A woman having her woman's day.

'But they seem very happy,' I suggested to the kulak.

With a bitter snort she dismissed the charms of momentary radiance. 'Aye,' she said, 'but it's naw night yet.'

Pink-blush bathroom suite, discreet wallpaper of tiny wild flowers, kindly smoked-glass mirrors, fitted shag pile of oyster grey. Glow of warmth from two rads and a heated towel rail. Authentic natural aromas permeating the hush. Everything pleasing to the senses – tasteful, reassuring, subdued. This was the humanist bathroom, heart of the whole operation. Here the odorous turbulence of life was converted into sweet-smelling calm.

A room that must have been heavily used – for all the humanists, parents and children, had the fantastic hypercleanliness of the provincial bourgeoisie, a pale washed-out look just this side of bleaching. Yet there was no trace of squalor, no rimed shaving mugs, shagged-out toothbrushes, twisted squeezed-dry tubes.

It was certainly a good place to recover from the fevers and manias of the wedding. According to modern theory hell is yourself, but the experience of living in Ireland had given me a paradigm shift. For me, hell was an endless party with a drunk in every room.

Holding on to the pink washbasin I studied the compromised features displayed in the blessedly kind smoked glass: a testing exercise in analysis and comprehension. Someone banged on the door. Certain no family member would be capable of such boorishness, I knew it was safe to indulge in irritation and petulance. *'All right!'* I snapped and went on with the study of my face in the mirror.

The door was rattled violently in its frame. Already the barbarians were at the gates. Not merely non-family, the intruder was also not a Protestant. I released the bolt with a dark frown of annoyance. Sure enough, it was a Fenian: Hugo Herron. But even for Hugo, the expression of bitterness and hatred was extreme.

He pushed me in the chest, driving me back a few steps. 'What'd you fuckin' say tay my mother?'

'Uh . . .?'

He pushed me again, more forcefully this time. '*What'd ye fuckin' say tay her?*'

'Nothing . . . I mean we just talked . . . I said nothing.'

'Then how comes I have to take her home now?'

'How should I know?'

Never answer an angry man with a question. He shoved me.

'Alls I know I have to take her home now she's that upset after you.' It seemed he might be calming down. But no. '*What'd ye fuckin' say tay her?*'

This thrust brought me up against the edge of the bath. 'I haven't a notion what you're talking about. If she's upset, it's nothing to do with me.'

Exercising a self-control more atrocious than frenzy, he brought his face close to mine and spoke in a low, measured tone. 'Ye know right fuckin' well what ye said tay her.'

'What did I say to her?' Again the foolhardiness of a question. He shoved me so hard I went over backwards into the bath.

'Ye know right fuckin' well what ye said.'

'*What'd I say?*'

Seizing the front of my shirt in his left hand, he hoisted me up and drew back his right fist. Try as we may there is no evading our destiny. It was an Irish wedding after all.

My life did not flash before me – but I was vouchsafed a sudden insight into the cause of the mother's pique. It could only have been my rhapsody on the three Herron girls. Seeking to please the mother in a way that was both intimate and sincere, I had launched into a long, rapturous analysis of her daughters. Liz, the pretty one, spoiled by the father – a candy-ass, a sweetie-pie. At the other extreme Frances – deprived, resentful, explosive. In between, Reba – a piquant mixture, a sweet-'n'-sour. All of which had been carefully expressed in non-judgemental and even flattering language. But in my drunkenness I had forgotten a crucial fact. The concept of reciprocity was entirely alien to the Herrons. They analysed you with pitiless ardour (biopsy without anaesthetic was a house speciality), but you could not subject them to even the mildest of conjectures. Not only had drink loosened my tongue, it had made me fatally blind to the mother's reaction. Now the consequences were incalculable. Instinctively I have always favoured silence. Here was proof of its value.

Certainly I said no more to Hugo – but some kind of primitive cry or squawk may have escaped me, something that revealed the smart aleck as only a pitiful, bare, forked creature. In any case, instead of delivering the punch he dropped me in profound disgust and, thrusting his face into mine, contented himself with a warning. '*Never you fuckin' speak to my mother like that again.*'

Some day a radiant imperious woman will seek me out and lead me to my destiny. All my life I have awaited the summons.

In the meantime I listen to assholes.

'I was buying gin and wine,' the man from the Arts Council smoothly began, 'and it came to ten sixty-six. *Battle of Hastings,* I said to this woman behind the counter and she turns round and shouts to this other woman behind her, *Have we a bottle o' Hastings, Roberta?*'

The question was delivered in a high-camp Belfast accent and rewarded by mature chuckles from journalists. New arrivals, invited only to the evening session, they were still fairly sober and restrained. Looking round, I saw more familiar journalist faces, including the patrician white head of Campbell Stanway. He seemed to get to a lot of parties for a mournful stylite. Even as I watched, another band with bright expectant faces surged into the drawing room. *All these people came to Gatsby's house in the summer.*

Where was everyone I knew? Kyle and Liz had disappeared. So had Mad Madge. Reba I had scarcely seen all day. Stupefied and distracted, I was only intermittently aware. Already it was dark outside. Night appeared to have fallen as swiftly and conclusively as in the tropics.

Another drink story was in progress. 'We were out in the wilds of Connemara, meself and this American woman. So we went into this tiny pub with a sort of half-wit character behind the bar. Generations of inbreeding, ye know.' The narrator, a journalist, froze his body and laid his head on his left shoulder like a terminally dispirited bird. Then he resumed his own easy stance. 'Pint of stout and a rum and black, says I.' Contracting his body again, he stared despondently at the floor. '*Blackcurrant man never come.*'

A hand was laid on my arm. It was Frances. I waited for her to speak but she simply jerked her head towards the door. Whatever her dark design, it could not be mentioned in public. I looked in her eyes – black, impenetrable, sybilline.

We went through the upper drawing room to the landing, but even in private Frances preferred to sustain the mystery. The face she turned to me was a bronze mask, inscrutable as Fate. 'I need a drink first' was all she would say.

Taking my hand (a tender dominatrice, most exquisite of oxymorons, most delightful of all the absurd and inconsistent fantasies), she led me downstairs to the kitchen and the big table laden with half-empty bottles. Solemnly we poured gins and touched glasses, regarding each other over the rims.

Unlike most of the women present she had not spoiled her looks with ornate special effects. Her wavy hair still enjoyed the freedom of the shaggy look and her female-executive suit, whilst expensive and well cut, retained some distant link with utilitarianism and the quotidian. Nowadays she was running the administrative side of Sean's building firm and the suit was most likely for meetings with clients and government bodies, at which she was incomparably more effective than her husband had been. Like Reba before her she had discovered the female cocktail that was devastating in male Ireland: a sophisticated Parisian elegance combined with language you wouldn't lift on a shovel.

'That fucker Hugo went for me in the bathroom.'

She sipped her drink with a shrug of detachment, even transcendence. 'Families.'

'He fucking *attacked me*,' I repeated, not above playing the child with the cut finger at times.

'I had a long talk with him earlier.' There was sympathy in her tone – but for the tortured aggressor not the innocent victim. Frances was even more up-to-date than I had thought. 'His marriage is a total disaster. Nothing but fights all the time. They had a fight today and Rosemary took an asthma attack. She has about twenty physical problems. Including frigidity. Hugo told me they haven't had sex for a year.'

'Oh terrific. Wonderfully Irish. He can't get his hole so he attacks me instead.'

Just as I had given up on reaching her caring/nurturing instinct, Frances leaned across and placed on my lips a kiss of surpassing tenderness.

Dominance and compassion! Power and tenderness! Order and warmth! Setting down her drink, she fell upon me with a ravening, despoiling mouth. I seized her with my free hand, not so much out of passion as to prevent her pitching me into the bottles like a skittle ball. Her bolero jacket was short and tailored to sit out from her back. My hand went under it to feel a silk blouse and taut strap, support for the warm freight I felt on my breast. An exquisite wash of discreet scent went over me. Sophistication, warmth, abundance, fragrance, power, and firm control.

Released, I looked at her and experienced a familiar vertigo – as when, after prolonged scrutiny of the bottom shelf in a bookshop, one suddenly straightens up for something recalled in the top row.

'Isn't that the wrong sister?'

McKenna. Frances took control at once. 'What's it to you?' He laughed knowingly. 'And where's your own wife, come to that? Haven't you a new young wife?'

McKenna laughed again. 'Let me tell you a story. These two bulls go out for a walk, an old bull and a young bull. They come to the top of a hill and see this beautiful green valley and a herd of plump young cows. *Christ!* the young bull shouts, tears off down the hill, screws the first cow it meets and falls down in a heap.' McKenna massaged his beard, regarding Frances with foxy eyes. 'Then the old bull walks down the hill and screws the whole herd.'

Grimacing as though in pain, Frances turned her head wildly to the dark night for succour. 'Was that supposed to be a *joke* or something?'

Dropping the banter, McKenna seized her arm and backed towards a chair. 'Come and sit on my knee.'

Frances, a model executive, was not only a negotiator and counsellor but a fit and agile squash champ. '*Lay off!*' She freed her hand

and pushed him back. 'I don't sit on knees.' Then she glanced down at his bulk with shockingly naked disgust. 'And how could anyone even if they wanted to with a belly like that?'

His eyes stationary and void, McKenna dropped heavily into a chair. It was what assassins describe admiringly as a 'no-reflex kill'.

Of course Madge had softened him up first – but even so. This was a man of stature and assurance, internationally revered. Frances coolly sipped her gin. Dig that hubris. No mere Andalusian insouciance, this was something more powerful from much further back. Beneath the executive-woman suit was a brazen Irish warrior queen.

I would have been happy to dance around McKenna's corpse but Frances led me off on the final stage of our journey, through the darkened back end of the house to a tiny pantry off at an angle and down several steps. It was certainly a magically secret place. We paused at the door to embrace and I experienced the strange debility said to steal over Gaels at the approach of the prodigious Queen Maeve.

Frances flung open the door. Sean and Reba hunched like furtive animals. I thought it was sex we had interrupted – until I saw the tray of smoked salmon. It was simply the servants pillaging. Frances had called me to share in the spoils.

Not a queen after all but a slave. Not the tradition of the Celtic warrior but that of the thieving Irish gyppo.

I don't even care for smoked salmon that much.

Her eyes shining with fulfilment and surcease, Frances lifted a slab onto a plate and held it out. 'It's absolutely gorgeous,' she breathed.

The arc broke, pattering, and steam rose from the glistening leaves of what estate agents call 'mature' shrubs. Better than whistling in the dark is peeing in the dark, an act not of fear but of affirmation and even defiance, briefly aiming the hot rank jet at the indifferent vault of the stars.

Even this moment of convivial autonomy was not to be

permitted without interruption. A figure came running from the house. I recognised John Herron: more family trouble no doubt. But instead of approaching he veered off and, flinging himself against a tree, violently spewed onto its base. John Herron, only begetter of all our troubles. If he had not invited me to chess all those years ago, none of this would be happening. Now he was sightless and vulnerable. I could kick him to death with impunity.

But someone else was approaching from the house. This was Caroline – sober, measured, righteous, *terrible* – advancing on her husband with calm purposeful steps. 'Nothing would do you but brandy,' she cried in violent sing-song distaste.

Without lifting his head, John groaned and extended an arm in desperate supplication.

Neatly sidestepping, Caroline peered intently into his mess. '*See!*' she cried in furious triumph. 'I told you you never chew your food.'

I penetrated further into the garden. Something stirred. Not a crazed intruder – I saw a cigarette glow. Another solitary – dark-suited, grave of mien.

'Jesus, Kyle. I thought you'd left long ago.'

'That was the plan.'

Even in my muddled condition the explanation seemed obvious. 'You haven't had a row already.'

'No no no no no.' Taking a packet from his suit trousers, Kyle lit a fresh cigarette from the one in his mouth. Then he offered the packet.

'Don't smoke.'

'They gave us this bedroom to change in. But Liz fell asleep and I couldn't get her to wake up.'

'I know how you feel. But free drink *plus* topping up. It's the Doomsday scenario, Kyle.'

'But on our wedding day . . .' His cigarette traced a vague, inconclusive arc.

'Impossible after a feed of drink.'

'With a little effort and good will you can win through to ecstasy in spite of the drink. We often have in the past.'

'So what happened this time?'

'She took one look at my prick and fell fast asleep.'

He didn't sound as though he was trying to be funny – but I laughed just the same. 'The most famous prick in Irish fiction.'

Even in this sensitive area Kyle was obliged to be frank. 'No no no,' he sighed. 'I have a very small penis really.'

In the silence that followed, he enjoyed a long, voluptuous, ruminating draw on his fag.

'Why don't you go back to the party?' I asked.

'Too much like a journalists' convention.'

He was suffering that extreme form of alienation best described as Gatsby Syndrome – the feeling of being not merely an outcast from the feast but an outcast from your *own* feast.

'I think Madge invited a lot of these people. What's become of Madge by the way?'

'Locked up in a bedroom.'

Internment without trial. The Fenian as eternal victim!

'For her own safety,' Kyle added. 'She fell down the stairs twice. Didn't seem at all concerned but it was felt she could do herself an injury.' He paused. 'So Liz was asleep in the main bedroom, Madge was next door . . . and that young wife . . .'

'Rosemary?'

'She was in another room having some sort of fit or seizure. But wouldn't open the door to anyone. I think the family here are getting alarmed. Downstairs is producing a lot of casualties and they're running out of rooms upstairs.'

The ultimate Protestant nightmare: being overrun by Fenian gyppos. For me, compassion had long since replaced resentment at the privileged lives of our hosts. In fact if they remained humanist after the party, I would have to consider conversion myself.

'Had enough of Fenians, Kyle?'

'I certainly needed a break.' He flicked ash into the shrubbery with seigneurial negligence. 'But of course only to return with renewed understanding and tolerance.'

As though in response there was an outburst of cheering from

Humanist House.

'Sidney Grey must be standing on his head again.' I was not referring to flights of paradoxical logic. Before I left, Sidney, a respected senior figure in local television, had actually stood on his head in the drawing room, keys and change spilling out onto the shag pile.

'You mean there are Prods left?' Kyle enquired in mock wonder.

'Your son's certainly going strong.'

Always a mistake to mention family. Kyle's frail insouciance was strangled at birth. 'Actually *he's* been a problem today as well. Aggressive and embittered. He said to me, *you're up in the clouds and I'm down in the gutter.* Both of which are manifestly untrue. He may be annoyed because I didn't see him in the States this year. I kept putting it off . . . thought there was plenty of time . . . at one point it looked as though I'd be staying on out there . . .'

'Extra teaching?'

'I met someone.'

Above us, the glittering void. All around, the campfires of mad tribes. Before us, mature shrubs. Underfoot, a trim lawn.

'But I made the decision to come back and settle with Liz.'

Silence, stasis, solemnity, bulk – dark shrubs presented us with the very essence of the mature.

'I'm sure Liz is right for me . . . a remarkable girl.'

Pitiless morning light, already in secure possession of the room. Though this was not what had wakened me. Involuntary love cries from upper floors can be almost unbearably poignant – but these raucous sounds smacked of showmanship and theatre. It had to be Madge and the criminal playwright she met at the wedding. Naturally Madge was a shouter and, from the sound of it, her lover had not been to Pussy Heaven since doing his time.

A sense of shame, bitter as gall, overcame me. Of the long glorious day nothing remained but fragments and snatches. Haziest of all, our bizarre return through the Protestant heartland in a taxi. Though I remembered being stopped on a lonely road by an Ulster

Defence Regiment patrol. The occupants of the overcrowded taxi were highly amused by the questioning. The patrol less so. We were asked to get out, in the course of doing which Reba ripped the leg out of her silk trouser suit. Immediately she started shouting at the soldiers. Madge joined in and the criminal backed her up in a strong southern accent. Hubris is often wonderful fun, but this was insanity. What probably saved us was the fact that the taxi driver was a Protestant. He mediated beautifully, placating the soldiers with one hand and shoving the harpies back into the car with the other.

Of the long wedding day itself little remained. Not only had I missed most of the company, I could remember practically nothing of the encounters that did take place. Whether or not it had been an Irish wedding I had certainly been an Irish guest: boorish, immoderate, drunken and loud. Not an outcast from the feast, merely too stupefied to partake. Certainly its like would never be seen again. Gatsby's last party was over. Winter was coming on.

Madge burst into the room, wrapped in a blanket. 'Have ye a fag? Jesus Ahm desperate for a fag.'

'Don't smoke, Madge.'

'*Fuck!*' So violent was the oath that Reba stirred and raised her head.

'Why are you up at this hour, Madge?'

'Oh I had a grand sleep.' She laughed. 'Sure didn't Ah tell ye last night. After Ah fell down the stairs there was a citizen's arrest. Ah was locked in a bedroom for most of the day.' Already it was a proud anecdote – the woman they had to chain up. Unafflicted by remorse, Madge laughed so uproariously that the blanket slipped to her waist. '*Whoops!*' Without haste she restored it. 'Reba, ye wouldn't have a fag at all. Kevin and me's *dyin'*.'

Reba shook a bleary head and Madge turned to go, then came back. 'Oh aye – can we borrow your car for a couple of days? Kevin and me's going to Donegal. He's never seen Donegal.'

'How are we supposed to get back to Dublin, Madge?'

'Sure stay here a few days. The crack's great.'

'I'm teaching this afternoon.'

At the thought of the long frantic drive a new and more terrible emptiness overcame me – hunger. Reba groaned and tried to pull me under the covers. I rose and dressed, shuddering a little at the crumpled Martini Terrace jacket.

Several sleepers were curled up in the living room (I had a blurred memory of dancing there) but the kitchen was empty. Empty of food as well as of people. No cereal or bread, not even coffee or tea bags. Only, sitting on top of the cooker, a gigantic vat full to the brim with kidney beans.

One of the sleepers rose and came drowsily down the steps. It was a girl I remembered dancing with the night before.

'Why the beans?'

'Madge was supposed to be doing salads for the wedding.'

'And the pot?'

'Belongs to one of Kyle's daughters. It's a catering thing.'

Now the most terrible loss of all overwhelmed me. Out of the fog of the long day came an image that was almost unbearably vivid and sharp: my beautifully garnished Chateaubriand taken away untouched. The phone rang in the hall. Someone came downstairs and took it.

Life strews its bounty and we scarcely take heed. Or not until too late. A survivor of Auschwitz has described a similar agony of remorse. All through his time in the camp a youth was tormented by a single memory: his refusal of a third helping of bean soup at a wedding. Imagine how the youth would have felt if he had refused the main course.

How long would it be before I ate? There was barely time to drive to Dublin for an afternoon of teaching. Reba would have to buy food and cook a big evening meal.

She came in from the phone, her face mottled and dark.

'*What'd you fuckin' say to my mother?*'

7

Stephanie of Monaco poolside with Delon Junior ('dans les bras d'Anthony Delon'), Belmondo Junior sick as a Skegness donkey ('C'est la fin de son amour avec Paul Belmondo?'), the magazines show beach life continuing, heady and narcissistic and frivolous – but we have left the scene to head north for Illiers, the fictional Combray of Proust, with whom I am in profound agreement on the subject of sun worship: 'Happiness numbed with cold, hunching its shoulders, shrinking into its core, is for me the most intense of all.' Joyce was less poetic but more terse: 'I hate a damn silly sun that makes men into butter.'

The company would not agree. We are with Sean and Frances and their children, eight of us crammed into Sean's battered van (from which he has at least removed his Kango hammer and drill, though not his nodding dog or sticker: IRISH BUILDERS MAKE IT LAST).

Originally we had arranged to go with Kyle and Liz. A villa on the south coast had been booked for two weeks and Kyle had arranged for us to stay with his northern French relatives on the way there and back. Then an Irish-American organisation, the Friendly Sons of Saint Patrick, invited Kyle and his wife on an all-expenses-paid trip to New York where they would be put up in a luxury hotel and generally looked after for the duration. Kyle could only assume that this was a reward for his pro-Catholic stance and was sheepish about accepting, especially in view of his commitment to us. Liz not only had no such scruples but she also added David to the guest list. Their replacements were Sean and Frances, in return for which I insisted on stopping in Illiers on the way home. Does not the spirit need pampering as well as the flesh?

The first snag is the French autoroute, which resembles so many of our avenues in life: a cinch to get onto but a bitch to get off.

There is no exit for Illiers and we end up twenty kilometres on in Chartres.

'Christ,' Frances cries. 'We're nearly in Paris. We could have spent the night in Paris.'

The complaint is immediately taken up by an adolescent in the back. 'Can we not go to Paris, Mam? Can't we go on to Paris?'

We turn south again, receive incomprehensible directions – and find ourselves back on the autoroute. Sean grinds his teeth at the approach of another toll. I frantically dig out francs. For the second time we pass within sight of the village. Then thirty kilometres to the *sortie* we missed first time and ten more back on bad country roads.

At last a welcome sight: our auberge.

'We'll stop here first,' Sean sighs.

It kills me to say it, but I have no choice. 'The Proust house closes at five.'

We make Illiers by four thirty. But it is far from the pretty village I have promised the others and myself. Instead, there is an ugly run-down Irish-style huddle of streets. Once again the shock of the ordinary and the bitterness of disillusion ('Desire makes all things flourish, possession withers them; it is better to dream one's life than to live it').

'Jesus!' Frances cries. 'Aughnacloy.'

Sean regards this as an insult to the Irish village. 'Aughnacloy has a Chinese restaurant now.'

I suggest that the air of desolation is due to the August holidays.

'Aye,' Sean says with grim irony. 'Ahm sure it's a great wee town on a Saturday night.'

According to the guide book the Proust house is open till five. And indeed we arrive to find the door open and a party being ushered out.

The last party. Sourly and grimly an old biddy clutching keys closes the door.

'Mais je suis venu d'Irlande . . . specialement . . .'

'Non.'

'Dix minutes.'

As implacable as de Gaulle on British entry to Europe. 'Non.'

No guides, maps or souvenirs, no posters of soulful Marcel to hang over the desk. She swings the door and hefts the keys.

'Cinq minutes . . . moi seulement . . .'

'Non.' The door slammed and locked this time.

Reba touches my arm. 'Come back in the morning.'

'It only opens in the afternoon.'

Leaving me with my grief she returns to the main square and the others. After a few moments of numbness and nullity I go around to the back to find the bedroom window from which Marcel tossed off onto the lilac tree. Needless to say, it cannot be seen from the street ('The traveller, that fond lover doomed to eternal disappointment').

At least the church of Saint Jacques is open. I explain to Reba that in the book this is Saint-Hilaire, where the young Marcel first sees, in the light of the stained-glass windows, the magnificent Duchesse de Guermantes, in real life the widow of Bizet, composer of *Carmen*. Looking out over the square, Reba listens while I try to establish a connection between her (tempestuous Carmen) and me (sickly, bookish Marcel).

'Is there not even a café open?' she suddenly calls out. Sean and Frances, prowling the perimeter, shrug in helpless disgust.

What am I doing in the company of such philistines? Kyle and Liz would have shown some interest at least. And all at once the thought of them touring Manhattan, of which I have dreamed all my life as Proust dreamed of Venice, is like a blade of cold steel in my spongy flawed heart.

Dear Frightened Fenian

In the rush of getting organised for the States I failed to question your strange decision to opt out of staying with my French relatives. Surely the fact of my not being with you is irrelevant? I speak practically no French, as you know. These are people of good will and you could still arrange a visit or even drop in unannounced. Most of the rest of the world is more adaptable than you. Why are you so terrified of life?

The equivalent exercise, my stay with Liz's uncles in the States, has been full of unexpected rewards and insights although of course I don't see eye to eye with them on many things. They're two fairly sad creatures despite their affluence. A lifetime of working their way up, bartending, then managing bars, then renting bars, then buying small bars and finally these enormous roadhouses outside New York, and yet all they seem to care about is Galway. All they live for is the annual three weeks in Ireland when they apparently spend their time standing around in yet more bars buying people drink. Their own roadhouses serve splendid American feasts like surf-'n'-turf (steak with prawns) but when they heard Liz and I were coming they asked her to bring two pounds of Irish pork sausages and a bag of steeping peas. This will be kept in the freezer for Thanksgiving dinner.

Both have been here over thirty years, all their adult lives, but without developing any interest in American life or culture. When I asked if you could still take the A-train to Harlem they were horrified. Why would anyone want to go to Harlem? Why would anyone want to go *anywhere* by subway? I had to point out that the popular music of the world in our century is entirely derived from the American negro and that Duke Ellington is a composer the equal of any. Liz was not too pleased with me on this. Like yourself she is always urging me not to confront people's prejudice.

But the uncles are always affable. Certainly very generous with the whiskey. And apparently willing to tolerate a certain amount of eccentricity in view of the way I have been honoured. Anyone all right with the Friendly Sons of Saint Patrick is all right with them.

That was a memorable few days with the Friendly Sons. I suspect that the much-vaunted Friendliness is limited to

Catholic or pro-Catholic whites but if you qualify, the generosity is certainly impressive. I did a reading in the Cuchulainn Room at An Claidheamh Soluis, a New York Irish centre whose name I happily understood from our visit to the Pearse Museum and when I tried to buy *Padraig Pearse – the Triumph of Failure* at the bookstall I was told there was no question of handing over money.

I've been wanting to read something on Pearse ever since our trip to the museum. I felt you were trying to be incredibly knowing and sophisticated that day and push me into accepting Pearse as some sort of repressed Catholic eejit obsessed with Gaelic sports and Celtic myths. Why could you not let me make up my own mind? It's not the first time I've noticed this urge to forestall criticism by getting in with your own first. Another of your phobias: neurotic fear of being thought a hick.

The biography is very anti Pearse so you have to scrutinise everything for opinions or loaded statements but even here the man's positive side comes out. In spite of all your sneering about Irish warriors and hurley sticks he seems to have had some good ideas on education. 'I interested a few friends in the project of a school which should aim at the making of good men rather than learned men.' And he sounds even more like me when he says that teachers should not be 'the rejected of all other professions' but 'the highest souls and noblest intellects of the race'. Am I not the perfect embodiment of his dream? And he has the measure of a certain kind of teacher like yourself. 'Many teachers fail because instead of endeavouring to raise themselves to the level of their pupils they endeavour to bring their pupils down to theirs.'

What an oddity U R. What an oddity U B. I think U may not B the 1 4 me.

But isn't there something wonderful in the idea of an Ulster Prod trying to sell Pearse to a Fenian? A thing whose like has never been seen. Life is full of these unique and unpredictable moments.

So does one not have to insist on being happy? Demand from one's self a positive attitude to the wonderful things that turn up?

Liz has been taking me round her old haunts, where she says she spent some of the happiest days of her life. What a wonderfully courageous girl she was and is. But nowadays she seems much more fearful about travelling in America. I have been explaining that to cultivate trust and sang-froid saves light years of trouble and worry and you seldom get ripped off. The only time I was robbed over here was when my ex-wife (the American one) got her new lover to climb in the back window of the apartment and steal my speakers. I only discovered this when I sat down to play an Ink Spots record and nothing came out. Thought I'd gone deaf until I saw the gaps on the shelves. An unalarming intimate sort of theft, inspired by love of music I hope.

How does your knowingness go with an inability to talk to people? Visit my French relatives and awaken them to the joys of Proust.

Live with a little more courage and dash.

Love

Kyle

The auberge is heartbreakingly cute, weathered old stone sumptuously gift-wrapped in ivy and garnished with an ornamental pond surrounded by white wrought-iron tables and chairs and a refurbished cart that is filled with flowering plants and picturesquely leaning on its shafts. A perfect setting for the cocktail hour though the tables are unoccupied, perhaps because of the three Doberman pinschers roaming the grounds.

'It's gorgeous!' the girls cry, but Sean reveals a Proustian scepticism.

'A fuckin' rip-off joint if Ah ever saw one.'

We are greeted by a *madame* glittering with tasteful ornamentation and flashing a smile as far from its original function as the prettified cart by the pond. As soon as I mention Proust she takes me to her office and produces *Le Parfum de Combray*, a hefty guide to Proustian Illiers which she proffers with another smile, enquiring pleasantly if we intend to stay long. Reaching out, I shrug helplessly. One could linger for ever on such hallowed ground – but with a family, travelling companions, the demands of this frenetic world . . .

'Une nuit,' she repeats, still smiling, but with the book stalled in mid-air.

'Une nuit,' I regretfully shrug.

'Ah,' she says, hefting the guide as though suddenly aware of its weight. 'C'est beaucoup pour une nuit . . . n'est-ce pas?' With a merry laugh she returns it to her desk.

In the corridor Sean is perusing the menu with a lack of rapture apparently lost on *madame*.

'Vous mangez ici?' she asks, subjecting him to full-frontal radiance.

He ignores her to scowl at me. 'It's a rip-off. Say ye don't know.'

I give her yet another helpless shrug, this one accompanied by a smile of apology sweet enough to disarm the most imperious and avid. She goes back into the office and slams the door.

Body language that needs no translation. Nevertheless I offer one to Sean. 'Not a happy lady.'

'Fuck her,' he growls. 'We'll drive round and see the score.'

Incroyable! My few brief hours in Illiers are to be spent driving round in a builder's van looking at menus. Sean goes off to inform Frances and I take my burning grievance up to Reba in the bedroom.

'*Christ!*' I shout. 'I have only a few hours here and he expects me to run around looking at menus.' Reba is concentrating on an open case laid on the bed. I have to go right up and shout in her face. 'Well I'm *not* going. I'm eating here . . . all right?'

'Keep your voice down,' Reba says grimly, taking my arm with a calm firmness suggesting, incredibly, moral superiority. 'Come here a minute.'

On the wall of the landing is a prominent notice:

SILENCE!

Guide d'Hôtels Silencieux

Beneath the title are several paragraphs describing the formation and growth of an association of hoteliers dedicated to maintaining oases of silence in our increasingly noisy world. At the bottom, on the dotted line, is the name of the auberge.

'When you were down with your woman,' Reba is saying, 'the kids were playing around and this character in a black suit . . .'

'The *maître d'.*'

'This comedian comes up and points to the kids and then to this sign. Then he stops and gives me this . . . look.'

Now I too am well and truly silenced. 'It was booked by post,' I sigh. 'The only hotel listed for this place . . . didn't know what it was like . . . had no choice . . .'

Reba grips my arm. 'When you're out with Sean *try* to be civil.'

Sean with only two weeks' holiday in the year. Sean who works like a dog only to be undone by fate. Sean whose beloved building firm is almost destroyed by recession.

'But guests aren't supposed to eat out. That bitch'll screw us if we go out.'

'How can she screw us?' Reba grimaces anew at my talent for worst-case scenarios. 'I mean, what can she do? We'll be gone in the morning. The price of the rooms is on the back of the door.'

Incredible hubris of the Herrons! They really believe they can tempt the Fates with impunity. No idea of potential disaster, the vindictive resolve of an implacable world.

For Kyle and Liz, the dream was a country house large enough for the kind of creative courses Kyle gave in England and the States. Despite the glory of its literary tradition and the unspoiled grandeur of its natural settings, Ireland as yet had nothing to offer in this line. The other essential ingredient was crowd-pulling tutors and here again they were on to a winner. Not only a star in his own right, Kyle was intimate with name performers on both sides of the Atlantic. As soon as he opened his doors famous tutors would flock to him, followed by cheque-waving tutees in droves.

Of course Altnagarvin would have been the ideal site and Kyle had long dreamed of saving the family home by such a scheme. The problem was always Olivia, who claimed that Kyle would swan about amusing the men and jazzing the women while she was left with the cooking, cleaning, admin et cetera. Liz had no such qualms. She knew that Kyle would never look at another woman and that no power on earth could turn her into a drudge.

They needed an idyllic setting close to an international airport. Also, since they could not afford a house big enough to accommodate students, there would have to be a nearby community capable of putting up guests. As for the house itself, it would have to have bags of character, large ground-floor rooms, and a large homely kitchen that preserved a traditional appearance while supporting all modern appliances.

The search began in the North and almost immediately threw up a magnificent old rectory not far from the airport that had begun as the splendid *Nutt's Corner*, then became the bland and tasteful *Aldergrove* and was now, in the age of neutral uniformity, *Belfast International Airport*. Kyle saw the house first; although the kitchen needed work, the price was reasonable and the setting perfect. Even better, the auctioneer had known Kyle's father and confided that the family was desperate to sell but that no one these days wanted big old houses so they could very likely get it for a song. Everything was fine until the second viewing, when the auctioneer was introduced to Liz in a southern-registered car. Fondly intending to ask all the questions, she found herself being interviewed instead. She would be living in Dublin, would she? Yes. And what would she be doing there? Aha. And for what newspapers? All this in a leisurely, unembarrassed way and when none of it was conclusive the key question in the same relaxed tone:

'So what denomination would ye be at all at all?'

Liz, naïve until now, shrieked with laughter and Kyle came in firmly to put a stop to this nonsense. 'We're both ecumenical Christians.'

'Aye.' This to Kyle with leisurely scorn, like a headmaster dismissing a feeble schoolboy cover-up. 'But what was she before?'

'Listen,' Kyle said, dropping the last pretence of friendliness. 'Are you selling this house as an auctioneer . . . or as a Protestant?'

It was the full shining armour of moral authority. Any mainland Brit would have cringed at such a brutal exposure of bigotry – but shame requires some awareness of liberal values. Secure and untroubled, the heartland has no fear of censure.

'Och now,' he said, grinning, a hand on Kyle's arm, 'it's a wee bit of both.' Not just unashamed, the man expected them to be amused at his candour.

It was at this point that I had to break into the story. 'Why didn't you throw the old cunt out of a top-floor window?'

But Kyle and Liz were amused. It was folklore, an anecdote. The incident did not touch them in any serious way.

They did, though, switch the search to Galway, which had many advantages: it was untarnished by the northern disorder, close enough to Shannon airport for the Americans, close enough to Yeats country for spin-off from the summer school. And as it was in the South, Liz had Dublin contacts who would help with grants, publicity, tax relief et cetera.

On the spot was her Uncle Tony, from whom they heard of a fine old farmhouse going for a song because the adjoining land and outhouses had been sold separately. A disadvantage was the lack of neighbours for B and B but the house more than compensated, an absolute honey in old stone with its own tiny orchard and birch wood.

Both Tony and Kyle were impressed by the trees, although for entirely different reasons.

'Jaysus ye'd never need to buy coal,' Tony muttered fervently.

Deep in a fantasy of reverent students strolling with magisterial tutors, like Boileau and Madame de Sévigné on the Avenue des

Philosophes at Chantilly palace, Kyle failed to see the relevance of the comment. 'Why not?'

'Why not? Look at those trees. Ye'd have enough blocks to last ye a lifetime, look see.'

Where the aristo pictured graciousness the peasant saw fuel.

The price was low and the offer, though on Tony's advice lower still, was accepted. Planning began at once – but when Kyle and Liz were measuring up a bedroom they saw from a window a heavy man in gumboots drag a sheep from a shed, straddle it, and in one fluid movement shoot it in the back of the head with a bolt gun and cut its throat with a butcher knife. The building next door was a slaughterhouse. Familiar with rural brutality from the poems of McKenna and Heaney, would the tutees accept this as authentic contemporary pastoral? In any case it could be seen from the upper floor only and no doubt the proprietor could be prevailed upon to keep the slaughter indoors. Kyle attempted to do so and was ordered 'out ta fuck'. Apparently this no-nonsense Catholic butcher wanted the house to remain empty so his slaughter wagons could monopolise the narrow shared laneway. On their next visit a load of intestines had been dumped just across the fence, well within sight and smell of the ground floor.

'We just turned around and left.' Liz, finishing the story, shrieked with laughter. 'But of course we'd been counting on the bedroom. So on the way back we just drove into this field and pulled the clothes off each other.'

After half an hour of driving round, Sean and I find a dingy hotel by the station where the Proust family must have arrived with their baggage and servants. Now station, street and hotel are deserted and silent – not the self-imposed sacred hush of a Hôtel Silencieux but the sullen, embittered silence of the rejected, the passed over, the fallen from grace.

'This hotel can't be full,' accuses Sean. 'And it would have done us rightly. Cheaper than the other place and in the town as well.'

'It wasn't in the book,' I explain. 'I had no way of knowing it was here.'

The menu is cheap and adequate. We place a booking with a morose *patron* who displays no sign of pleasure or gratitude. At least the search has not taken too long, but before I can speak Sean has ordered two beers.

Of course I should have known. All through the holiday we have been playing this game, Sean attempting to drink at every opportunity and I as persistently attempting to thwart him. Something about the guy always drives me to the negative joys of perversity and mischief. In his company, as with many of my compatriots nowadays, I find that the profoundest intoxication is that of going to bed sober.

To resist or not? *Try to be civil.*

Incredibly, I have to drink and piss away my time beneath the sorrowful eyes of Proust himself on the wall. Marcel complained about the deadening effect of habit, but he had only self-imposed routine to contend with. What if he had had to endure its monstrously reinforced social forms of ritual and convention? For instance, the rapture-inducing group rite of holiday afternoon boozing.

Time, the grieving eyes say, *time, time, time, time.*

Sean follows my gaze. 'Cheerful fucker.'

'Barrel of laughs.'

It is the early orchid portrait by Jacques-Émile Blanche. Formal and lifeless in the past, it now speaks to me with passion and eloquence: 'I believe it would still be possible to get well if it were not for *les autres*. But the exhaustion they bring about, one's helplessness at making them understand the suffering – sometimes lasting a month – that follows the foolhardiness one has committed for what they imagine to be a great pleasure: *all that is death.*'

And now I am subject to that most inflexible and binding of all cultural imperatives, the need to be not a bit slow with your round. Sean drains his glass with a meaningful sigh – but it is now or never for my pilgrimage ('that grain of poetry indispensable to existence'). I rise and inform him that I must see the village before dark. Overworked and persecuted, stranded with an idiot in a dead town, his holiday rapidly ebbing away, Sean is forced to resort to an abandoned evening newspaper in a foreign language. He opens *France Soir* with a defiant flourish, even a paper he cannot read better company than a crank.

'Pick ye up at the church at eight.'

Yet one hour of freedom and joy! In spite of everything I feel the excitement of expectation, the lure of rich and meaningful alternative realities. Even as a child I was a Proustian. In the pungent dark of the Palace the trailers always appeared more interesting than the film I had just paid to see. Desire makes all things flourish; possession withers them. I could have sat through a programme of trailers alone.

At the street map in the square I memorise the Itinéraire Proustien, then immediately take a wrong turn. *Peu importe*, or as we say in Ireland, matter-a-fuck. It was youth, Proust's youth, that invested certain streets with magic. Youth enchants everything; adults have to wrest significance from the world. For me one dingy lane is as good as another.

By keeping to downhill streets I arrive at the stream and the footbridge that leads to the site of the famous hawthorns. No hawthorns – or none that I can recognise – but the road to Tansonville stretches out, deserted and enticing, cornfields on either side, just as it must have looked on the Proust family walks.

But how can an hour have gone by already? If time goes at such a pace here no wonder Marcel complained.

On my way back uphill to the square a heavy vehicle rounds the sharp corner just ahead. *What reckless mortal seeks my death?* Braking abruptly, Sean opens the door and waves the evening paper open at an inside page: RICHARD BURTON EST MORT.

'Uhn?' he grunts angrily, as though the death is another consequence of my obsession, this insane quest for high culture killing off mainstream entertainment all over the world.

But it is not Sean's attitude that gives me a moment of vertigo. This is brought about by a sudden premonition: blinding overhead light, a masked face and a gloved hand producing a scalpel that blazes with purity and zeal.

'What did he die of?'

'See for yourself.' Sean hands me the paper. 'Heart attack, I think.'

We had never taken out essential health insurance in the South. Why waste the money when we were young and strong? But after a series of steep bills when the children needed hospital tests we had decided to call in the insurance man. A medical was required, a mere formality of course. The doctor took my pulse, grunted, took it again, was silent for what seemed an eternity. An irregular heartbeat, he announced at last. *Sky-high premiums* was my first response, rather than any thought of illness or treatment. Then he mentioned the word 'specialist' and all at once Dublin lost its charm. I wanted to be heavily sedated, then rushed out to a waiting car and driven north to the UK and the National Health Service.

The problem was microstenosis, a faulty heart valve, the valve probably damaged by rheumatic fever in youth. I could have had rheumatic fever without knowing it, the specialist explained, causing in me a surge of murderous hatred for my mother and Aunt Lily. To have suffered obsessive fear without its only benefit, protection. A childhood of fanatical warnings and prohibitions (about knocks on the head, cold stone, wet grass, sharing my sandwiches, the swimming baths) and right under their noses was what they feared most: 'somethin' that'll come back on ye in later life'.

The specialist recommended the National Heart Hospital in London. For free treatment I had to consult my old family GP in the North, pretend to be still resident there (though without actually mentioning this) and request a referral. He wanted to send me to the Royal Victoria in Belfast. Certainly Ulster Prods imbued with the work ethic were more reassuring than hearty southern Catholic clubmen – but state-of-the-art English know-how was more attractive than either.

Having imagined a vast high-tech complex in perfectly manicured grounds, I was shocked to find that the National Heart

Hospital was two small and nondescript mismatching pieces, one Victorian and one newish, stuck together and forming part of a dingy inner-city street. In fact, the new part resembled my Dublin college: unattractive postwar modernism ageing ungracefully. Here was an outpatients department like the wages office in an Ulster shirt factory. It was clear that I was not to be spared the unsightly. The waiting room was full of grey-faced old wheezers wearing jackets over naked torsos hideously marked by huge vertical scars from throat to stomach. This was our resting place on the Stations of the Cross: ECG, X-ray, sonic scan, examination. For each it was necessary to strip to the waist, but in between the nurses allowed at least a partial cover-up: 'You may put your jacket back on if you wish.'

Waiting was devoted to silent meditation, but I was unusual enough for a blue-faced old cockney to waste a little of his hard-won breath. 'Bit young for a dodgy strawberry, mate?'

I could scarcely have agreed more, but it was not a matter of choice. Before we could investigate the injustice he was called for his ECG and I went in for an examination that confirmed the original diagnosis: a damaged heart valve, probably requiring surgery within a few years.

'Risky surgery?'

Instead of upper-class English conviction, socially vile but reassuring in a consultant, I had a scruffy young Scottish doctor who cheerfully admitted to partial knowledge. 'Who knows?' He shrugged.

Goddam it, I didn't want honesty. It was reassurance I needed. I wanted to be daddied.

'There's always a risk,' he added helpfully at last.

So the best I could hope for was a scar like the old wrecks, and before that to be sliced open, with soft innards spilling, like a cooking tomato. Not an easy thing to assimilate. We know that all good things must come to an end – but it is a nasty shock to discover that mediocrity is also finite.

Across the street was the King's Head, a dainty little London pub.

The Dodgy Strawberry would have been a more appropriate name. Not that I wanted alcohol. Consumption of drink would have to be curtailed. Ditto for almost every other pleasure in life. ('What about sex?' I asked – and he laughed. The bastard laughed. 'No problem – within reason.') What attracted me was the English pub menu. The time for dilettantism was over. I needed hearty traditional fare.

'While you've your health you've everything,' my mother used to say, so often that I took it up as a mocking catch phrase. Here is another chilling fact that lies in ambush for youth: the sayings you thought were a joke and applied to fools are not amusing at all and apply to you.

After steak-and-kidney pie I had apple crumble and custard. Then coffee – and another coffee. How cosy pubs can be! Even the noise was comforting, a kind of warm human surf. But the lunch-hour crowd thinned out and all too soon it was closing time. Nothing for it but the street.

You may put your jacket back on if you wish.

Careful budgeting is necessary if we are to afford a wine lake to take home and a *déjeuner sur l'herbe* en route. With the carelessness so typical of males, I obsessed with literature and Sean with drink, we forgot to check if the Hôtel de la Gare had a children's menu. It does not and the children's refusal to share meals will make the dinner almost as expensive as the auberge which, for all its faults, did have a children's rate. Many ingenious combinations are worked out and put to the younger members of the party. They refuse to share meals.

Yet among the *hors d'oeuvres* are frogs' legs, rare in cheap restaurants. Reba cries out in ecstasy. I opt for *pâté maison.*

'Aren't you having the frogs' legs?' she asks in a loud voice. 'Thought you always wanted to try them.' In her superior tone is an unmistakable imputation: that the only Francophile in the group is squeamish about the quintessential French delicacy.

'I'd love to try them, but you ordered first.' I should stop at this, but there are times when the truth will out at whatever cost. 'You *know* you never allow me to have the same course as you.'

Fair exchange: in return for an accusation of cowardice an accusation of bullying.

'For Christ's sake!' Reba shouts. 'That isn't true.'

'Why else would I not have them? You always make me have something different so you can try it. You'd be furious if I ordered the same.'

Reba glances about to establish her rational calm. 'Seems to me *you're* the furious one.'

When the starters arrive she tries to pass me the frogs' legs but of course I insist on the martyrdom of the *pâté*, which resembles the liver of a dead alcoholic.

One of the adolescents pushes hers away in disgust. I could hug her – until she takes up an old theme. 'Can we not stop in Paris tomorrow, Mam?'

At the expense of enormous effort Frances manages to stay calm. 'I've told you already. We have a boat to catch.'

Reba refrains from offering me a single *cuisse de grenouille*. Needless to say I would die sooner than ask.

Although we are the only diners, the main course takes for ever and is profoundly dull when it arrives. I refrain from pointing out the probable superiority of the auberge. In fact I refrain from speech altogether ('The children of silence should have no portion with the children of the word'). My communication is with the variously aged Marcel who stares down on us from all four walls of the dining room. Young or old, the eyes are full of sorrow.

'And old Dickie Burton's gone,' Sean sighs, affected at last by the morbid atmosphere.

'It's sad,' Reba readily agrees. To atone for her brutish husband she will take upon herself the burden of sustaining conversation.

Sean stares moodily into his wine. 'You know, the first picture Ah ever saw was Richard Burton in *The Robe*. The whole school was taken to it ... Ah suppose because it was a religious thing. In the Palace, that was. Ah mind it as well. It really was a palace to me.

Plush seats . . . the big velvet curtain . . . the gilt . . .'

As so often it is the violation of truth that goads me back into reluctant speech. 'The Palace was a dump. It stank of piss, there was a bald woman at the cash desk and the guy that took the tickets was a cripple with a club foot and a withered arm.' Contorting face and body, I crush my right arm against my side and extend an open hand to Sean by awkwardly advancing my entire body. Looking up, I seem to see Marcel's sorrow tempered by gratitude at this rare victory for unpalatable truth.

'That was the first picture in Cinemascope,' muses Sean, '*The Robe* . . .' He tosses off the last of the wine. 'Another bottle of this?'

But already the *patron* is morosely and noisily stacking chairs.

'He wants to close up,' Frances says.

'Fuck this for a geg. We'll have to have a few in the hotel.'

For once the auberge is on my side.

'Hôtel Silencieux?'

It was an isolated building on scrubland, a battered old hangar brought to brief summer life by a neon sign and the thunderous repetitions of contemporary dance music. In front, groups of slim dark youths bestrode the lightweight machines Sean dismissed as 'fuckin' egg-baters' or 'fartin' bikes'. We were parked across the street watching the arrival of patrons, all incredibly young: not just foreigners, creatures from another species, another galaxy.

'The average age is about twelve,' I said at last.

'Oh come off it.' Frances turned to smile over the back of the passenger seat. 'You're not old.'

An invitation not merely to a disco but to the Dance of Life itself. She would rip open my shirt – maybe even hold my dick. An offer strictly limited, hurry now while stocks last. Nevertheless I could not accept. It was too late for Club Med.

'Plus it'll be a rip-off,' I heard myself saying. 'There'll be a membership fee or some other stunt. The drink'll be astronomical.'

My crippled-insect posture was destroying the entire holiday. Yet I was powerless to stop it. Failure of self-esteem is the root of all evil.

All around us the void, cold as my flawed heart, black as a loyalist village.

Sean took off with a scream of tyres. When we got back to the holiday house, he and Frances headed silently for the stairs.

'What about a drink?' I suggested, a pathetically feeble concession that got the treatment it deserved. They went on without looking round.

And on the beach I could not participate in the ritual chasing and splashing and ducking. I sat on the sand with a book, fully dressed, as though already carved by the surgeon's knife. Not a mark on me but already behaving as though hideously disfigured.

One especially sunny day Reba urged me to take my shirt off and 'get a bit of colour'. It was a relaxed and propitious moment, near the end of the third litre of wine.

'Look,' I said. 'I'm not a beach boy. I'm having an operation soon and after that I'll be scarred.'

'What's wrong with scars?' Sean said. 'Ye can tell everybody ye were gored by a bull.'

'You haven't even got it yet,' Frances urged. 'And anyway no one worries about a scar.'

'Then how come you won't wear a bikini yourself? How come you only wear swimsuits?' Not merely destroying her insouciance, I was doing it with information imparted by Reba in strictest confidence. This is how it goes on the third litre. 'How come you can't let anyone see your stretch marks?'

Sean scowls at the dark and silent auberge. 'They'd never get away with this in Ireland. Fuck, we were doin' this job down the country an' stayin' in this hotel next to the site. Manager tries to close the bar at two in the mornin' . . . *two in the mornin'*. The boys keeked up fuck. Seamus Roddy was goin' tay tummle the hotel. Goin' tay demolish the whole fuckin' place. Went out and started this big JCB an' everythin' . . .' As though feeling a powerful machine throb beneath him, Sean lurches a little and has to regain his balance.

'What happened?'

'Seamus? He fell against the cab door an' knocked eesself out.' Burgeoning laughter is shushed by Frances. Sean glares malevolently about him. 'Jeesiss Ahd love to fuck that auld cart into the pond.' He turns to me. '*Eh?*'

This is mere teasing, motivated more by mischief than outrage. And the reason for his lack of concern is soon evident. Shooing the three adults into our room with much admonitory body language, he goes off with the children and returns alone with a bottle of wine and a corkscrew.

Once again he has outsmarted me. Irish builders make it last.

'Knew this dump'd be dead,' he explains. 'So Ah took the necessary precautions.' He draws the cork and flourishes the bottle. 'The night is but a pup.'

Climbing onto the bed beside Reba, he gallantly offers her first swig. 'Funny business, isn't it . . . ye know, the way women never go bald and men do.'

Reba's luxuriant black tresses would make any older man nostalgic. Or it could be the memory of the cashier at the Palace. Certainly there is a wistful acknowledgement of his own eventual fate. He has the signs, unmistakable to the fellow sufferer, of male-pattern alopecia in its early stages. Of course this may never be mentioned, despite his own brutal frankness in the matter. How sweet to chuckle comfortably to Sean as he did to me, 'Ah see you're losin'a few slates on top.'

'Hormones,' I tell him instead. 'Get castrated before puberty and your hair'll never fall out.' I stare pointedly at Reba. 'Prevents a lot of other problems as well.'

A dig about our scant physical intimacy over the fortnight. My unsociable behaviour has had an inevitable consequence. You have to frolic on the sand if you want to frolic between the sheets.

She takes a swift second belt of wine before passing the bottle to Frances, who drinks deeply and offers it to me with a renewed smile of invitation. I decline, having conceived a bold plan to rise early in the morning and strike out cross-country for Tansonville.

Her arm continues to offer the bottle while her brain grapples with this new refusal and her eyes search my face for an apology or explanation. Sean gets off the bed to relieve her of the bottle. Still looking at me, Frances utters the words more atrocious than a sentence of death to Irish ears.

'God there's no crack in you any more.'

'I suppose not. One day you wake up to find Madame Verdurin is the Duchesse de Guermantes.'

Sean the holiday boy nudges Reba. 'What's he on about?'

She studies me, renewing an old perplexity and sadness. 'How should I know?'

'You think you're too good for us, don't you?' Frances looks increasingly bitter and angry. 'That's the real reason. You never joined in anything this holiday. You've been withdrawn the whole time.'

'I'm fucking sick of crack,' I shout. 'I've had a lifetime of crack and I'm sick of it. I'm sick of pretending everything's a scream. It fucking well isn't a scream.'

My unexpected virulence has a calming effect.

'We all have our problems,' Frances says quietly.

'But not when you're around,' I sneer. 'No one's allowed to have problems round you. All you want is good-time people. Good-time people . . . and crack.'

She rises abruptly. 'Come on, Sean.'

Mr Club Med staggers upright, wits astray from the hammer blows of obscure and capricious destiny. Another hour's drive and he could have been in Paris, knocking back Pernod and *demies* in the Crazy Horse Saloon. Instead he is marooned with squabbling relatives in a stuffy hotel in the sticks. Uttering a confused churl grunt he half offers the bottle to Reba. Frances seizes him violently and points him to the door, turning to give me a look no longer so much angry as disappointed and hurt.

Bière! Cola! Gini! Schweppes! Orangina! North African hawkers pounded the beach with massive freezer boxes slung from their shoulders, their litany as immutable as our indifference and torpor. Then something came between us and the sun. It was Sean, back from his jog but with a more inflamed and excessive panting than was merited by exercise. As we squinted in irritation he astounded us by flagging down a hawker and buying a cold beer at a price far above that *à la terrasse* which in turn exceeded that at the bar which in turn . . . but you get the idea.

'The top end of the beach is nudist. Completely. All shapes and sizes and ages. Mixed doubles. Beach tennis.' He took a long swig of beer. 'Mixed volleyball.'

After lunch there was further astonishing expenditure. Sean enrolled all the children in the Club Micky, an outrageously expensive beach venture he had bitterly opposed till now.

The adults walked up the beach but when we paused at our usual spot Sean kept going. No one asked questions or even commented. In silence we traversed the buffer zone of partial nudity.

'You won't be able to keep your shirt on,' Reba muttered.

'Not planning to.'

I was more interested in Frances, who ploughed ahead with a grim expression. Was she doing this to give Sean an unforgettable touch of Club Med? If so she would make him pay. He would have another importunate creditor in the long nights after Samhain.

Instead of our usual beach formation, myself-Reba-Frances-Sean, we reorganised ourselves as Frances-Sean-yrs. tly.-Reba. A profoundly equivocal and disturbing experience, I found myself lying naked next to a naked Irish builder. Beyond her husband, Frances undressed with disapproving reluctance. I snatched a brief glance, devout and illicit, as when a child lifts a bowed head to watch a priest open the tabernacle at the consecration. And now I understood the wisdom of Destiny in substituting Frances for Liz. It was to vouchsafe me a glimpse of the third Herron beaver: extravagant, lustrous and charged, bristling with an energy and confidence that were yet only the outward manifestation of a true and secret power, like a busy military base above an underground silo. At once I was dazzled, humbled, fulfilled. This was the apotheosis of my love for the Herrons. Now my dodgy strawberry could fail and I would die replete.

She lay down in the sun but her body was not like those of the sun worshippers around us. Inferior, Frances herself seemed to suggest, with her awkward, brusque movements and poignant hunch of concealment. Foolish child of little faith. These burnished beach bodies were public and hence worthless and empty, mere images robbed of integrity and substance. The public realm nullifies all that ascends to it. Only the private has meaning. Only the private has value.

Never exposed to sun, her flesh was pale and even flabby in places, the breasts no longer firm, aureoles mahogany-dark from motherhood and sprouting a few vigorous hairs. It was indisputably private and real, charged with a terrible authenticity that would have torn a sob of compassion from a stone. And of course the stretch marks themselves, exquisite silvery striations like spirit trails in the ether.

Why have we banished ourselves from the paradise of the real? Even after a century, Degas is regarded as a misogynist for painting women as they are. I would love to extend the tradition with *The Stretchmark Paintings*, a series of sumptuous masterpieces to crown the early studies: *Woman Inserting a Tampon* and *Woman Peeing Herself Laughing*.

Sometimes the need for expression is as mordant and imperious as a bodily function. I understood the frustration of the mystic, overflowing with tumultuous but ineffable emotion. I wanted at least to take Frances by the hand and communicate my gratitude by an ardent squeeze. Sensing an imminence, a quickening, Reba warned me with a look. No doubt she thought I was about to make a cheap joke. Even after all these years she has failed to comprehend the religious side of my nature.

Exalted and pure as a youthful priest newly ordained, all I wanted now was for High Mass to continue, organ resounding as voices filled the vault of the cathedral with joyful hosannas. I don't believe I even had to turn on my stomach to conceal a hard-on.

It was a profoundly spiritual moment.

A troubled night haunted by an ancient dilemma: to yield to *les autres* or insist on the hegemony of the spirit. The more vital the question the less chance of an answer. At six thirty I rise to silence and darkness, mist thick on the ground. Plenty of time to get to Tansonville and back before breakfast. But as soon as I touch the front door, the Dobermans rush it in a snarling pack. Bloodthirsty growls pursue me back up to the bedroom.

Reba stirs drowsily. 'You all right? Sounded like they got you.'

I go into the bathroom and switch on the light, one of those harsh overhead strips so unkind to men losing a few slates on top. Beneath widely spaced hairs, naked scalp gleams obscenely. Tilting the head to hide scalp only reveals the black nasal cavities sprouting growths of hideous vigour and fecundity. I may have spoken of 'hair loss' – but the term is inaccurate. Hair is not strictly lost – it just relocates, first to the nostrils and then to the ears.

Reba has gone back to sleep, sprawled across the bed whose covers, disturbed by my restlessness, conceal only her lower back and upper thighs. Just enough to make the composition perfect, an exquisite natural voluptuousness no model could catch.

And the three beavers! Liz sweeping her skirts up with one hand and lowering her pants with the other, Frances spread out in the sun, Reba straddling the bath, one foot on the ground and one against the tiled wall, pointing the cheap rubber shower attachment into her streaming abundance. What heart-rending images I could give the world if I knew how to paint.

And of course the arm Reba has flung out is the one with the vaccination mark. Even asleep she knows how to intoxicate and madden. I suppress an overpowering urge to get back into bed, an act of selfless heroism that will never be known. Goodness has to be invisible.

Not that such restraint is typical. Intimations of mortality have violently inflamed my desire. The cold breath of the void, that snuffs out so much, fans the flames of lust. As the things of this world fade, the flesh increases its power. Meaninglessness is the true aphrodisiac. Increasingly these days I am haunted by a character in *Salammbô*, a lascivious Carthaginian with a hideous disease that consumes what remains of the rotting flesh carried about by slaves in a canopied litter. As the decomposition accelerates so does his lust, requiring more and more young girls to be brought to the litter where he flings aside his mask and falls upon them with a ravening mouth, or rather a ravening hole where the mouth used to be.

Perhaps my obsession is an example of the inoculation principle: for immunity to permanent oblivion I take regular doses of the temporary version. Whatever the reason, my need is becoming an addiction. I am taking to sexual intercourse the way other men take to drink.

Now the sky lightens, the mist rises, common day takes from the ornamental furniture its fantasmal and sinister look. Still the dogs patrol the grounds. At seven o'clock footsteps crunch on the gravel and I spring to the window in time to see the brutes led away.

Reba stretches and opens her eyes. 'I'll go with you.'

'But the kids?'

'They can go to Frances when they wake.'

'Are you sure?'

Can it be that there is no resentment about the previous evening? About the whole holiday? About our whole life together?

Reba laughs. 'I'm sure.'

To side with me instead of her sister and leave in the cold dawn for an unknown destination of uncertain access – such is the faith of women that saves men's souls. Reba dresses and we leave warily, elated and fearful, like adolescents sneaking out of boarding school.

Prepared to rough it, we find a track going in the right direction.

'Look!' Reba cries. 'Hawthorns.'

'But not *the* hawthorns.'

'What do you want for nothing?'

As we follow the track I tell her about Tansonville and Swann, the sensitive man among boors, the obsessively jealous lover who marries his courtesan mistress and suffers both the death of love and the ostracism of his friends – a disappointed man on the way to a premature death.

'You saw some of his story in the movie – except that Swann wasn't handsome like Jeremy Irons. He was red-faced and bald.'

'You're not still obsessed with going bald? Does it worry you that much?'

'It does during cunnilingus. I mean, all you can see is the top of my head.'

'But I'm not in any condition to study it.' She laughs ironically. 'I'll still love you when you're bald.'

'According to Proust love is impossible. We want only what we can't have. As soon as we get it we're no longer interested.'

'Do you believe that?'

'There's a lot of truth in it. You certainly had a dramatic loss of interest immediately after we were married.'

We have come to the river of the famous walks. I had pictured a mature and tranquil waterway with willows overhanging the paths that follow its sinuous curves. In fact it is a mucky, babbling Irish stream.

On the other side we peer through the gates of a cool austere chateau – Tansonville surely – and, pointing to a plaque, Reba cries out with the delight of a lifelong Proustian. I scramble up a grassy bank and reach over the wall to a pear tree. Reba cries out again, this time in fear. If an auberge has Dobermans, what will be guarding a chateau? I slither back with two pears and present her with the largest. Pears from Tansonville in the early morning with the mist not off the ground! Good too: hard, but sweet and full of flavour. As we cross back over the river a tractor sways round a corner towards us.

'Quick!' Reba cries in mock alarm, pushing me off the road onto the verge. 'Hide the pears!'

Something of my old gallantry returns for a moment. '*Your* pair could never be hidden.'

And in her eyes the old loving mischievousness. Desire surges back in a wild, imperious flood.

'Well,' Reba says calmly as I seize her. 'Somebody's in the mood.'

As though this were a caprice, a mere whim.

'Mood has nothing to do with it. I'm a desperate man.'

'But it's a bit damp still.' She glances about with a dubious expression. 'Ah could toss ye off.'

For a long time now I have appreciated with all my heart that the best is enemy of the good. Oddly enough, this was a French saying originally – *Le mieux est l'ennemi du bien.* Reba sets to work with skilful, oblivion-bearing hands.

Profoundly grateful, I offer in a hoarse tone what seems to me the most affecting sexual compliment a man can pay a woman. 'You know it's only you I think about when I'm whacking off.'

Tansonville. Hawthorns and pear trees. Joy of pantheistic surrender in our moments of remission.

'Have you a tissue or something?' Reba murmurs.

Somewhere a single bird carols in ecstasy. *The kindness, infinite, of her hands.* Gently, expertly, tactfully, they harvest pleasure. A whimper of gratitude and veneration escapes me.

Reba glances round. 'No one's coming.'

But she's wrong.

Dear Festering Fenian

Writing for the second time without a response reminds me of how few letters you have written. Do you not value the delights of correspondence? I have compared notes with Liz and we both find you increasingly surly and withdrawn. What we both loved and admired was the beautiful farouche young man living on national assistance in a shabby bedsitter, putting his heart and soul into the reading of masterpieces and the preparation of simple but healthy tuna salads, his mind razor-sharp and his integrity absolute.

America continues to be all niceness and kindness and generosity. But what a careless and wasteful country. In New York we went to see Dickie Wells, perhaps the greatest trombone player in jazz (his only rival is Vic Dickenson whom I once saw described as 'the bucolic Hamlet'): an elderly man who ought to be revered but playing a dingy little bar where no one paid him any attention. I nearly got into a fight for asking people not to talk. They seemed to think I was a nutcase, as did Dickie himself when I went up to tell him he was a genius.

And when I take David to see softball in the local park what excites him most is that no one bothers to search for or even pick up the stray balls. After every game we go round the park collecting them. So far he has twenty-seven.

I see a lot of David because Liz has been away interviewing prominent Irish Americans. A true journalist, she can never miss an opportunity. Also I suspect she enjoys a break from David. I don't feel any resentment. A certain weariness comes with the years but also greater patience. The patience wins out by and large.

What I do grievously miss is my Selmer Mark 6. After being inspired by Dickie Wells I made desperate enquiries – but saxophones are unheard of among the Irish American community. Perhaps I should take up the piano accordion. At least I have a box of watercolours and I appear to be improving. I know my technique is limited but I have good draughtsmanship and a boldness that makes my clumsy efforts not boring. Van Gogh did all his work in ten years. I have burgeoning notions to do for Ulster what Hopper has done for America. Can't wait to get to grips with those marvellous Ulster gasworks and graffiti.

This chatty letter has lain in the typewriter all day. I see I am using the same model as Saul Bellow.

Remember Sam, my handsome son you met at the wedding? He married and had a child and invited us to the christening. They live in a place called Brockton, south of Boston. Liz was apprehensive about meeting my first wife but in fact it went well enough with Jean. The problem was all with Sam. He claims to have given up liquor but drinks beer continuously. In America beer seems not to count as alcohol. After a long spell of bumming around he has settled down with a pretty wife and a well-paid job as a construction worker. Yet towards the end of a pleasant afternoon he directed a violent outburst at me. Why do children need to make these hysterical and baseless attacks on their parents? It reminded me of your own exaggerated ravings about your mother.

Liz's uncles continue to ply us with free whiskey, which is pleasant but does nothing for our sexual life. To get her back into the swing of it I bought a book of female sex fantasies called *My Secret Garden.* I certainly found it rather exciting to read about women copulating with their boxer dogs on long car trips. But the most encouraging thing is confirmation that women are as hopeful of pleasure as men. It was this aspect of Liz that renewed me after a long barren period in my life. As no doubt it will again though she refuses to look at the book. Now that our holiday is coming to an end she is concerned about where we will eventually settle in Ireland. Every location has its problems, but I tell her that wherever we move it will be somewhere new and exciting or else we will find exciting reasons for staying in our rejuvenated old beauty where we are.

Be good, be happy, learn to talk to your fellow human beings and love Dickie Wells.

Love
Kyle

At L'Auberge des Trois Dobermans, *madame* enjoys an exultant revenge. After breakfast she presents, with a wicked flourish, the international money order sent as a deposit months before, describing it with malicious contempt as 'le cheque'.

'Pas un chèque,' I say, pointing helplessly to the printed

description. 'De l'argent. C'est à vous. Moi, je ne peux pas l'encaisser maintenant.'

Grinning confidently, enjoying herself, pausing every now and then to gaily salute passing guests, *madame* rejects my pleas one after another, varying her objections with a blithe disregard for consistency. In the first place she denies the authenticity of the order – impossible to accept it in payment. Second, they cannot cash a 'chèque', they are neither a bank nor an exchange bureau. This is an *auberge*, the word spat out with fierce hauteur. And in the third place she objects to it in the first place.

If she does not accept the order we cannot meet the hotel bill and our return expenses. The bitch is screwing us. I turn wildly to Reba. 'Get the dictionary.'

To *madame* I explain that other establishments have taken similar orders, there has never been a problem.

'Mais c'est la campagne ici,' she laughs. This is the country. They are simple folk. Traditional fare and lodgings for coin of the realm, foreign pieces of paper they do not understand. Several guests have lingered to enjoy the fun and she shares her laughter with them, teetering slightly on red stilettos that match the tight belt encircling her pencil-line skirt and the gleaming nail polish of the bronze hand laid on her black silk blouse as her ancient bronze features crease further with mirth and her heaving breast gives off waves of Soir de Paris. Every inch the toiling peasant. Her affluent guests laugh along with her. *C'est la campagne* – a good joke.

Now she has thought of a new humiliation. Still laughing, she picks up the phone, dials, talks incomprehensible French, then suddenly leans into me holding out the receiver and envelopping me in a fragrance as potent and disabling as mustard gas.

'La banque!' she cries in triumph, pushing the receiver into my chest and turning to alert the audience to cabaret.

'Pas un chèque,' I bleat into the phone. 'Een ... ter ... national Mawn ... ee Ord ... errr.'

Satisfied, *madame* and guests enjoy a rich laugh.

Reba arrives with the dictionary and squeezes my hand. 'You're doing really well.'

As I hand back the phone, Sean rushes in from the forecourt. To engage my attention fully he seizes my shoulder, swings my body back towards him and, to dispel the last traces of dreamy absent-mindedness, thrusts an insane, livid face into mine. 'Those fuckin' dogs are attackin' the kids. *They just bit Eamonn's trousers.*' He turns a hate-filled countenance to the she-devil. 'Tell her. Go on. *Tell her.*' Then he looks at me again and waits.

It is better to dream one's life than to live it. 'For fucksake, Sean.'

This intervention has spoiled the fun. *Madame* swiftly and coldly lays it on the line: cash from us now, then Patric her *maître d'* will accompany us to Illiers to cash the order. I point out that since it is in her name only she can cash it. She dismisses this pedantry with contempt. Everyone knows Patric.

'You're not going to pay her,' Sean howls.

'What's the choice?'

'The order's good, isn't it? Get the fuckin' police.' Terminally disgusted, he walks off.

I pay cash and accompany the impassive young *maître d'* to his car. Sean's battered van follows behind. On the main road, attempting to prepare a speech for the bank, I remember that I have returned the dictionary to Reba. *Peu importe.* The sun is shining, the corn-fields are richly golden. It occurs to me that we must be driving along the Guermantes Way, which in Proust's novel symbolises money, arrogance and insensitivity. One has to admit that some of the mischievous god's effects reveal a fine ironic zest. I glance at Patric – and am deeply shocked. In repose his handsome features have slumped into an expression of bitterness and nihilism terrifying in one so young. *Pauvre* Patric – *madame* has fed his nuts to the Dobermans. They never told him about *her* in catering college. An impulse of solidarity makes me reach out across the barriers of enmity, language and generation.

'Toujours les problèmes,' I softly suggest.

'Uhrn,' he grunts, in fierce ineffable disgust.

In the bank the order is passed around with much discussion and shrugging. Patric and the manager confer at length. The manager rings head office, then confers again with Patric. I gather that he is guaranteeing payment in a week when the order has been processed. In the meantime, Patric is to give me cash from the *auberge* account. Profoundly unhappy, Patric phones *madame* and gets into a violent argument. Reba appears at the window, wincing and tapping her watch. We were supposed to stop for a leisurely picnic en route to the ferry.

At least one conclusion of Proust's has been proved: 'True wisdom would consist in replacing nearly all travel by study of the railway timetable.' From now on I will read books and absorb their message instead of chasing after authors. No more hero worship, no more cults, above all no more pilgrimages to literary shrines. Henceforth let the search for truth be confined to the leather sofa in the through lounge.

Patric comes off the phone, his blank features offering no consolation.

'Bon?'

'Pas bon,' he says, making for the door.

I scurry after him. 'Mais . . .'

'Une autre banque.'

Since the *pas un chèque* routine is wearing thin, I ask Reba for the dictionary.

Her face contorts wildly. 'I left it in the hotel.'

Patric drives in silent fury across the village. In the second bank the cycle of discussing and phoning begins again. This time the order is acceptable – the only problem is that it is in *madame*'s name. Reba appears at the window tapping her watch. Already it is too late for the *déjeuner sur l'herbe*. Now we will be lucky to make the boat with a nonstop drive.

On the counter is a magazine about Illiers produced by the bank. As the manager phones head office and confers with Patric, who in turn phones *madame*, I flip through the details of bank-financed building: chalet bungalows, new *complexe sportif*, *restauration des WCs* in the Collège M. Proust. On the last page, under the heading of tourist attractions, is a set of photographs of the interior of the Proust house – exactly what I came to Illiers to see.

At a desk in front of me a man is trying to work in spite of the commotion (Patric is shouting down the phone at *madame).* I wave the magazine suggestively and he shrugs assent – it is nothing, take it. I ought to leave him in peace but am grateful for a last-minute blessing which proves Marcel wrong. There is always something beyond the cycle of obsession and disappointment. Not a thought that can be easily communicated in a phrase – but I manage it with expressive body language and a mature tone richly freighted with suffering, endurance, and resignation.

'Quelque chose,' I murmur, and oddly enough he seems to appreciate the complexity and weight behind the words. A man my own age, harassed, fatalistic, wry, losing a few slates on top.

'Quelque chose,' he agrees with a smile.

Notown

8

My desk has been tidied again. The unsightly but meaningful disorder of brochures, letters, folders, memos and circulars ('ZEN AND THE ART OF MANAGEMENT: a talk on how the West is losing the Third World War *without even knowing it's begun*') has been gathered into a neat stack by Ken Sutherland who keeps his own desk clear but has hung all the pegs with clothing, draped the radiators with towels, filled the cupboards with ropes and climbing equipment, obstructed the floor with a rucksack and running gear, loaded the shelves with geological specimens, his diary of potholing on Tonga, a video on Tonga, Whole Earth magazines, *Modern Rope Techniques for Mountaineers, A Thousand Great Tunes for the Banjo,* and placed under my feet (*my* feet), the actual banjo itself in a battered case covered with stickers.

It is not hard to deduce that Ken is a bachelor who uses the office as a combined attic, campsite and changing room. Such is the person I see more of than anyone other than Reba and the children, a roommate dismissed as impossible by colleagues and banished with yrs. tly. to a Celtic ghetto.

To the average London civil servant, Ken is a lunatic in a world of calm sanity. In fact, the crucial difference is that his madness is visible whereas theirs is concealed. At all times and in all places he can be no other than what he is, a startling achievement anywhere in England and especially in the English civil service. To have remained singular in the ultimate conformity culture – for this a man must be forgiven a great deal indeed.

But not tidying my desk when the rest of the room is a pigsty.

'You've been at it again,' I accuse as soon as he enters the room.

Grandly settling himself in his swivel chair, Ken spreads the fingers of each hand and triumphantly lays them on bare wood. 'Clear desk policy. I learned that at Shell.'

I indicate the disorder of the room. 'You create all this mess and then just because your desk is clear you object to a few papers on mine. Untidiness I can understand ... but this is something else. This is neurosis. This is obsession. This is mania.'

At once he disintegrates, burying his face in his hands. 'I know that. I know. I know. You're absolutely right.' He springs up and grabs the nearest item, the banjo book.

'No, Ken, that's OK. All I want is for you to leave my desk alone. A little mutual tolerance, all right? You obviously have no experience of cohabitation.'

'Oh you're right. You're right. You're right. I live like a peasant. Like a peasant. What I need is a woman. I know that. But I might be getting married. See, I met this woman out on Tonga.'

Joyce, an American nurse also doing a stint in the Third World and like himself an active, outdoor person. Together they ran along dazzling beaches (pausing in wonder to watch the surf boil as a consequence of distant erupting volcanoes), forged deep into the jungle with rucksack and tent, pierced the hymens of the incredible virgin potholes of Tonga. Instant physical and spiritual rapport – they were made for each other. At the moment Joyce was on a two-year contract in Saudi Arabia but they corresponded regularly and even spoke on the phone at enormous expense.

'You mean you haven't seen each other since Tonga?'

'She came to London once but it wasn't a great success. It was the time of the FIXER project. I was a bit preoccupied ... you know?'

'You mean you neglected the love of your life *for a project?* And you weren't even part of the official team on that thing. You neglected her for a project you didn't have to work on.'

An advisory and training department, our function is to help other departments select and use computer software. I am an Information Systems and Decision Support man. Ken is an expert on Expert Systems, a fashionable new type of specialist known as a Knowledge Engineer. Our role is to provide advice, and I am implacable in keeping to this – but Ken can never resist plunging in over his head. A crazed Scottish Calvinist, he has had the superstition of activity in his blood for centuries now. Where other men are ruined by gambling, stimulants, greed or sex, Ken is incapable of restraint at the siren call of a project team.

'I know. I know. I know,' he says. 'I can't help myself. I know.'

'So she arrives expecting a firm commitment. Instead you piss her off and send her back to an environment with a million sex-starved men and practically no attractive women. She's bound to meet someone else, Ken.'

'I wrote to explain and apologise.'

'She'll meet someone else.'

Once again he buries his face in his hands. Attacks of violent self-loathing are of course a feature of Calvinism. 'You're right. You're right. God I was mad. You know, you're talking a lot of sense now.' He lays a hand on my arm. 'Fancy a drink after work?'

'Family man, Ken. Have to get back.'

'Of course, of course.' Fresh guilt convulses him and he lowers his head. An endearing sight. As with so much that is noble, the practice of self-laceration seems to be dying out in the world. Calvinists and Catholics should form a protection group: a Society for Laceration And Self-Hatred (SLASH).

'I mean, rejecting the love of your life for FIXER, Ken. What did that team achieve in the end? Bet you can't even remember what it's an acronym for?'

He looks up at me, wild, broken, distraught, a Scottish Lear on the heath.

'Remind me. What does it stand for?'

I never miss an opportunity to let it roll off the tongue.

'Fault Isolation eXpert for Enhanced Reliability.'

'I hardly ever see Kyle,' Liz said in good-humoured amazement. 'I'm only here half the week and he's always away that half. This weekend he's going to Yorkshire to give a creative writing class.' She looked from us to Kyle as though he might even yet cancel the booking.

'The arrangement was made a long time ago, darling.'

They were showing us round their new Belfast home. Liz was in Dublin from Tuesday to Thursday and tried to spend the rest of the week in the North – but she had many weekend assignments, as Kyle pointed out.

'You're just as often not here yourself.'

'I know,' Liz said, shaking her head.

Although this had been inevitable, it seemed to come as a surprise to Liz and thus, she imagined, to everyone else. We were in a familiar situation with Liz – that of being offered as startling news a development long foreseeable and foreseen.

But the excitement of showing us round took her mind off the cost of living. She had a right to be proud. The lounge was a triumph of comfort, style and individuality, both a revelation and a reproach to Reba and me for it lacked even one item of conventional furniture. Here everything was at once striking and virtually cost-free: Kyle's gasworks paintings (unframed, on stretched canvas, but all the more immediate for that), a huge battered bureau that had once been in Kyle's father's office, a massive, scarred, cigarette-burned table seized by Liz when on the point of being dumped from a newspaper print room, as had been the unit that served as a coffee table (a heavy wooden stand brutally scored by the equipment it once had supported – I thought with shame of our chrome and smoked-glass monstrosity), a rickety hat stand on which sat a huge broken chamber pot from whose many cracks and apertures a hanging plant dangled anarchic and luxuriant tendrils, shelves packed to overflowing with records, tapes, books and fat American quarterlies, and finally, from Altnagarvin, several frayed armchairs and a chipped piano on which Liz was learning to accompany Kyle (and ultimately blow great piano with the Kyle Magee Quartet).

It was a magnificent combination of the utilitarian and the artistic. Even Reba was moved to shame at the limitations of her conventional taste.

'Why couldn't *we* have a room like this?'

The kitchen, however, was less impressive, marred by a sink full of dirty water piled with dishes, cutlery and pots.

'We had a few people in last night,' Liz explained.

'My wife is a slut,' Kyle gaily informed Reba.

Upstairs only the main bedroom and study were finished. The other rooms were stripped and would be redecorated as soon as the builders finished converting the roof space into a studio for Kyle.

We put the children to bed and settled gratefully in the lounge – only to discover that we were going out. This was the night of Kyle's session with the Billy McKnight Trio in the Imperial Hotel.

'We're producing our own LP,' Kyle explained. 'Though the financing of it is tricky.' Without further ado he fetched my copy of the appeal going out soon to all his admirers and friends. At the top was a logo, a silhouette of a jazzman leaning back to project notes from a saxophone, and under this the name of the new label: Woke Up This Mornin' Records.

> I have reason to believe that you care for my work. Having no funds for advertising or distribution, I would like you to listen to the enclosed record and decide if you could distribute copies, selling it or giving it as a present to those who appreciate good mainstream jazz. You are of course under no obligation but I would appreciate return of the record if you are not interested.

'Isn't the Imperial one of those awful suburban places?' Reba asked. Most likely it was the music she dreaded more than the venue. If anything, her hatred of jazz had intensified over the years.

'Kyle would perform anywhere,' Liz laughed. 'You know, in the States he got up at one of those do-it-yourself comedy places and did an act.'

Novelist, painter, critic, jazzman . . . and stand-up comic.

'Can't remember a thing about it.' Kyle said. 'The auld drink.'

'But *Carmen*'s on TV' was Reba's last protest.

'We'll tape it,' Kyle cried. 'We finally gave in and got a machine. Great fun. Found a remarkable video last week.'

'Not bad at all for that kind of thing,' Liz agreed.

'Wish we could remember the name of it. I just stopped for petrol and picked it up in the shop. There was a daunting middle-aged lady at the till – but she only smiled sweetly at me.'

'This was in Protestant Ulster, Kyle?'

'Even here times have changed.'

But when the baby-sitter, a friendly local girl, arrived and I looked at the books she was carrying (others study clothes and features, I peer at the books), wicked fingers of bone played an arpeggio on my spine. Instead of the expected dog-eared best seller, she was carrying a black bible and a work of biblical exegesis.

'She's an out-and-out loyalist,' Liz agreed. 'Everyone round here's the same: fundamentalist and loyalist. But they're friendly enough really. Fine if you keep away from religion and politics.'

'But we have a Dublin-registered car,' Reba wailed. 'Will it be all right here?'

Liz laughed. 'You're being driven in a Dublin-registered car.'

Kyle suddenly pounded the wheel in high spirits. 'You know the black version of *Carmen*?' He inclined his head to Reba. '*Carmen Jones* with Harry Belafonte and Dorothy Dandridge?' Actually turning round to her, he adopted an exaggerated American accent. 'Hi there, Heatwave! You is what folks back home call a real hot number.' Raising her head from the Woke Up This Mornin' Records publicity material, Reba gaped at Kyle in amazement. 'Of course it was boxing instead of bull fighting. Husky Miller was the heavyweight who ruined her.' Turning back to the wheel, Kyle pounded it and lustily sang, to the tune of the Toreador Song, 'Stand up and fight until you hear the bell, stand toe to toe . . .'

'Stop clowning, Kyle,' I said, 'and try to remember the name of that video.'

Only now was Reba able to voice her alarming discovery.

'Billy McKnight's the Billy from *Teatime with Billy*.'

'Enjoy music?' Ken asks and like Pilate does not stay for answer. 'Come and hear the group some time. We play in a pub every

Friday night. Not the greatest musicians in the world – but we have a good time. A good atmosphere . . . you know? Come along some Friday night.'

At once I see a crowded basement and beards growling about exile in Van Diemen's Land.

'Not into folk, Ken. More of a jazz man myself.'

'But come along and meet the guys and have a few drinks. We have this Irish fiddler, Frank Kelly . . . a great character.'

What saves me is the arrival of Benny with the internal mail. Ken rises with a solemn look and, putting an arm round Benny's shoulders, leads him gently to the wastepaper basket.

'Straight in there, Benny. The whole bunch. File under w.p.b.'

Benny laughs uproariously, glancing sideways to make sure that I too am taking this as a joke.

'Happy, Benny?' Ken asks with mock severity.

Benny nods, laughing still.

'We'll have to put a stop to that.' Ken looks to me for support. 'Can't have that sort of nonsense.'

'Out of the question,' I agree, bringing down a fist on the desk. 'All happy staff to be dismissed without notice.'

Now Benny is laughing so hard he can scarcely deliver the mail. And these people are supposed to be serious Technical Advisors. This pair of maniacs. Wacko zany goofballs.

'From the Random Memo Generator,' Ken cries, riffling his mail in real disgust when Benny leaves. 'Don't you get sick of this place sometimes?'

Like everyone else Ken is constantly whingeing. But for me the Advisory Department is a sufficiently tranquil niche.

Has the present moment not a kind of magical eternity? On the wall above my desk the sun etches a rhombus of bright gold, and the only sound is the muted beeping of feather-touch computer keys. Ken is playing with new software, the Automated Reasoning Tool (ART). Not an official evaluation, this is a purely gratuitous enthusiasm: ART for ART's sake.

'Ken, what's a warm boot in MSDOS?'

'Control, Alt and Delete,' he sings out.

But I have broken the spell and have cast us out into self-consciousness.

'Happy yourself?' Ken suddenly asks, with an intense and searching look. No wonder colleagues think him insane.

Certainly I am content. The move to England seems to have worked out well. With the money from our own house and that left by my mother (she and Lily died within six months of each other) we have been able to afford a reasonable house in London. Reba has found congenial work, which she never managed in Dublin. The children have settled in new schools. As for me, hair loss and greying proceed at acceptably slow rates and even my troubled heart seems to have settled, the horror of major surgery indefinitely postponed. Very likely the proximity of the heart hospital has a stabilising effect. Already, binding new habits and routines have developed – but I am no longer in search of transgression and outrage. All I want is the long tepid dream of the plateau years.

'Happy, Ken? I'm not sure. Can we be consciously happy?'

He stares into my soul. 'You tell me.'

'I think not. That phrase *the pursuit of happiness* is a terrible thing in the American constitution. Pursuit is always self-defeating. Proust said it: Happiness may be found only by seeking something other than happiness.'

'But what's the something other?'

This is why I like Ken. He too suffers from the increasingly rare twin diseases Beckett ruthlessly diagnosed and cured himself of: 'the malady of wanting to know what to do and the malady of wanting to be able to do it'.

'You want the knowledge for a system – RUle-Based Expert System for Happiness, acronym RUBESH.'

'I like it!' Ken shouts, pounding the desk. 'I like it a lot.' Elated, he switches on the electric kettle and spoons instant coffee into two filthy chipped mugs. *My* coffee, Continental Blend, the second jar I have had to buy despite an agreement to take turns. But who could be petty on the verge of a major breakthrough in philosophy? At last the Advisory Department is living up to its name.

'Let's consider your approach first, Ken. Total immersion. Ecstasy of the project. Arbeit Macht Frei.'

'I don't have German.'

'Work Gives Freedom.'

'I like that. Who said it?'

Of course Ken is too easy.

'A sign on the front gate at Auschwitz.'

Liz came to the door of her Belfast terrace house with a pretty black-haired child in her arms.

'Our secret.' She laughed. 'We never told you about this.'

'One of my many love children,' Kyle said.

'No, it's Renee's wee one,' Liz explained. 'This is Helen. Isn't she a dote?'

'Liz has more or less adopted her,' Kyle said. 'It's the best she can do. Poor Liz won't be having any more of her own.'

'Actually she's due back with her mum. Kyle, would you mind taking her? I can't face getting into that car again.' Liz turned to us. 'I didn't get up from Dublin till all hours last night.'

'Certainly, darling.' He took the child. 'Come on, wee pet.'

Our own children clamoured to keep Helen or else go with her in the car. Remembering Kyle's style of driving, I persuaded them to stay and watch cartoons with David.

The three adults went down into the kitchen for coffee. Once again the sink was full of dishes.

Reba went straight at it. 'What's this about *poor Liz* and not having any more children?'

'I agreed at the start there'd be no kids. Kyle said we'd three families between us already and that was enough.'

'You mean you actually want a child?'

Liz, career girl and free spirit, nodded in solemn agreement. 'I'd love to have a baby with Kyle.'

'You're insane.' Reba said. 'Haven't you enough trouble looking after David?'

I had never heard Reba speaking to Liz in this way before. In fact their relationship was almost completely reversed. Now it was Reba who had the authority and Liz who deferred and made excuses.

Reba: 'How are you managing with David anyway?'

'He misses two days of school when I come up here, but some weekends he stays down with friends. Kyle's been great, I must say. He plays with him and takes him to football matches on Saturdays. He's teaching him chess at the moment.'

'And what about all this travelling?'

'Oh, it's desperate. I can hardly stand the sight of a car. Actually I've been looking round for something up here . . . but it's even harder to get in than down south.' Liz turned to me. 'My experience in Dublin actually goes against me. You know how it is here if they think you're too Catholic.'

'Remember the Fenian rejected for a job as newsreader?' I jerked my head wildly. 'F. . .f. . .f. . .f. . .fuckin' discrimination again.'

'But Renee has this great idea for the Little Theatre. She says a lunch thing would do a bomb there. I mean, there's all those offices around it and the foyer's really nice and it's lying empty at lunchtime. Health food, we thought . . . you know? Nice salads and quiches . . . she thinks we could really do well.'

Indeed how could it fail: state-of-the-art product, upmarket site and a sales team that combined brutal Parisian depravity with the innocent sweetness of the Irish colleen? You would have to be some kind of pervert if you didn't get stiff in your pants.

'You'll have every guy in town,' I said. 'Or all except Kyle. I don't suppose he's taken to health food yet?'

'It's hopeless!' Liz cried, happy again. 'He has to have his fags and chips and Ulster fries and butter and full-cream milk. No substitutes and no cutting down. Costs a fortune to feed him. And even worse, he insists on going into wee shops round here. Says we have to be part of the local community.'

'Prod shops?' Reba asked, resuming her stern and mistrustful demeanour.

'*Loyalist* shops. And of course Kyle takes David in for sweets and they pump him like mad. *Oh isn't that the great wee man. And who would this be now? And tell me this, son, where do you go to school?*'

School = Religion, the most practical and widely used equation in Ulster life. Once a Protestant newspaper described my language as that of the public lavatory wall, ending the review with the name of my old school. Gutter = Fenian. QED.

'So of course David says he goes to Miss Kearney in Dublin. Oh . . . Dublin . . . well isn't that nice. And Kyle the big gawm doesn't even see what's going on. Thinks they're being civil, for Christ's sake.'

'Oh my God,' Reba said.

'And you know the joke of it of course. David goes to a Protestant school in Dublin . . . same as your kids.'

'You'll have to get this across, Liz. Leaflet all local businesses. *Miss Kearney is a Protestant*.'

'And that bar at the end of the street's supposed to be a UDA hang-out. Kyle insists on going in to play pool with them. I just don't want to think about it . . .'

'But can't you move somewhere safer?'

'Too expensive,' Liz sighed.

Outside, the silent dark city. Inside, the lamp, leather sofa, dense print. An old story: man alone in the night, beating feeble wings against the infinite.

The stubborn last dream: to understand.

In bursts Reba, excited and flushed, bearing with her an invigorating aureole of cold. 'God Ahm foundered. It's freezing. Feel that.' She bends to my hand a cheek tingling cold. Shrugging out of her coat, she flings in my lap a crumpled sheet, her Management Committee agenda, covered with doodles and secret messages: 'I need a drinky pooh', 'Will Kate ever shut up?', 'Pat is a werewolf – look at his hands'.

'For Jesus' sake get us a drink!' she cries now. 'I thought that fucking meeting would never end.'

After a bracing gulp of G and T Reba launches into her story. The centre has had its grant cut and the Management Committee wants to bleed successful ventures to support lame ducks. In particular, they covet the proceeds of the Women's Open Day, which Reba is determined to reinvest in women's activities, a growing list that includes Screen Printing, Pottery, Computing for Women, Health and Fitness, Female Massage, Assertiveness Training, and Housewives in Dialogue.

I asked if she had made up the last title herself.

'Why?' she snapped, deeply suspicious. 'Do you think it's stupid?'

'On the contrary,' I answered gravely. 'It's touched by genius.'

'I do know where to draw the line. Kate wanted to call the lesbian counselling session Lavender Horizons. I put my foot down there.'

I have no doubt that she did. The development of her authority has been astonishing. For while London has merely accommodated me, to Reba it has given a vocation. Or, rather, renewed and sanctioned an existing vocation. What was the Herron shop but an unofficial community centre, and what was Reba's function but that of unofficial women's worker? Now she has discovered the joy and wonder of the metropolis: what you did for love at home you can get paid for here.

Reba is a star again, as I discovered when I ran the inflatables on the open day (my function both practical and symbolic, a man in the menial, supportive role). As soon as they learned I was the husband, the mothers leaving children were lavish in praise of Reba's work. A joy to note the veneration in their voices and eyes.

A joy to be driven home by Reba in the centre's minibus, a huge, ramshackle, ancient, syphilitic structure, Reba stomping the slack pedals, seizing the juddering gear stick, hauling the great horizontal wheel, propelling the shrieking, reluctant monster through the clogged streets of London.

'Well there was uproar,' Reba says now. 'Remember Sally from the Young at Heart Club?'

Could I forget Reba's most bitter rival, a pensioner certainly young in her lust for domination and conquest?

'The women wrote a letter about her carry-on at the open day. I mean she came in without paying and started selling tickets for the Young at Heart raffle. This was just before the draw for *our* raffle. Loads of people bought tickets thinking they were for ours. Then she goes to the food stall and demands a free lunch as one of the workers. One of the *workers* – and her only there to cause trouble. Of course she went apeshit when the letter was read out. Said we should never have been allowed a raffle so close to the Young at Heart social. But we had her on that one. The open day was booked *long before the social.* She was in the wrong *herself.* Oh she was livid! Livid! Then she was just saying *anything.* That we neglected the mayor and left him sitting in a corner. I said he was resting after a go on the inflatables.'

'I'll back you on that.'

'So everyone laughs and she storms out – but the rest were still licking up to me to get their hands on this money. Jim's planning this family social and he says they're thinking of getting an Irish band *which ought to be good news for Reba* . . . you know, grinning away, a real lick, and I say, Jim, over my dead body, I'm here to get away from that and if it's bloody piano accordions you can manage without me. That shut him up. You know, one of these second-generation Irish, full of sentimental crap about Irish music and the IRA.'

'So what band *are* they getting?'

'It's a disco now. I've put you down to barbecue . . . *all right?*'

'So you're happily married,' Ken says.

'Apparently.'

'Reckon I should take the plunge?'

'Unless you're going to be extraordinary. Hardly likely at your age.'

'That's what I thought. So I rang Joyce and proposed . . .' He lifts his chair and turns it round to face mine, always an indication of a lengthy counselling session.

'Coffee first, Ken.'

He buries his guilty face in his hands. 'I forgot again.' But immediately he is on his feet, rooting in the rucksack and producing two pieces of green fruit. 'Used to do this all the time in Tonga. Cut limes from the jungle and put them into hot water. Lovely refreshing drink it is.'

'All right, all right . . . lime tea.'

He prepares mugs of fragrant hot water and eagerly resumes his seat. 'So I told her I was ready to marry her and she burst into tears. Completely hopeless. Had to ring back half an hour later. Then it all comes out. She's met this other guy in Saudi. Only a few weeks ago but it's a whirlwind romance. Guy already wants to marry her. So now she's totally screwed up. Says if I'd asked even a month ago . . . '

'I told you to make a commitment, Ken. You have to pee or get off the pot.'

'I know that. I know that . . . God don't I know it.' He lays a hand on my arm and bows his head in anguish. 'But this guy's from London and she's coming over to meet the family. I asked her to come and stay with me instead. She said no but she'll see me at least . . . and she wants to stay in a hotel to be independent of us both. What do you *make* of that?'

'Sounds like you might be still in with a chance.'

'But I can't afford to fuck up again. I need to know what to do.'

'You're talking serious research, Ken. Love is a steep learning curve.'

'I know that – but I need expertise. I want the rules.'

It takes me a few moments with paper and pencil. 'OK . . . Heuristic Advisory System for a Sensitive Loving Environment . . . HASSLE.'

'That's the one.'

'Let's pinpoint the problems. First, we're dealing with a knowledge-rich domain.'

'I know that.'

'Second, even lengthy experience seems to teach people nothing. We meet another old friend.'

'Yeah . . .?'

'The knowledge acquisition bottleneck.'

'Caused by?'

'The illusion that there is nothing to know, that it's easy, that all you need is to find Mr or Mrs Right, that the problem was where you were looking not what you were doing.'

'So where do I start?'

'You need to buy two things.' Ken seizes a pencil and the nearest piece of paper (a circular for an executive briefing on FORCEFIELD ANALYSIS OF TOTAL QUALITY). 'First, a key text: *The Art of Loving* by Erich Fromm.'

'Ah ha.' He scribbles with furious zeal. 'And the second?'

The guy is a sweetheart. How could women reject him?

'A jar of Continental Blend.'

Fame is like money – no one ever has enough. No layman ever has sufficient cash and no artiste is ever as famous as he or she feels is deserved.

Kyle too was discontented. Expecting universal recognition and respect in the middle years, he found instead that his reputation was stuck at a certain level. Despite all his efforts, it refused to reach critical mass and commence what economists call the 'take-off into self-sustained growth'.

I put it to him that there were several reasons why this should be so.

First, both rabblement and critics were impressed only by mystery: as with nuclear physicist and neurosurgeon, the more minuscule our understanding the more enormous our respect. What was needed was an intricate and intriguing machine, something for rabblement to marvel at and ingenious critics to tinker with. But Kyle's self-commenting novels were without mystique. Their simplicity was despised as lack of intelligence and their autobiographical bias as lack of imagination. Instead of being a virtue, his honesty was gauche and naïve, an embarrassment. And in a new puritan ice age his sexual candour was *passé*, in bad taste.

Nor was he saved by shrewd marketing. All his paperback editions came from downmarket pulp houses and were intermittent, fugitive and disposable, with coarse paper, small print, and pathetically tasteless covers adorned by models in dated clothes. Utterly lacking the austerity and gravitas of the upmarket imprints, Kyle's work belonged not in the quality bookstores where baroque music noodled discreetly, but in the half-a-dozen-for-five-bob bargain Westerns box in Woolworth's.

As for promotion, he certainly had energy and enthusiasm, but these were cancelled out by naïveté. The way of the world is solemnity for the cameras followed by frankness and smut in the bar. Kyle's reversal of this procedure made him a dangerous lunatic in the eyes of media people.

And on top of it all he persisted in reviewing his peers with a devastating candour he thought, in the touchiest of professions, would be respected. Almost every review he published made him lifelong enemies; I was sure unscrupulous editors used him as a hit man to settle scores.

Given so many formidable obstacles it seemed to me a miracle that he was still being published at all. Surely he was doing as well as could be expected?

Not a bit of it, no. He was not half famous enough.

In any case, enormous fame would destroy him, I argued. Given an urge to say yes that made Molly Bloom seem like a Carmelite nun, the demands of international stardom would eat him alive in no time.

'No no no no,' he insisted stubbornly. 'I could work wonders with fame.'

A change of some kind was inevitable.

During his summers in America, Kyle was increasingly involved with creative writing classes – he had no taste for academic criticism or heavy reading – and even in winter he was now a regular tutor at fiction writing courses in England. Everywhere, writing was being promoted as a skill that could be taught and learned. Like kings, bishops, presidents, film stars and whores, the writer was merely another professional doing a day's work for pay. And the craft work produced by such professionals was exactly what rabblement and critics admired.

For Kyle the solution was obvious: his next book was a *project. Show Them the Instruments* was a contemporary Ulster love story (and hence a relevant today thing) but loosely based on the legend of Diarmuid and Gráinne (and hence acquiring timeless solidity and affording scope for exegesis). A fine piece of machine tooling, it boasted exquisite symmetry (boy sax player from republican family with Sinn Féin brother, girl singer from loyalist family with paramilitary da), perfect resolution (symbolic ending in an English abortion clinic, new Irish life snuffed out by cold indifferent Brits) and several ingenious devices (for instance the paramilitary and Sinn Féiner, bitter opponents in theory, actually colluding over rackets and to crush the romance). There was even a symbol of hope at the end – the saxophone of the lover with smashed hands being taken up by a younger brother who appears to prefer jazz to pop.

Here was a perfect image for the final credits: the youngster attempting a first solo that is soaringly taken up on the soundtrack as the camera pulls back for the final wide-angled shot of the city. In fact the whole thing cried out to be filmed. Already I could see the poster: right foreground, passionate girl singer at mike; left background, cool youth blowing up a deep mood on sax; in between, exploding cars, burning buildings, sinister figures in balaclavas and shades.

This was one issue that could not be debated by mail. It had to be hammered out face to face.

'You think it's bad?'

'It's worse than bad – it's competent.'

'Of course, you always want something sophisticated and knowing.' Agitated, Kyle walked up and down, driving a hand through his hair. 'But that sort of thing only appeals to initiates and the elect.

Public taste may be vulgar, but the public wants more than it knows. You have to take what people think they want and slip in more. The Elizabethan public wanted blood and thunder. Shakespeare accepted the formula and gave them *Macbeth*.'

'But your Catholics are ridiculous, Kyle. The Sinn Féin people spout your Pearse research. And your unemployed Catholics are even worse. Enjoying their freedom, discovering themselves through music and literature. They behave like liberal arts professors on sabbatical.'

For a novelist Kyle was strangely short of empathy. His own self-esteem may have been too massive. He could imagine himself in different circumstances, but not as the product of those circumstances.

'What do you want? Characters who aspire to nothing and achieve nothing? We see people like this all around us. Yourself for instance. But it doesn't jolt us into renewal. We have to imagine a better way.'

'Well . . . if you're talking about fantasy . . .'

'The abortion scene . . . wasn't that sordid enough . . . even for you?'

I had to concede that this was convincing. Highly convincing.

'Was that Liz, Kyle? Did Liz have an abortion?'

His conversion to professionalism could not outweigh a lifetime of candour. 'A while ago . . . just after the wedding.'

Hence her dislike of the novel, the first time she had given a negative reaction to Kyle's work. However much we enjoy seeing others' foibles revealed, we are rarely amused when it is done to ourselves. Expectantly we raise the mirror – and a misshapen mutant stares back.

In public Liz did not admit the real basis for her dislike. Instead she too criticised the depiction of Catholics. 'If you want to know unemployed Fenians, look at our Hugo. A far cry from your version. He hates being out of work.'

'But think of the movie, Liz,' I said, indicating the great screen with a sweeping gesture. 'Their chords said yes . . . their cards said no.'

Typical Fenian cheap sneer. Liz laughed. Incensed and frantic, Kyle retaliated by denouncing her lousy journalism. Thanks to him she had broken through into features, interviews with Kyle himself, Tom McKenna, others ... including American pulp writers using Ireland as a tax haven.

'You jeer at me,' Kyle shouted, 'but look at this. Look at this.' He rooted desperately, eventually producing a newspaper with a triumphant flourish. 'Some science fiction hack. Instead of asking why he writes garbage she goes on about how he's converted a bloody eighteenth-century farmhouse. *It is not a plushy past-obliterating conversion.* Interior decoration, this is the important issue in life.'

'This is what happens with every piece I write.' Liz got up and left the room.

Kyle went on shouting at me. 'You know what she does is utterly meretricious. Promoting these rich hacks. The very trash we most need to get rid of. You know that.'

'I know that.'

'Then why don't you speak up? Why don't you attack *her?*'

'I never expected anything else. She's a journalist, Kyle.'

'And if it's not rich hacks it's republicans. You know this eejit Madge ... the one who ruined our wedding ... you know she's an out-and-out IRA supporter ...'

So this can of worms was now open. Kyle had never mentioned anyone's politics before. Had his work on the book made him sensitive to such things?

'You hang out in a UDA bar yourself.'

'You know that means nothing.'

'Neither does Liz being friends with Madge.'

Kyle appeared to accept this analogy. Either that or the issue of the novel was too pressing to abandon for long. He returned to the attack, as he would at every opportunity, till death did us part. 'But the book ... there's so much in it ... even the title is marvellous ... you've seen this of course ... instruments in the two senses ... instruments of music and instruments of torture ...'

*

If I prefer hardback books it is not out of snobbery but for practical reasons. A paperback must always be held, whereas a well-produced hardback will remain open on a desk, leaving both hands free for a lightning concealment operation. As soon as some-one opens the door it takes only a second to slide adroitly across your book the minutes of the last Ad Hoc Users' Group meeting or the details of a training course in Power Communication Skills ('Make your idea "their idea", gain credibility with subordinates, win over opponents').

Of course, the trick is more difficult with those in the know. Ken passes my desk (being next to the door is a grave disadvantage) with the kind of ironic, negligent laugh that should be exclusive to me.

'The Irish hard at work as usual.'

This kind of thing is always tricky. Not only the words but the tone must be analysed carefully for provocation and insult. But in this case the meaning is beyond doubt. What we are dealing with here is the stereotype of the feckless Gael.

It will have to be explained to Ken that, far from ethnic determinism, my position has been deduced with philosophical rigour and adopted and maintained at great personal cost. What appears to be a layabout Paddy in reality is an *existential hero of sloth.*

'Ken,' I begin, with a gravity that makes him turn his chair at once, although he has already logged on and keyed a screenful of data. 'It's time to get to the root of your obsessive worship of activity.'

Clearly Ken would let pass from him this particular cup. 'Obsessive ...?' he pleads, with a vague appealing glance at the evidence of alternative orientation: Whole Earth magazines, banjo, rucksack, climbing gear. 'Didn't I go to Tonga to get away from the rat race?'

Not so easy, old friend. Cross the world to escape your demons and you find them waiting in the arrivals lounge.

'But in what capacity, Ken?'

'Head of Financial Systems for the administration.'

'Not exactly Gauguin. And how did you spend your spare time?'

'Caving.' He comes forward on his seat. 'But these were virgin caves. Never explored. No potholer could pass up a chance like that. And when you're down there, you know ... up to your waist in water, holding a lamp for someone to take photographs ... you just don't think about anything else.'

'Exactly, Ken.'

With the consummate skill of the barrister I have led him to incriminate himself. Now I have him where I want him. Full of the clinching argument to come, I rise swiftly to put on the kettle. The adaptor is full of plugs so I yank one out. Ken's screen goes blank.

'Was that important, Ken?'

'Go on,' he says wearily.

'We have to start with Calvin who postulates the transcendental God and double predestination. This unknowable God will save some and damn the rest. No one can tell why or whom, and nothing you do can change your fate.'

Ken makes an impatient gesture of dismissal. 'No one believes that crap any more.'

'Of course not. But these things create a mentality... which becomes self-perpetuating. The key features were isolation, doubt and fear. Ceaseless activity was necessary both to distract and provide outward signs of election, namely worldly success. The anxiety was relentless: no release through the cycle of sin, confession and forgiveness ... but if you could demonstrate you were one of the elect you could let off steam by loathing and despising the others, the damned ... scarcely human at all ...'

Ken's phone rings. Without turning his head, he tilts back his chair, lifts the receiver and slams it back.

'This survives in two strands: the work ethic in Calvinist countries and racial hatred in Calvinist outposts like South Africa and Northern Ireland, violent feelings of superiority to and contempt for the subhuman natives. If your Scottish forebears had joined the Ulster plantation you'd be playing in a kick-the-pope band instead of working yourself to death.'

'Now hold on.' Finally he bursts into heated protest. 'Those crazy preachers. Don't associate me with that crowd. Gothic monsters. Jesus. Gothic.'

'Your soul brothers, Ken.'

'Fuck off! I mean, who's more superior than *you*, for fuck's sake? Isn't Catholicism as bad? Obsessed with superiority too?'

'Catholic triumphalism is different. Also murderous, indifferent to good works, incapable of compromise – but not for the same reasons. The Catholic obsession is with authority. What you do doesn't matter as long as you bow to the authority of the true Church. Authority is always the crucial issue. The southern Irish fought a civil war over the precise wording of an oath of allegiance to the British Crown that would have been meaningless in reality.' I come forward with a grim intensity that makes Ken draw back. 'The Protestant obsession with superiority is the perfect sanction for colonialism and the Catholic obsession with authority is the perfect sanction for nationalism.' I let him suck on that for a moment before producing the clincher. 'So the beauty of Ireland is this: religion produced a doomsday cocktail on both sides at once.'

In the pewter light of late afternoon, Ken's face is ghostly and pale – as though convinced that our world is the realm of the Prince of Darkness, the Evil Spirit, the Hooded One.

'So there can never be a solution in Ireland,' he whispers in dread. These Calvinists slip so easily into despondency and despair.

'Of course there can. Remember that reality is unimportant. Only symbols count. So it's a problem for a pure mathematician like yourself. Devise a set of symbols to make the Protestants feel superior and the Catholics convinced the authority is theirs.'

Even before dropping his suitcase, Kyle wanted to know who had done the paintings in the lounge. They were Reba's, the fruits of an art class at the local community centre (and part of the involvement that led to her job). Kyle studied them thoroughly, both from a distance and up close, offering lavish praise tempered with just the right amount of constructive technical advice. Then he insisted on seeing all her work, even exercises, rejects and preliminary sketches, giving to each the same prolonged and concentrated attention.

Uttering short strangled cries, Reba walked about with jerky movements, abrupt halts, sudden violent changes of direction. No mere anxiety about Kyle's opinion, this was a profound perturbation due to the breaking of an old and powerful taboo. For the first time in her life Reba was violating the Herron principle of scornful non-participation. Even by displaying two paintings in her own lounge she was entering the public arena and committing the greatest sin in Fenian subculture: that of making yourself out to be somebody.

'Your own style already, strong and bold. You definitely have talent.'

Reba snorted and made extravagant dismissive gestures. Nonsense, vanity, eejit work, madness. All the same, she was pleased.

Then Kyle really spooked her. 'Have you thought of exhibiting?'

This was like thrusting a blazing brand at a newly captured wild mare.

'*No!*' she shrieked, rearing away.

Even so, it was an auspicious beginning. Kyle had asked us to put him up because he felt his agent was not promoting him with sufficient enthusiasm and to stay with her as he usually did would make him less businesslike in negotiations over the new novel. Reba had objected on the grounds that she would be treated as a skivvy. Instead she was fêted like Picasso in his sun-'n'-chateau years.

'You'll be pleased to know there's a lot of interest in the novel,' Kyle informed me ironically. Not a hint of rancour.

'Just goes to prove my point.'

As well as doing deals he stocked up on culture. Every day he staggered in laden with books, records, prints and cards which he added to his acquisitions section on the table in the lounge. Nor did he forget his genial hosts. There was often something for the kids: one day, two-inch fun-sized booklets of Wordsworth and Keats (greatly appreciated though never read); another day, cards of animal paintings from the National Gallery. For me an LP of the great Dickie Wells (*Four in Hand*, also featuring the bucolic Hamlet, Vic Dickenson) and for Reba a remaindered art book (*Techniques of the Great Masters*). And for everyone every day a bottle of wine and extravagant patisserie in a gold box tied with ribbon.

Reba had vowed not to go out of her way, but we could not avoid rising to the occasion. Thus the house would be full of rich cooking smells as everyone awaited the starting gun – Kyle's dramatic entry, weighed down by the eternal briefcase as well as several carrier bags and the shining, beribonned patisserie box. 'God but London's exhausting.' And while the wine was breathing and/or chilling we would all have a whiskey and soda and marvel over the day's art treasures.

Soon the acquisitions overflowed the table and even the lounge itself, but Reba did not resent the untidiness, not even the dirty glasses, packed ashtrays and the coming down in the morning to find the lounge stinking of smoke and the record player still on (Kyle stayed up alone into the small hours drinking whiskey, listening to music and writing his diary). Only one prospect alarmed Reba (and luckily it did not come to pass): that Kyle would doze off and burn a cigarette hole in the leather suite.

What disturbed me was the way Kyle left his diary among the records and books on the lounge table. I could never commit my atrocious thoughts to paper, and if I did the results would be locked away in a vault. But when I mentioned the diary Kyle only laughed.

Evening meals were long, noisy and convivial, followed by whiskey and further melodious discourse and disputation in the lounge. Always there was music in the background. Kyle would play his new records and I would counter with classics from my own collection. Of the two great schools of tenor saxophone playing, those founded by Lester Young and Coleman Hawkins, Kyle favoured the light, airy, genial style of Lester whereas I preferred the buzzing vibrato and uningratiating classic austerity of the Hawk. Even more divisive, Kyle had a fondness for the many white imitators of Young, men like Zoot Sims, Lee Konitz and, above all, Stan Getz. All these seemed to me to be skilful but bodiless.

'*Listen!*' Kyle would shout, turning up the volume.'Getz is always so *musical*.'

'Mere talent, Kyle.' And with a superior air I would put on a record by Hawkins or his great disciple Sonny Rollins.

Not even Kyle could fail to deduce my assessment of his own playing. If I was sniffy about white Americans and dismissed the British out of hand, who would doubt my opinion of a tenor man from mid-Ulster? He drew the obvious conclusion but did not take offence.

And at least we could agree on Duke Ellington, who transcends every category and faction. Even the implacable Reba was prepared to unbend for the Duke, especially numbers featuring the swooning *glissandi* of Johnny Hodges.

'Hodges is on the sweet side,' Kyle said to her. 'But the sweetness of good Sauterne not the sweetness of saccharine.'

Whatever the music, he involved Reba in the discussion. And relentlessly probed the depth and extent of her newfound fulfilment.

'So you're helping other women to find themselves as you've done?'

'That's one way of putting it.'

'Certainly more worthwhile than your sister's employment.'

And always the surprises. After several days he suddenly remembered he had taped the black *Carmen* for Reba. So that evening we had Husky Miller and his seventeen decisions in a row (but only three on points, the rest was all KO). Kyle sang along lustily, promising to fight till he heard the bell, to keep punching till he made his punches tell.

'Of course I feel an affinity for Husky. Used to box a bit myself.'

'Kyle's a terrible eejit,' Reba said to me. 'He's a case.'

Inevitably the original *Carmen* followed and Reba could not refrain from tempestuous flamenco-type stomps. Taking a swift swig of Jameson, Kyle sprang up and joined her on the shag pile. Zorba and Carmen, perfect couple for the Dance of Life.

When Liz rang, I assumed she would be delighted at how well things were going – but her laughter at my account of the gypsy dance struck me as feeble and forced. The next night she did not get in touch at her usual hour and Kyle, after asking our permission to ring, required a detailed explanation from Liz.

A bizarre truth was becoming apparent: that these two free spirits, famous champions of sexual liberty and uninhibited to the point of caricature (the Happy Hooker and the Laughing Cavalier) were both in fact almost insanely possessive and jealous.

Whether or not Liz put a stop to the partying with Reba, on the following night Kyle offered to babysit for us. It was the least he could do in return for our hospitality, he said. When we protested, he came up with an even more compelling reason: the Benson & Hedges Snooker Classic on TV.

On his last day he was participating in a lunchtime seminar at the Institute of Contemporary Arts and I presumed he would spend the evening with groupies and fans. But just before teatime he rang to say that he would stand us a meal out if we could find a babysitter.

By now we were accustomed to whiskey aperitifs. Kyle's Jameson was on the table among his cultural acquisitions. Next to it was the diary, not only still available but *open at the current week.* Now despite my insatiable hunger for knowledge I have a fairly good record on invasion of privacy (certain letters of Reba's remain untouched to this day). But I defy anyone to refrain from glancing at an open diary. Most of it concerned the marketing of his novel, but Reba and I got a comment apiece.

'Reba's paintings have a strong, chunky, individual style. Definite evidence of talent. Must get to know her better.'

And on yrs. tly. 'Seems more serene and affable. Stabilising of his heart condition? Or maybe London's his spiritual home.'

Resisting a strong desire to turn back the pages, I called Reba for a look. She studied the week's entries for a long time. 'There's no harm in him really . . . is there?'

I did not share the thought that had just pierced me. What if the diary was a plant? What if he wanted us to read it? Only a Fenian could think such a thing.

Emerging from the underground, Kyle dropped his briefcase and embraced us both happily.

'Where shall we eat?' he cried, producing an envelope and waving it. 'Just been given this cheque I'd completely forgotten about.'

Reba was now confident enough to be sassy. 'Depends on how much you got, Kyle.' And she mentioned an exclusive wine bar we would never have considered if obliged to pay ourselves. Kyle immediately agreed.

'So how did it go today?' I asked.

'Extremely well. Several ageing courtesans came up to reminisce about former pleasures and hint at renewing them. But I resisted temptation.' He stopped and opened his arms to us. 'I told them I was dining out with my charming and talented in-laws.'

Even the menu and wine list, instantly sobering to Reba and me, failed to dampen Kyle's enthusiasm. He ordered with reckless abandon and produced his purchases of the day: for Reba the original Carmen story by Mérimée, for me a second-hand Stan Getz LP (*Sweet Rain*) and, for himself apparently, a book of North American Indian astrology.

'Let's look you up first,' he said to Reba. 'Your moon or month is Strong Sun Moon. Carnelian agate's your stone, the wild rose is your plant and the flicker's your animal.'

'What's a flicker?'

'A kind of woodpecker.' Kyle consulted his text. 'According to legend, the flicker has red wings because he went too close to a fire set by the Earthquake Spirit. But let's see. Flicker people are deeply attached to home. A comfortable and attractive dwelling is essential to them and they will go to any lengths to make it beautiful.'

'Hah,' I cried in triumph. 'The leather suite.'

'Or Reba's paintings,' Kyle said. 'But you see what I mean. There's something in this. Listen. Their moon, the Strong Sun, gives them powerful feelings. Their hearts are overflowing with love and like their plants they have a wild untamed beauty.'

'That's more like it,' Reba/Carmen said. 'But what about *him?*'

Kyle looked for my month. 'Freeze-up Moon.' They both hooted. 'Copper's your mineral, your plant is the thistle.' Louder laughter. 'And your animal's the snake.' Pandemonium, uproar, other customers turning.

'Kyle, you bastard, you're making this up.'

'Like their plant they are covered with prickly sharp spikes that keep people at bay and often hurt even those they love.'

'Perfect,' cried Reba.

Suspecting that Kyle was only reading out the bad bits, I seized the book. 'Snake people tend to be intellectuals, keen observers and analysts of life.' Even better, 'Because of their vital force, Snake People are said to be intense and exciting lovers.'

Bored with this positive stuff, Reba now seized the book. 'And you, Kyle?'

He chuckled, shifting in his seat, repeatedly driving a hand through his hair. Food arrived but was barely acknowledged.

'Earth Renewal Moon,' he said, signalling to the waitress for another bottle. 'Quartz, birch tree and snow goose.'

'Earth Renewal people are gregarious,' Reba read. 'They need company and can act as receivers and transmitters of the great powers of the universe.' Zorba, teach me to dance! 'Like the Snow Goose they fly high above the earth and impress those upon it with their beauty and continual distinctive honking.' The Kyle Magee Quartet! 'Above all they stir our imaginations to wonder about where they are bound and what sustains their flight.'

Elated by the success of the book, Kyle did not seem to mind that the food was dull and overpriced.

'And what's Liz's moon?' Reba asked with her mouth full.

Which reminded Kyle to go and phone.

Reba poked at the astrology book. 'What *is* all this? Does he believe this stuff?'

When Kyle came back he said, in the jovial tone of the astrology exchange, 'We have an appointment with a marriage guidance counsellor next week.'

We waited for the punchline, but none came. Either he was serious or the humour of the Snow Goose is beyond those on earth.

'Is it as bad as that?' Reba asked eventually.

'We've been in fairly bad odour for a while now.'

'What do you mean by bad odour?'

'No sex.'

'None at all?'

'Virtually none.'

We considered this in silence.

'It's the travelling,' Reba said. 'Liz having to go up and down all the time. Dragging David back and forth. Trying to run two homes.'

'Liz does precious little in the Belfast home.'

'I can well believe that.'

'I do almost all the housework and shopping. Whenever she arrives I've always a hot meal ready. I take David away in the morning so she can have a lie-in. Often she lies in to lunchtime and well beyond.'

'Rollin' in her bed,' Reba said. 'That's what my mother used to call it. Liz is still up there rollin' in her bed.'

'I take David to a football match almost every Saturday.'

Over the last of the second bottle we digested the evidence. I ordered a third.

'What about the Little Theatre business?' Reba asked. 'The lunchtime thing?'

'That ended in acrimony even before it got off the ground.'

Another pause.

'But sex is always the weakest link,' I said. 'The first thing to go under pressure. It needn't mean a total breakdown.'

'It's the travelling,' Reba repeated. 'Is there no chance of cutting that out?'

Encouraged by her sympathy, Kyle explored the options in detail. None appeared to offer a quick and easy solution.

'In the meantime,' I said, 'couldn't you come to some sort of temporary arrangement?'

'Such as?'

'The sins within marriage, as the Catholic Church calls them.' He stared at me blankly. 'Gettin' your mickey pulled, I mean.'

Now he understood, but his lack of enthusiasm was total. Like all stick men he was deeply devoted to full vag. pen.

'Surely you can work something out. Ask her to lie on her stomach and let you go in from behind.'

'That's disgusting,' Reba shouted with surprising fury. 'Using Liz like a slab of meat.'

They glared in mute but powerful joint reproach. Reba and Kyle in alliance against me, this experience was certainly new.

'That's what Caroline does for John,' I said at last. 'John told me himself. And isn't this adult life as we know it: compromises, coping strategies, bargains . . . imperfection . . . second best . . .?'

This philosophy disgusted both of them and the evening ended on a sour note. When we got home, Reba went straight to bed. Not only disillusioned with her husband, she had Housewives in Dialogue first thing in the morning. Kyle went into the lounge for whiskey and jazz. I too was tired but felt it callous to abandon a man who had so generously opened both his wallet and his heart.

I swayed in the doorway. 'We must exchange recipes some time. What's your specialism, Kyle?'

'Casseroles.' He seemed to be in fairly good spirits. 'And yours?'

'Curries and chilli,' I told him.

Not only is Ken never late, he is usually the first into the building and the last to leave, better known to porters and cleaning staff than his bosses. But today there is no Ken. I have to cover for him on calls from repro, two project leaders and a department head wanting to know about ART.

Eventually he bursts in, gaunt and wild. Already thin to the point of emaciation, today he resembles a camp victim coming to meet the liberators with staring eyes and a skeleton trembling with inchoate emotion. Dropping the rucksack, he flings his bones into a chair and lays his skull on the desk.

'Jesus, Ken.'

'It's Joyce,' he says after a while. 'I've been up all night.'

'How long's she been here?'

'Four days.'

'*Four days.*' Despite his condition I cannot suppress my annoyance. How can these people expect advice if they withhold essential information? If there has been a disaster he has only himself to blame.

'I've been seeing her every day. Just chatting, not putting on any pressure. It seemed to be going well. Then last night she turned up at my place out of the blue. In a terrible state. Distraught – almost hysterical. And it all came out. She wasn't here to see me – or his people either. She was here for an abortion. This guy said he'd marry her if she had an abortion. They were supposed to get married here. Then as soon as she has it the guy gets cold feet. Says it's too much of a rush, he needs more time. I mean, can you believe this bastard? So of course Joyce freaks and rushes straight round to me.' He pauses, apparently from exhaustion.

'I'll make some coffee.'

'So we sit up most of the night talking. She's really grateful to me . . . good old Ken, blah blah blah . . .'

'But she might mean it, Ken. This could work out for the best.'

'No no no. It's too late. I'm just a shoulder to cry on.' He laughs bitterly. 'I offered to marry her myself first thing this morning . . . but she wasn't interested.'

I hand him the coffee, which he gulps down. 'Thanks, mate.'

'Had any breakfast, Ken?'

'There was another crisis. Eventually we got to bed, but half an hour later she was knocking on my door. Bleeding. Had to phone my doctor and get him out. You know what that's like in London. Had to threaten . . . shout . . . swear. So he turns up, furious. Not his patient, not a clinic he recommended or is responsible for. Convinced it was me who got her pregnant and arranged the whole thing. Really nasty and sarcastic when I tried to explain.' He buries his face in his hands. 'A fuck-up, in other words . . . a total fuck-up.'

'That's some night, Ken. But when she calms down she'll appreciate all this.'

'No, it's too late. It's over. Maybe next time, eh? Now that I know what to do. See, I've been reading your book.' Reaching for the rucksack, he pulls out and displays *The Art of Loving*. Out of print when he went in search of it, this is actually my copy. Ken shows it almost daily to reassure me that it is in safe hands, cherished and being closely read – but each time the book is in worse condition, creased, dog-eared, frayed, cruelly cracked down the spine. A sight that presents Fromm's alternatives in a brutally practical way. To hoard or to give? To have or to be? So far I have not complained.

'Fresh start, eh? A fresh start all round. You know I've had an offer?'

'Didn't know that, Ken.'

'Software house in the City. Name my salary. Choose my company car. Shares in the deal too. New young company and if it takes off I can sell out and retire in a few years. And these people know what they're doing, believe me. None of this fucking shambles here. Professionals . . . you know?'

'I thought you wanted to go back to a warm climate?'

In the act of raising his cup he pauses, eyes occluded and blank. 'I did say that, didn't I?'

'You definitely said that.'

Another lengthy pause. 'Moving the goalposts, eh?'

'Changing the spec as you go along. Ultimate analyst's nightmare, Ken.'

'Yeah,' he nods, frowning anxiously. 'Yeah.'

'You're thrashing around, Ken. Starting a new job is not a cure

. . . it's the disease. What you need is rest . . . time to think . . . time to relax.'

He nods in eager willingness. 'Practise the banjo, eh?'

'Practise the banjo, Ken.'

Suddenly he springs to his feet. 'Look . . . thanks a lot. I mean for everything. You must have covered . . .'

I wave airily. Anyone can pretend to a knowledge of ART.

'And for listening to all this . . . all this crap.' I wave again. 'No seriously . . . it's been great . . . *do you mind if I pull down this blind?'*

Before I can answer he has done so, plunging the office into alarming semi-darkness. Then he pulls down his zip and opens his trousers.

Every analyst knows of the problem of transference. But how many have had to face sexual assault?

'Jesus, Ken.'

He removes his trousers and hangs them carefully over the back of his chair. Then he takes off his jacket and shirt.

'I need to go for a run.' From the rucksack he takes shorts, a singlet and shoes.

'Is this wise, Ken? I mean, without sleep or food?'

He dons the gear with a happy, concentrated look. 'I need to run when I'm under pressure. This is how I deal with it.' He laces his shoes ferociously tight and jogs ecstatically on the spot. 'When the shit really comes down I just get out there and *run*.'

The inside of marriage is stranger than the interior of the atom. And, like the atom, it is subject to Heisenberg's Uncertainty Principle: every attempt to determine current status alters that status. Thus Liz was annoyed about what she saw as Kyle's successful public relations exercise in London. Yes, everything he had said was true, but his evidence was fantastically selective. For instance, did we know that Kyle had given her an infection by using a dirty vibrator? Hardly an unforgivable crime – except that he had made the condition unbearable by insisting on subsequent penetration. And he was equally insensitive during her frequent attacks of thrush. *Even after the abortion* he insisted on his conjugal rights. And while he always had a meal ready as claimed, he also started drinking in the afternoon so that by the time Liz arrived from Dublin he was high as a kite.

'I mean you work all day and then drive up from Dublin absolutely knackered. And of course David fed up and cranky as hell. All you want is peace and quiet and instead you have this eejit rushin' out of the house singin' like something out of light opera. Recently he's even started coming out into the street playing the saxophone. I wish you'd never played him that bloody Sonny Rollins thing . . . what's it called again anyway?'

'Don't Stop the Carnival.'

'That's the one – I wish you'd never played him that. All you want is to drop onto the sofa and you have Kyle slobbering and pawing over you, stinking of whiskey. I mean I enjoy a drink myself, but Kyle's at it every day in life.'

'*Every day?*'

'Starts every afternoon at four or five o'clock.'

Thus what Kyle was broadcasting as pathological frigidity was, according to Liz, only the natural reluctance any girl would feel.

And *everything* was broadcast, this of course was another problem. Kyle told everyone everything and you knew it was only a matter of time before it turned up in his work. Already he had used the painfully intimate details of her abortion. 'But that's been Kyle's stock-in-trade all his life,' I said. 'This is what makes the books you admire so much. You could hardly be surprised or shocked.'

Liz listened sullenly. Not only surprised and shocked, but intensely annoyed at my attitude.

Then there was Kyle's claim to be exploited and abused, a poor neglected housewife abandoned to feather duster and valium. This had been literally broadcast on radio. 'My wife goes to work while I cook and look after the house and my young stepson.' As there was still a severe shortage of 'new men' in Ulster, this line was hugely successful with women. Yet Kyle was constantly on the go himself, doing his regular jazz gig as well as one-offs and tours, increasingly in demand as a tutor on fiction writing courses, performing regularly on local radio and sometimes even TV, agreeing as usual to everything he was offered.

One extreme example. Renee goes off for the weekend and dumps her mother and child on Kyle and Liz. A bit much, a young child and a geriatric – but OK, fair enough, Kyle is guilty about Renee having the mother full-time. Then, on Friday night, some painter in Fermanagh rings up wanting to do Kyle's portrait. So on Saturday morning Kyle heads off to Fermanagh *in Liz's car* (his own is in the garage after a smash-up), leaving Liz who never walks anywhere to do the shops on foot with two children and a cripple in a wheelchair.

Bad? Outrageous? Grotesque? Wait till you hear the end of the story. At midnight Kyle arrives back full of complaints, expecting sympathy for having had to sit in a hard chair all day.

'And sporting an incredible hard-on,' I suggested.

'*But it's Saturday night*, he said to me.'

It was as a result of this weekend that Liz had fallen out with Renee and the lunchtime plan had been aborted. Already money had been invested in catering equipment which Renee had more room to store. Did Liz ever see any of it? Did Renee return any cash?

All this we got from Liz on our way in from the airport. Kyle had always picked us up before, and it was obvious that Liz had come out herself to set the record straight.

At the house, Kyle was friendly but less extravagant than in London. Immediately the adults split by gender, another innovation. Reba and Liz went into town, taking Sarah and leaving Emma and David. Kyle suggested a country walk on the far side of the motorway.

We set out in a quiet, sober mood. Even the children were subdued. It was a raw and lowering Irish day, heavy with non-deliverance. As it has been, so shall it be. Here nothing would ever change – or only for the worse.

Kyle began by thanking me gravely for the advice.

'What advice?'

'On sexual relations.'

It took me a moment to understand. Truly Kyle is not as other men. If you offer him advice he not only remembers but acts upon it.

'Hardly a permanent solution.'

'It helped for a while.'

On the other side of the motorway, widely spaced wooden steps zig-zagged up a hill next to a stream. We climbed in silence. I had never seen Kyle so morose. He paused and looked back down at the road.

'Who could have foretold that the heart grows old?'

This famous question has an obvious answer: anyone but a self-indulgent Big House Prod. And I could have added a personal objection: many like myself would be glad of a heart that grew old. But I was feeling too compassionate to quibble. When it comes to banishment from Pussy Heaven all men are one.

'What about the marriage guidance thing?'

'Liz's idea. We saw this large, formidable lady who asked a great many questions. I said, can we ask *you* a question. Are you, or have you ever been, married yourself? When she said no I terminated the whole thing. You can scarcely offer advice on an area you have no experience of.'

'That would put most advisors out of business. Me included.'

'But you're qualified on the subject of matrimony. You seem to have made a go of it. What's the secret?'

The famous lover and husband really wanted to know. I experienced a familiar sensation: that of feeling like Kyle's da. A sensation less bizarre than before. Now I looked like his da.

'Maybe it's only the fact of being a Fenian. Our parents stuck it out so we do the same. Yours split up – you split up too. We do what we see done by and large.'

'There must be more to it than that.'

The mucky slope was hard work, especially in white London

casual shoes. We paused on an open-air landing enclosed by a graffiti-covered fence. Expecting exuberant sectarian vileness, I could see only names of heavy-metal rock groups: Anthrax, Iron Maiden, Megadeth. Even at slogan level, indigenous culture is dying out.

'Maybe also the absence of high expectations, Kyle. I've never believed in romance. If we know there's no such thing as a free lunch why does everyone expect a free candlelit dinner? Love is like everything else, largely a matter of work. What you get out depends on what you put in. You know *The Art of Loving* by Erich Fromm?'

'A kind of semi-pornographic sex manual?'

'That's *The Art of Love* by John R. Eichenlaub MD. Very different book, though also a classic of its kind. Remember the Ice-spurred Special?'

'You'll have to remind me.'

'Girl claps a handful of ice on your balls just when you're coming.'

'A little ambitious for me at the moment.' He sighed heavily. 'But didn't you have problems too? Didn't you nearly split up?'

'Every couple nearly splits up. I think all women feel contempt for their men at some time. A public man can look contemptible in private, and vice versa. The problem is that the contempt seems to hit women suddenly. It's difficult for both partners to cope with: very sore on male self-esteem. This is the danger period. Of course the contempt may be permanent, but you can come out on the other side too. You just have to put in the work . . . and then, even harder, have faith in the work.' Was it really this simple? 'And of course you have to not be married to a shithead in the first place.'

Kyle seemed to be pondering deeply. 'I've certainly put some work into this marriage.'

We had finally attained the summit. I felt a little mild triumphalism was justified. 'I have survived to see the victory of scepticism. History has absolved me, Kyle.'

'A fine phrase. Hardly your own.'

'Fidel Castro.'

Kyle was gazing out over the recreation area like an English lord surveying his Irish estates. 'The natural world is always my consolation. Beautiful here, isn't it?'

Actually I thought it was scabby enough. Nothing natural about beer cans and cigarette packets. And the civic tameness failed to impress one with the wild rugged grandeur of the Mass Rock in his blood.

However, the Anglo-Irish Agreement had just granted the Fenian South a say in Ulster's affairs and Protestants were still smarting at having to suffer the pope's nose. There was much talk of 'safeguarding Protestant culture' and 'preserving the Protestant identity'. No one was sure what these were – but it paid to be careful about what you disparaged.

'The other marriages were different,' Kyle went on. 'The first was just youthful madness. The second failed because of me – I was away all the time and made no effort. Really just stayed with Olivia till the children were grown . . .'

'And how is Olivia?'

'Fine so far as I know. Back in Yorkshire with a man who makes garden gnomes for a living. Art of a kind, I suppose.'

'Popular culture?'

'But with Liz it's different. I've tried so hard this time.'

Downhill the going was easier. The walking at least.

'But you could give a lot more. The running around for instance. I mean, have you ever in your life refused an offer to perform?'

He said nothing, even turned away to call to Emma and David down by the stream. But answered in the end – and honestly, as I knew he would.

'I suppose I have something of the actor's temperament.'

You could ask this guy anything.

'And the drinking,' I murmured. 'Why do you drink so much?'

For me regular heavy drinking was a response to Fenian-type problems: failure, inadequacy, lack of self-esteem, despair. But Kyle was supported by the pillars of the contemporary Hercules:

money, looks, charm, a name. According to Liz, the drinking was simply another aspect of his hedonism. Whatever the pleasure, Kyle indulged it to the full.

This time it took him even longer to reply.

'It's a familiar friend,' he sighed. And then, perhaps feeling this was too resonant, too much of a phrase, 'And I find it difficult to sleep without a couple of whiskeys.'

After this, I gave him a rest until we got back to the main road. But the sight of the southbound carriageway brought unavoidable associations.

'And all the travelling, Kyle. That has to be a factor.'

'I suppose so,' he said at last.

'The logic's inexorable. The travelling can't go on. But Liz needs to work to pay the mortgage. And can't get work up here. Whereas you can be based anywhere . . .'

I let him suck on this for a while.

'Bizarre as it may seem, Kyle, the road to Pussy Heaven seems to lead through Dublin.'

In happier times he would have reacted to the Americanism. Now he appeared not to notice. Things were certainly serious.

He laughed bitterly. 'Just when we've got the house fixed up. The roof space was finished only last week.' He turned back and took in the hillside with a grand sweep of the arm. 'Just when I've discovered this lovely walk.'

And, he could have added, just when Protestants were most resentful about the Fenian South. Apart from the pope's visit, it was hard to think of a less propitious time for a move to the Vatican's most loyal colony.

'You moved out of the South yourself,' he said, 'and yet you're recommending it to me.'

'Health reasons. For the NHS. There are imperatives that override everything else. I mean, I'd live up the Shankill if it was the only way to Pussy Heaven.' There was a pause while we got the children safely across the road. 'Also, I'm resigned to the grotesque and the absurd. *Any view of things that fails to recognise their oddity is false.*'

Again he was too absorbed to request an attribution. 'Paul Valéry,' I had to add myself.

Across the road were large detached houses with immaculate and sumptuous gardens. In our morbid preoccupation with the ugliness we tend to overlook the many positive aspects of Ulster. Away from the lights and cameras, caring and nurturing quietly proceed. The cities may be in ruins – but the gardens are flourishing.

'Perhaps you'd like to meet John Goodall,' Kyle suddenly said.

'*Who?*'

'He was one of the actors in Robbie Semple's revue years ago. You and Reba gave us all a nice salad once.'

'Not just at the moment, Kyle.'

'We meet to play chess. Intelligent fellow like yourself. Job, wife and children, struggling to survive and understand.'

'Not just at the moment.'

In one of the gardens a woman was kneeling by a flowerbed. Mature, protected, lush and lovingly manicured herself. I might have desired her once – when I was young and foolish and imagined the suburbs full of sensitive neglected wives yearning for spiritual growth.

Kyle stopped to praise the garden and she blossomed like a Climbing Mrs Sam McGredy (another of Ulster's positive contributions). Kyle especially admired one flowering plant and she offered to do him a cutting. He protested, but she rushed off for instruments and an old yoghurt carton to take the shoot. (Tip for stick men: if the way to a Fenian woman's heart is by praise of her children, admiring the garden may be the secret with Prods.)

Kyle thanked her with extravagant courtesy. What pleased him was not so much the cutting as the proof, arriving just when it was needed, of the warmth and generosity of the province that had borne him.

'Now wasn't that a lovely gesture,' he said, flourishing the carton. 'You see – they're fine people. Fine people.'

9

Grinning, handsome, effusive, an unchanged Kyle met us at a Dublin airport unchanged except for a giant billboard: DON'T BRING AIDS HOME. At the door of the terminal building he made a grand sweeping gesture and uttered his own *céad míle fáilte.*

'Welcome to southern Ireland where nothing moves except the statues.' A reference to two recent events: the collapse of a government 'crusade' to purge the constitution of Catholic elements and the 'movement' of a plaster Virgin in a country grotto at Ballinspittle, a phenomenon that drew crowds of twenty thousand daily. To Kyle these two events were exquisitely linked.

Not that it seemed to depress him – any more than the Irish drizzle or the habitual traffic jam on the quays.

'The statues move faster than the cars,' he said, rooting among the rubble of cassettes and cassette boxes and putting on Ella Fitzgerald singing *The Cole Porter Songbook.* 'But the Ha'penny Bridge is very picturesque – especially at night.'

What shocked me was how little I seemed to remember of Dublin. Buildings, street names, districts, nothing readily came to mind. Normal brain cell burn-out – or was there a suppression factor at work? Even the South Circular Road was not particularly familiar.

The new home was in Terenure, the last outpost of sleazy flatland before the interminable primness of the suburbs. A dim decaying terrace, just like their street in Belfast. And just as in Belfast, Liz explained that they were recovering from a heavy night, this time with Tom McKenna and his young second wife.

Typical of Kyle not to mention Tom. Yet, not only a household name as a poet, McKenna was now in the news as the leading figure in a group of artists and academics dedicated to establishing Ireland as a leading exporter of intellectuals rather than of labourers, bar staff and nurses. They had a magazine (*Eriugena* – Latin for Irish-born, and the name of the first Irish thinker to win international renown), a publishing house (Peregrinatio – Latin for the intellectual emigration common on the part of early Irish scholars), organised readings and symposia, and had been the subject of admiring profiles on television in the UK, where it was recognised that Ireland was a world leader in the growth area of cultural nationalism. I had seen McKenna on the box describing Eriugena as 'poet, translator, teacher, controversialist – above all an original thinker of world class'. After explaining that in the Carolingian era the Irish were in demand as the best Greek scholars in Europe, hence the prominence of Eriugena at the court of Charles the Bald at Laon, Tom as always lightened it up beautifully with the legend of the great man's death – he was allegedly stabbed to death by the *styli* of envious scholarly rivals.

'So what was McKenna on about last night?' I asked.

Liz laughed. 'He told this really good joke . . . if only I could remember it. I'm hopeless with jokes. Something to do with cunnilingus . . . and the punchline was *smokey bacon flavour*.'

Kyle also laughed. 'Tom and I compared notes on the problems of demanding young wives.'

As though their attractive young women were a burden imposed by fate. As though Kyle had been wise and detached about Liz, instead of dazzled by her rowdyism and promiscuity.

'Yes,' I said, 'while the young wives compare notes on the problems of ageing, egotistical husbands.'

'No no no,' Liz cut in. 'Dara could never have a problem with Tom. She thinks the sun shines out his hole.'

Another detached observer. Another Tiresias. Who would guess that Liz herself had barely emerged from uncritical awe? But this had always been her greatest talent. What totalitarian regimes had to toil and sweat for – the rewriting of history to suit the current perspective – Liz had always achieved effortlessly with a wave and a laugh.

Kyle cackled delightedly. 'She put her arm round him and said,

What I like about Tom is that he never hustles.'

It took me a while to accept that this was not a gag.

'Never hustles,' I shouted at last. 'McKenna? He fucking *invented it.*'

Kyle was pleased with this reaction. Not usually fastidious about self-promotion, even he found the vignette bizarre enough to demand recording. And went off to fetch a cartoon of the young Mrs McKenna staring worshipfully at her husband, the immortal sentence issuing from a bubble over her head. But what struck me was the depiction of Tom, a ruthless caricature emphasising the big belly and seigneurial manner.

'Of course I can't paint properly without a studio,' Kyle explained. 'But it has something . . . no?'

We all agreed, even the children. So convivial was the atmosphere that Liz suggested a drink. Only mid-afternoon, but goddam, it was Christmas. Reba produced our duty-free litres of whiskey and gin, which did nothing to dispel the high spirits.

I even indulged myself, despite having frequently reminded Reba of all the drunken Christmas explosions: Sean and Frances one year, John and Caroline the next, Hugo and Rosemary every year. Had we not ourselves once fallen out of bed at 5 a.m., trading punches and screams on the bedroom floor? Reba had not denied these facts, but derived from them a precisely opposite conclusion. Instead of promising more of the same the unbroken series of blowouts meant that this year everyone would be making a special effort. By now they would know when to be cautious and what to avoid. This time it was going to be different.

So the children were sent upstairs to play, and Liz questioned Reba on her new career – a little mistrustfully, it seemed to me, reluctant to believe that backward Reba could have landed such a desirable job. For Liz herself was finding it tough. Not only were female journalists old hat but new journalism courses were pouring ambitious graduates onto a limited job market.

'Remember Campbell Stanway?' Liz said to Reba. 'The new tabloid he was editing flopped so he started a news agency. It's doing really well now – all the English papers use him. I get quite a bit of work there myself. But he's throwing a do today at five. I ought to show my face. Fancy coming along?'

Liz rushed this out in a bright but tense tone – like someone trying to interest you in double glazing before you slammed down the receiver. Or perhaps the sudden silence only made it seem so. It certainly exaggerated the sudden thump on the ceiling.

'*David!*' Liz screamed.

Reba studied me, then Kyle. Then took a sharp belt of gin.

'Well . . .'

Liz resumed her sweet-pants telephone manner. 'Just for five minutes . . . to show my face. And it won't be the usual journalist hooley. You know Campbell. Very discreet and civilised.'

When Reba detected no resistance in my expression, she tried cautious agreement. 'If it's only for a minute . . .'

'I'll put the casserole in the oven and we'll be back in time to eat.'

All that remained was Kyle's blessing. He swirled his drink, finished it in a gulp and continued to stare into the empty glass.

That ancient Irish custom – augury from whiskey dregs.

'I notice you haven't invited me. I notice you don't want me at the party.'

Upstairs the noise was getting worse. Shrieks, bumps, hysterical laughter, a situation moving inexorably to crisis.

Speaking slowly, with great caution and delicacy, Liz put her case. 'In the first place this is not a party, Kyle. It's a staff do. Second, I get more work from Campbell than from anyone else. I want to put in an appearance because we can't afford to lose the money. And I asked Reba along because she was friendly with some of the people – whereas you have always said you hate the sight of them.'

Dignified, well-structured, plausible. Except of course for her claim of an 'appearance'. Most likely she would stay till the small hours.

Kyle chose to defend his low opinion of her colleagues. 'You can't expect me to admire meretricious work.'

Liz stood up decisively. 'If it annoys you that much, we won't bother. I'll put the casserole on and take the kids for a walk.'

Punishment by martyrdom – I never thought to see it from Liz. And an especially hopeless tactic with guilt-free Kyle. For Kyle, the self-denial of others was merely the homage due his talent.

We all set out on a straggling, uneasy walk, out one end of the Terrace, then along the banks of the Dodder and back in at the other end. For all his love of the natural world Kyle had nothing to say about it on this occasion. In fact, there was little talk.

Reba came alongside at one point. 'I didn't want to go to that to see you-know-who. I just wanted to support Liz. I think she should be able to get out on her own.'

More nobility and denial. Was ever the motivation for partying so selfless?

The meal was also an uneasy affair, despite two rounds of aperitifs and a box of wine to wash it down.

I questioned Liz on her agency work. What sort of Irish stories did the English press buy? As usual I made the implication too obvious. She could scarcely admit to supplying the English with caricatures of Paddy.

'Bet you made a few bob out of the moving statues.'

Her laughter was a pale ghost of the old demonic hilarity. This polite amusement would never endanger her pants.

'Are you really interested in all this?' Kyle snapped at me.

Did he feel I was neglecting him? Making overtures to Liz? Certainly he saw motives other than the disinterested quest for truth. Always the problem with unhappy couples. Anything friendly you say to one is interpreted by the other as taking sides.

'We had another big seller recently. Priest found in gentleman farmer's wife's bedroom . . . head smashed to pulp with the leg of a chair torn apart in blind fury.'

'Wow,' I cried. 'Tell me more.'

Now she laughed with some of her old zest. Her pants might even have been in jeopardy – had not Kyle intervened.

'Since you're so interested perhaps you'd like to see her latest work.'

He went away to fetch a newspaper and came back to throw it in my lap. Liz had a half-page spread, most of the space taken up by photographs of Irish writers, underneath each of which was a paragraph describing the writer's plans for Christmas. McKenna made a lot of having to spend it in England – a ludicrous jest of the gods.

'This is her literary contribution.'

'It keeps you in whiskey,' Liz said, 'and that's no easy thing with the price of it here.'

Kyle turned to me. 'Perhaps you'd like to meet Tom again. He's still in town.'

Was he trying to cause trouble? Widen the rift? Implicate me on his side?

'What?' I gasped. 'Not now surely?'

'As you wish,' he said, rising abruptly.

'You're not *going?*' Liz cried.

'Only to get cigarettes.'

'Then don't take the car. You've been at the drink all day.'

He left without answering. We heard the front door slam and the car start up.

At length Liz broke the silence. 'This is what it's like all the time now.'

'And the sex business?' Reba enquired.

'Bad as ever. You know I was in for a D and C? He was looking for it as soon as I got out.'

Kyle returned in angry silence, poured himself a large whiskey and knelt to select a record. Something to distract us, a fresh start – good thinking.

We fixed fresh drinks and moved to the soft seats.

'Listen to this. Chet Baker. He's lost all his teeth and can't play the trumpet. So he sings instead. "My Funny Valentine".'

We listened in respectful silence, sipping.

Eventually Kyle turned to me. 'What do you think?'

The evening was delicately poised. It was a crucial moment. All my life I had taken the path of least resistance and now it was surely more imperative than ever. Appeasement could mean peace in our time, confrontation could bring about a ruinous war. On the other hand, I was being questioned by a man who had made a career out of honesty. Surely it had to be a two-way process. And of course, as the court reports say, there was drink taken.

'I think it's a man who can't sing attempting "My Funny Valentine".'

At once Kyle was on his feet shouting. 'Can't you see it's heroic for crissake? He's lost all his teeth – but he won't give up.'

I tried to temper my disagreement by expressing it as quietly as possible. 'I don't see any point in singing if you can't sing.'

'But you're so mean-spirited. You can't respond to anything noble.' Kyle swung his arm wildly, seeking evidence for the wider accusation – and having little trouble finding it. 'It's the same with my novel. You can't see the generosity of vision. If you'd read it with proper care . . .'

'I did read it with care,' I shouted – but Kyle was already going for the manuscript.

Chet struggled on, heroically or embarrassingly, according to your bigness of heart.

'The tune the auld cow died to,' Reba said with a titter.

Kyle soon wiped the grin off her face. Obviously giving up on me, he went straight to Reba and placed two heavy binders of typescript in her lap.

'Have you read this?'

She gaped at him. 'No.'

'I'd like you to read it and tell me what you think.'

Suddenly Reba looked drunken and stupefied. '*Now?*'

'You don't have to,' Liz said quietly.

Kyle turned and bore down on his wife. 'I have asked Reba to read this and she has agreed.' He was standing over her chair now, leaning down. '*Why do you feel obliged to intervene?*'

Calmly taking up her drink, Liz rose and left the room. Kyle went to the sideboard to fix another whiskey. Since coming back with the manuscript he had not looked in my direction, so I was free to study him at my leisure. His expression had changed. As though he had given up attempting to convert fools and withdrawn to an inner world of certainty and comfort. He smiled to himself – not the usual boyish grin but a contemptuous, lopsided leer.

'Remember the scene outside the club?' he said suddenly, turning to me. The incident in the novel where Protestants offer the sax player Irish-style discouragement in a car park. Kyle's tone was untroubled, his eyes calmly glazed. Everything in his manner now suggested satisfaction. Obviously he was no longer trying to sell me the novel. The question had no aesthetic import. And yet it was heavily charged with significance.

'You're threatening me!' I shouted in amazement. 'You're actually *threatening* me, Kyle.' Instead of denying it he sat down with a peculiar inward-looking grin of contentment. 'You're actually threatening me with physical violence,' I said again, looking around as if for recording equipment and camera crews. I badly needed this scene on film. How else would anyone believe it? Kyle Magee the liberal humanist. At the very least I needed reliable witnesses and all I had was Reba with her mouth open, not in astonishment but abandon, fallen asleep over page one of the novel.

'So what do you intend to do? Beat me up if I refuse to admit you're wonderful?'

He laughed comfortably, dismissively, thoroughly pleased with himself.

I had a couple of swallows of gin. Possibly not a good idea if we were going to settle things in a car park. Nevertheless I went for a refill. My hands were trembling badly. I was trembling all over.

Liz returned with a grave but decisive expression. 'I've been speaking to Campbell on the phone. There's still people there, Kyle. If you don't calm down I'm going now.'

'Go,' Kyle said. 'Go to your young republican friends.'

'Campbell is a middle-aged, white-haired, conservative Englishman.'

'But all the rest are republicans. Wasn't I set upon by one of them as soon as I met you?'

For the first time Liz lost her head. 'And who put him out?' she shrieked. 'Who put him out of the house?'

'Then how come you're always arguing the case for the IRA?' Kyle suddenly turned to me. 'Tell her about the IRA. Tell her what you said to me. Tell her what they're really like.'

So – one minute he threatens to knock your melt in and the next he asks you to lecture his wife on the Right-thinking Citizen's attitude to terrorist violence.

'Liz isn't a republican for crissake,' I snapped. 'You pick on her for consorting with them and yet you lick up to McKenna who's the worst kind of narrow nationalist bigot.'

It seemed to me that, beneath its state-of-the-art European intellectual jargon, McKenna's Eriugena movement was nothing but old-style Catholic nationalism. The same exaltation of Gaelic culture, the same patronising dismissal of Protestant Ulster, the same contempt for and rejection of all things English. As with so much in life, only the language was new. Where pro-British sentiment would once have had you denounced as a 'Castle Catholic' or, more recently, as a 'West Brit', now you would be accused of 'post-colonial servility'.

Liz and an awakened Reba were also shouting, loudly proclaiming the Herron tradition of independence. Ten years of trying to run a business in a lawless area and yet never once had the mother appealed to the self-appointed law enforcers, the IRA.

Kyle ignored them to answer me. 'Tom McKenna has shown me nothing but friendliness and generosity.'

'Oh yes,' I sneered, 'that's why he asked you to be part of his movement.'

Just an instinctive reaction shot – but it dropped him white and sick in his seat like a kick in the stones.

Of course – McKenna had realised Kyle's lifelong dream of a cultural movement with popular support. Old wine in new bottles is eternally popular, and McKenna's movement was probably the greatest success in marketing since the launch of Bailey's Irish Cream. He had created an incredible dissemination machine but denied his faithful old buddy access.

'I think I could have made a contribution,' Kyle said, with a simple wounded dignity that should have softened the hardest heart. Liz certainly seemed to regard him with fresh compassion and concern.

Instead I gave him a touch of his own medicine – the bitter, vindictive, contemptuous laugh.

'You're a fuckin' eejit, Kyle. You know nothing. McKenna has never had an ounce of respect for you. Even if you *were* a liberal humanist . . . and this is increasingly doubtful . . . he would have nothing but genial contempt. There's nothing a nationalist despises more than a wishy-washy liberal. He wouldn't let you within a thousand miles . . .'

Before I could finish Kyle was upon me, seizing my head in both hands. At the crucial moment he avoided delivering a blow, but not before my spectacles flew away across the room. Reba and Liz rushed between us. Kyle withdrew, drained his glass . . . and smashed it against the opposite wall.

I retrieved the spectacles – unbroken. The development of lightweight plastic lenses has certainly improved my quality of life. Now Reba can knock my glasses off with little risk of inconvenience and expense. The knowledge of this is an enormous comfort, especially over the Christmas season.

Not that the lack of damage in any way condoned or diminished the offence.

'You hit me,' I said to Kyle.

'I didn't hit you. If I'd wanted to do that you would have known all about it. I trained as a boxer, remember.'

'So what were you doing – *asking me out for a dance?* You knocked my fucking glasses off.'

'I didn't mean to knock them off.'

I laughed unpleasantly. 'The liberal humanist.'

He fetched a new tumbler and half filled it with whiskey.

Unrepentant and angry still. But at least with the sense to leave the room.

It was hard to believe that this day had begun in the uneventful calm of London. All I wanted now was to get to bed, but Liz poured herself a tumblerful and sat down to tell sad stories of the deaths of kings. 'This is what it's like now. Everything leads to a row.'

We listened in glum silence. She took a hefty swallow and considered where to begin.

But Kyle never found it easy to relinquish the limelight. He appeared in the doorway with an empty glass.

'Well I hope you're satisfied,' he said with heavy sarcasm, going to the sideboard for a refill. 'You're the people who advised me to come to this ridiculous country. Everything would be fine if I just came down here.'

'You brought it on yourself,' Liz shrieked. 'I could have had work in the North and you deliberately sabotaged me.' She turned to us. 'Madge put me in touch with these people in the North – editors and so on. We were to meet them for a drink and then have them back for something to eat. I phoned Kyle from the pub to make sure he was doing the salads. Of course, he says. So then we arrive back and nothing's done. Kyle's sitting playing chess with John Goodall, the house is a shambles and David's asleep on the couch piggin' dirty. So of course there's a screaming row in front of everyone.'

'*You* had a row,' shouted Kyle. '*You* did the screaming.'

'Know what he said?' Liz hooted. 'Chess is a very absorbing game.'

With a powerful two-stride run-up, Kyle drew back his arm and launched the contents of his glass at Liz.

She shook her head free of liquid. 'You know what I said about violence. *I'm warning you, Kyle.*'

He paused, frustrated, then found relief in the familiar way: smashing his glass on the wall and walking out of the room.

'Chess is a very absorbing game,' Liz shrieked.

*

Even after all this Reba had high hopes for Christmas, arguing that it might be a good thing to get the quarrelling over early. In accordance with another of her theories – that the best way to approach Mrs Herron was in the safety of numbers and under the protection of the festive season – we were to visit Harvey Terrace in a two-family group (though Kyle was to call on his children and join us later). But the closer we got to the kulak the more ill-judged this strategy seemed. For me, association with Kyle and Liz was part of the problem, not the cure.

Even worse, the kulak's natural misanthropy had been exacerbated by ill health. On top of chronic cystitis and insomnia she now suffered from arthritis and attacks of vertigo (possibly an occupational hazard of nihilists, the result of a lifetime of staring into the abyss) and bitterly resented her daughters' absence and the necessity of relying on Rosemary, who had become a sort of unofficial health visitor, drawing on her own lifelong experience with a variety of ailments (including high blood pressure, asthma, eczema, migraine, mastitis and a tilted womb). Rosemary was only too glad to get in with the mother (for help in controlling Hugo) but retained undiminished her extraordinary talent for espousing what would most offend the older woman. For Rosemary had found religion – or, rather, she had upgraded to state-of-the-art, abandoning saints-'n'-sorcery for the Charismatic movement, which was anathema to traditionalists like the kulak for whom religion was sombre, immutable, silent, concealed, something never to be mentioned, much less proclaimed in tongues to the sound of guitars and tambourines.

As soon as we arrived in Harvey Terrace she burst into a lengthy complaint. 'That Rosemary has me head deeved about all this Charismatic carry-on. She wanted me to go to these meetins with her on Tuesday nights. I mean . . . did ye ever? Can ye see me batterin' a tambourine and shoutin' hosannah? Says I, Ahm not fit for meetins. So she gets tapes of the meetins. Says I, Ah can't play them. So she gets me this contraption.' Going to a kitchen cupboard, Mrs Herron retrieved and dropped on the table a carrier bag containing cassettes, headphones and leads. Rosemary had bought the kulak a Walkman. Easier to imagine Napoleon directing his marshals by cellular pocket phone. One of the cassettes spilled onto the table – *Methodology for Living: Redesigning the Spirit, Talk 6.*

'Can't you tell her politely to leave you in peace?' Liz suggested, setting herself up for a sucker punch.

'But sure I couldn't manage without her now,' Mrs Herron cried in triumph. 'Sure not one of me own daughters ever darkens me door.'

Family squabble, time to disappear. The big front room was bitterly cold but had a portable gas heater. I sat down with two books I had borrowed from Kyle's study: his own *Bolt the Stable Door* and an American edition of an Alice Munro story collection not yet published in the UK. Although Kyle had yet to arrive, his presence was everywhere: in the typewriter, saxophone case and massive cassette player we had brought up for him in the car, and of course in the act of reading itself, not just through his novel but because in our recent encounter my glasses, which had seemed undamaged, had actually been bent.

Just as I was starting to appreciate the solitude, Liz came in, took a seat and made a great show of warming herself at the heater. Terribly humble and self-effacing, don't bother about me, get on with reading your book. As an attention-seeking ploy it was devastating, breaking down my defences in an instant. Obviously I am nowhere near perfecting the body language for *eff off.*

'Rosemary's arrived,' she said with the peevishness that was becoming habitual now. First resentment spreads to every area of the marriage; next it engulfs colleagues, friends and relations; finally it encompasses everyone and everything. Soon I would have to rename her Sour Pants. 'She's down in the kitchen yapping away about women's health problems. I just had to get out. And then of course David arrives into the middle of it. *What's a D and C?* he says. I had him well warned not to butt into adult conversations, but he's so used to it. And if you'd seen Mammy's face when he said it . . .'

Not hard to imagine. For Mrs Herron, civilisation's crowning horror was the precocious, spoiled child. And in this respect David was certainly state-of-the-art: intrusive, over-familiar, boastful, impertinent, aspiring to worldly assurance and bonhomie, insisting on adult company and adult television, impossible to feed or get to bed.

David blossoming already and Kyle yet to arrive. It was shaping up nicely. A swell bag of nails.

'Why are you reading Kyle?' Liz suddenly asked with keen interest. If she had not noticed the novel, she would have found another cue. Every conversation now was sucked into the black hole of the marriage.

'Checking for anything anti-Catholic,' I had to admit, the public confession bringing home the difference between this and the first reading, when the book seemed not so much a call to freedom as a shout of triumph at a liberation already accomplished. All we had to do was go forth and the husks of the old dead cultures would simply shrivel up and blow away behind us in the wind.

I put it to Liz that the move south had brought about a change in Kyle's attitude on religion and politics. She claimed it had begun during an election campaign in the North. Arguing that IRA atrocities had more than cancelled out unionist injustice (which Catholics had in any case grossly exaggerated), Kyle voted unionist for the first time in his life. In classic tit-for-tat style, Liz then gave her vote to the Catholic party.

At least this was her story. But was she as innocent as she claimed? It was certainly a long time since her support for the liberal Garvin Dodd. And of course Kyle was right: most of her journalist friends were republicans. Madge, for instance, had just come out in open support for the IRA campaign of violence. What did Liz really believe? What did Kyle really believe? As soon as doubt and mistrust are entertained, the questions multiply to infinity. It is nearly always Question Time in Paranoiaville.

One thing seemed certain – the two people I thought least affected by tribalism were now both retreating to entrenched tribal positions. What hope for poor benighted Ulster? Even the butterflies were taking sides.

And myself, the Master of Nonattachment, poring over an old novel for anything to fuel the ancient grievance. At the merest hint of a religious slight anywhere in these pages, all the old resentments would burst out afresh.

In the innocence of youth we think we are healthy and pure – but all the time the virus is in us, lying low in its cosy nest at the base of the spine. And when we are hurt or sick or tired or confused, the deadly lodger spies its chance and rushes out to assume control.

'So there it is,' Liz said. 'On top of sex, where we should make our home, what I should do for a living, we now have religion and politics to argue about as well. We can hardly talk at all without a fight. There isn't a safe topic left.'

'Snooker?'

'We fought about who did the cooking all through the world championship.'

Certainly it was hard to be positive. 'Seems a miracle you're together at all.'

'We already separated.'

'!?!?!?'

'Kyle was back in the North on his own for six weeks.'

'And what happened?'

'He came down on my birthday with champagne and this beautiful slinky silk nightdress. Just a gift from an old friend, he said. Just in memory of old times. So we drank the champagne in memory of the good old days.' Her tone was sombre, with none of the familiar mischief, but the careful timing revealed a residual concern for effect. 'Then he asked me to try on the nightie . . . just to see it before he left . . .' And at the memory of herself in black silk she could not suppress a laugh touched with the old exquisite silver, a broken quivering shaft of moonlight on a magical sea.

It could have been just like old times, but at Christmas there is no room for self-indulgence or pleasure. Reba came in with a passionately talking Rosemary at her side.

'I don't know *what* to get her for a present. See that good Walkman Ah got her and she wouldn't use it. Wouldn't put it on her even. And ye know that time she fell outside Poundstretchers? One of her vertigo attacks. Really hurted herself. She was in bed for days and I got her this lovely thing and she wasn't one bit fussed about it. She has it shoved away in here. Look.' Rosemary took from a drawer an article which she showed to Reba who studied it for a time before bringing it across to Liz and me.

It was a large rectangular plate designed to look like an open book, binding and pages painted in around the sides to frame bold Gothic script.

FOOTPRINTS IN THE SNOW

A man dreamed that he was walking alone across endless fields covered in snow. Just when he felt he could go on no more, God appeared in the grey sky and said to him, 'My child, you are not alone. Look back.' The man looked back and saw two sets of footprints in the snow. And above these were displayed all the scenes of his past life. But as he followed the panorama into the past the man noticed that beneath certain scenes there was only one set of footprints in the snow.

'Lord,' he said, 'at the most difficult periods of my life there is only one set of prints. Why did you abandon me when I needed you most?'

In the sky the Lord shook his head and sighed. 'My child, my poor child,' he said with infinite sadness, 'do you not know that those were the times when I carried you?'

The last time I had seen Kyle was the morning after the affray. As we were having breakfast in the kitchen he came downstairs barefoot in a shiny silk dressing gown that barely covered his ass. It was not a garment to confer dignity but he more than compensated by means of his defiant carriage and resolute stride. With the curtest of nods in our direction he turned into the living room.

'The floor's still all glass!' Liz warned, but he took no heed.

Broken glass, burning coals, water: this man could walk on any surface whatever.

'But where did he get that dressing gown?' Reba asked.

Liz was trying to interpret the low, indistinct sounds. 'What's he up to?' Wearily she palmed her troubled brow. 'He's not starting to drink at this hour?'

From the living room came the answer: a brave or foolhardy attempt to transcend the limitations of nature, namely Chet Baker trying to sing 'My Funny Valentine'.

After this intransigence (at almost *No Surrender* intensity) I was not looking forward to Kyle's arrival in Herrons' – but he blew in with all the old gusto and cheeriness. Not a trace of anger or resentment. On the other hand no apology either, and after all my glasses had been noticeably bent.

As soon as the hugs and kisses were distributed he retired with his true love, the Selmer Mark 6. High-ceilinged, uncarpeted, sparsely furnished, the Herron front room was a perfect echo chamber. Soon a startlingly loud 'Loverman' took possession of the house.

Wanting to keep away from the family, I went in to watch him blow his soul. The shut eyes, the grimacing in ecstasy, the hunching and twisting and dramatic hoisting of the horn. This was the problem with Kyle's playing: you could always see the veins standing out on his sax.

'Well?'

'Great stuff, Kyle. It's just a little hard to get used to in a Fenian house.'

'This music was born in a ghetto. It was born in deprivation.'

A familiar fallacy, the homogeneity of the under-class. Harvey Terrace was not a ghetto but a sought-after location. To most Catholics in the area, the Herrons were impossibly stuck-up.

'Easy to be romantic about blacks,' I suggested. 'Harder with Fenians.'

'But I seem to be spending my life among Fenians. I'll have to find a way.'

Certainly the spirit of reconciliation. Perhaps even a kind of apology.

'Fenians and blacks aren't as separate as you'd think. There was once a colony of Gaelic-speaking blacks in the West Indies.'

'My God,' Kyle murmured. 'What a subject for a novel. I could learn to love Gaelic culture . . . and the book would make Fenians respect the negro.'

On this supremely hopeful note we went down into the kitchen where the natives had a cup of tea ready. Kyle, at his most charming, described to Mrs Herron the difficulties of visiting children in outlying parts of the province.

'But of course exploring the wilderness is a well-known Ulster Protestant trait. Daniel Boone and Davy Crockett were both Ulster Protestants.'

'I never knew that,' Mrs Herron said mildly.

'Oh yes. And many more besides. I have a book at home somewhere. *Ulster Goes West.* Perhaps you'd like to see it some time?'

We looked at the Incredible Scoffer Queen, the Empress of Nay.

'Yeeesss . . .' she murmured unhappily. Not exactly Molly Bloom, but it was definitely affirmative.

'Sounded like someone on the piano with you,' Hugo said.

'Play an instrument yourself?' Kyle enquired in sudden hope.

'Couldn't carry a tune in a bucket.'

Undeterred, Kyle laid a hand on Hugo's arm. 'Come and I'll show you. It's a minus-one tape. Everything except the main instrument so you can play along.'

First the kulak, now Hugo the Brute. We waited, hopeful and touched in spite of our cynicism, as, in a Western, the hardened saloon drunks hark to the back room for the cry of a newborn child. And sure enough it came to us – comic, halting, laborious, gauche – the sound of an absolute novice extracting a squawk from a tenor sax.

'Jesus Mary and Joseph,' Rosemary said, getting up to see what this man was trying to do to her husband.

But there was no miraculous rebirth. Hugo soon came back enraged.

'He thinks it's great to be unemployed. He thinks Ah like sittin' about *pullin' me fuckin' wire.*'

Rosemary, however, stayed on with Kyle.

'She'll have his head deeved,' Mrs Herron said.

'Don't you worry about Kyle.' This was the first contribution from Liz on the subject. Obviously she was trying to lie low.

When Rosemary came back it was only to pick up her *Methodology for Living* cassettes.

'Kyle wants to hear these,' she announced in triumph. 'He says he'll type some of it out for me.'

To convince Mrs Herron of Christlike sacrifice and boundless love there was no surer way than to tolerate Rosemary and her religious obsession. 'He's the only one had any time for that wee girl. Typin' out all that stuff . . . *and him not even a Catholic.*'

Needless to say it did not last. In the morning Mrs Herron was shocked to return from the shops and find Kyle out on the front street *in his incredible shortie dressing gown,* happily waving goodbye to the two startled binmen who had called with seasonal good wishes.

'If ye'd seen him. Like a figaroo, look see. And of course the whole street with their eyes out on stalks.'

'But did he know . . .?'

'Thanks be to God he had the wit to give them the price of a drink.'

Then however, instead of apologising for a garment that would be ludicrous even in a Hollywood sex comedy, instead of rushing off to make himself decent, Kyle actually follows her down into the kitchen and starts making himself his breakfast and chatting away *as cool as you please.*

'Says he to me, *Have ye a banana? I like a banana chopped into my cereal.*' I had the feeling of her shaping the anecdote for a more important audience still to come, like a director in the provinces before an opening in the capital. 'And next thing, says he, I'd like a bit of a fry, I'm very partial to Ulster fries. *Have ye any bacon in the house at all?*' Here she paused to let us marvel at the impertinence. 'Says I, there's only a bit of streaky for coverin' the turkey. Oh says he, I suppose that'll have to do. *I suppose that'll have to do,* says he, and starts cookin' himself a fry. Still in the dressin' gown of course and cookin' away and singin' out of him. Not a care in the world. Gay as a lark. *Gay as a lark,* look see.'

Soon she made another shocking discovery: that Kyle had completely appropriated the front room, adding to his heavy equipment a strew of cassettes, books, magazines, notes and typed manuscript.

'It's like Paddy's market in there,' she said to Reba and me, adding, in a tone of grim significance, 'That's a fella that's never had to pick up after him.'

After a lengthy session at the typewriter, Kyle produced the first fruits of his collaboration with Rosemary.

There's something in my heart like a stream running free
And it makes me feel so happy, as happy as can be.
Now I'm living in a New Creation.
Now I'm drinking at the Well of Salvation.
Praise the Lord, I'm satisfied.
Every need has been supplied.

'I heard about *this* character,' Mrs Herron said. 'He says don't worry about the brown envelopes with the windows. Don't bother your head about bills. The Lord'll look after everything.'

'But his theme is spiritual rebirth,' Kyle explained. 'Something we need and that can only come from inspiring individuals like this man. It certainly won't come from the established churches. At one time I thought they could be revitalised from within . . . I even considered becoming a minister myself . . .'

Mrs Herron failed to suppress a fright reflex. Beneath the charming surface was an unregenerate Protestant . . . a black-enamelled Orange huer.

Reba laid a hand on her sister's arm. 'How would you like to be a minister's wife?'

Ignoring this, Kyle went to the front room and returned with the massive ghetto blaster and *Methodology for Living* cassettes, one of which he placed in the machine, resolutely pressing the *play* button. 'Beneath the clichés what he's saying is fairly sensible. What any sensitive thinking person would say.'

'Are you going to make us listen to a sermon?' Reba cried out in dismay.

'Here is God's master plan, the Divine Design for Mankind. First, no other human being has power over you unless you allow it. Regardless of your situation you have been and will always be free. God has forgiven you; now forgive yourself. God loves you right now; now begin loving yourself. God is love. Remember this when you are tempted by reason and logic – the truth is so simple that smart people miss it. Smart people don't get into Heaven. Grown-ups don't get into Heaven. *Unless you become like the little children* ... Whether you're fifty ... or sixty ... or seventy ... Though of course I know all the women here haven't reached forty yet ...' (Background female laughter.)

'Religious humour certainly hasn't changed,' I said to Kyle.

From the kulak issued a prayer at once heartfelt and fervent. 'Please God Rosemary won't be round here tonight.'

As the girl's new mentor, Kyle felt obliged to speak on her behalf. 'She's desperate for someone to talk to.'

'Sure me head's addled listening to her. She's me head deeved about Hugo. As if Hugo hadn't enough to worry about trying to find work.'

'I've been thinking about these marital problems.' Kyle frowned in concentration, oblivious to the general stiffening and murderous warning looks from Liz. 'Liz and I have had problems of our own' – Liz tilted her head and rolled stricken eyes at the ceiling – 'and I've done quite a bit of reading in the area. *Now* ... ' Coming eagerly forward on his chair, Kyle addressed himself specifically to Mrs Herron: 'I was wondering if there could be anything behind this persistent frigidity problem.' He paused to ensure the woman's undivided attention. '*Was the girl ever sexually abused by her father?*'

Is there a truncheon in the house? Somebody coldcock the eejit. Nothing less will restrain Kyle. He would shite the bed if there was a hundred houlin' him.

'I know her father well,' Mrs Herron said with frightening coldness. 'A decent hardworking man.'

Would anyone else in the world persist in trying to sell psychotherapy to a kulak?

Kyle, with a quizzical tilt of the head: 'And her brothers?'

But on Christmas morning everything is forgiven for the moment. Downstairs plunge the children, closely followed by Kyle in his notorious mini dressing gown, only taking time to nip into the front room for his Selmer and then accompanying the opening of the presents with chorus after chorus of 'Don't Stop the Carnival'.

Mrs Herron, who hardly ever sleeps, is not only up but back from Mass, observing with a bemused look the unprecedented commotion. Reba and Liz arrive on the scene with a camera apiece. Kyle switches to Christmas carols but with no loss of brio, lifting his Selmer in a Dionysiac abandon that threatens to expose his all. With every crescendo he hoists the horn higher ... soon his mother-in-law will have the Christmas present of a vertigo attack. Heedless, the girls crouch with cameras.

'*Liz* ...'

'It's all right. I know. He's wearing underpants underneath.'

Reba aims her camera at Kyle, who obligingly raises his sax.

'Where in under God did you get that dressing gown, Kyle?'

He interrupts a spirited bebop 'Jinglebells' to answer. 'Birthday present from my wife.'

And resumes with an enthusiasm that even draws grudging acknowledgement from the kulak. 'He has plenty of go in him anyway,' she says to me. 'You have to give him that.'

Nor does she seem to mind, now, that Kyle once again remains in the ludicrous garment for breakfast, a deluxe Christmas version of the Ulster fry with black pudding, mushrooms, sausages and fadge. Still unsatisfied, Kyle the connoisseur calls for fried bread. Mrs Herron watches in amazement as he devours it with relish. Even the kulak has long since given up on this most lethal of Ulster delicacies.

'You're not a great one for the health food anyway.'

'We have nothing to fear but fear itself.'

At least he gets dressed for the adult present-giving, an orgy of consumerism in which he and I could of course never participate. Instead we exchange jazz tapes.

'Chet Baker?'

'You'll love him in time.'

Kyle has a weakness for mere *entertainers* and is even prepared to indulge Uncle Toms and clowns. This year he has added to Chet Baker a duet between Bing Crosby and Louis Armstrong. Jazz indeed. I myself favour purist austerity, but in honour of the festive occasion have taped a rambunctious Charlie Mingus selection. Agreeing with Bird that *now is the time*, Kyle rushes off for his ghetto blaster so that Mrs Herron unveils her new microwave oven to the boisterous sounds of 'Ysabel's Table Dance' and 'Wednesday Night Prayer Meeting'.

'Sure I'd never be able to work a contraption like that.'

'It's really handy for cooking on your own, Mammy,' Liz explains. 'It's from all of us here, and Sean and Frances and John and Caroline too.'

Stimulated almost to frenzy, Mingus adds his raucous shouts to the exuberant cacophony of the musicians.

'Let's all go up and see John and Caroline,' Kyle cries, springing immediately to his feet.

Mingus utters a climactic shriek. Wincing, Reba turns down the volume.

Once again Kyle shites the bed. In the first place all the world knows that Mrs Herron detests Caroline. The kulak of course quarrels with everyone – but Caroline has mortally offended by refusing the intimacy of the squabble. In the second place, even if she loved Caroline like a daughter she would never visit. The kulak did not visit you, you visited her. And in the third place she cannot stand Caroline in the first place.

'Sure what would take ye up there?'

The sudden grimness would alert anyone but Kyle. 'Then we'll ask them down here.'

'I'm not having those weans on top of me all day.' Needless to say, Mrs Herron finds these grandchildren also to be monsters of precocity and disrespect.

Instead of abandoning the project, heedless Kyle goes to the phone and arranges a visit. The kulak of course refuses to come along, plunging into a black and bitter mood from which she will not be easily raised. Now she has what she most enjoys; grievance and martyrdom.

John and Caroline live in a private park of homes in the style of the colonial courthouse, flat symmetrical façade set off by a pediment on pillars (of white fibreglass), the pseudo-classicism a bid for the graceful, serene and above all timeless authority craved by the parvenu desperate to conceal the fact of recent arrival. It is a style increasingly popular with affluent Fenians. The native bourgeoisie are the new colonists.

We are greeted by Caroline in a well-cut suit of bolero jacket and long skirt with patch pockets from which she must frequently draw a hand to fling back the girlish long hair her bold resolute movements continually cause to fall over her face.

'It's absolute *bedlam*,' she cries. 'Come on in.'

The interior has none of the suffocating plushiness and clutter of my mother's generation, the Persian carpets, velvet curtains and dark, ornate reproduction furniture. Instead the tone is cool, muted, unadorned, simple, light. Few patterns, pastel shades, clean shapes in lots of space. A style that would have us believe all the ponderous baggage of the past has been jettisoned in favour of bracing clarity, nonattachment and infinite potential. In other words, pseudo-airiness has replaced pseudo-pomp.

'The champagne, John!' Driving a hand through her hair with a clash of bracelets, Caroline turns to Kyle who sits beside her on the oyster-grey leather sofa. 'This is the only day we drink before lunch.'

'Caroline seems very friendly with Kyle,' I suggest to Liz.

'He stayed here a couple of times when he was doing gigs with the quartet.'

In the corner a giant television, austerely black, flickers in silence. Caroline has merely turned down the sound – a revealing touch of vulgarity amid the good taste.

And in the kitchen, an affront to the shining units, tiles and split-level oven, lurks an unregenerate guilty furtive hangdog Fenian male.

'So Kyle's actually stayed here?'

John laughs briefly. 'Rang us up to say his quartet was playing the Holyrood and perhaps we'd like to come along. We both hate jazz – but what could we do? Then during the show he comes down to our table and asks if we can put him up for the night. Fair enough, we do that – and we're up to three in the morning finishing all the drink in the house. Then a couple of weeks later he rings up again.' Pause for a bracing swig of champagne. 'The second time he propositioned Caroline.'

'Propositioned?' I took a hefty snort myself. 'What's the *mechanics* of that?'

'Mechanics?' John laughs harshly. 'He waited till I went out for drinks and then asked her to go to bed with him.' Together we drain our glasses. 'Caroline declined ... but apparently the offer stays open.' Morosely he studies the flecks of foam. There is never enough champagne. Although elsewhere lift-off is apparently being achieved. Bursts of shrill laughter reach us from the lounge.

'But surely it's not much to do for a genius, John. I mean, your drink ... a bed ... your wife ...'

'Don't forget the full Ulster fry in the morning.'

We return to the lounge where Caroline is explaining to Kyle the plight of the liberal agnostic trapped in traditional Catholic culture. The need to send children to Catholic schools. Then your vulnerability to pressure and bullying. The envelope for Planned Giving. The priest at the door.

'Of course we have the kids well warned,' Caroline laughs. 'They know to say they've been to Mass if they're asked.' With a clash of bracelets she drives back her hair to turn on Kyle the full effulgence. 'We actually took them along a few times so they would know what it was. Of course they were bored out of their minds and never wanted to go back.'

Instead of probing to the heart of her ambivalence, Kyle is content to nod gravely, sipping the Irish whiskey that has promptly followed the champagne. On the coffee table before him is a newly opened bottle of Jameson.

Getting the guy out of here is certainly going to be a bitch.

And all the time the kulak building up a head of steam. *Think they can leave me to cook their dinner. Think they can sit up there drinking and leave me to skivvy.*

Reba leans to me to whisper, 'Mammy'll be sittin' wi' her arms folded and her mouth in small plaits.'

Surprisingly, it is Liz who gets us out and back in reasonable time.

'That bird'll be dried up to nothin',' says the mother at once.

In fact the turkey is not at all overdone – but she has decided to punish us by being awkward, claiming lack of sleep, painkillers and a stomach upset have combined to destroy her appetite.

'But you'll have some turkey, Mammy?'

Long grudging pause. 'Maybe a wee pick then. Just a wee pick to taste me mouth.'

'Sprouts, Mammy?'

Further unforgiving silence. 'Maybe a wee wee taste.'

Kyle has one of the turkey legs. David insists on the other, and then hardly touches it. Instead he seizes Kyle's glass. 'Gimme a taste of your wine.' He grimaces. 'Ugh! This stuff is rotten. Think I'm going to be sick.'

Kyle tolerates David's behaviour and even coaxes the kulak with questions about her American trips. Since losing the shop, the old girl has become quite a traveller, though with little evidence of the much-vaunted broadening of the mind. What has impressed her most about the New World is the extravagance and ingratitude of its children.

'You know my brothers have lovely homes . . . beautiful homes. Well you've been in them yourself. But their families are never in them. Never in them, look see. I remember Paul, Danny's oldest boy, going out to *buy* his breakfast somewhere. Lovely homes . . . beautiful homes . . . and yet they won't even sit down to eat their *breakfast* at home. I just said to Danny, says I, you give them too much . . . they get *far too much*.'

'Your brothers are extremely generous,' Kyle agrees. 'But perhaps a little uncharitable to coloured people.'

Seldom is a Christmas dinner visited by the terror of intergalactic silence. Only Kyle continues to eat in happy unconcern. How typical of his reckless extravagance to follow great play with an own goal. No sooner a hard-won advantage than it is thrown away. He would shite the bed if there was a hundred houlin' him.

'Maybe they have their reasons' is all the kulak will say.

Kyle continues to attempt conversation, but there is no chance of a second recovery. All we can do now is gorge on food, drink and junk television.

Exactly the kind of sullen torpor Kyle can never accept. Just after the start of the big movie he announces he is going for a walk. Even on Christmas Day the thought of Kyle tramping Fenian back streets is cause for alarm.

'You could be kneecapped,' I warn him.

Liz laughs equivocally. 'Kneecapped in the head.'

She does not intervene, however, and Kyle sets off with a determined expression, returning an hour or so later with kneecaps intact.

I myself abandon the big movie to follow him into the front room.

'Tired of life among the Fenians?' Testing and probing him seems to have become a compulsion with me.

He is not in the mood to take it lightly. 'I'm tired of the group ethos. This perpetual clinging together for reassurance and support. It seems to me that Catholics only want shared emotions. That business of jeering the Queen's message today. A narrow solidarity of hatred . . . and a total absence of genuine morality. No one here is capable of facing anything alone.'

Who was this anchorite? An advocate of solitary enlightenment who would scarcely go to the corner shop without a minibusload of disciples. And who is he accusing of herd conformity? The glittering heresiarch of youth, now an advocate of solitary withdrawal, perhaps the only adept of nonattachment ever to come out of Ulster.

'You're beginning to sound a bit anti-Catholic, Kyle.'

'So be it. Just as McKenna's reverting to tribalism, so I feel less inclined to be sympathetic to Catholics. Especially after the way those two soldiers were murdered. Protestants used to be the worst for brutality. The Shankill butchers and so on. But now Catholics have definitely taken the lead.'

'Your atrocities are worse than our atrocities. Are we down to this level?'

'And the Protestant excesses of the past have been grossly exaggerated. Another example of group myth. Ulster was never fascist. It was never South Africa.'

'Only because it was part of the UK. But imagine the Protestant State with its own legislative powers . . . and an army to enforce its laws . . .'

Once it was all so different. Once we sought the beam in our own eye rather than the mote in our neighbour's. On *Born-again Ulster*, without any conscious agreement between us, Kyle had attacked the unionist ethos and I did my best to pillory Catholic nationalism.

Like schoolboys with stamp collections we had exchanged religious grotesquerie. He showed me the metal emblems and insignia that marked his father's rise through the Orange Order, the Royal Arch Purple and all eleven degrees of the Royal Black Institution:

lips stamped with the word SILENCE, clasped hands, seven-stepped ladder, skull and crossbones, Aaron's rod, crossed trumpets, square and compass, seven-pointed star and red cross. I showed him scapulars, a Saint Joseph's cord, a Sacred Heart picture (rays of light emanating from a gashed heart garlanded with thorns and bearing a blazing cross on top) and the miraculous medal that is sewn onto underclothes, or dropped in the garden of a house to facilitate purchase or rent.

We even began to spend money on grotesquerie. Kyle bought me a *Protestant Telegraph* with lurid denunciations of 'The Purple Harlot of the Seven Hills'. I bought him a *St Martin Monthly* in which, under 'Thanksgiving for Favours Received', grateful readers recorded the saint's help in passing the driving test or the civil service exam.

'In southern Italy there's a statue of the Virgin that secretes human blood. And in northern Italy there's a Church of the Holy Prepuce.'

'You mean they claim to have . . .'

'Absolutely. He was a Jewish boy, remember.'

Kyle was impressed, but far from beaten. On my next visit he presented me with a record currently charting in the Protestant heartland – 'The Pope's a Darkie' by the Bitter Orange Band, a jaunty country-'n'-western-style song that begins with the pope's consternation on awakening in the Vatican to discover he has turned into a black man.

We agreed that our communities, divided in so many ways, were at least united in racism.

'But wasn't Saint Martin de Porres black?'

'Half-caste. Spanish father, black mother.'

'Then why is he so popular in Ireland?'

'He knew his place. Remember his life story in the magazine? *I am only a poor half-caste servant. Sell me.*'

We planned to write a play in which Martin de Porres, product of two bitterly opposed cultures, returns to earth to put his experience to use in healing divided Ulster. Despite the surpassing sweetness of his temperament he is everywhere subject to contumely and rejection, including torture by loyalists with butcher knives and, finally, kneecapping in the head by an IRA convinced he is a British army undercover agent.

It was obvious how we would share the writing – Kyle would take the Protestant and I the Catholic scenes. In Altnagarvin we sat up to the small hours, throwing back the Jameson and shrieking with laughter.

Late on Christmas night Madge Dillon rang to say that the local team was enjoying a revival and *everyone* went to the home games now. You didn't have to be a soccer fan to enjoy the crack. Liz emerged from her inertia to set about organising a party: 'We can bring all the kids, it's a family thing.'

But on Boxing Day David has a stomach upset. To Kyle there is no problem – leave him in bed. Liz has to point out that her mother is no Florence Nightingale. David is vomiting regularly and roaring for attention, sympathy and service.

'I promised Madge I'd go, Kyle.'

Long, profoundly troubled pause.

'In other words you're telling me to stay.'

'It's the obvious thing. You know you don't get on with Madge any more. And I hardly see her these days.'

It is true that Kyle has never warmed to Madge since the wedding whereas the rift between Liz and Madge was healed when Madge had a serious breakdown immediately after the marriage. At once her eccentric behaviour was forgiven as mental ill health.

And now Madge is restored to her former harmony and confidence.

'*How're ye doin', Mrs Herron!*' Doubts, qualms, grudges, sulks – every form of reluctance and pettiness is swept away by her boisterous entry. Settling happily in the kitchen, she informs us that the team is under dynamic new management and now includes a North African and even, would you believe it, a Brazilian.

'A Brazilian,' Kyle repeats in soft wonder, staring at Liz, who keeps her attention fixed on Madge.

Also an over-the-hill Scottish player, once a well-known star with a major English club, Madge cannot recall which at the moment.

'Arsenal!' Kyle howls in anguish. 'He was a striker for Arsenal.'

I am aware of Madge's interest in the local soccer club. Purely professional at first, a couple of colour pieces on the revival of the team. Shattered community . . . restoration of much-needed pride et cetera. Magnificent response from the fans . . . not a trace of English-style hooliganism, practically no policing needed. Beneath the chatty cosy surface a subtext: that, unlike the loutish Brit, the Gael is *incredibly responsible* if given *control of his destiny* and that this is scarcely surprising since the Gael had a civilisation and culture when the Brit was still wiping his arse with a tuft of grass.

Now Madge has become a real fan herself, although as much for the atmosphere on the terraces as the play on the field.

'It was great when they got the Brazilian. All ye ever heard from the terraces was *Give it tay the darkie!* Of course the minute they did he was hacked down. *Hi, ref! Where are ye, ref! Sen' off the huer!*'

Outside the ground we meet up with Frances and Sean and their children, just arrived to spend a few days with Sean's family and recruited by a Christmas-night phone call from Liz. Frances appears to be dubious, but the enthusiasm of Madge and Liz will brook no negative thoughts, sustaining the carnival mood even after the bitter news sweeping the ground: North African injured and Brazilian gone home for Christmas.

'What!' Sean shouts at Madge. 'You mean there's *no darkies at all?*'

By way of consolation she hands him a half-bottle of Teacher's. At least the Scottish striker is on – but my allegiance goes to Badger, a local grey-haired winger who defies the pitiless years with a performance as lively as any on the field.

'*Come on, Badger!*' I shriek, a carnival contribution rewarded by Liz with a look of melting intimacy and gratitude that does more than hard liquor to keep out the cold. Several in the crowd also look round in surprise. For, contrary to Madge's promise, there is no brilliant repartee. Nothing but a sullen silence punctuated by sullen roars.

Frances the sports girl is also silent.

'Still go to squash?' Vivid is the memory of our single encounter when she held the centre of the court in casual, strong-thighed arrogance, lashing the ball into corners and making me pant, sweat, slide, fall and run into walls.

'I gave up the club.' Bitter shrug of contempt. 'Nothing but men trying to get off. All the socialising and drinking got me down in the end. That's all they think you're there for – to get off.'

'So what do you do now?'

'I weight-train.' The chill of late January afternoon? A shiver traverses my spine. 'I go to this gym with a women-only session. You can work on your own there in peace. No one bothers you.'

So Frances has also arrived in Notown. For her too, maturity has meant isolation. Every honest road leads to a lonely place.

When the bottle comes round I take a hefty swig and pass it to Frances in the silent solidarity of the mature disabused. After a long snort she holds it up to what's left of the light. Not worth passing on. She puts it back to her head.

There are no further stimulants. Play slops from end to end in untidy waves. With ten minutes remaining, Badger floats in a cross. The Scottish star jumps and misses, but it falls to a gamely scuffling local who manages to poke it into the net.

Madge appears to be satisfied and sets about organising the victory celebrations. After a home match 'everyone' goes to the Avoca Hotel for a drink. Win or lose it is always great gas. She will introduce us to the players.

Sean and Frances make the excuse of having to visit Mrs Herron. Liz lays a hand on my arm.

'Come and congratulate Badger.' The old mischievous laugh. The entrancing profligate eyes.

'He'd enjoy it more from you, Liz.'

Her gaze sweeps the dear silver that shines in my hair. 'I'll tell him I love mature men going grey.' The eyes drop to mine. Magical intimate laugh. Enslaved, I am given my chore. 'Tell Kyle I won't be long. One drink.'

If I can say this as though I believe it my performance will merit an Oscar. But when we get back to Harvey Terrace we find that Kyle is long gone.

Mrs Herron, explaining the situation, demonstrates that reporting can never be value-free. Although scrupulously calm and objective, her attempt to render mere facts is almost insanely judgemental.

'He's gone to John and Caroline's. Ah ha. Just after you left.'

'And David?'

'Wrapped him in a blanket and took him with him in the car.'

We ponder this in a silence heavy with kulak resentment.

'Oh yes. And then says he to me on the way out, says he to me, *don't you think Caroline's a most attractive girl.*' She looks round the company with an air of detachment and calm. 'So. There you are now. That's the way of it. There you are.'

Is there no limit to Kyle's indiscretion? Not only damning himself he must also bury Caroline even deeper in the shit.

Only now does the kulak miss her third daughter. Reba explains that Liz has gone off with Madge.

'So she's gallivantin' as well. Oh they're a pair, the two of them. They're a pair all right. They've that poor child carted everywhere from pillar to post.' Finally all pretence at objectivity is cast aside. 'Ye see, Kyle's gettin' too old for all this carry-on. He's too old to be runnin' about in auld vans with pop groups. There's too many young ones at that carry-on now. He'd want to sit down a minute at his age. And her too.'

This is blowing up into a classic shit storm. After savaging Liz, the kulak will turn on Frances and Reba. Finally she will accuse all her offspring of blighting her life ('Ah lived before Ah saw one of yese, look see').

The children of Frances and Sean, expecting generosity and good will, regard in amazement the older Catholic tradition of universal contempt expressed in mounting peevishness and anger.

Neither offering presents nor hospitality, the kulak has yet to even acknowledge their presence.

'We'll have to go,' Frances says curtly. 'Sean's mother'll have a meal ready.'

Too late, Mrs Herron realises that she has overdone it again. 'Sure there's a whole heap of turkey here and no one to eat it.'

When the guests continue to prepare for departure Mrs Herron is driven to something resembling an apology. 'I never got those children anything. I wasn't fit for the shops.'

My fear is that we will now be left alone to face the music. But resourceful Reba expresses a sudden concern for David, claiming she promised Liz to minister to her son.

'But there's no call to go over there. Give them a ring.'

'We'll just nip over for a minute.'

'But ye'll be back for a bit of turkey?' Mrs Herron cries, caught in the bitter trap of the misanthropist. However you loathe the human race you need at least one of its members to heap scorn upon.

Having had enough of aged parents, Sean and Frances cancel the family trip and come along with us.

'This is a terrible crowd to land on you, Caroline.'

'We'll never notice a few more.' Once again Caroline presents a dazzling contrast to the kulak, dismissing the problem of numbers with a bracelet-clashing wave of the hand.

David, fully recovered, is watching television with the other children in a kitchen littered with the happy detritus of the season. In the lounge Kyle is comfortably settled in an armchair, tea and Christmas cake in his lap, a glass of whiskey by his side.

Reba seems to enjoy explaining the whereabouts of Liz. 'It's where the women all go to get off with the team.'

Frances adds a brutal thrust. 'Wouldn't have minded going myself. That Scottish fella had a great pair of muscly thighs.'

Laying cup and saucer on the floor, Kyle turns to Caroline with unmistakable queasiness. 'Can I use your phone?'

'They're only teasing you,' Caroline says.

He returns looking angry and miserable.

'Get her?' Reba asks lightly.

'Madge.'

There is an awkward silence, tactfully broken by Caroline taking a drinks order (which John fills). Then she engages Kyle on the subject of a new play from Tom McKenna's Eriugena movement. Currently touring Ireland, this must-see production draws on the latest historical research and dramatic technique to present a vivid picture of the culture clash between Planter and Gael. Certainly it undermines the colonial stereotype of potato-eating priest-ridden Paddy, revealing for instance that divorce was permitted by Brehon law and that the pre-potato diet was remarkably modern. Not merely the first saint and scholar, the Gael was also into health food a thousand years before anyone else.

Just as I am about to enter the discussion, Madge and Liz arrive by taxi.

'Good to see you're so concerned about your son,' Kyle says at once to Liz.

'David's *absolutely fine*,' Liz roars, glancing round to see if we have taken note of the unprovoked aggression. 'I've just talked to him in the kitchen. He's watching James Bond and he's *fine*.'

'Any of you folks hungry?' Once again Caroline's intervention is perfectly timed. Grossly under-utilised in accountancy, the girl should be fronting controversial live television. 'There's loads of turkey and ham. We can have a cold plate.'

Though lightness, even insouciance, is the predominant style of the house, in the dining room traditional values prevail. Long table of polished mahogany. Rows of high-backed dark chairs. Massive sideboard with dinner service and cut glass. Tradition, authority, order, calm.

'Beautiful room,' Kyle says.

'But we're never in it,' Caroline cries. 'John only ever wants to eat in the kitchen.'

Despite lack of experience with the room they prove an effective team, John in the kitchen passing plates through the serving hatch and Caroline in the dining room distributing them round the great table. Liz and Kyle are at opposite ends but apparently happy, impatiently calling for the box of chianti slowly going the rounds. Kyle in particular looks entirely at home, eating with as healthy an appetite as those who have been freezing on the terraces and, 'not a bit bird-mouthed' as the kulak would put it, calling for the mustard and cranberry sauce John has forgotten to pass through the hatch.

Liz turns to me with that low, intimate voice that goes below the social superstructure to speak directly soul to soul. 'I wasn't neglecting David. I just had to get out of that house.'

'Who said you were neglecting him?'

She lays a hand on my arm. 'I just had to get away from my mother . . . and above all from Kyle. I needed a while away from everyone. And it was beautiful over there in the Avoca. A big fire . . . hot whiskeys . . . but I had no intention of staying all night. I just needed a while away. Madge was furious when Kyle rang . . .'

Our heads, which have been drifting together, instinctively part and lift to look down the table. At once Kyle drops his eyes to his Christmas pudding.

'Caroline, a wee bit of brandy butter and this would be perfect. My mother used to make beautiful brandy butter.'

'There's no brandy butter here,' Caroline laughs.

'Sure it wouldn't take you a minute to make some.'

Although his tone is playful it is obvious that Kyle would not object if she granted his wish. Caroline utters a laugh with just a hint of naked steel. A hostess is not a skivvy. Never mistake charm for subservience.

'There's mince pies for after. Home made.'

'Only Protestants can make proper mince pies.'

How to counter a joke that may not be a joke? For Caroline the answer is simple. With a laugh that may not be a laugh.

Subtleties lost on the rest of the company who are becoming increasingly boisterous and convivial. When the lateness of the hour is mentioned, John suggests putting the children to bed upstairs.

The real problem now is lack of drink. Spirits practically gone, chianti box finished, off-licences shut. Reba points out that Harvey Terrace is well stocked – and every drop of it ours, chosen, bought and transported by no one but us. It is only a matter of calling in to collect what we want.

How wonderfully simple a course of action when you are recommending it to someone else. For of course there is no question of Reba herself making the trip. It is obvious that no blood relation could raid the kulak and live.

What she has in mind is equally obvious. I decline to go alone, hoping for support from Sean, the favourite son-in-law. Easy to see why he is favourite. The canny fellow holds his peace – and Kyle pipes up instead. Once again Destiny is making me his accomplice in pillage and rape.

The kulak is watching *Columbo* in the living room and to her already black mood is added the fury of the aristo at being caught out in vulgarity. I produce a cover mission – David's pyjamas and ventilator – and Kyle sits with her while I sneak clinking carrier bags out to the car. Not that there is any hope of fooling the Ancient One, but being candid with elders is not in my power. Furtiveness is second nature after a time.

In the car Kyle's expression takes an ominous turn. Once again leaden sludge has replaced the sparkling house wine.

'Why didn't you say what you came for really?'

'This is our culture. A lie for a lie and an untruth for an untruth. Our parents concealed everything from us so we conceal everything from them.'

'I can't understand why you're so pusillanimous.'

'I can't understand why you're so angry.'

'It's the way you treated Mrs Herron . . . lying and walking out on her.'

'What?' I shout in amazement. Once again it is sheer surprise that sends me over the top. 'Don't give me that, Kyle. You don't give a shit about Mrs Herron. You're the one who walked out on her in the first place. It's not that. You're angry with me for some other reason.'

He turns to give me the benefit of his new expression. Half a ton of rapidly solidifying slurry.

'Don't be so fucking stupid.'

As always, tone is the crucial thing. Often the most brutal content is essentially inoffensive. But now Kyle's tone is unmistakably heavy with contempt. I'm not crazy about the actual words either. Colour starts to drain out of me. My body contracts.

It seems we even get angry in opposite ways. Kyle's face darkens; mine goes white.

'Listen.' I thrust a blanched countenance at him. 'You're no fucking intellectual giant yourself.'

He nods grimly, vehemently. 'Oh you're frequently clever. You can be very sharp at times. But Goethe talks about this. He says God gave man cleverness as he gave claws to the cat. You're clever all right – but all you can do with it is wound.'

For a sage supposedly lacking talons, he's drawing a lot of blood himself. Fair enough. It's a cutting fight.

'At least I don't beat my wife.'

Anyone else would have stopped the car and thrown off his coat. But Kyle is never a predictable opponent.

'She drove me to it,' he says with surprising calm. 'It shows what I've had to tolerate.'

The logic is breathtaking, exquisite. His violent acts do not reveal a violent man. Quite the opposite. If someone as gentle as he lashes out it shows that the provocation must have been beyond human endurance. Clear proof that Liz is the guilty one.

Dig that casuistry! However slow-witted in the rest of our lives, when it comes to self-justification we discover the subtlety of Aquinas and the daring of Einstein. Even so, Kyle's defence is in a class of its own, right up there with Proust's proof that sadism reveals 'a gentle and scrupulous nature' (because, to the purely virtuous sadist, pleasure appears so wicked that it can only be enjoyed by impersonating wickedness).

My fascinating speculations are cut off by the sight of a

mesh-covered Land Rover and heavily armed RUC.

'*Jesus, Kyle.*' I brace myself as though for a head-on collision. 'You've been drinking all day. You'll be done for sure.'

'Calm yourself.' Kyle rolls down the window and shrewdly takes the initiative. 'Has there been an incident?' Exactly the right tone, concerned but not obsequious, a confident law-abiding citizen offering co-operation and support.

'Just routine.'

This is the new breed of RUC man: youthful, courteous and handsome, with the neat short hair and moustache of American homosexuals in the seventies. Where are all the glorious rednecks of yesteryear? Retired to isolated hill farms? Emigrated to Canada? Dead of apoplexy at having to endure the pope's nose?

The one at the window scrutinises Kyle's licence. 'What are you doing in this area, sir?'

'Visiting in-laws.'

Bending to return the licence, the officer subjects me to an experience rich in reactions for Fenians – that of staring into the eyes of an RUC man. Immediately I feel the pull of apparent opposites that are in fact the same. Ingratiation or defiance would be equally natural. The really difficult thing is not to react at all.

'You *see*,' Kyle cries as soon as we are out of earshot. 'This Fenian fear of the police is absurd. With Liz it's almost pathological.'

'Where do we get these ludicrous notions?' Ironic detachment is the intention – but I remain far too jumpy to bring it off. 'Why do we fear our impartial police force? Especially after decades of community work by the B Specials.'

'The B Specials were farm boys protecting their homes from the IRA.'

If the Friendly Sons of Saint Patrick could hear him now.

'You sound like a unionist politician, Kyle.'

Again, what ought to be a grievous insult draws a surprising response.

'I've often thought of becoming a unionist politician. Trying to swing the tribe. I've just too many other commitments.'

This at a time when political prospects are so bleak that moderates are abandoning their parties in droves for media and public relations jobs. Even now Kyle believes he can save the province. You certainly couldn't accuse the guy of *je-m'en-foutisme.*

'And it's time you Catholics stopped exaggerating. The B Specials were never the Klu Klux Klan.'

'*Ku* Klux, Kyle. *Ku* Klux.'

'Ku Klux.'

The agreement is prompt and amiable. His anger seems to have subsided and a hero's welcome from Caroline entirely restores his good humour. Glass in hand, he calls for jazz. Grimacing, John explains that they have only Caroline's classical records, Mozart mostly.

'I *like* Mozart,' Caroline says with the firm simplicity of conviction, flashing her husband a sharp but useless reprimand. Fenian through and through, John would apologise even if he *was* Mozart.

'A young man with real talent,' Kyle agrees, as though he has just auditioned Amadeus for the Kyle Magee Quartet.

'*K467!*' commands Caroline. 'Piano Concerto 21.'

Revived by the arrival of drink, the party breaks into voluble groups, Sean and Madge discussing football, Reba and Frances and John conferring on tactics for handling the kulak, Kyle attempting to sell Caroline jazz, our hostess listening with interest and appreciative laughter but remaining entirely unconverted, indissolubly wedded to the concerto and the symphony.

Liz squats on the floor by my chair, a troubled Magdalene, sore, afflicted and perplexed. Sipping gin, she talks of Kyle's relentless and savage abuse. Describing her as an IRA sympathiser is only the latest accusation, one to add to a growing list: journalistic whore, slatternly housekeeper, neglectful mother, frigid wife.

'I can't take much more,' she says. 'I need people to like me. I need to be well thought of.'

'I know that, Liz.'

She sips her gin, frowning, unable to understand where it went wrong. 'It's really starting to get to me. All my confidence is going.

I'm getting nervous and flustered at work. I can't make decisions. I can't organise anything.' A familiar tale, damaged self-esteem crippling the psyche as a damaged heart cripples the flesh. 'Worst of all, I'm starting to feel unattractive. Unattractive and old.'

From the way she concentrates on her gulp of gin it is plain this is sincere candour and not a bid for flattery.

'I don't think you need to worry on that score, Liz.'

She moans in authentic gratitude and lays a hand on my knee. Imagine a mangy old bear having a gallon of wild honey poured over his head.

As a result I fail to notice Kyle until his contused and congested features are looming directly over us.

'I've just about *had enough*,' he shouts, seizing Liz by the arm and dragging her to her feet. 'We're going.'

She breaks free. 'I've warned you, Kyle. Any more violence . . .'

'Kyle, it's only . . . she was just . . .'

He ignores me to concentrate on Liz, lapsing into a strong mid-Ulster accent. 'Ye'll get no divorce in Dublin.'

'But I can get it up here.'

'Then Ahll show ye up in court for the huer and irresponsible eejit ye are.'

By now Caroline and Madge are between them.

'You're *over-reacting*,' Caroline sharply informs Kyle.

Liz to Madge: 'I'd better go.'

'You're not going off alone with him in that mood.'

Reba and Frances also try to persuade her to stay.

'I'll have to go. It'll be all right.'

She turns to thank Caroline for the meal and apologise for ruining the party. Kyle waits by the door in angry silence, demonstrating the advantage of the Zorba ethos. A life force need never apologise. Everything is justified because everything is life.

After they leave, Sean ('the night is but a pup') attempts to rally those of little faith. 'Sit down a minute and have a drink,' he says to Madge.

For once she is not in the mood, turning angrily to John as the male relative and, with no apparent sense of breaching feminist principle, upbraiding him for not applying the patriarchal heavy hand.

'You shouldn't have let her go with him when he's in one of those moods.'

'She's a grown woman, Madge. I can't dictate to her.'

Disgusted, she asks permission to phone a taxi.

John glumly goes to kill Mozart, still gamely promoting harmony and elegance in the background.

'You know, I could see that coming,' Caroline says to me. 'He was watching you and Liz all night.'

Frances, accepting a drink from her husband, demonstrates the Herron love of terseness at the expense of nuance and scruple.

'He's a bastard,' she says.

Sean, approaching me cordially with the bottle: 'Sure we're as well off without the fucker.'

Terminal desolation settles on me like a nuclear winter. Nothing could be less attractive now than a wallow in tribal solidarity.

'No thanks.'

Reba gives me a sharp look. 'You're not going to try to defend him after *this?*'

As it turns out, Sean is right. The night *is* but a pup. No sooner has Madge left than there is a commotion in the hall and Liz bursts into the living room, shrieking, her head bent to the hand holding one side of her face. Everyone jumps up. She runs into my arms.

'We had no keys to get in.' Her speech is thick and slurred, as though from a local anaesthetic. 'Me mother was in bed with a sleeping pill and we couldn't get in.' Her head lifts a fraction. 'You have the keys.'

'*Keys?*' I repeat stupidly, forgetting the booze raid.

'So we had to come back here. Then we had a terrible row in the car . . . and *he thumped me in the face.*' She buries the damaged side on my shoulder, groaning.

'Where was this?'

'Just outside.'

Vigilantes make for the main door. Liz cautiously lifts her face and takes her hand away. Cuts on the lip and nose, the whole side of the face puffy and swollen.

'Anything broken?'

'Don't think so.' With trembling, slow fingers she probes mouth, nose and cheek. 'Last time it was a broken nose. Had to go to Casualty. He kicked me in the face.'

'*Kicked?*'

'Kicked. And broke Olivia's nose too a couple of times. Among other things. She did a sworn affidavit for the divorce case.'

So the charm is far from free. You have to pay through the nose.

Sean returns, frustrated and unappeased. 'He must have cleared off. The car's there – but no sign of your man. Unless he's hidin' in the bushes.'

John brings the answer. Kyle is in the dining room with Caroline, who has locked the door on the inside. At once a hanging-mad mob attempts to storm the room. Speaking through the door, Caroline suggests that there has been enough trouble for one night.

'Worried about your Waterford glass?' Frances shrieks. 'We won't break your good glass.'

Moving to the front, Sean lays a calm hand on the knob and reveals an intuitive grasp of a basic truth – that obedience is commanded by lowering rather than raising the voice.

'Open the door.' A low growl of authority, straight up from the balls.

Certainly it impresses Liz, forgotten at the back of the group. 'I don't want to see him. *I don't want to see him.*'

Reba leads her away upstairs.

Through the door Caroline directs us to the serving hatch in the kitchen. This implies concessions but when we get there it is she who makes the demand.

'Two cups of coffee, John.'

'*Coffee!*' shrieks Frances. 'Coffee for that pig.' She thrusts her head into the hatch. 'I'll fuckin' well throw it round him.'

Even John is no longer docile. 'Maybe he'd like some more of your Christmas cake,' he says with quiet impertinence. 'Or a mince pie. No – I forgot. Fenians can't make mince pies.'

Caroline regards him coldly. 'That sort of attitude is no help at all.'

He leans into the hatch, calm but intense. 'Maybe you haven't noticed – but the man has just smashed up my sister's face.'

Further encouragement to Frances. 'I know what he'd like,' she cries to Caroline in a perfectly insane parody of brightness and gaiety. 'He'd like a wee ride.' She puts her head through the hatch to address Kyle. 'The offer's still open . . . *yes?*'

Reba must have passed the story of the proposition to Frances. Needless to say I promised John not to breathe a word to a soul. Caroline slams down the hatch. Even if we get through the night alive, the fallout will poison the earth for a hundred years.

'*You're not making him coffee!*' Frances shouts at John now. 'By God she has you well trained, that one.'

Will there be two among us still on speaking terms in the morning?

'I'm making us all a cup.'

Good idea: mugs will give us something to do with our hands.

Frances pounds at the hatch. 'Coffee for her ladyship. *Get your knickers back on.*'

Caroline collects in dignified silence and slams the hatch shut behind her.

Reba appears with the medical report on Liz: nothing broken, merely exhausted and sore, almost asleep already.

By and by Caroline resumes negotiations at the hatch. 'Kyle wants to go now.' She looks to Reba. 'But he needs the keys.'

'Ahll fuckin' dance to him,' Reba shouts, rushing to the hatch. '*You're not fuckin' wanted in our house.*'

'You can't send him on a long drive at this hour. He's had a lot to drink. He wants to stay here but I told him that's not on either.'

'You mean you'd love to go to bed with him but you don't want your face rearranged.'

I take the keys to the hatch, getting a glimpse of Kyle slumped at the far end of the long table.

'You expect us to sleep in the same house as that bastard?' Now Reba is furious with me, face flushed and mottled, eyes hot and wild. Contrary to Hollywood cliché ('You are beautiful in your wrath' – John Wayne to Susan Hayward in *The Conqueror*), an angry woman is just as ugly as an angry man.

'You mean you're going to let him walk out of here?' This is Sean to John, the last possible pair to fall out with each other. If there is anything more infectious than acrimony I would not care to encounter it.

No, I tell a lie – Frances and Sean appear to be still on good terms.

'We don't want any more trouble,' Caroline is saying now. 'Kyle isn't proud of what happened. He says it's the fault of his boxing days. He's cursed with a good right hook.'

'Oh isn't that too bad.' Another chorus of bitter scorn from the Herron girls.

But eventually a peace formula is hammered out. Kyle will be granted safe passage if he goes to Harvey Terrace before us, leaves the key beneath the doormat and disappears at once to bed.

But his departure does little to lighten the mood. Caroline makes for the stairs in mute, white-faced fury. John goes after her and they launch into a screaming row on the landing.

'Time to go, folks,' Frances declares.

Knowing Kyle's disregard of constraints, I can imagine him roaming Harvey Terrace waiting for someone to try to send him to bed. The official whiskey bottle is here, but he may well have a stash. Better another cup of coffee in the exhausted calm after the storm.

By the time we follow him, the dawn chorus is starting. As agreed the key is under the mat and no one lurches out of the living room whiskey in hand. Reba goes straight to bed and falls at once into a deep sleep. Usually I go out like a light myself – but tonight something keeps me awake, no doubt the presence of Kyle in the house.

A few hours of tossing with intervals of nightmarish sleep is even worse than insomnia. I rise and go downstairs. The Selmer is still in the front room so he has not slipped away. Probably sleeping like a baby. Once again I marvel at his sense of invulnerability. One phone call to Hugo and the guy would be dead meat.

Needless to say, Harvey Terrace does not have the corrupting luxury of central heating. Whoever is first to rise lights the fire in the living room. An ancient skill, long since lost to London Irish like myself. I gather poker, tongs, coal bucket, newspaper and a box of Zip firelighters whose spirit smell and friable texture take me back to my bedsitter days (at home it was always newspaper and sticks). The tiny freezing dank room. The overcoat on the bed. Carefully retrieving reusable cinders. Carefully emptying the cinder tray into an empty coal bag.

The pleasant sensation of ancient ritual is disrupted by something unusual in the grate. Among the ashes are scraps of fabric partially burned. Something soft, with a dull sheen, frilly in places. The charred remains of silken knickers. In the freezing dawn Kyle must have squatted here and made a fire out of his wife's pants. Always a man to invent his own rituals. And a solemn Burning of the Pants might be as good a way as any to mark the end of a marriage. But the honey-soaked gusset of Liz would not be easy to set alight.

Someone comes downstairs and goes into the front room. Then out through the front door. Then back again to the room. Obviously the man himself, shifting his gear.

'Goodbye, Herrons!' a voice sings out with biting irony, more of a taunt than a valediction. Unrepentant, unhurried, uninhibited, unashamed. But no, he is leaving without an Ulster fry so perhaps he is harder pressed than he sounds.

There is no response from the sleeping house. Squatting, I stare in a trance at the ashes and charred scraps of pants. The guy is leaving. Now is the Time.

Already behind the wheel, he rolls down the window and presents a face of ancient sediment: misshapen, thick, dirty, caked hard.

'Don't hit Liz again.'

His eyes lift briefly, full of the new thing – contempt.

'She deserved it,' he says, bending to put in the key.

To retaliate or not? Even respected Zen masters have been known to strike wayward pupils to bring them back to their senses. And still he has no sense of danger, eyes firmly fixed on the ignition. You can get terribly tired of being dismissed as pusillanimous. I punch him in the face as hard as I can. And indeed there is instant enlightenment, though not of a particularly spiritual kind.

'*Ye dirty wee fucker!*' he roars, pushing violently at the door.

As always, failure to think the thing through immediately causes a problem. Efficiency would trap him in the car. Fair play would let him out. Decisiveness has never been my strong point. I lean on the door – but only half-heartedly, so that he has no trouble forcing me aside and bursting out onto the street. On the pavement he assumes an alarming crouch: disciplined, purposeful, wary, compressed. A boxer's crouch. All at once I feel uncoordinated and insubstantial. A strong gust of wind would knock me down, never mind the legendary right hook of a champ. Will he go straight for the KO – or tee me up first with a left jab?

Zorba, teach me to dance.

Despite expecting it I entirely fail to see the punch. Only instinct makes me sway back. The fist brushes my cheek and clips the edge of my nose. An inch closer and I would be out cold. I flail back inexpertly, wildly. Sucker punching a seated opponent is infinitely easier.

Only now is the full absurdity made manifest. In all my years I have never thrown a punch, much less pursued a fist fight. A man entering middle age, with a damaged heart . . . an *advisor.* And on the very spot where I courted Reba. *Make love not war* was our generation's slogan. Everything is going in the wrong direction. Backwards, backwards, backwards, backwards.

'I don't want to fight you,' Kyle says, backing off.

I pursue him, shaking uncontrollably, like a rogue washing machine shuddering across the kitchen floor. Gradually the surroundings come back into focus. Already we have travelled halfway down Harvey Terrace. Kyle slows and drops his guard. There is blood on his face. Beside us people emerge from a front door, shouting. In the middle of the road a car slews to a stop, the woman driver getting out to remonstrate. No doubt these are genteels who take us for brawling nouveaus. Little do they realise that the pugilists are scions of the Protestant and Catholic bourgeoisie.

Someone seizes me from behind – Reba.

I permit her draw me back to the house and push me into the front room.

'Jesus, you look *terrible.*'

I can imagine. Pinched, white, shaking, manic, wordless, wild-eyed.

The room has been stripped bare. Even the book I left on the mantelpiece is gone.

'The Alice Munro!' I howl in anguish. 'I was only halfway through.'

This seems to affect me more deeply than anything. From Zorba you expect enormities – but not pettiness.

Reba is peering out of the window. 'Some woman's looking at his face.'

Two secondary aches finally get through to my consciousness. The left side of my nose hurts like hell and my right hand is cut. Most likely the blood on Kyle's face is my own.

'Now he's getting back into his car . . . I think he's going . . .'

Involuntary memory. Kyle skipping down the steps of his home, squatting happily on the floor of my bedsit, grimacing over his Selmer, helpless with laughter on a bench seat in Grogan's . . .

'He's starting up . . . definitely going now.'

But surging back stronger than ever in memory.

The Irish madeleine – a punch in the face.

10

For the even-tempered and competent it is almost impossible to resist promotion in a state-run bureaucracy. To evade major responsibility requires almost superhuman vigilance, fortitude and stamina. Carving out and preserving my niche has been far from easy. I have had to fight my way to the bottom.

This morning I am preparing a training manual, as always taking infinite pains over wording and structure, arduously producing a distillate of absolute purity, a limpid essence unadulterated by familiarity or ingratiation. Not for me the desperate need to reassure and be reassured.

Of course the rigour is not appreciated. A few discriminating souls admire the clarity but increasingly there has been dissatisfaction with what has been seen as inhuman exactitude. They want a user-friendly interface: the enthusiasm of the sales pitch, the breeziness of breakfast-time television, the vacuous effluvium of DJ babble. An attitude that has received a powerful boost from a new man, a clown who gives his demonstrations a 'welcoming ambience' by decorating the computer room with a minivanload of his own potted plants. When this first happened, the discriminating few waited for ridicule to do its work. Instead the practice was hailed as a breakthrough. Emboldened, the man had the impertinence to criticise what is perhaps my finest manual, my *chef d'oeuvre.* And to criticise its *style* of all things.

Needless to say I have made no concessions. We all have our standards and our carefully delineated areas of slippage. I will stoop to ingratiation only for sexual favours from Reba.

Now the writing is finished and I am about to add an appendix of diagrams stolen from textbooks. To conceal the source the procedure is as follows. First the textbook page is photocopied and the diagrams are cut out. Then the cut-outs are pasted onto a blank page, care being taken to avoid telltale skewing. This page is photocopied and the copy is carefully examined for dark lines and smudges around the edges of the cut-out. These are treated with correction fluid and a further copy is taken. Usually this third copy is good enough to be added to the text and sent to the reprographic unit with a signed statement to the effect that none of the material is protected by copyright.

It is a peaceful and pleasant chore. But first a coffee. I take my own jar of Continental Blend from a drawer (for me, coffee sharing has been no more successful than other communal ventures). Miraculously the kettle on the windowsill has enough water to cover the element so there is no necessity to descend to the Gents three flights below for a fill. This could be one of those rare days when happiness makes up in height what it lacks in breadth. A perfect, untroubled, plateau-years day. While the kettle boils I watch the street below, a narrow alley leading past the front offices of several wholesale clothing companies. In the doorways, bosses loiter sullenly, middle-aged men with heavy brutal faces, blow-dried hair and expensive leather bomber jackets the colour of child's excrement. This is the market place that is sucking us all into its hideous vortex. An edict has just announced that all advisory staff must work for a time in the real world. These days no niche is safe.

Some are winkled out – but as many are lured. Discontent and restlessness are the dangers of the plateau years. Incorrigibly perverse, for us appreciation is rare and only easy in retrospect. To learn to savour our moments of peace as they occur is the difficult but necessary lesson.

Another tremendous boon is that Ken is out of the office today, an increasingly regular occurrence. At the end of the month he leaves to join a City software house for whom he is more or less working already. Even better, there is no sign of Alanna, Ken's new Australian girlfriend who shares his interests in mountaineering and folk music and has submitted to a crash computing course from Ken in order to better her status as a swimming pool attendant. For several months Ken has coached her in the office, laughing fondly at her mistakes and shrieks of frustration and glancing over at me for approval like a doting parent. Few things are more embarrassing than the love play of other couples but, having counselled Ken to spend more time with his women, I can scarcely complain when he takes my advice – even though Alanna is a biker and has added to the chaos of the room a studded leather jacket and an enormous crash helmet.

'She may not look it but she's very shrewd,' Ken said to me. 'I'm getting her into the new firm as a word-processor operator. I've no doubt she'll go far. And now we have almost identical interests. We can work together, sing together, run together. You know we abseil Thursday lunchtimes in the gym. *Why not join us some time?*'

'I don't think abseiling's for me, Ken.'

'How do you know till you've tried it?' He pulled his chair across to mine. 'But it's great being with an athlete. You know . . . the muscles all taut . . . stomach flat and hard . . .'

So many things can never be said. How to explain a preference for women marked by childbirth and the punishing years of parenthood?

But today no Alanna, no Ken. In glorious solitude I cut and paste with a pair of sharp scissors and a new Pritt Stick. Who is happier than a craftsman with proper tools and peace to get on with the job? Happiness is absorption, says the sage. At such times I feel a continuity in my life. Despite all that has happened (or failed to happen), I am still the schoolboy who worked for hours at beautiful multicoloured maps of the relief and drainage of obscure river basins. That schoolboy was not deceived – he knew the effort was pointless. Yet he was happy to be sequestered and engrossed, a monk embellishing an illuminated manuscript far from a coarse and venal world.

The first letter from Kyle was surprisingly mild. Two thirds of it described his recent activities, including an Ulster tour with the Billy McKnight Trio and the successful launch of the new novel.

> There is an air to the reviews of *we didn't realise he was so good.* I enclose a few to show how isolated you are in your response. Perhaps now the Ulster public will follow the critics. Although when I was installed in a Belfast bookshop last week to sign copies, most of the customers took me for a security man and showed me their bags. But every experience teaches us something. Next time I will not let myself be positioned near the door.

Then, after a page or so:

> I understand why you wanted to hit me but expect you to understand why I thought hitting Liz none of your business. It was one tormented blow, unfortunately accurate and hard (cursed with a good right hook) and regretted as soon as it happened.
>
> Liz and I seem to be sorting out the separation amicably enough though some animal within howls at loss. Certainly it is very satisfactory to be on good terms again. You have no idea how traumatic it is for someone as noble and kindly as myself to be hated.

I wrote back in what seemed to me a similar vein, devoting the first two thirds of the letter to a discussion of the novel and related issues. Then I agreed that marital problems are no one else's business but added that couples who fight in public and appeal for support can scarcely complain when the bystanders get involved. Also, my right hook was so much less powerful and effective than his. Perhaps he could coach me? Purely out of academic interest of course. Hopefully, now that the dust had settled, we could all go back to the calmer relationships of happier days.

The response was instant and dramatic.

> Your letter is really an exercise in a certain style and it is pretty good of its kind. One smiles at witty turns of phrase that soften up the reader for the short breaks into apparently profound sincerity. But the total effect is as ugly as your mean anger on the

pavement. Generous spirits do not have to be told that certain blows are expressions of frustration and love.

To encourage Liz to free herself from this violent monster is a grotesque distortion of truth and a terrible disservice to Liz. *Calmer relationships of happier days* is really awful. Growing souls need a fair amount of violence. I could have saved her from the tribe and the world of hack journalism you have driven her back into. When David grows up he will not thank you for your intervention.

As to your right hook the sneaky blow through the window connected but caused no damage. Out on the pavement, bored stiff and frightened by your anger, I was glad to feel that I could have hit you at will and your comparative youth would not have made up for physical incompetence. One can be almost glad of going to a public school at times.

I do not hate you or anything but you have a sort of meanness that only my love for Liz could have made me work at. It seems clear to me now that your contribution was a chance to express your envy and resentment, sexual as well as literary. It must have been galling to be impotent in both fields but close to someone who was not. Your furtive and timid desire for Liz has been a particularly pathetic thing to watch.

Renee agrees that there is something unhealthy and disgusting about your Peeping Tom attitude to sex. Repression has made you malicious and destructive and I think that, consciously or unconsciously, you have been quietly poisoning the marriage from the start. If you are unable to enjoy Liz you will see to it that no one else does either. It is certainly something you could do well. And it explains so much: the strange frigidity of Liz after a glorious beginning, your callous suggestion that I use her body, your insistence that I move to Dublin, your hatred of a novel that was obviously destined for success. My tragedy is that I failed to understand this until too late.

Out in the big world life is far from the crippled and limited thing you seem to think is inevitable. Even now as I write there

> lingers in my nostrils the scent of a courageous and attractive young woman with as much going for her as Liz. More in fact for unlike Liz she has genuine talent and a desire to dedicate herself to it. An embryo jazz singer of great promise, she came up from the crowd last night to do several songs with the quartet. And sexually she is a strange heroic offspring of Henry Miller with amazing natural sexual gifts to make all fantasies real. I have no idea how it will work out in the long run but excitement is there and available in quite real and practical terms.
>
> Almost every day offers happy surprises to those with the courage to accept them. All the time I meet people with more positive attitudes than yours and no less intelligent. I do not feel like an oddity.
>
> 12.40 a.m. I write consoled and heartened by the music of the great Scottish tenor Kenneth McKellar.
>
> Where I may have done Liz wrong is by telling lies or modifying my normal behaviour to get at her lovely body. We had more going for us than most, and reform and discipline would have produced results. I know that, like telling a good steak from a bad steak, I was trying to bring out the best in her and when I hit her it was a demand that she choose between love and bullshit.
>
> I have not yet accepted that it is water under the bridge and now that I understand your influence I may be able to counteract it. Obviously I cannot prevent you talking to Liz but I have no desire to see you again myself.

It was one of Kyle's midnight specials, the angry whiskey letters that were legendary even in the rancorous local arts world. Though aware of these for years, I had never actually seen one, much less been on the receiving end. I read it several times a day and it always said the same thing. The limitations of my right hook no longer seemed a laughing matter. I added ten extra press-ups in the morning and took to shadow boxing in the mirror.

A week later a second startling letter arrived. This was from Kyle's new London agent, a Simon Broderick, who said Kyle had spoken highly of my volume of uncollected stories. Would I care to send it along for an opinion?

Was the pope a Catholic? Did a bear shit in the woods? We pretend to be detached but our vanity has feather-touch controls.

I phoned the agent immediately, assuming Kyle had put his word in before Christmas and would withdraw it as soon as he remembered. But in fact he had made his recommendation only a week earlier, possibly even on the same day as writing the letter. Somehow it was exquisitely characteristic. The guy was promoting me in the morning and sending me hate mail at night.

The Resources Committee has been scheduled at short notice over the lunch hour, something that I am pleased to see annoys even its English members. For, contrary to popular belief, *la vice anglaise* is love of meetings, not beatings. As soon as they gather officially, otherwise sane and intelligent English adults lose all sense of time and proportion, debating the most trivial details with fanatical enthusiasm into the lengthening and derogatory dark. Reluctant to generalise about a people, I used to blame personal circumstance – work obsession, bad marriages et cetera – but I have come to see the phenomenon as the wornout fag end of a shining faith. Radical ends usually deteriorate into a fixation with means – a technique is easier to apply than a principle – and the great English religion of democracy has petrified into idolatrous worship of committee procedure.

And of course the meetings phenomenon is particularly weird to someone of my background, a northern Fenian whose main experience of lay gatherings is a stone-throwing mob.

Nick Ackerly breezes in, ignoring the atmosphere of sullen resistance exuding from Dave Fox with his crash helmet ostentatiously before him and Chris Hartley entirely absorbed in his sandwich tin and flask.

'Now as you know we put in our bid for a new system some

time ago.' He pauses and looks round, alerting us to a witticism. 'But these things are like elephants mating – much high-level huffing and puffing and no results for two years.'

Everyone laughs happily, including Chris and Dave. So much for the English Resistance.

Ken Sutherland rushes in, gaunt and wild-eyed, blundering his way to a seat with many muttered apologies.

'Now,' Nick continues, 'the powers that be . . . *in their wisdom*' (light laughter) 'have finally approved – but they've given us only a week to put our views.' He pauses gravely. '*We'll have to get our skates on.*'

'But we don't want *another Mickey Mouse set-up,*' Ken bursts out with a passion suggestive of momentum gained in a previous encounter. 'I mean, if you're a Noddy user . . . fine – but many of us here are doing *serious work.*' Growls of agreement and approval. 'We need power and high-res graphics if we're to run the new packages. What we need now is a *network* of *proper work stations.*'

There is a ground swell of serious mature support, something a master like Nick Ackerly would never deny. 'I couldn't agree more, Ken. *I'd* love an all-singing-and-dancing system too. All the bells and whistles. Power and high res. Screens everywhere . . . even the *loos.*' He pauses to let the laughter die and ensure we appreciate his sincerity. 'But we have to accept that this is the era of cuts. You're talking telephone numbers, Ken. You're talking two hundred thousand to crazy.' He pauses again to let this sink in. 'Now I'd like you to listen to Irene and her proposals for enhancing the existing system.'

Irene rises, Nick's creature, unmoved by grimaces and groans. The existing inadequate system was her baby but she has consistently refused to acknowledge the mistake. For her, as for so many others, success is the triumph of will over intelligence.

Ken is first to break the dismal silence left by her proposal. 'But we all know the system is rubbish, Irene. Why throw good money after bad?'

'Well,' Irene sneers. 'Of course the macho types always want new toys.'

Macho? Caring supportive Ken? A man who carried *The Art of Loving* until it almost fell apart. The charge is so monstrous that he can scarcely articulate an answer. Stumbling to his feet, he blurts out mangled sentences in which the f-word is clearly indicated without actually being pronounced. A pathetic technique I had thought exclusively Irish. Here it has the effect of handing Irene an undeserved moral advantage she immediately exploits to the full.

'*Well* . . . I really don't think there's any need to swear.'

'Ken,' Nick begins – but Ken is already on his way out, white-faced and trembling, bumping tables and chairs.

Now the proposal to enhance the old system is only tepidly opposed. At just the right moment Nick throws in the decisive sop – he will not buy an all-singing-and-dancing network but in acknowledgement of a genuine need he will acquire two sophisticated work stations.

'If we keep the old system where would they go?' A sullen Dave Fox tacitly accepts defeat by questioning the details instead of the principle.

Nick shrugs lightly. 'My room? I could move out.'

Once again we are outclassed, struck dumb by this unexpected generosity.

'It's the biggest,' Nick says simply. 'And central as well.'

'But where will *you* go?'

He shrugs dismissively. This is not important. Rejecting status symbol management, his only concern is for the department.

'Just as long as your back's protected,' Chris Hartley calls out, and everyone enjoys a much-needed laugh, none more hearty than that of Nick himself.

It pleases Nick to imagine he survives by his wits in a dangerous and unpredictable environment. He likes to think the advisory department is a seething, murderous Borgia court.

Liz came over to visit us, supposedly to forget the separation in

London's Disneyland of the arts. In fact she scarcely left the house, lying in bed almost until we got home from work, then waiting for us to cook and get the children to bed so that the serious business of the day could commence: drinking monstro boss gins and complaining bitterly about Kyle.

'We're supposed to be separated but he's never off the phone. He just can't take it. No one's ever rejected him before. He's never off the phone – and he keeps turning up out of the blue in Dublin. I thought I'd be safe when he went back to the North. Then of course he gets really narked if I'm not around. *I don't know why you had to have the house*, he said, *you're never in it. Where have you been anyway?* None of your fucking business, I said. And then he keeps demanding things out of the house. This is after taking a removal van full of stuff. I was interviewing a guy by phone when he arrived with the van and he had half the house away before I could do anything. I had to stand in the hall and watch it all going past. And still he has the nerve to demand more. He even wanted stuff out of the garden. I said, *for fuck's sake Kyle you're not going to start digging up the garden.* So then he accuses me of being bourgeois, obsessed with property and gardening. I mean you know our back yard – a skittery wee bit of concrete with clay round the edge. About four fucking daffodils. *Oh it's all right for you*, he says, *but I have no flowers.* I went out and cut the fucking daffodils and handed them to him. *Take the fucking flowers then. Now are you happy?*'

We would start between nine and ten and by midnight Liz would be warmed up. Reba and I usually faded round one but Liz invariably stayed on, drinking in angry solitude. God knows what time she went to bed. After a few days I took to pouring myself a mineral water instead of gin and tonic. Liz suspected nothing, but Reba caught me at once. I expected her to be furious. Instead she joined in the subterfuge.

But hangovers were only a minor part of the strain. The main problem was the no-win nature of the discussions. Liz had a burning need for self-justification and an anger desperate for release. Possibly common in separating couples, both were certainly familiar from Kyle's letters. When *he* punched *Liz* it was love and frustration; when *I* punched *him* it was cowardice and envy. When I expressed myself well he could jeer at me for being clever; when I expressed myself badly he could jeer at me for being gauche. Now Liz angrily demanded our support in her accusations against Kyle. But as soon as we gave it she would start to defend him and just as angrily turn on us. It was impossible to agree or disagree. Worst of all was to try for objectivity and detachment.

'I've never seen her like this,' Reba groaned. 'I'm even starting to sympathise with Kyle again.'

Haggard and haunted, Reba looked like the one with the broken marriage. For another source of resentment was Reba's new job. To Liz, Reba was the know-nothing shop girl, later the know-nothing housewife. Her destiny was to stay in the background and support those bound for glory. Yet while Liz was getting nowhere, here was Reba in a sought-after job and actually selling paintings on the side. I tried to explain this to Reba. Few afflictions are as painful and humiliating as that of eroded differentials.

With me, Liz was deeply suspicious of the letters to Kyle. Either they were angry and usurping her privilege or sympathetic and betraying her. When I showed her Kyle's side of the correspondence the jazz singer episode seemed to affect her in a way that went beyond jealousy and scorn. It seemed to me that she was afraid of Kyle bragging about something else.

'She's screwing him,' I said to Reba.

'*No!*'

'You think Kyle drives to Dublin to argue about flowers?' I quoted him: '*You have no idea how traumatic it is for someone as noble and kindly as myself to be hated.*'

'Wasn't that a joke?'

'Was it?'

Reba ruminated in silence. 'But she *couldn't*.'

I let this one float up and away over the trees.

When it was out of sight Reba said, 'He must be laughing up his sleeve at the lot of us.'

'And at me in particular. Though not being able to throw it up to me must be killing him.'

Another oddity – in her incessant analysis of the dying marriage Liz had never once alluded to the Harvey Terrace brawl. Not that I expected or wanted any form of approbation. I did it for myself not her. But to talk continually around the incident without ever mentioning it required both concentration and will. It occurred to me that she disapproved on religious grounds. Though she liked to project independence and spirit, when it came to the arts Liz had the piety and subservience of a Muslim child bride. Whatever the provocation you did not storm the mosque and punch a Holy One in the face.

'What are you looking forward to?' she asked me one evening, late, when she was tanked up on gin.

I shrugged lightly. 'Early retirement.'

Unamused, she grunted contemptuously and continued to stare. More was obviously coming. Women always empty the magazine.

'To do . . . *what* . . . exactly?'

The words were pronounced slowly and carefully. She was very drunk.

'To squat in silence in a dark pool . . . at the heart of a dark forest.'

Not bad for an impromptu answer. The Frog Prince in reverse would be my fairy tale. Liz continued to stare heavily, but with something disconcertingly new in her eyes. What accountants call 'negative goodwill'.

Note the protective ironic phrase. Kyle was right about many things, including my use of flip language as a distracting evasion. Let me be plain and direct for once. I am not detached from emotional life. I can be hurt as easily as the next man. What I saw in her eyes was dislike.

'And that's it?' Again she was choosing her words with great care. 'You're not much . . . of a *specimen . . . are you?*'

She would probably have forgotten this completely by morning. Whereas I would remember it to my last breath. I shrugged, waving the mineral water I wished was a drink.

Women always empty the magazine.

I get back from the Resources Committee to find the blinds down, the light off and a body stretched out on the floor of the office. A partially naked man's body, hairy white legs glowing in the darkness with a ghastly phosphorescence. Profoundly disoriented, I stand in the doorway for a long time.

The man appears to be seriously ill – but not dead. After a few moments he stirs and turns to me with a groan, solving at least the problems of identity and dress.

'Jesus, Ken.'

'Sorry...'

'Why the running gear? *What's wrong?*'

'I'm sorry...' With much groaning and trembling he pulls himself up and drops into his chair. 'Everything was getting too much so I went for a run in the park ... must have blacked out or something ... don't remember much about it...'

'Jesus, Ken. Get to a doctor.'

'That's just it.' He buries his face in trembling hands. 'I can't go to a doctor. I have none.'

'?!?!?!'

'The business after Joyce's abortion. Doctor thought it was me knocked her up and I was spinning him a line. After he saw her he gave me the push. *Mr Sutherland, I'd appreciate it if you found yourself another* GP.' Ken sighs deeply. 'But what with one thing and another...'

We sit in silence in the gloom. A faint memory stirs.

'But isn't there a doctor for staff? A Civil Service Medical Unit somewhere?' What I recall is a circular urging staff to fight for a service in danger of being cut. 'Petty France?' The number is still in the internal directory and the unit is still alive, no thanks to me. I get Ken an appointment for an hour later. 'Now... *coffee.*'

He writhes in a paroxysm of guilt and self-loathing. 'I can't use your jar again.'

'Exceptional circumstances.'

I boil the kettle and prepare two mugs, one of which Ken seizes eagerly, cupping his hands round the heat.

'Now what is it? The meeting? Irene the bitch?'

'Fuck Irene,' he says, taking a long bracing sip. 'It's Alanna.'

'Gone?'

'Worse than that.'

'Gone with your money? Your belongings?'

'Worse,' he says, beginning to take a certain grim pleasure in the extremity of his case.

'Gone with all your computers?'

'Gone with a guy in the band. Frank Kelly.'

'The Irish fiddler!'

Ken sits his mug on the desk, rests his elbows on his knees and hangs his head. 'So it's a beautiful fuck-up. My personal life is fucked up. My professional life is fucked up – I mean, she'll be there at the new job, won't she? My recreational life is fucked up. I mean, the band has a gig tomorrow night.' He seizes his mug and drinks avidly, grimacing a little at the acrid aftertaste that makes Continental Blend worth the few extra bob. (Like Flaubert, I need a touch of bitterness in all my pleasures.) 'A total fuck-up. But you know what's the worst thing of all?'

'What's that?'

'Knowing it's all your own fault. Knowing there's no one else to blame but yourself for the whole thing.'

'You're wrong, Ken. That's the best thing. The inevitable journey has three stages – Innocence, Disillusion, Acceptance – but hardly anyone goes the whole way. How many blame themselves for anything? You've taken a major step, Ken. *The adept has reached the third stage.*'

Ken regards me in amazement. Advisors should not get excited. The phone rings.

'*Fuck!*' Ken screams, with a jolt, as though viciously stabbed in the back.

A soft Irish brogue asks for Ken.

'I'm not here.'

'I think it's personal, Ken.'

I hand him the receiver and start to back out of the room, recording an image that will live in the memory: Ken in his running gear at the desk, naked legs phosphorescent in the gloom, haggard face watching me with a blank, faraway look.

At last he drops his eyes to the receiver.

'Frank,' he says.

We saw Kyle again: on television, a half-hour interview on Channel 4 as part of an Irish festival. *Show Them the Instruments* had just won a major new literary prize (set up to reward works that promoted peace and reconciliation between the communities in the North). With his mostly intact French good looks and checked, open-necked lumberjack shirt, Kyle resembled Jack Kerouac or some such American beat saint. The interviewer was classic southern Irish spoiled-priest: twitchy, sanctimonious and superior, obviously anxious to nail Kyle. As yet the Académie irlandaise had admitted no beats.

After a brief discussion of the early books he homed in on the broken marriages, no doubt expecting Kyle to retreat in a defensive confusion of guilt and shame. Instead Kyle gave himself enthusiastically to the subject, frowning in concentration and speaking in the hesitant, fitful manner of a serious man grappling with a difficult problem.

'The first marriage was very short of course. We were both too young and wild, I guess.' His rueful sigh and *I guess* made him seem like an American movie star sincerely expressing regret. 'The break-up was both our faults. But the failure of the second marriage was almost entirely my fault. I was too busy writing, performing, travelling . . . building myself a career . . . *several* careers. I didn't put enough into it . . . and a marriage can only thrive if both parties work at it constantly. It's just like writing or playing saxophone or any other worthwhile activity – you don't get a lot out unless you put a lot in.' He nodded several times in a self-accusation that would have lasted much longer if it were not for the waiting audience. For their sake he roused himself with a sigh. 'And with the third marriage . . . well . . . I thought I did put enough into it this time. I worked so hard at that marriage. I was determined not to make the same mistakes again. So I became a sort of house husband. My wife went to work and I cooked and cleaned and so forth. I even moved to the Republic for the sake of my wife's career . . . and many aspects of southern Ireland I find deeply repugnant. And I think I was a better step-father to her son than I was a real father to my own children . . .' Once again he drifted off into a troubled reverie.

'So what went wrong?'

Kyle started slightly, as though surprised to find himself still in company. 'She kicked me out,' he said with a quick laugh, the terse demotic producing an effect of total candour and sincerity.

During the break, Reba and I stared at commercials in stupefied silence. We were trying to cut back on midweek drinking but as soon as she expressed the wish I sprang to my feet and made stiff G and Ts.

'The instant this ends,' I said, 'we'll have Liz on the phone.'

Far from showing Kyle up, the impertinent probing was infinitely better for his image than the usual bland cosy kiss-ass. It was the interrogator who was coming across as an asshole – but all he could do now was press on.

'Wouldn't you say that your life and work reveal a profoundly ambivalent attitude to women? That in fact you hate women really?'

Chuckling in delight at the absurdity of this armchair psychoanalysis, Kyle drove a hand several times through his hair. 'I *adore* them,' he sighed with a fervour that must have had female viewers swooning all over the land.

'But perhaps you'd be wary of another marriage?'

'Not in the least.' He grinned disarmingly. 'I'm a born husband.'

Having failed totally in his bid to get Kyle, the spoiled priest fell back on routine questions about the new novel. The final query: what challenges remained for an actor, jazzman, radio star and prize-winning novelist? Where to next?

Kyle chuckled and drove a hand through his hair. 'To find the fourth Mrs Magee.'

I was wrong about Liz. The programme was over twenty minutes before she rang. I took the call because Reba was fixing fresh drinks.

'So you've seen him.'

'*Seen* him? I'm just off the phone to the bastard.'

Attacking a hero in his moment of triumph seemed to me a grave mistake. Even with my limited experience of glory I knew the acclaimed performer's high.

'So what did he say?'

'*Say?*'

Distracted and incoherent with rage, her account of the conversation was fragmentary and jumbled but a piecing together of her random comments to me (and, later, to Reba) suggested an exchange on the following lines:

KYLE: Are you ringing to congratulate me, darling?

LIZ: Like fuck Ah am.

KYLE: But didn't you think I looked marvellous? Everyone said I looked marvellous.

LIZ: Why did you talk about me? I don't get half an hour on TV to put my side of things.

KYLE: This is fame, darling. I can't help it if you married a famous man. And I can't do anything about it if you're not famous yourself. That's one thing at least you surely can't blame me for.

LIZ (*shrieking*): I'd like to get half an hour to say a few things. Like you coming down to Dublin to argue about a fucking potato peeler. *I'm very fond of potatoes and I bought that peeler.* Why didn't you tell everyone that kind of thing instead of the other bullshit?

KYLE: No one else thought it was bullshit, darling. Women have been especially sympathetic. Immediately after it was recorded one of the technicians came up to tell me how shitty their interviewer looked and how sensitive and sincere I was by comparison.

LIZ (*screaming*): Great! Great! I hope you'll be happy with her and give my fucking head peace.

KYLE (*laughing lightly*): She wasn't attractive enough for me.

Ken returns in late afternoon, chastened and wan. 'He did lots of tests and there's nothing wrong with me. I have no sinister brain disease.'

'But you have, Ken. You have.'

'What?'

'The disease of the project.'

He buries his exhausted face in his hands. 'I know. He said that. He said it's due to overwork. He said I'll have to slow down.'

'So no more work. Look – there's a presentation in the board room. Let's go down and have a glass of wine.'

'I can't face them all after that meeting this morning.' He pauses, seeming to relent a little. 'Who's leaving?'

'Tina Bergsen from Publicity. The American woman. Going into one of the big advertising agencies.'

Nick Ackerly is in the doorway of the board room, legs apart in a comfortable straddle. A Colossus, to be sure – but a modern, caring, sympathetic, user-friendly one.

'Ken!' he cries, the earlier disagreement apparently forgotten or forgiven. 'We'll be doing this for you next month. *Why are all the good people leaving?*'

'Incentives,' I tell him. 'Or, as we used to call it, money.'

Practised manager that he is, Nick ignores the jibe – but gauche innocent Ken is stung into response.

'No!' he protests. 'It's to work with professionals.' And now he too fixes Nick with a bitterly judgemental look.

Immediately agreeing with Ken, Nick lowers his voice in conspiratorial intimacy. 'I know *exactly* what you mean, Ken.' He glances quickly about, as though for eavesdropping senior executives. 'I feel like moving on myself. What with these cuts . . . and more coming up . . .'

'No!'

'Oh yes . . . and anyway two years is enough in one job.' Ken goes off to get wine and Nick's glance falls on me. 'How long have you been with us now?'

'Four years.'

'Any career plans?'

'No.' Of course I am stabbing myself in the back. The concept of the niche is anathema in incentive culture. Career moves should be like Irish rain – if not actually happening then anticipated soon.

'No thought of a move at all?'

'No.'

Surly monosyllables (the urge to self-abasement before authority is at least one Fenian instinct I have managed to control). Yet Nick nods wisely, as though I have offered an original, thought-provoking and perhaps even conclusive argument. 'The devil we know . . . *hn?*' He nods decisively, swirling his wine. 'It's just I get restless from time to time.' Leaning towards me, intimate, familiar, confiding. 'The truth is . . . *I'm a bit of a gypsy.*'

Ken returns with two glasses of wine. Time for Nick to commence the presentation.

Tina's two great loves – art and horses. Must have derived former from Bostonian roots. Boston Museum of Fine Art best collection North America. No surprise Tina whiz at art and design. No surprise editing whiz either. New England – Poe, Hawthorne, Frost, Emerson, Thoreau. Should really have been working in New York with Norman Mailer or Saul Bellow (light laughter) instead of disentangling civil servants' prose (loud laughter). Horrors to match stories of fellow Bostonian Edgar Allan Poe (loud prolonged laughter).

Other love horses. Own horse retired steeplechaser name of Whoomph. After famous painting by Roy Lichtenstein? Or was that *Wham?* (laughter). Loving art and horses should have made Stubbs favourite painter but not so. World not always tidy (light laughter). Favourite painter Monet, French artist immortalised in Beatles song (loud laughter).

But despite love of Impressionists, light shed by Tina more akin to golden glow of Italian Renaissance . . .

'He's fucking her, isn't he?' Ken snarls.

'These are PR people, Ken. It's all image. All front.'

Nick resumes, solemnly now. Not a good time for Renaissance light. Gathering dark clouds of redundancies, reorganisations, budget cuts (murmur of melancholy accord). Tina perhaps wise to depart. Did not have to be meteorologist to see ill winds coming. Hence to most important part of occasion. Knew Tina also liked Michelangelo so had spoken to 'businessmen' from Italy (light anticipatory laughter). Alas told transfer of Sistine Chapel ceiling a little too 'high-profile' (loud replete laughter). Had to set sights lower. Knew Tina collected nineteenth-century watercolours. Hence final choice of . . .

'Let's get out of here,' Ken growls.

During the storm of applause it is easy to slip away. In blessed silence we descend in the lift and cross the foyer.

'How can you put up with that bunch of shits?' Ken asks in the righteous purity of rejection. Wonderful ecstasy of contempt! Sweet indeed to sneer and walk away. For a moment the criminal joy of youth is restored. Except that five minutes later you have to kiss a new ass.

'As well this bunch as another, Ken.'

We pause on the front steps, contemplating the streets of Notown, where renegades flock from all over to find the insubstantiality and weightlessness of freedom. Though the highway before us is scarcely inspiring: a multi-lane one-way thoroughfare flanked by undistinguished buildings (the Victorian redbrick tavern opposite retaining a certain character and warmth) and currently jammed with increasingly impatient tailed-back traffic. Ken too shifts impatiently. Disillusion and restlessness are in the air. Yet I feel strangely reconciled. It's the marvellous long tepid dream of the plateau years, our unglamorous circumstances long since accepted, bitter shocks of self-knowledge and mortality long since absorbed (my operation postponed so often I can almost forget about it). Not that I no longer want anything to happen – but I have certainly arranged my life so that uneventfulness is likely. Today I wouldn't know imminence if it crapped in my hat.

'Fancy a quick one?' Ken asks, nodding across at the tavern in a manner apparently casual and blithe but heavy with emotional undertow.

'Naaaah.' I am getting better at resisting emotional pressure. Too good, some would say. 'Have to get back, Ken.'

'Sure. Sure.' He nods brusquely.

Of course I will miss old Ken. But I have permitted myself to be persuaded into contingency. He is still only a colleague. Someone else will take his place.

'We'll have a drink when you're leaving.'

'Sure.' Not at all pleased. Not one bit.

He wants me to be his guru – but healthy relationships have to be two-way. Who will be *my* guru? Who will instruct me in non-attachment? Who will show me the fourth stage?

Besides, I'm trying to cut back on midweek drinking.

Picture a meeting, not just among the Irish (profoundly averse to the mechanisms of consensus) but in the very temple of Nietzschean anarchy: the Herron living room on Harvey Terrace.

A chamber that will not survive in even its present adulterated form. Mrs Herron too has had to yield to the punishing years. No longer able to flash her antlers from the crags, she has exchanged the house on the hill for a cosy bungalow in the suburbs. Exactly the kind of home for which I was once ruthlessly pilloried in this very room. Needless to say, it would never do to remind anyone. The more exquisite the ironies, the less we are free to point them out. Increasingly now I understand the loneliness of God.

Mrs Herron has taken Sean to the bungalow to get his professional opinion. John has also gone along, leaving the three sisters who have held me in thrall twenty years. They look as splendid as ever, or so it seems to me. Beyond the inevitable thickening there is little excess weight, the luxurious black is barely tinged with grey, the strong Herron bone structure has outlasted mere prettiness. In fact Frances, once so unappealingly angular, now seems to me the most attractive, although this could be due to the sprinkling of grey I find almost unbearably stimulating. What they have lost is their aura of hubris, gaining instead knowledge, stamina, resolve and a strong dash of the essential adult seasoning, disappointment. (Is it absence of this that makes youth so insipid?) Now I could only love a woman who has known a measure of disappointment.

All the Herron girls have been beautifully seasoned. I could happily have spent my life with any one of the three. A sentiment not reciprocated by at least two of them. Frances has been openly contemptuous since the French holiday, Liz abrupt and cool since the affray with Kyle. I will just have to love all three in one. All beautifully seasoned mature women in one.

'How's the civil service?' Frances enquires in an insolent tone that suggests I have found my true level.

'Fine,' I tell her with equal asperity. 'Still pumping iron?'

It is almost a relief when the kulak returns.

'Good house,' Sean announces with the gruff mature terseness of long-established authority.

Liz goes to make tea, an uncharacteristic gesture that reveals her unease. For the purpose of the meeting is to settle her affairs. In southern Irish law Kyle remains the sole owner of the Dublin house. In theory he could sell it any time and put Liz on the street without giving her a penny. Another exquisite irony – the Fenians trapped by their own repressive laws. No doubt Kyle is highly amused, but amusement will not buy a new life. In exchange for signing over the house he wants four thousand pounds. Liz, with an overdraft, no collateral and a dwindling income, could not raise a bank loan – so Reba, Frances and John are jointly lending her the money instead. Originally the kulak was not meant to know but the thought of her fury on finding out was more than even Liz could contemplate.

'There's no rush though,' Liz babbles now. 'I could maybe get something out of him if I started divorce proceedings in the North. I'm just not sure of my legal position. I'd need to see a northern solicitor. Maybe just threatening to take him to court . . . the whole violence thing coming out . . .'

Mrs Herron laughs harshly. 'That wouldn't worry him one bit, look see. Sure isn't he well used to that sort of carry-on? Hasn't he been at it a lifetime?'

'But I'm not planning to move house and Kyle would hardly put David and me out on the street. I know he wouldn't do anything like that.'

'You surely don't want him holding this over you?' John asks.

The kulak leans forward, fierce. '*Don't ye want to be rid of him completely?*'

'Of course I do.'

'But are ye *sure* of that?'

The suspicion and snappishness of an aged confessor. Is there a firm purpose of amendment? Will you avoid the occasions of sin? At the same time there has been no mention of the Catholic position on divorce. Once again Mrs Herron is blatantly ignoring the party line. In the crucial affairs of property and money, religion takes a back seat.

'I'm sure,' Liz protests. 'It's just I hate borrowing money.'

At once the siblings pledge their unequivocal support. With a typically fine sense of theatre, the kulak lets them finish before making her move.

'Yese'll do no such thing. Not one yese'll pay out a penny, look see. Yese all have families of your own and I'm not havin' yese going into debt with your whole lives to live. If anyone's to pay out money it'll have to be me. There's money left from the shop compensation . . . and from selling this house . . .' – raising a hand to silence protests – 'that's the way of it now. I hate paying out to the likes of him – but sure what can we do?' She laughs bleakly, not without a certain grim relish at the novelty of a kulak paying off a son of the gentry. It is certainly an exquisite *bouleversement*, a rare treat for the voluptuary of the grotesque. 'He's a remittance man!' she suddenly bursts out in triumph, hitting on the term she will use to describe Kyle from now on. ('Saw the remittance man on

TV again' – malicious cackle – 'he's no more of a Peter Pan nor I am.')

No doubt Kyle would take this scene as proof of Liz retreating from his world of freedom and truth (concepts that often need to be defended by force) into the comforting bosom of Catholicism and family. But Liz scarcely looks either comforted or content. More like humiliated and angry. 'I'm paying all this back,' she keeps insisting to the company. No one believes her for a second.

It is obvious that she is about to take the money and run. Nor is there any great warmth or solidarity among the rest. Significantly, no one suggests a drink.

Even if deep family feeling exists, there will shortly be nowhere for the family to gather. The new two-bedroom bungalow will not accommodate couples and children. John's house would certainly be big enough, but no one has been there since the night of the drama. Nor has Caroline issued any invitations to her in-laws.

'I think I'll go on up to bed,' Liz says now. 'I have to go back first thing and it's a terrible drive.'

Mrs Herron cannot resist a last jibe. 'And you never done telling me how generous he was.'

'Who?' Deliberate obtuseness, rather impertinent of Liz with a cheque for four large in her bag. On the other hand it is obvious that the kulak wants to twist the knife.

'The remittance man – who dye think? Ye used to never be done goin' on to me about how generous he was. *Oh he's as generous. Doesn't care a hoot about money. Give ye the shirt off his back.*' Pause to set Liz up for the *coup de grâce.* 'All I have to say is this. God protect us and preserve us from generous people – they always end up costin' ye a fortune.'